THE DOMAIN
OF ARROGANCE

THE DOMAIN
OF ARROGANCE

Charles David Grotsky

To order additional copies of this book, contact:
Xlibris
844-714-8691
www.Xlibris.com
Orders@Xlibris.com
834407

CONTENTS

DEDICATION

To my late parents, Jerry and Sunny Grotsky, who taught me to write at an early age and greatly influenced the enjoyment I get from reading.

To my late grandparents, Matthew and Minna Artson, for their opening the world for me as a young child by taking to me to visit the great natural history and art museums of New York City.

ACKNOWLEDGEMENTS

I would like to acknowledge the following people who contributed in the writing of "The Domain of Arrogance":

My cousin, Brenda Lowen, and my friends, Wynette Weaver and Ann Mullen, who offered suggestions that helped me to make various clarifications. My good friends, James Green and Traci Livingston, who enjoyed the story and made important observations. The head of a writer's group, David Rosenberg, for his important opinions regarding structural changes. Tom Halfhill for pointing out needed corrections. And my late friend and spiritual teacher, Dawna Su Maria Burhman, for her love and support. Last, but not at all least, my Senior Publishing Consultant, Dean Summers, who guided me along the path, and added to my overall understanding of self-publishing my book.

CHAPTER ONE

14 AD

Yeshua's hands rested on the railing as He stood on deck and gazed north across the channel. The breeze played with the many curls in His long, dark hair.

"What is the matter? I sense that something is bothering you," asked His uncle, Joseph of *Arimathea.*

"It is difficult to express in words, but I will attempt to do so. I am feeling an intense negative force. Whatever this force is, it has a great power of pure evil I have not

encountered before. As we draw nearer to Briton, the source of this terrible power gains in strength."

The journey from *Judea* had lasted six months. They had crossed from *Corbilo* in *Gaul* earlier that morning and sailed toward Briton. Joseph was a trader of tin; a valuable commodity required to make bronze. They would be guests of *Gorust* Cadwallan, the owner off lead, tin, and silver mines. His son, *Kenau*, and *Yeshua* were both fourteen years old.

Their ship docked in mid-day at the port of *Padstow* in Cornwall. A young man in his twenties greeted them as they stepped onto the pier.

"My name is *Brychan*. News that

your ship was seen crossing the channel reached us this morning.

I will take you and your nephew to Mr. *Cadwallan's* residence on *Looe* Island, where he and his son await you."

The man helped them load their bags into a row boat, and they set off east.

A small wooded island came into view as they rounded a headland, and they saw a handsome two-story house of stone and timbers standing a good distance from shore. The house was fronted by vegetable gardens and rows of fruit trees. *Brychan* assisted them onto a pier and hefted their bags out of the boat.

He then took them to a path leading to the house.

"I will take my leave now, fine sirs," he said.

Yeshua and Joseph carried their bags and followed the path. As they drew near the house the front door opened, and *Gorust* and his son, *Kenau*, appeared.

Gorust stood a good six feet tall, and his graying hair was worn in a pony-tail. When he smiled, his blue eyes twinkled.

"Welcome to Cornwall," he said in a jovial voice. "Please come inside."

Kenau was tall as well, with blonde hair, and his eyes were also blue.

Yet, in contrast to his father, *Yeshua* sensed his deep

unhappiness. He appeared to be sullen and withdrawn. And *Yeshua* was acutely aware of something else.

Gorust led them through an entrance hall, past a stairway, and into a large dining room. They were seated, and servants brought platters of venison, duck, and earthen bowls of cabbage soup with leeks and boiled carrots. Joseph and *Yeshua* recounted the many trials, experiences and adventures of their long journey. When all had had their fill, *Gorust* patted his stomach and cleared his throat.

"*Kenau*, be a good lad and show *Yeshua* around the property while Joseph and I discuss business."

After the boys left, the two men faced one another.

"Your son has matured since the last time I was here," remarked Joseph.

"Three years ago, was it not?" asked *Gorust*.

"Closer to four."

Gorust settled back in his chair.

"Yes, I agree with you, Joseph. My son has matured. *Kenau* has a bright mind, which has often surprised both myself and his tutors. He seems to have been born with fluency in Latin, Greek, and Aramaic and abilities in mathematics and geometry. He is also a natural horseman with great skill."

Joseph observed *Gorust* avert his

eyes and heard him let out a deep sigh.

"There is something troubling you, my friend."

Gorust looked at Joseph and attempted to smile, but failed. He laced his fingers together and spoke.

"*Kenau* has a strong personality that is negative and is often expressed in anger. I have heard many reports from my gardeners that he has been seen being cruel to small animals.

He will frequently fly into tirades.

I have done my best to raise him. Perhaps he misses not having had a mother. I chose not to remarry after my wife died. I must admit that

I am greatly disturbed by *Kenau's* unhappiness."

Gorust leaned forward and managed to smile.

"But enough of my problems, Joseph. Tell me something about your nephew."

"*Yeshua* is turning out to be a fine young man. He enjoys studying our scriptures and takes delight in teaching others. He too seems to have been born with a keen mind and language abilities, but I think his main attribute is one of love, respect for others, and Goodness."

"Perhaps He will have a positive influence on *Kenau*, then."

The two strolled through the garden, past planted beds of

vegetables and many rows of fruit and nut trees.

Yeshua walked alongside *Kenau,* who halted and turned to face Him.

He pushed his arms outward with great force. A strong gust of wind carried *Yeshua* backwards a dozen feet and sent Him sprawling. *Kenau* raced toward Him and picked up a shovel. He raised it over his head to strike *Yeshua* who motioned with His hand and bent it in half. *Kenau* unbent it and swung the shovel in an arc which missed *Yeshua's* head by only inches. *Yeshua* motioned with His hand again and sent the shovel flying.

Kenau frowned and broke into a run. He halted, faced *Yeshua* and raised his left arm. An intense red-hot beam of light issued forth from his finger. *Yeshua* raised His right arm and held His palm outward, but He had moved too slowly. The beam seared His forearm and wrist.

Yeshua winced in pain. He waved His left hand and the burns healed instantly. He saw that His palm had deflected the red-hot beam and that it had struck *Kenau* squarely in the chest. The force of the blow had propelled him backwards and slammed him against the trunk of a large chestnut tree.

Kenau sprang to his feet and rushed at *Yeshua,* who took two steps backward and opened his arms wide. He brought His hands together with a thunderous clap. A whirling column of air appeared and swept *Kenau* aloft ten feet off the ground. *Yeshua* allowed him to spin clockwise for a few moments. He opened His arms wide once more. The vortex dissipated, and *Kenau* fell heavily to the ground.

Yeshua strode up and looked down at him. *Kenau's* eyes had changed from blue to a fiery crimson.

"I know who you are, *Yeshua ben Yusef.* My mother died giving birth to me. We were both born at the exact same time, and you are *Ur,* The Christ."

"And I know who you are. You may

use the name *Kenau*, but you are *Chosech, The Antichrist.*"

Kenau's fiery, crimson eyes blazed and were full of hatred.

"You will die a horrible death nailed to a wooden cross in less than twenty years, and, mark my words, I will be there in person to witness it."

"Our Father has made this known to Me. So it is written. You, on the other hand, will die and be reborn countless times on this earthly plane. And unlike mortal humans, you will be cursed with the recollection of your past lives. They will haunt you until the day when you shall meet your final end."

"My final end?"

"Yes. You shall be consumed by

the fires of a great comet. Your body shall be incinerated by that of My own fiery breath. In that moment your vital essence, indeed, your very soul, shall be utterly extinguished and cease to exist."

"Souls cannot be extinguished."

"Our Father may choose to permanently terminate a soul if He so desires."

Kenau glared up at *Yeshua* and his angry face broke into a wicked smile.

"Until that moment, I intend to do all I can to eradicate the whole doctrine of Goodness, which is like a vile, sickening, contagious disease."

Yeshua smiled down at him with love.

"Our Father created us as opposing forces so that those who dwell on this plane may have a clear understanding of the difference between good and evil. He has provided them with a clear choice between the two."

"Evil is the far better choice."

Yeshua smiled with love once more.

"I suggest while My uncle and I are here we two agree to a truce."

"A truce? Why should I agree to a have truce with you?"

"Because, as I have just demonstrated, the Forces of Light are far stronger than the Forces of Darkness. You cannot now, and never will be able to, defeat Me."

"We shall see about that. For the sake of my father and your uncle, I will agree to your truce, but for only as long as you remain here."

Yeshua saw that *Kenau's* fiery crimson eyes had returned to blue.

He pulled him up by the right arm and hauled him to his feet. The two boys walked back to the house in silence.

ALBUQUERQUE, NEW MEXICO

"Damn!" swore Janey Spadaro upon realizing she had just driven in a big circle. There was the same lighted candy cane on the lawn again. She crossed herself, looked up, and whispered, "Sorry". Now, where was that Christmas party she'd been invited to?

A few minutes later, she saw a house ablaze with holiday lights atop a small hill. Janey drove up a long driveway and parked. She smoothed and straightened her bright red, white, and green knit sweater as she walked in the open door. Hungry, she filled a plateful of food from a buffet table and looked around while she ate. She recognized a few people from town and some from the university, but no one from her laboratory. Janey realized she must be at the wrong party and felt guilty about the food she'd just eaten.

A tall, pretty, blond woman walked slowly toward her and smiled.

"Hi, Merry Christmas." She offered her hand. "My name is Andrea. What's yours?"

"Janey," she answered and shook her hand. "I'm so sorry, but I think I'm at the wrong Christmas party! I drove all over the place and couldn't find it."

"Really? Well, you're welcome here anyway. What do you do, Janey? For work, I mean."

"I'm a hydroponics engineer and instructor at the university. I thought this was my lab's Christmas party, but obviously I made a mistake."

"How interesting," Andrea whispered to herself. She caught the eye of an imposing man with dark, gray hair. She slightly nodded and then glanced at Janey. The man approached them.

"This is my husband, Michael."

"Andrea, sorry to interrupt you," the man said, "but we really could use four more bottles of wine from the cellar."

"Sure. I'll go get them. Janey, would you please give me a hand?"

Janey put her now-empty plate on the table. They descended some stairs in semi-darkness. She saw a wall in front of her with many rows of bottles lying on their sides. Then Andrea struck her on the back of the head with a wine bottle and all went black.

FIRST MESA, POLACCA, ARIZONA

Cheveyo (spirit warrior) stood on the roof of his house at First Mesa and gazed at the setting sun. He looked up as a black helicopter flew overhead, going west toward the Grand Canyon. The old man nodded in the direction of a group of Hopi elders, who stood on a nearby rooftop. "*Nukpana* (evil)," he muttered.

The black helicopters had first appeared three years earlier. Since then many people from the area had mysteriously gone missing. The number of helicopters had greatly increased in the past few weeks.

They usually appeared near sunset and were often spotted at

night. *Cheveyo's* son Robert, whose Hopi name was *Kwahu* (eagle), and his sixteen-year-old grandson, *Tewa*, joined him on the roof.

"A beautiful sunset," commented Robert, as the sun dipped behind some clouds, sending shades of magenta, orange, and yellow across the sky. Robert was a U.S. National Parks ranger and had determined the helicopters were landing in the vicinity of a prominent sandstone formation named Isis Temple in the Grand Canyon.

"I'm going to take *Tewa* on a river rafting trip down the Colorado to Trinity Creek over the weekend," Robert said. "We'll be back on Sunday. I want to get a closer look at

Isis Temple and see what in the heck is going on."

OFFICE OF THE FBI, PHOENIX, ARIZONA

"Today's case-loads are done," said Susan Johnson as she swiveled around in her chair. Her shoulder-length red hair swirled in the same direction. "One more day till the weekend. What are you going to do?"

Jenny Spadaro smiled at her assistant.

"I thought I'd go up to Flagstaff and then visit the Grand Canyon. I haven't seen it in quite a while."

The phone rang, and Jenny answered, then listened.

"Yes, sir. I'll be right there."

Susan gave her a quizzical look.

"The Special Agent in Charge wants to see me," Jenny said.

"Uh, oh."

Jenny walked down the hall and stood in front of his door. She quickly checked her cell phone for a message from her twin sister, Janey, but there was none. Nervous, she took a deep breath and knocked twice.

"Please come in, Agent Spadaro."

Jenny sat in a chair in front of his desk and waited. Her mind raced to uncover some reason for her presence. She couldn't recall anything she'd done that required her to be disciplined. She smoothed her dark, curly hair, sat up straight, and forced a smile.

"My records indicate that you have accumulated sixteen days of paid vacation time in the past two years. Your work here is exemplary, Agent Spadaro, and I commend you. Your assistant, Susan, will cover for you. Your vacation starts effective tomorrow. Have a good time."

Jenny walked back to her office in a daze. Sixteen days? Yes, she knew she was a workaholic and used her job as a distraction. She had somehow let the fact that she hadn't taken any time off in two years go right past her. Many thoughts and images crowded one another. Where would she go? There were so many possibilities.

"What's wrong, Jenny? Bad news? I hope not," said Susan.

"You'll be running the show here while I'm away on my sixteen day vacation!" Jenny exclaimed and smiled brightly. "I start tomorrow."

"That is so fantastic! Don't worry about anything. I can handle it."

"I have complete confidence in you, Susan. Call, text or email me anytime, okay?"

"You got it."

Jenny's phone rang and she answered it.

"Phoenix FBI. Missing Persons Division. Agent Spadaro speaking. How may I assist you?"

"My name is Sheriff James Burch up here in Keams Canyon. We've spoken a few times over the past year. I'm calling to report a rash of missing people from our general area, particularly in the last three weeks. Sorry to call on such short notice. It would be great if you could attend a meeting we're having tomorrow, Friday, at our town hall. I put it on the web, but I guess you missed seeing it, because I didn't hear from you."

"What time is the meeting?"

"It's scheduled for two o'clock in the afternoon. We'll have law enforcement officials from four states as well as representatives of the

Hopi Tribal Council from each of the three Mesas."

"Count me in, Jim. I'll drive on up."

"Great. I'll see you tomorrow."

Susan looked over at Jenny.

"But, your vacation starts..."

"I know, but we've been following these missing persons events for almost two years now. It's our division, Susan, and we're good at what we do. One more day on the job and then..."

"Paris, London, Rio?"

Jenny laughed.

"We'll see."

She hugged Susan.

"Happy holidays!"

Jenny walked out to her car and tried calling her identical twin sister,

Janey, for the tenth time. Once again there was no answer. The two of them had always had a strong psychic, telepathic connection with each other ever since they were children. Yet, for some reason, Jenny couldn't connect with her sister's mind. She sent her yet another text message and also an email. Janey lived in Albuquerque. Where had she gone for the last three days?

Jenny drove home and pulled into her driveway. She checked her cell phone once more, but there were still no responses from her sister. She now became greatly worried.

GRAND CANYON, ARIZONA

Janey slowly awakened to a loud noise. She opened her eyes but couldn't see. She tried to speak, but something was covering her mouth. Her hands, she found, were bound together, and the back of her head throbbed with a persistent pain. Fear gripped her and soon grew into terror. The noise increased in volume and then stopped as the ground beneath her abruptly jerked. Then she heard voices.

A pair of hands grabbed her by the arms and lifted her to a standing position. The covering over her eyes was removed, and she blinked in the bright sunlight. A voice spoke from behind.

"Move forward quickly. Follow the man in front of you."

She obeyed and determined that she was in a helicopter. The man in front of her climbed down some metal stairs onto rocky ground. She followed him along a steep path leading to an opening in a sheer rock wall. She hesitated, and the man behind her placed his hand on her back and roughly pushed her forward.

"Keep walking straight ahead," said one of the men. Both carried automatic rifles.

Janey walked toward a large square structure standing against the far wall. It appeared to be metallic. Lights all around gleamed off its surface. As she stood in front of it, she saw that the middle of the square was empty, but Janey noticed that she couldn't see through it to the other side. The middle was blurry and undulating.

Fear and nausea rose from her stomach. The man behind whirled her around and with one quick motion removed the tape covering her mouth. The other man cut the tape binding her hands.

The two men were large and had crew cuts. They looked her up and down.

"Very nice," commented one.

"Too bad she has to leave us so soon," said the other.

Both men laughed. One said to her,

"Walk straight toward the square."

She turned around and screamed as a pair of hands suddenly shoved her forward into the square, and Janey Spadaro was engulfed in darkness.

TRINITY CREEK, GRAND CANYON, ARIZONA

The desert sun peeked over the eastern horizon as Robert and *Tewa* ran through a list of items they were taking on their rafting trip. *Cheveyo*, *Tewa's* grandfather, stood nearby.

"I'm sorry you're going to miss the meeting at the Keams Canyon town hall this afternoon," he said. "I hope it's constructive. I'll tell you about it when you get back."

"I'll be interested in hearing how it goes. Many have gone missing, like my friends *Honovi,* (strong deer), and *Tuwa*, (earth)," said Robert, "and that was nearly three years ago."

He paused to reflect on the recent government cutbacks that had resulted in his loss of a day. He now worked Monday through Thursday and was a ranger at *Canyon de Chelly* National Monument which was a forty-five minute drive from home.

"*Tewa* still has Christmas vacation, but I have to be on duty Monday morning. See you Sunday late in the afternoon."

Cheveyo wished them both a safe journey and went into his house.

"The inflatable raft, oars, and pump are stowed" Robert asked. "Do we have the life vests?"

"Check."

"Sleeping bags and camp pillows? Our jackets?"

"Got em'."

"Tent, shovel, camp chairs?"

"Check on each."

"Grill, charcoal, waterproof matches, lighter fluid?"

"Yes, Dad. We've got all of them."

"Cooler should have water, sandwiches, fruit, and chips for our lunches, then raw venison and veggies for dinner."

Tewa methodically answered

"check" for each item. He made sure they each had LED flashlights and extra batteries. He felt in his jean pocket for his flashlight and made sure his knife was in its holder on his belt.

"Okay, let's roll," said Robert. "We've got a three-hour drive ahead of us. I'll gas up in Tuba City."

Cloudless, blue skies lay overhead as they glided down Trinity Creek. The steep sided canyon cliffs, bathed in mid-day sunshine, cast reflections in the smooth water. *Tewa* remembered many rafting trips along this creek with his father and mother, *Sihu* (flower), who had died of pneumonia three years ago. He saw her sitting beside him in his mind and missed her terribly.

"White water up ahead, Son," warned Robert.

Tewa tightened his life vest and steeled himself. They felt the raft dip low, and then they were flung up and then down again. *Tewa* rowed with all his strength.

"Watch out for that log sticking out over there!" shouted Robert.

"I see it," *Tewa* shouted back.

The two of them maneuvered safely around it as the raft bucked back and forth. Then they were through the rapids and floated leisurely on calm water.

Another hour passed, and both felt hungry. They each ate a sandwich as the raft slowly floated down the creek; they took in the vegetation along the banks, and the beauty of the cliffs on either side, now bathed in afternoon sunshine.

"Our camping spot should be around the next bend, *Tewa*. Let's get the tent set up first and then build a campfire pit."

They tied the raft to a branch and quickly cleared rocks from a flat area. Then they hauled the raft safely onto shore and stowed the oars. While Robert set up the tent, *Tewa* placed large rocks in a circle. Then he used the shovel to dig a fire pit.

Robert came over and was

pleased to see *Tewa's* initiative and good work.

"A fine job," he said.

He poured charcoal briquettes in the pit, doused them with lighter fluid, and placed a circular metal grill on top.

"I'll let that soak in for a while. Let's gather some dry branches for an after-dinner campfire."

Tewa walked over to some bushes, which lay in dark shadows. He surprised a ringtail cat, which is related to a raccoon, and watched as it scurried away into the brush. *Tewa* had an arm full of branches, and his dad carried two small logs.

Robert watched the shadows climb up the canyon walls as the sky darkened. He lit the briquettes with a wooden match and settled back in his camp chair. The creek flowed on past as it had for two million years. He thought of *Sihu*, and of how they'd snuggled together in this very spot.

A long sigh escaped him, and he wiped tears away with his sleeve. Although his grief had lessened, her warmth, smile, and laugh were always with him.

A cool breeze wafted down the creek and signaled the onset of night. He and *Tewa* put their jackets on and prepared dinner. Green peppers, onions, and tomatoes were cut and put on skewers along with chunks of venison. Robert placed them on top of the grill to cook.

Darkness descended fast, and the sky was filled with stars. Robert pointed up.

"That is called the Orion Arm, which is part of the spiral galaxy called the Milky Way. Our solar system is in the Orion Arm. The Earth is but a tiny speck in the grandness of the universe. We're both made of dust from stars that have exploded, and someday both of us will return to dust again. But, *Tewa*, our souls, and your mother's soul, will always live on."

After breakfast they broke camp and continued their journey down Trinity Creek. At about ten o'clock in the morning, they rounded a bend and beheld Isis Temple. A loud sound startled them as a black helicopter flew directly overhead, straight for the prominent formation.

"That's unusual to see so early in the day," said Robert.

He found a sandbank, and the two of them hauled the raft out of the water and secured it to a nearby tree with a sturdy rope. They climbed up a rocky slope and looked up. Isis Temple rose above them for more than seven thousand feet.

"I want to get a good view of the area," said *Tewa* as he began to scramble up the slope.

"I'll stay here," said Robert. "Be careful and don't go too far."

"Okay, Dad."

Tewa soon found that the going was tough, and he had to climb in a zig-zag pattern, jumping from one rocky ledge to another. Then he saw a dark depression in the cliff wall above him. He managed to position himself in front of it on a narrow shelf of rock.

A large pile of rocks blocked what was clearly a cave entrance. *Tewa* began to carefully remove the rocks, placing them on one side of the narrow shelf. He was able to squeeze his body into an opening and found himself standing inside a dark area. He took out his LED, turned it on, and froze because he stood no more than three feet from the edge. *Tewa* carefully inched his way forward, looked down, and saw a drop of at least twenty feet. He got on his knees, turned his LED off, and saw something that both surprised and scared him.

The area below was as big as a supermarket parking lot. He noted that it was hard-packed earth, level and well-lit. A square structure with a wide opening stood against the back wall. Then he heard voices. Two men dressed in camouflage uniforms with rifles escorted a woman wearing a red, white, and green sweater. *Tewa* watched, open-mouthed, as a man pushed the woman into the square, and she disappeared. He inched backward, got to his feet, and exited through the hole he'd created.

Tewa carefully made his way down the slope and reached the bottom only to find his father surrounded by five men armed with what looked like AK-47 rifles. A large man with a shaved head, tattooed arms, and a holstered revolver scowled and shouted at him.

"Where have you been?" he demanded of *Tewa*. "What have you been up to?"

Tewa was scared. Three of the men pointed their guns at his dad, and two others pointed guns right at him.

"Nothing. I mean, I just went to find a place so I could go to the bathroom." He tried to smile but couldn't because he was shaking with fear.

The man glared at him, then, apparently satisfied, spoke loudly and in a stern voice.

"You are in a restricted area. No one is allowed anywhere in this vicinity. Do you understand? I don't want to see either of you around here again. Get the message? Now shove off!"

They untied their raft, got in, and left.

"*Tewa*, look at me," his father said, "I know you're very scared, but I need your concentration. Row in tandem with me. They may change their mind, and I need for us to get out of firing range and around the bend up ahead."

Tewa began to row along with his father in long, steady strokes. Soon they cleared the bend and kept going for another half an hour. They began to feel safe. Robert opened the cooler and tossed a big red apple to *Tewa,* who caught it.

"Eat the whole apple. You'll feel much better."

Tewa smiled and took a bite, then another.

"Those men meant business. We're okay now. You don't have to be scared anymore."

Tewa finished the last bite of the apple. He was feeling better.

"Yeah, those men with guns

were pretty mean, Dad, but I saw something just before I climbed down that was even scarier than them."

"Really? What did you see? Tell me."

Tewa related finding the cave and seeing the woman walk into the square and disappear.

"Are you sure? Maybe the angle was such that she was blocked from your view."

"No, Dad, I was looking almost straight down, and she just vanished."

Robert loved to read science fiction.

"It sounds like she walked through some kind of a teleportation device or what is known as a Jump Gate. But that's not possible!" He paused. "Or perhaps it is. I recently read an article about two physicists at the Max Planck Institute who were able to briefly send sub-atomic particles through the intervening space and then made the same particles appear in another place!"

"Wow! Like in *Star Trek*! Maybe that's how all of the missing people are being taken. But the question is, *where* are they being taken?"

"Let's tell *Cheveyo* what you saw as soon as we get back. And I also want to find out what happened at the meeting in Keams Canyon."

HIGH PLATEAU DESERT, ARIZONA

Dr. Marc Prentis tilted his cowboy hat up and wiped his forehead with a handkerchief. He took a few steps forward, looked to his right, and stopped as his trained eyes spotted a pictograph painted on the canyon wall. Though it was faded, Marc was able to make out three dark, elongated figures wearing cloaked, hooded robes. He used his large knife to remove bushes partially blocking a low entrance. He bent down, crawled through, and stood up on the other side. Marc followed a narrow, worn path through a cleft in the rock wall. He walked forward ten feet and looked down. Waste flakes in many colors littered the ground.

These were commonly found at archaeological sites and were the discarded fragments left over from tool making. Many were utilized as small knives.

Marc continued down the path between steep rock walls until he entered an open area. Rubble covered the ground. He knelt in the center and pushed aside rocks, pebbles, and decayed tree branches. A flat stone was revealed. Once more he used his knife, carefully running it along the edges of the stone, and lifting it at the same time. He cautiously peered inside and held his breath. There were no rattlesnakes. Instead, an ancient Anasazi storage cache was revealed.

As a professor, Marc knew that the politically correct term used today for Anasazi is Ancestral Puebloans. Their pueblos, now in scattered ruins, covered most of the American southwest; the civilization had reached its height in art and architecture between 1100 and 1300 AD. *Mesa Verde* and other major cliff dwellings had been constructed during this period. Advances in pottery, incorporating black-and-white designs on orange backgrounds, were achieved. The Hopi, thought by many to be the most mystical of Native Americans, are the direct descendants of the

Anasazi, whose culture lives on in their myths and legends.

In his mid-thirties, Dr. Marc Prentis was a professor of archaeology at Northern Arizona University in Flagstaff. He had two months left on a six-month sabbatical to write a book on the early Anasazi culture; he had rented a house in Keams Canyon.

He was friendly with many in the Hopi community at First Mesa and knew that their Anasazi ancestors had first migrated from the *Hovenweep* area of Colorado and Utah.

Marc stood up and removed his digital camera from its case bag. He took some photos, using natural light, because flash shots can damage artifacts. He put the camera away and took a closer look into the cache pit. Three finely chiseled arrow-heads of brown, blue, and white chert lay below. Next to them was an unbroken pre-historic large *olla* or bowl. Marc guessed its age to be between 250 and 500 AD. Its designs were black and orange, crudely drawn, yet they had a pleasant flow to them.

Lying in a small, open *olla* was the most beautiful necklace Marc had ever seen made of turquoise, hematite, and onyx beads of various sizes. There were many more objects in the cache, but late afternoon sun had taught him it was better to head on home and return another day. Then he could do a proper job. He replaced the flat stone and covered it with rocks and dry brushwood. On his way out, he photographed the painted pictograph of the hooded figures.

He threw his gear in the passenger seat of his truck and headed west, trailing dust down the rough road. When he got into cell phone range, he checked for messages. There was one from Dr. Thompson, his father's doctor in Maryland. Marc stopped the truck and listened.

"Marc, your father is at death's door and may not last the night. But he's a fighter, so my suggestion is for you to get on a plane ASAP and come to Bel Air."

"Oh, Dad!"

He pulled out a handkerchief as tears streamed down his cheeks. When he got home, Marc made reservations for the first flight to Baltimore, which left at ten a.m. from Phoenix's Sky Harbor Airport.

He'd known this day was coming, for his father, Admiral Bill Prentis, had been in ill health for the last two years. Marc was his only child, and they had always been close. They'd grown even closer after the death of his mother, Iris, five years earlier. She'd been a Navy wife and had become his partner in a highly successful business begun soon after his father retired from the Navy. Marc had also loved her deeply.

He ate an early dinner, set the alarm for six a.m., and soon fell asleep.

KEAMS CANYON, ARIZONA

"Crap!" swore Jenny Spadaro after checking for any messages from her twin sister, Janey. There were none. She crossed herself, looked up, and whispered, "Sorry". With her handbag over her shoulder, Jenny rolled a small suitcase to the car. Keams Canyon lay a good three hours away, but she'd given herself an extra hour. She wanted to get there before the meeting started to conduct interviews with those whose friends and family members had gone missing. She pulled out of her driveway, got on I-17, and headed north.

Jenny turned on the radio, and her hands tightened their grip on the steering wheel. The song she heard caused her to have painful thoughts and memories. A wave of grief seized her heart, and she felt her eyes brimming with tears.

"Oh, Mitch, my darling. I miss you so much! I think of you all the time."

She quickly switched the radio to another station. Jenny kept one hand on the wheel while she dried her tears.

Snow covered the branches of pines along the freeway, and the air was cold when she stopped two hours later to get some lunch and coffee in Flagstaff. Jenny got onto I-40 and headed east toward Albuquerque. She considered calling the FBI office there and reporting Janey's disappearance, but decided to wait one more day. Jenny took AZ-87 at Holbrook and headed due north to Keams Canyon.

Located within the Hopi Reservation, Keams Canyon is not a Mesa village, but an administrative center with many U.S. Government offices. Jenny drove east on Route 264 and entered a scenic area of forested hills. She passed Saint Joseph's Mission Catholic Church and continued along the Main Street.

There wasn't much there besides some office buildings, a motel, and a café. She parked by the town hall, walked in the front door, and looked inside.

"Agent Spadaro? I'm the sheriff, Jim Burch."

A tall man with dark blond hair extended his hand. Jenny shook it and smiled. The sheriff smiled back.

"Thanks for driving all the way up here."

Jenny saw that a crowd half-filled the town hall.

"You're welcome. Sorry, but somehow I totally missed seeing your posting on the web about the meeting. Can I have your overall review of the current situation?"

"Certainly. I'd like to have the tribal leader of First Mesa join us if that's all right."

"Of course."

"He was reluctant to speak with you. Relations between the FBI and Native Americans have improved, but distrust remains. I convinced him that you were here to offer assistance."

'Thank you, sir."

The sheriff signaled to an older man with gray hair worn in a pony-tail, who approached them.

"Agent Jenny Spadaro of the Phoenix FBI," she said and smiled.

"My name is *Cheveyo*. As a member of the Hopi Tribal Council, I welcome you here. Any help you may give to our community would be greatly appreciated."

Sheriff Jim Burch, Jenny, and *Cheveyo* took seats at a table.

"Here are the facts. Three years ago we began getting missing person reports at our office," said Jim. "But not just Keams Canyon. We got reports from other jurisdictions across Arizona and many from Utah, Nevada, and New Mexico. All told, there may be as many as a thousand people who have mysteriously disappeared. Of course, some may be homicides or accidents, but those would be a small percentage. Then, in the past three weeks, we've seen an escalation over a wide area, I decided to have this meeting. We have posted it on the web, and I have representatives here from police departments in four states."

Cheveyo looked grim.

"It all began with the appearance of black helicopters," he said. "They fly low over First Mesa, heading west toward the Grand Canyon. Usually, we see them in late afternoon, near sunset, and even at night. My son, Robert, is a U.S. National Parks ranger who sometimes goes to staff meetings at the regional headquarters. He used a mounted telescope there a few weeks ago in late afternoon, and observed the helicopters landing in the vicinity of a large formation called Isis Temple.

He and my grandson, *Tewa*, went on a rafting trip this weekend to get a closer look."

"Please, sir, if you'd be so kind," asked Jenny, "could you introduce me to some of the people present who have loved one's missing?"

Cheveyo nodded and led her across the room to a group of Hopi men, women, and children.

"Jeez, we're finally here," said Jack as Augi parked across the street from the town hall. He reached for the door handle.

"Not yet," said Augi. "We sit and wait. The boss said not to call attention to ourselves, so we'll stay until we see more people show up. Besides, we got here early."

"But I gotta go pee," whined Jack.

"Hold it."

Both men were large and crammed into their compact rental car. Augi opened all the windows.

"It took us three and a half hours to get here. Look at this place! You call this a Main Street?" Jack laughed.

"Is this a joke?"

"Listen, the boss sent us here because he saw the meeting posted on the Internet. He's concerned that the cops may catch on to what we've been up to, okay?" responded Augi. "We're supposed to record what goes on and report back to him." He glanced in his rear-view mirror and saw a group of two dozen people walking toward the town hall. "Okay, let's go."

The two men had crew cuts and wore khaki slacks and extra large blue dress shirts. They took seats in the last row. Augi removed a small notepad from his shirt pocket along with a pen while Jack went to find the men's room.

Jenny Spadaro had conducted five interviews when *Cheveyo* walked up and led her to four Hopi at a nearby table.

"*Yamka* (blossom) and *Tocho* (mountain lion), I'd like to introduce FBI agent Jenny Spadaro from their Phoenix field office."

Jenny shook hands with them.

"And this is *Pamuya* (water moon)

and *Mongwau* (owl), grandparents of *Honovi* (*strong deer*), who has been missing for three years. *Yamka* and *Tocho* are his mother and father."

"Pleased to meet you," said Jenny. "Can you tell me what facts you may know about his disappearance?"

"*Honovi* was a construction foreman on the O'Callaghan-Tillman Memorial Bridge spanning the Colorado River over Hoover Dam. It's an extension of US 93 that connects Arizona and Nevada," said *Yamka*. "He always sent us money from his pay-checks and called us regularly. Then the money and the phone calls suddenly stopped. We don't know why."

Her voice faltered, and she wiped

away some tears. *Tocho* took hold of her hand.

"Was there anything he said, looking back, that you now consider to have been odd or out of place? Anything unusual?"

"Yes," answered *Tocho*. "He told us that over a dozen men from the construction site had gone missing. Many of the other foremen and supervisors just thought they had simply decided the work was too hard and left. But he didn't think so. And *Honovi* said something else."

"What?" asked Jenny.

"That often, just before sunset, they would hear and see many black helicopters flying overhead toward the Grand Canyon."

Jenny looked at *Cheveyo,* who nodded as Sheriff Burch walked over.

"Jenny, we are about to start the meeting. Please take a seat on the stage. Your name tag is on your chair."

Jenny smiled and thanked the four Hopi.

Jack returned from the restroom and sat down heavily. He looked around.

"Jeez, the room's full of freakin' Indians!"

Augi, who was part Cherokee, rolled his eyes.

"Oh, so sorry. I forgot to use the politically correct term, "Native Americans," Jack snorted.

"Will you keep your voice down? In fact, just shut up. The meeting's starting."

The Keams Canyon sheriff spoke to the audience and summarized the situation of the past three years. Then he introduced law enforcement officers in attendance from four states. There were chiefs of police, homicide detectives, crime scene investigators, and even a state attorney general.

They each spoke briefly about the missing persons in their state, but no one could pin down a reason behind the nearly one thousand people who had simply vanished. Then Sheriff Burch introduced Jenny Spadaro.

She walked up to the podium and looked out at the assembled people.

"My name is Jenny Spadaro, FBI agent with the Phoenix field office. My team is in charge of our Missing Persons Division."

Augi and Jack's eyes opened wide.

"That's the same woman we pushed through the Jump Gate a couple of days ago. That can't be possible. We both saw her walk through it!", Jack said.

"I agree", said Augi. "Now will you shut up and listen?"

"First of all, I'm taking this personally," Jenny said. "My identical twin sister, Janey, disappeared from Albuquerque four days ago. She's a hydroponics engineer and teaches at the University of New Mexico. I've drawn some insights from my interviews prior to this meeting. Sheriff, do we have a data-base on the missing people?"

"Yes, we do, and it's pretty extensive."

"Then I ask that you please make it available to all of us on stage. I would like to review the average ages and various professions of those who are missing.

Second, I plan to meet with the Special Agent in Charge at our Phoenix office next week and recommend that our Directorate of Intelligence at FBI Headquarters in Washington, D.C., be involved in gathering information. We all need to work together on this situation. I have received disturbing reports from my interviews about black, unmarked helicopters being involved in a majority of the missing person reports. Many people from the Hopi Three Mesas area have seen them near sunset and even at night.

Finally, It is my opinion that there is something strange going on in the Grand Canyon, and I will suggest to my Special Agent in Charge that an FBI SWAT team be sent to the area around a prominent sandstone formation there known as Isis Temple."

"Oh, so that explains it," said Jack. "She has a twin sister! But Augi, I don't like what she's saying. What do you think we should do about it?"

"I think that we give her a dirt nap."

"Are you nuts! We can't kill an FBI agent!" declared Jack.

Augi looked around nervously.

"Will you keep your voice down?" he whispered. "Look, she's gonna bring the federal heat down on us. Besides, we're both wanted for murders in Florida and Texas. Tell me, what difference could one more possibly make?"

Jack shook his head.

"I still don't like it. Too risky."

"The boss told me that the operation is almost finished. They're gonna close the whole thing down next week."

"I don't care if Victor's shutting it down. I still don't like offing a fed," stated Jack.

"We're forbidden to say his name."

"Yeah, I know. But it's his last name that *really* cracks me up. Victor..."

"Shut up, Jack. Don't say it," Augi said through clenched teeth.

"Okay, okay."

"Look, we gotta buy us some time."

Jack couldn't argue with that. He nodded.

"Okay, how do we do her?"

"We follow when she leaves, wait till there's no one around, and run her car off the road," answered Augi.

"Okay, but I still don't like the idea."

"Neither do I."

BEL AIR, MARYLAND

Dr. Marc Prentis said a silent prayer of thanks as his flight landed safely at Thurgood Marshall Airport. He rented a car, drove through Baltimore to the freeway, and arrived in Bel Air, Maryland, about thirty minutes later. There were large areas of snow along the roadway to his father's estate. Rows of maple trees on either side stood with their branches bare of leaves. The three-story, colonial-style house sat on five acres with broad lawns in the front, back, and sides.

The house was painted a light orange, and the shutters and front door, were dark red. There were two white columns on either side of the door, and the lintel above proudly displayed an American eagle. Marc parked in the driveway beside two other cars. The air was freezing, and he hurried inside. Marc rolled his suitcase in and left it in his old bedroom. He heard some voices on the second floor and climbed the stairs. Dr. Thompson, his family's physician, greeted him, and he was introduced to three nurses.

"Marc, I'm so glad you came. He's not long for this world. I shall miss him dearly."

"Thank you, Doctor."

Marc walked through the open doorway and stepped into his

father's bedroom. Things were arranged as he remembered them. A chest of drawers with a wood-framed antique oval mirror on the wall above it. A desk and chair in the corner. A Persian carpet lay next to the four-poster bed, which had a night-stand on either side. Everything looked the same, except now there was a medical monitoring machine near the bed, and an IV bag ran something into his father's left arm through a transparent line.

The admiral was asleep. An oxygen tube had been inserted in his nostrils. His breathing was labored, but steady. Marc pulled up a chair and sat at the bedside. He looked at his father with love as memories from their lives together played in his mind. Despite his having been an admiral on tours of duty during the Cold War in many locations around the world, his father had somehow always managed to find time for his son. Then he'd been given a hush-hush desk job at the Pentagon. He'd eventually retired and become a successful and wealthy businessman. The admiral suddenly opened his eyes.

"Marc! Oh, Son. I'm so glad you came in time," he said in a weak voice. "Your mother's calling for me to join her." Then Marc heard his father's voice grow in strength. "I don't have much time left, and there's so much I have to tell you."

"Tell me?"

"Yes. Remember the desk job I couldn't talk about? I was with the Office of Naval Intelligence. I was assigned as the commander of the Special Devices Center at Area 5."

"Don't you mean Area 51?"

"No. Area 5 is at the Great Lakes Naval Training Center north of Chicago. Area 51 is in Nevada."

"What do they do at the Special Devices Center?"

"I'm going to get to that. I'm dying, Son. Won't last much longer. I must get this off my chest. Been sworn to secrecy forever, but they can't hurt me now."

"Hurt you? Why would anyone..."

The admiral reached out and tightly gripped Marc's arm.

"Listen to my words carefully and have no doubt that what I'm about to tell you is God's truth. I'll swear on a stack of Bibles, Son."

"Go on."

"We've had a secret space program for many years with established bases on the moon and Mars since the mid-1970's. NASA is just window-dressing; a dog and pony show. Further, our technology is at least fifty years ahead of what is known by the general public. Advances include both anti-gravity and variable-specific impulse magneto-plasma rocket engines. They use radio waves to ionize and heat a propellant, thereby accelerating magnetic fields that create plasma and generate thrust. We use these engines in two large, triangular-shaped spaceships. The Space Fleet is known by the code words, 'Solar Warden'."

Marc felt hot tears run down his cheeks.

"Father, you're delirious. I'll go get Dr. Thompson."

"No, I am *not* delirious, and I am *not* drugged. My mind is clear, and I need you to listen to me. Pay attention, Son."

The admiral continued.

"There is a blue-colored comet heading straight toward Earth. I don't know how long we have before it comes near us, but when it does, it will directly strike our planet and annihilate all life."

"Oh, my God!"

The admiral continued.

"Do you know what a plutocracy is?"

"I'm not sure."

"Marc, there exists a worldwide taxonomic group that controls all the governments, military, wealth, and power on the planet. A taxon is a specific type or family of people, and a plutocracy means government ruled by the wealthy class. These people make up about two percent of the world's population."

"Oh, come on. That sounds crazy!"

The admiral recited from memory.

"Some of the biggest men in the United States, in the fields of commerce and manufacture, are afraid of somebody, are afraid of something. They know there is a power somewhere, so organized, so subtle, so watchful, so interlocked, so complete, so pervasive, that they had better not speak above their breath when they speak in condemnation of it."

"What crazy conspiracy theorist said that?"

"President Woodrow Wilson said that in 1914. Son, the country I grew up in, and later defended, no longer exists. We don't have a democracy anymore. The wealthy now buy and choose our politicians, especially our presidents. Marc, there are just sixty-two people who have combined assets among them that equal the wealth of three billion five-hundred million people. That's half the population of the entire world!"

"Are you kidding me? I find that hard to believe, Dad."

"I know you do, Son. However, what I'm saying is the truth. As a matter of fact, one percent of the extremely rich have amassed more wealth than the rest of the entire world. Fifty-two percent of our nation's wealth is owned by the top one percent of the population, and there are now just ten banks that control nearly all of the world's financial wealth. According to the latest statistics, over the last thirty years, the wealthiest one percent of Americans have seen their net worth grow by twenty-one trillion dollars, while the wealth of the bottom half of Americans has fallen by nine hundred billion dollars."

Marc slowly shook his head.

"How much money do you have to have in order to be counted among the top two per cent?"

"A minimum of two hundred and fifty million dollars."

Marc slowly shook his head again.

"How much do you have to have to be in the top one percent?"

"A minimum of one billion dollars."

"Oh, my God."

"This culture of wealth has

reduced the size of the middle class and greatly widened the gap between the super rich and the very poor," said the admiral.

Dr. Thompson gently knocked on the door and entered the room. The three nurses stood outside in the hallway.

"Sorry to interrupt you, Marc, but it's time to administer Bill's pain medication, and we need to check his vital signs and wash and clean him."

He glanced at his watch.

"It's almost five. It appears to me that the admiral will still be around to continue your conversation after dinner. Come back here to his bedroom in an hour and a half."

Marc went downstairs and unpacked his suitcase. He found there wasn't a lot of food in the fridge or kitchen cabinets. The roads had been cleared of snow, and he drove to a nearby restaurant and read the local newspaper while he ate. Dr. Thompson met him at the front door when he returned.

"Your father sure has a bee up his pants and kept asking for you all during dinner. He still has a pretty good appetite. I listened to his heart, Marc, and I'm afraid he's on his way out."

"Thanks, Doctor. I'll go see him now."

Marc entered his father's room and sat down beside the bed.

"I'm glad you're back, Marc. I know I don't have a lot of time left, so listen to every word I say. Now, back to my main topic. The elite have known about the blue comet for many years and have used their vast wealth and technology to construct a clandestine base beneath the surface of one of the two moons of Mars named Phobos. They plan to escape to this base, named Sub Rosa, which means "secret" in Latin, when the comet gets close to Earth. Then nearly one thousand five hundred of the very wealthiest and powerful will escape with their families to Phobos, and everyone else on our planet will die."

Marc wore a stunned expression.

"Their plan is to eventually return to earth. It may be dozens of generations on Sub Rosa, but someday they intend to repopulate the planet. They have put together a genetic biological library of DNA from all Earth's life forms, and it is stored at sub-zero temperatures on the Phobos base."

"The Hopi have long held to a prophecy concerning a blue comet that will utterly destroy Earth. They call it *Sakwa Sohu* or "The Blue *Kachina*.""

"I know, Son. Many indigenous peoples around the world have a similar prophecy. Unfortunately, it looks that they're about to be proved right."

The admiral briefly paused.

"Where was I? Oh, yes. There are two large triangular ships in the Space Fleet and each is capable of carrying over seven hundred people plus cargo. They're in underground facilities at a secret spaceport on *Hoste Island* in *Tierra del Fuego*, Chile. That's at the extreme tip of South America, and it is completely uninhabited. These ships can travel from the Earth to Mars in three days."

"If what you say is true, Father, why are you bothering to tell me this? I mean, if Earth gets destroyed and these elite people escape, what difference could it possibly make?"

"None, I guess. It's just wrong. You

see, Son, they've been abducting innocent people for three years now because they need skilled workers in many areas to run the base for them. They must know that the blue comet is approaching and getting close.

So far, almost a thousand people, composed of specialists in their fields, have been taken. The majority of them have gone through a device called a Jump Gate."

"A Jump Gate? What's that?"

"Something developed at the Special Devices Center at Area 5.

A Jump Gate is a stable traversable wormhole between two locations. It's a teleportation device. You just walk through it and end up on Phobos. It's located in the Grand Canyon, not far from where you live."

"Are you serious?"

"Yes, Marc. I couldn't be more serious. Those people at Sub Rosa will essentially become slaves when the elite and their families arrive. And that's why I'm telling you this at the end of my life. Because it's wrong. What these people are doing is morally reprehensible. Sub Rosa is their secret domain, and they are utterly arrogant. What's worse is that I've gone along with it, knowing it's wrong. May God forgive me. Both of us are on the evacuation list. So was your mother."

The admiral reached for a tissue

and dried some tears. He cleared his throat and began to cough violently.

Dr. Thompson and one of the nurses walked in and ushered Marc outside.

After about five minutes, Dr. Thompson informed Marc that he'd sedated Bill and that their conversation would have to continue in the morning after he'd had his breakfast.

"Will he, I mean, is he going to make it through the night?"

"I think so. I caution that you don't want to get him excited tomorrow because that just might do him in.

I think he'll be okay. We'll keep a close eye on him through the night and awaken you if necessary. I'll see you in the morning."

Marc woke up slowly. He was warm under lots of blankets and quilts. His eyes focused on the bedroom window, and he saw snow falling lightly outside. He dressed and made his way to the kitchen. The nurses had gone out and brought hot coffee, bagels, and cinnamon rolls. He enjoyed his breakfast and then climbed the stairs to his father's room.

"Good morning, Marc," said Dr. Thompson. "I'll be frank. This may be his last day. So let him talk to you about whatever he has to say and try not to interrupt him too terribly much, okay?"

Marc nodded and entered the room. He sat in the chair. Once again Bill reached out and firmly gripped his son's arm.

"This is the most important part of what I've got to tell you, so listen carefully, Marc. The fact that a blue comet will destroy the Earth has been concealed for a very long time. Our church and the Vatican first learned of it with the three prophecies of *Fatima*, Portugal, in 1917. That's when three children claimed to have seen and spoken with The Virgin Mary. They said She had revealed the prophecies to them. The first two prophecies were made public and involved the hell of World Wars I and II. The third prophecy was kept secret until it was finally released by the Vatican in the year 2000. But, probably for fear of causing a world-wide panic, the official Vatican version didn't speak of a blue comet striking the Earth. Instead, it said the third prophecy was primarily about the fall of the Soviet Union and communism and the attempted assassination of Pope John Paul II."

The admiral coughed violently and quickly recovered.

"Marc, I refuse to believe that Our Heavenly Father would bring a comet to destroy the Earth. And I don't believe that The Blessed Virgin, or her Son, Jesus, would allow all of their children to perish, either. And why should only the rich and powerful elite be spared? I tell you that it's wrong. There must be some way to divert the comet and cause it to miss the Earth."

"But how?" asked Marc. "We haven't the technology to divert a comet. Or maybe, based on what you've told me, we do."

"No, I'm afraid we don't. But I have my faith. And so do others. Somehow I'm convinced that we can save our planet. There is a man named Colonel Jason King. He was an F-15A Eagle Squadron Wing commander when I headed up a carrier task force out of *Yokosuka*, Japan, during the Cold War. We became good friends. Now he's the pilot of the USS *Excalibur*, one of the two large triangular ships in the secret space program. His wife, who is a medical doctor, and their two young daughters, are being held against their wills at the base on Phobos. Jason has had a change of heart. I want you to contact him. The two of you must work together. Find allies you can trust."

Marc wiped tears from his eyes with a tissue and then focused on a black-and-gold lacquered box on the night-stand by his father's bed. Its lid bore the image of a full moon casting its light on an ocean framed by stands of bamboo. The box had been a gift to the admiral from the Japanese government.

"Open the lid. There is a false bottom. Pry it up with your fingernail. You'll find a key taped to the underside. Use the key to unlock the bottom drawer of my desk."

Marc got up and did so. He removed a thick, black three-ring binder and brought it over to the bedside.

"Everything I've told you is carefully documented in there. Guard it with your life. They can't hurt me now, but if they find out you have this information they'll kill you. I'm sorry, Marc, but now I've put you in harm's way."

Marc's father gripped his son's arm tighter, and he gazed at his son with his steel-gray eyes. He began violently coughing again, and his chest heaved up and down. Then the coughing subsided. The admiral's eyes closed and then suddenly opened.

"I see your mother standing over there in the corner. She's waiting for me to be with her in heaven. It's my time, Son. Know that I'm proud of you. You could have joined us in our business and made lots of money, but archaeology has always been your passion. I'm leaving my inheritance to you. I know you'll use it wisely."

He coughed, wheezed, and his face became pale. Then his voice grew in strength.

"Do whatever you can to stop

these evil people. And remember to always have faith. The information for contacting the colonel, Jason King, is in the black binder. Find him. Promise me."

Marc leaned forward. He kissed his father on the cheek and spoke through his tears.

"I give you my word, Father. I promise. I love you so much."

"I love you, too, Marc. I always have."

The admiral's grip on his son's arm went limp. He inhaled and exhaled his last breath, dying with a smile on his face.

Marc sobbed and took hold of his father's hand. He lay his head on his chest.

Dr. Thompson opened the door and entered the room. He placed his hand on Marc's shoulder to comfort him, and the two men cried together.

CHAPTER TWO

Vatican Advanced Technology Telescope (VATT) Mount Graham, Arizona

The sky conditions in southeastern Arizona are among the best in the world, and the Vatican operates a 1.8m telescope there known as the Pope Scope. Mount Graham rises ten thousand seven hundred and seventy-one feet above the surrounding desert and is home to the Vatican Observatory Research Group.

Dr. *Aldo Lanza's* loud shouts from

the telescope above brought Father *Guido Sabelli*, the director of the VATT, out of his downstairs office.

"Extraordinary!"

"Straordinario!"

"Oh my God! What am I saying? It is heading straight for us!"

"Oh, mio Dio! Che cosa dunque intendo dire? Essa è direttamente per noi!"

"What is it, *Aldo*?"

"Ma che cos'e, Aldo?"

"The comet we have been searching for. It exists!"

"La cometa abbiamo cerato. Esiste!"

"Do not worry my friend. We are both on the evacuation list. Please, give me the details."

"Non ti preoccupare, il mio amico. Ci sono nella lista. Per favore, dammi i dettagli."

Father *Sabelli* returned to his office. He looked at his wall clock. It was now 10:45 p.m. A nine-hour difference made it 7:45 a.m. in Rome. He called the private number at the Vatican.

"Good morning. Cardinal *Lorenzo Perizzi* speaking."

"Buon giorno. Il Cardinal Lorenzo Perrizzi parlando."

"Good morning, Your Excellency."

"Buon giorno, Vostra Eccellenza."

"Qual è la password?"

"What is the password?"

"Solar Warden."

"Guardiano solare."

"How may I help you, Dr. *Sabelli*?

"Mi dicca, Dottore Sabelli?"

"We have seen it!"

"Abbiamo visto che."

"Are you certain?"

"Vi sono certi?"

"Yes, confirmed."

"Si, confermato."

"How long do we have?"

"Quanto tempo abbiamo?"

"Less than four weeks."

"Meno di quattro settimane."

"What color is it?"

"Di che colore è?"

"Blue."

"Azzurro."

"Thank you, Doctor."

"La ringrazio, dottore."

"I must call him now."

"Mi deve chiamare lui ora."

Xavier del Mundo returned to his desk and and looked out the window at the New York skyline. He reflected on his life and how he had pursued his goal until it had become a reality.

A memory formed.

He was a young boy standing in front of the bathroom mirror.

He reached for his toothbrush. Then he would comb his hair, get dressed, eat breakfast, and take the bus to school. He was seven years old. He looked up and noticed that a mist had begun to form around the mirror's edges. Soon the mist began to grow at the top, bottom, and sides. It crept steadily toward the center until the entire mirror was fogged over. Then the center began to clear, and, instead of his own image, *Xavier* found himself staring into the blue eyes of a Roman soldier in full army uniform and helmet.

His toothbrush fell from his fingers onto the counter, and he gasped.

The soldier smiled and nodded at him. As the image began to fade, the soldier's blue eyes flashed a fiery crimson. *Xavier* grabbed hold of the counter and knew in that instant, without a doubt, who he was. He was The Antichrist. Then many dozens of faces, both male and female, began to appear in the mirror in quick succession. Only a few of them lingered long enough for *Xavier* to view and recognize. One was a feudal lord in Brittany, another a Spanish conquistador, and yet another a German U-Boat captain. As each image faded, their eyes flashed a fiery crimson.

Xavier then saw a vision in the mirror and knew without a doubt that he was looking at himself as an older man. The man sat behind a large desk in a beautifully decorated office.

The vision was accompanied by a strong feeling that he was seeing himself as the secretary general of the United Nations. If he could someday reach that position, he would be able to control and manipulate the world. He vowed that day, at the age of seven, that he would someday make that goal a reality.

His father had then shouted on the other side of the door.

"*Xavier!* I must use the bathroom. Finish and open the door. Hurry up!"

¡" Javier! Debo usar el cuarto de baño. Termine y abra la puerta. ¡Apresúrese!"

Through the years he had kept his goal in mind and ingratiated himself with members of a global network of criminal enterprises while being employed as an accountant and manager for the local diocese. Growing up in Cordoba, Spain, he studied and earned degrees in law, political science and business administration at the University of

Cordoba. He decided to legally change his name from *Xavier* de Vega to *Xavier del Mundo* and liked to chuckle at the play on words; "Savior of the World".

Eventually he gained a position with the Vatican as an emissary in the diplomatic corps. While he lived in Rome, he became fluent in Italian. And he had eventually learned to live with the inevitable mind-trips that frequently haunted him as he re-lived many of his past life experiences.

Xavier knew that when the day came and he achieved his goal as secretary general of the UN, he would use his position to benefit a separate, secret, technically advanced break-away organization with trillions of dollars that had been embezzled, corrupted, and subverted from member constitutional governments.

The ultimate goal would be to establish a one world government under their total control and to accomplish this under the guise of world peace.

As the years passed by, his positions brought him wealth and importance. *Xavier* and his elite friends oversaw the development of weapons of mass destruction and, learned how to use the media to sway the minds of the vast population, and indoctrinate generations through the control of educational systems worldwide.

Ultimately, they envisioned an entirely depopulated world in which no more than a half-billion people lived and flourished. Their need for the accumulation of money, power, and control was endless, and their greed was unstoppable.

Xavier leaned back in his chair and smiled. He had achieved his lifelong goal and was secretary general of the UN. He had already served for the last five years and had recently been appointed for another five-year term. The concentration and control of the world's finances in the hands of him and his friends were a reality. *Xavier* would, as The Antichrist, become the supreme leader of the new world order.

His secretary buzzed him. "Cardinal *Perrizzi* is calling from Rome."

SUTTON PLACE, MANHATTAN, NEW YORK CITY OFFICIAL RESIDENCE OF THE SECRETARY-GENERAL OF THE UNITED NATIONS

Xavier del Mundo looked down at his large gold ring, which was richly encrusted with blue-white diamonds in the shape of a cross. His desk phone rang and he picked it up.

"Good afternoon, Mr. Secretary. Cardinal *Lorenzo Perrizzi* calling."

"What is the code word?"

"Sub Rosa."

"And the second code word?"

"Solar Warden."

"Please continue."

"VATT has confirmed the comet. It is coming."

"What is the ETA?"

"Less than four weeks."

"What color is it?"

"Blue."

"Then the third prophecy of *Fatima* is true. The time has come, at last, my dear friend."

"Poi la terza profezia di Fatima è vero. Il tempo è arrivato finalmente il mio caro amico."

"Yes."

"Si."

"Initiate the escape operation."

"Iniziare la fuga."

Xavier del Mundo ended the call. He looked down at his gold ring once more. The blue-white encrusted diamonds in the shape of a cross now blazed with an intense bright, red light that reflected his fiery crimson eyes. His mind instantly transported him to *Golgotha* and the crucifixion scene of *Yeshua* on the bloody cross. Then his thoughts carried *Xavier* farther back in time to the early years of his first past life when he had been a young man named *Kenau* Cadwallan, living in Cornwall, Briton. The year was 16 AD.

The fat merchant from *Gaul* uses his sleeve to wipe his mouth, which disgusts me. How best to manipulate this fool to pursue my aims?

"*Kenau*, please pass the gravy to *Monsieur Neve.*"

"Yes, Father."

I wait for the merchant to eat the last of his venison and drain his wine glass.

"*Monsieur Neve*, do you know anyone serving in the imperial Roman army in *Gaul*?"

"Why yes, I do. Why do you ask, *Kenau*?"

I smile at the thought of witnessing the death of *Yeshua* on a cross. I have seventeen years to bring my plans to fruition.

"I wish to join the Roman army as

an auxiliary soldier and serve in the cavalry."

The look of surprise on my father's face delights me.

"You wish to become a Roman soldier?" he exclaims. "Why? I do not understand. You are only sixteen years old!"

"A good age to join," says *Monsieur Neve*. "I know your riding skills are excellent, and *Gorust* tells me that you are fluent in Latin, Greek, and Aramaic, which serves you well."

"And *Kenau* is proficient in mathematics and geometry," offers my father.

"I want to see the world, have adventures, fight battles, and seek excitement. I find my life here in Briton to be boring."

"Very well. I shall make inquires on your behalf. I am friendly with an officer who serves as a recruiter. I will endeavor to make arrangements for him to pay you a visit."

"Thank you, *Monsieur Neve.*"

I watch him wipe his mouth with his sleeve once more and smile to myself.

Quintus Atrius drinks some wine and sets his goblet on the table.

He is here at my father's house to interview me.

"Your riding is exemplary, young man. And the fact that you are conversant in our Roman language, as well as in Greek and Aramaic, is in your favor. But I warn you. The life of an auxiliary soldier in our cavalry will not be one of ease. You will work hard, face danger, and follow orders. After your retirement in twenty-five years, you will become a Roman citizen.

I now ask if you are willing to make a commitment to serve the glory of Rome and the emperor?"

"Yes, Your Excellency, I am."

Quintus turns to face my father across the table and smiles.

"I propose a toast. I accept your son, *Kenau,* as an auxiliary cavalryman in a *cohors equitata* under the command of *Prefecti Titus Caratacus*. He will be assigned to an *alae*, or cavalry wing, and reside in the provincial capital of *Gaul* in *Lugdunum*. May he serve with valor."

My father, *Gorus*t, *Quintus Atrius*, and I stand on the pier. *Brychan* lays my bags down and bids me farewell. My father is crying. He gives me a long embrace.

"Take good care of yourself, *Kenau*.

I will write letters to you. Answer them if you so desire. I wish you a happy life."

I follow *Quintus Atrius* up a wooden ramp and onto the deck of his ship. My father stands below on the pier. I know I will never see him again.

CAESAREA MARITIMA 29 AD

Our ship sails toward the expansive harbor at *Caesarea Maritima* after a ten-day journey from the city of *Ephe*sus. I must soon organize my *cohors equitata* of cavalry and infantry into a caravan, but I decide to take a moment to reflect on my life as a Roman soldier.

It is the fifteenth year of the reign of Emperor *Tiberius Caesar.* I stand on deck and watch as our ship, *Jupiter,* begins to make its way into the vast enclosed harbor, which is capable of accommodating nearly three hundred ships. She is a Roman army troop transport with forty rowers on either side and square-rigged sails.

I am now a thirteen-year veteran in the army. I received training and gained valuable experience for eight years in *Lugdunum,* the Roman capital of *Gaul.* I relive my first combat as I did battle with my *cohort* in 21 AD against two rebellions of Romanized *Gauls* and served under the commands of *Visellius Varro* and *Gaius Silius.* Under *Publius Vellacus* I fought against open rebellions in *Thrace* in 21 AD. and again in 26 AD. I could see the agony on the faces of my enemies as I slew them with my sword.

The memory brings a smile.

I received many decorations and was promoted to *Decurion*; second in command.

I was garrisoned and served the emperor in the Roman port city of *Ephesus* in Asia for the last five years. At long last I am being sent to

Jerusalem in *Judea*. Four years hence, I intend to witness the crucifixion of *Yeshua*.

I end my reverie and approach my *Prefecti, Marcus Fabius*, who orders me to use my knowledge of Aramaic to make arrangements with local herdsmen and negotiate with the transportation outfitters for our caravan.

"We will need oxen to pull two-wheeled wagons, mules for four-wheeled carts, and donkeys and camels for pack animals. The journey will take five nights, and we will arrive in Jerusalem on the sixth day. The area our caravan will be traveling through is full of bandits. We will set up our own camp outside of the nearest cities and post guards. We will carry all of our own food provisions and buy fresh fruits and vegetables along the way. Altogether we have four dozen cavalry and seventy-two infantry foot soldiers. We are reinforcing the soldiers in Jerusalem on orders from Governor *Pontius Pilate* due to increased political insurrection and agitation among the Jewish population."

My *Prefecti* points to our right and speaks. "The herdsmen and outfitters are a five-minute walk to the south."

I salute, walk down the ramp, and step onto the dock. Before me is a remarkable scene. Long rows of white marble columns line the road leading into the city beyond. I can see magnificent palaces and public buildings in the distance. I hear the voice of my *Prefecti* and turn to look up at him as he stands on deck.

"The harbor and city have been constructed within the last twelve years. *Marcus Vitruvius*, the great architect during the reign of Emperor *Augustus Caesar*, provided the guiding principles to build the massive breakwaters. *Herod* built the Temple of *Augustus* that you see before you. He also built the forum to your left and the theater and amphitheater to your right. The buildings are all made of the local *kukur* stone and are coated with polished white stucco."

I point straight ahead to a large rectangular walled pool of water. Three niches in the wall are adorned with statues. Horses drink, and many women fill vessels of various sizes.

"What is that structure?"

"That is the *nymphaenum* which is a fountain and a source of fresh water for the people of *Caeserea Maritima*. The three statues are of Emperor *Augustus Caesar*, *Hygieia*, the goddess of health, and *Asclepios*, the god of medicine."

I thank my *Prefecti* for the

information and proceed to carry out his orders.

Our caravan leaves the city on the main road, named the *Decumanus Maximus*, and heads southeast. Although we are starting in mid-morning, we intend to reach *Hedera* before sundown. The Roman road crosses the fertile Plain of *Sharon* in the region known as *Samaria*. It is *Aprilis* and the fields shimmer green with barley and golden wheat in the sun. Groves of olive trees stand on either side of the road, and rows of them recede in the distance.

Sweat pours down my cheeks and neck under my helmet, and I wipe both with my scarf. My oval shield and javelin are firmly secure on my horse, and my short sword and dagger are sheathed on my military belt. The threat from bandits is real, and they have been known to attack caravans of Roman soldiers such as ours in the past. I ride in front of my *alae* alongside my *Prefecti*. Behind me are our *cohors equitata* of cavalry and foot-soldiers. Oxen and mules pull heavy wagons and carts, and long lines of donkeys and camels kick up clouds of reddish-yellow dust. The heat is intense. It is fifteen *milliarium* to *Hedera*, where we will establish our camp for the night.

At long last, we arrive at the fortified rest stop we call a *castra* or encampment, and set up our tents within the high defensive walls, known as *vallum*. They are made of tightly packed earth and large stones and surround a rectangle with two entrances to the east and west. The sun is low on the horizon by the time the camp is complete. We enjoy a hearty dinner, and, of course, our cook includes *garum,* which is made by crushing and fermenting the intestines of fish, such as anchovies, mackerel, or eel, in saltwater. He seasons it with herbs of fennel, coriander, and oregano. The mixture is left to ferment in the sun for a week and then kept for a further twenty days or so. He stirs it daily until it becomes a liquid, and then it is poured into jars.

I admit that it is an acquired taste.

Night falls swiftly, and guards are posted, to be relieved every two hours. I pause before entering my tent. A fire burns brightly in the center of the *castra*, and I turn around to gaze at the myriad of stars above me. I breathe in the cool air and smile in anticipation of tomorrow's journey. I am one day closer to Jerusalem.

We are on the road shortly after sunrise. The morning air is pleasant, and we move at a good pace. The heat builds as the sun reaches mid-day, and we halt for a rest and a meal. Orchards of grapes and groves of olive and pomegranate trees border both sides of the road.

Samaria is made up of broad valleys lying between steep hills. I can see two high mountains far to the east as we continue our journey. The road begins to ascend, and our caravan leaves the valley; we are now traveling between outcrops covered with rock cliffs on either side.

I order units of my cavalry to ride in the front and rear since this terrain is perfect for anyone intent on ambushing us.

Near late afternoon, we approach, the city of *Sebaste*, which is built on a large hill with steep slopes on all sides. My *Prefecti* tells me that *Herod the Great* rebuilt the ancient city fifty-six years ago and that the name *Sebaste* is Greek for

Augustus. Soon we see an amazing sight. We ride past six hundred stone columns, which line the road leading to the city. The *castra* lies to the north, and we set up our camp there for the night.

The third day of travel takes us through hilly country, and the road winds steadily upward. We pass through a valley lying between two large mountains, named *Ebal* and *Gerizim.* The city of *Shechem* is on the southern side of the valley, and the *castra* has a spring of fresh water nearby, which is a welcome sight. Three more days remain during our journey to Jerusalem.

Our caravan leaves *Samaria* and enters *Judea*, and we head southwards. We camp the next two nights at the *castras* near *Shiloh* and *Gideon*. The morning of the sixth day greets us with bright sunshine and clear blue skies as we eat our meal. I inwardly prepare myself to enter the city of Jerusalem. We have our midday rest and meal at *El-Birah* before resuming our journey. Soon afterward I catch my first glimpse of Jerusalem sitting atop two hills and surrounded by massive, protective, gray stone walls. *Marcus Fabius,* my *Prefecti*, rides beside me.

"I was garrisoned here eight years ago" he says. "Jerusalem is a wonderful city. The *Kidron* Valley lies before us. That large hill is called the Mount of Olives."

"What is the building atop the hill?"

"That is the gold-embellished Jewish Temple. The Jews believe it sits on the most holy spot in the world. The city is divided into two parts; the Upper and the Lower.

The rich and very rich live in white marble palaces in the Upper City. The Lower City is for everyone else and consists of narrow, twisting, unpaved streets. The high, thick gray stone walls you see encircle the city, and there are massive gateways at intervals along the wall where publicans collect taxes on all goods being brought into or taken out of the city. We will enter through the Damascus Gate."

Our caravan approaches the

high arched gate, which is wide, and we easily pass through it. Red-caped Roman soldiers clear the area and hold the crowds back as our wagons, carts, infantry, and cavalry enter. Marcus and I dismount and lead our horses forward on the cobblestones. We walk past merchants and craftsmen sitting behind their stalls. An old *Bedouin* woman places a date in my hand. I put it in my mouth, and it crunches as I bite down. I taste its sweetness and remove the pit. I smile at her as we walk on. I hear Greek, Hebrew and Aramaic, being spoken. Peasants drive their flocks of bleating sheep along the road inside the gate.

I drop some silver Roman coins down on a table and drink a cup of cold licorice tea. The air is filled with smoke, incense, and the smell of perfume.

My head is spinning! More *Bedouin* women, their heads covered in brightly colored scarves, sell carved wooden boxes, knitted bags, figs, grapes, okra, dates, and tea.

"This way," says *Marcus,* and we follow a road that forks to the left.

I make sure that our caravan is behind us.

"We will stop at a rest area up ahead," he says. "There our goods, weapons, and supplies will be unloaded and the herdsman and outfitters paid. They will return to *Caesarea Maritima* in the morning. We will see to it that all of our troops are installed in their barracks. Once that is done, you and I will enter the Fortress *Antonia* and present ourselves to the *Tribune,* who is named *Demetrius Aquila*."

I see the walls of the fortress rising above me. Four stone towers stand solidly at each corner above the battlements. *Marcus* and I walk through a gate guarded by two armed Roman soldiers, who salute us. We climb a series of stone stairs to a platform and then mount another flight of stairs.

"*King Herod* built this strong fortress around sixty-five years ago to protect the Temple Mount," *Marcus* says. "He named it after his friend, *Marc Antony.* An underground passage goes from the fortress to the Temple. There are usually around six hundred Roman soldiers garrisoned here and another four hundred at the palace of the *Tetrarch, Herod Antipas.*"

We reach yet another platform and stop. Two more armed soldiers stand guard on either side of a door and salute us. One of them knocks on the door, and a tall, robust man with graying hair opens it and gestures for us to enter. The door closes behind us, and we stand in the office of the *Tribune* of Fortress *Antonia.*

He is dressed in a full Roman army uniform.

"Welcome to the Legion X *Fretensis*," he says and smiles.

"I welcome you and your reinforcements. The Jews in *Galilee* are known as *Zealots*. They disparagingly refer to us Romans as *Kittam*. There have been attacks on our soldiers and open rebellion. A new edict issued by Governor *Pontius Pilate* states that no more than twenty adult males are allowed to assemble at one time. Recently the Jews are being greatly agitated and incited by a rabble-rouser from *Galilee* who speaks about a Kingdom of God."

"Does he go by the name of *Yeshua*?" I ask.

"No. He is known to his followers as one named Jesus."

Demetrius Aquila sits at his desk and motions for us to sit, as well.

"I have read your military record, *Decurion Cadwallan*. You have faithfully served the empire and I commend you. I see that you are fluent in Greek, Latin, Aramaic, and Hebrew. Therefore, I am assigning you to be chief liaison officer between the Roman authorities here in Jerusalem and the high priest of the Jewish *Sanhedrin* Council, *Joseph Caiaphas*."

"Thank you, sir. I am honored."

We both salute him. Our meeting

is over. *Marcus* and I climb yet another flight of stairs and exit onto the roof of the northeastern tower. The city of Jerusalem is spread before us. The Temple sits above all in its splendor with golden-topped decorations and white marble columns. Many structures have orange or red-colored roofs, and there are quite a few domed buildings.

I walk over to a far wall and stand alone. The heat is intense, and I use my left hand to shade my eyes as I look out over the city. I have, at long last, arrived at my destination after many years of planning. Four years hence, I intend to witness the crucifixion of the man I know as

Yeshua, who is apparently known locally as Jesus. I am certain they are one and the same.

JERUSALEM 33 AD

The year and my age are the same—33 AD. The day is *Martius* 20th.

I am at a meeting of the *Sanhedrin Council*. Present are the high priest, *Joseph Caiaphas*, various members of the Jewish *Pharisees* and *Sadducees,* an elder, *Jonathan Annas*; and a man known to us Romans as *Judas Sicarius*. I receive a report and a request from those present. The man named Jesus went into the Temple of God and overturned the tables of the money changers. He cast out all who sold and bought in the Temple and then prohibited sacrifices from being offered for several hours.

I asked what the Roman authorities wish, and they answer as one that they want to silence Jesus once and for all and request that He be arrested, tried for political insurrection, and crucified.

I return to Fortress *Antonia* and have a meeting with the *Tribune*, *Demetrius Aquila*.

"Why do the Jews want this man arrested?," he asks.

"They claim that he threatens their authority, and the sacredness of their traditions. Also he is anti-Roman, and outright rebellious."

"Tell *Joseph Caiaphas* that I order him to take a force of officers to arrest this man. I want you to accompany them with a squad of eight of our Roman soldiers."

"Yes, sir."

The man, now known as Jesus, was called *Yeshua* when we first met nineteen years ago. I decide to bring *Judas Sicarius* along to identify him.

"Where is He?" I ask *Judas*.

"In a place called *Gethsemane*. We must go out through the north Temple gate, go down into the *Kidron* Valley, cross the river, make a right, and then take a left turn," answers *Judas*.

"Let us make haste."

We approach a walled compound.

Judas opens a gate, and we enter. A group of men are standing in a garden with rows of olive trees. *Judas* walks up to one man dressed in a white robe and kisses him on the cheek. I nod to my soldiers, and we place the man in white under arrest and lead him out through the open gate. We return to the city, where Jesus is given a quick trial. He is found guilty of both blasphemy and insurrection. I am authorized to interrogate him before he is crucified.

I order my men to strip Jesus of his clothes and watch with delight as he is pinioned and bound by ropes to a tall wooden stake. His bare back beckons for chastisement. My *flagellum* is no ordinary whip, and each end of its twelve leather thongs has metal, bone, or sharpened nails. I remove my helmet. Jesus looks straight at me without any response.

"Do you not recognize me?"

"Your intense negative energy clearly identifies you as Chosech, or The Antichrist."

"Are you not surprised to see me after all these years?"

"Our Father long ago foretold all that is about to occur. Proceed."

I rear back and whip his back over and over. He does not utter a sound.

I order my men to untie him and carry him to the wagon. *Yeshua* turns and looks straight at me. I see a single tear form and roll down his right cheek.

"Is that all I get for the pain I just inflicted on you? Only one tear?"

"The tear is not because of any pain. It is for your inability to give and to receive love. Hatred shall never prevail, and in the end Love shall always triumph."

My squad transports the man known as Jesus outside the northern wall to a place called *Golgotha*.

A cross has been placed atop the hill.

I see to it that Jesus is staked through His hands and feet to the cross, and we depart. I return with one of my men named *Longinus* three days later.

I order Him to pierce Jesus's right

side with his spear point. A mixture of blood and water pours forth.

"*Mithtra*! He lives!"

A bright, golden halo appears over Jesus's head, and *Longinus* falls to his knees. Jesus opens His eyes, looks straight at me, and our eyes meet.

My eyes glow a fiery crimson.

"I have long planned to witness your death. I, who alone represent the Darkness of Chaos, have come to watch you die. And when you die, so will Goodness, and I will at last reign Supreme."

Yeshua smiles down at me.

"And you, my brother, shall be consumed by the fires of a great comet. Your body shall be

incinerated by that of My own fiery breath. In that moment your vital essence, indeed your very soul, shall be utterly extinguished and cease to exist."

My face contorts with rage. I scream and spit on Jesus, who stares down at me.

"Although My own physical body may perish, you and I shall meet again many more times in the future."

"How will this be so? You will be dead."

"If Spirit came into being because of the body, it is a wonder of wonders.

At this moment know that I both love you and forgive you."

SUTTON PLACE, MANHATTAN, NEW YORK CITY

Xavier del Mundo's heart beat loudly in his chest. He opened his blue eyes wide, blinked a few times, and looked around him. He found that he sat at his office desk. Outside was the skyline of New York City. He shook his head vigorously in a concerted effort to return to the reality of the present. He picked up the phone.

KEAMS CANYON, ARIZONA

"Jeez," whined Jack. "Where is she? There's only five cars left on the street!"

Augi sighed.

"Be patient. You got some hot date you gotta get to or something?"

"No, I'm just bored sitting here. That's all. And I'm nervous, too."

Jenny Spadaro stayed after the meeting to converse with the sheriff and other law enforcement officials. The hall had emptied out by the time she returned to her car. She opened her small suitcase in the back seat and put her laptop inside. She still planned on staying in Flagstaff and visiting the Grand Canyon over the weekend. She wondered how her Special Agent in Charge would react when she walked into the office on Monday morning.

Augi glanced in his rear-view

mirror as the FBI agent walked out of the hall.

"There she is. We'll wait till she drives away and then follow her at a distance. Buckle up."

Marc Prentis headed east in his truck down Route 264. All he wanted was to get to his house in Keams Canyon. He sighed, and tears formed because he suddenly felt very much alone in the world. Two months remained before he returned to teaching at the University of Arizona in Flagstaff. In the meantime, he had only his cat, *Mansi*, to talk to.

Marc used his handkerchief to dry his face. He was both physically and emotionally exhausted from the incredible deathbed confession of his father, the long flights there and back, and the endless memories constantly playing in his mind. Altogether they'd taken their toll on him, and he looked forward to a relaxing, hot shower followed by a good ten hours of sleep.

Jenny headed west. Once out of the canyon, there was nothing but flat desert on either side of the road. Tall *saguaro* cacti grew in abundance. She saw no other cars approaching and only one car a good distance behind her. The meeting had been intense, and she put on a classical music CD to ease her nerves. She noted that the road directly ahead crossed a deep ravine and then began to steadily rise.

The calmness brought on by the music ended abruptly by the sound of shattering glass and the thump of something smacking into the left side of her car. She quickly turned her head and got a good look at two men using their car to push hers off the road. They were both smiling.

Jenny grabbed the steering wheel, prayed to Jesus, and held on as she took out the guardrail and sailed through the air. Her car crash-landed on a steep, rocky incline and then plunged downward at a fast rate. The front end smashed against a boulder at the bottom, and, as the air bag inflated, she was thrown forward into her steering wheel and knocked unconscious.

Marc reached the top of the hill and smiled. He was almost home. Then his smile vanished when he saw a car push another one off the road. He hit the gas and drove downhill. The other car sped past him in a blur.

He parked his truck and looked into the ravine. There was a vehicle at the bottom, and he could see someone in the driver's seat. Marc quickly made his way down the slope. The driver was a woman.

He opened the door. She was slumped forward. He felt her neck for a pulse and found one. She was alive. Marc unbuckled her seat belt and lifted her out of the car. He gently laid her on the ground and stood up. His heart was racing, and he used a handkerchief to wipe sweat from his forehead.

Then the woman groaned and opened her eyes.

"Who are you? Where am I?"

"My name's Marc Prentis. You've had an accident. Can you walk?"

Jenny painfully sat up and felt for anything broken. She was okay. Marc reached down and helped her get up. He stood by her till she was steady on her feet.

"I smell gasoline," he said. "We'd better get away from your car."

He took her hand and they began to make their way uphill.

"My handbag is in the front, and my small suitcase is in the back seat," she said. "I can't leave them."

Marc ran to the car. He grabbed her bag, but the rear door was stuck. He reached behind and hauled her suitcase up and over the front seat. Then the two of them scrambled up the slope. They made it to the road just as Jenny's car erupted in flames, followed by a tremendous explosion.

"Oh, crap. I loved that car," moaned Jenny. She looked up, crossed herself, and whispered, "Sorry," then smiled at Marc.

Augi drove up the hill. Jack turned to look back and saw a column of black smoke billowing up from the ravine. He smiled broadly.

"She's toast."

"Good," said Augi. "Let's get outta here."

The woman gently touched her bruised forehead and winced in pain.

"Someone just tried to kill you. Why?" asked Marc.

He watched the woman rummage through her handbag. Marc's eyes went wide when he glimpsed a revolver.

"My name's Jenny Spadaro," she said and produced a gold badge. "I'm an agent with the Phoenix FBI."

Marc sighed with relief.

"My name is Dr. Marc Prentis. I'm a local professor of archaeology."

"Where are we going?"

"I'm taking you to my house. I live

in Keams Canyon. Your body will go into shock soon and you'll need to lie down and get some sleep."

"Thank you for saving my life, Marc. I'm forever grateful."

"You're welcome, Jenny, but I ask again. Why did someone want to kill you?"

"I attended a regional meeting at the Keams Canyon town hall concerning a thousand people who've gone missing in four states. My guess is some bad guys didn't like the idea of an FBI agent investigating whatever it is they're up to."

Marc nodded. He drove past St. Joseph's Catholic Church and made a right turn. His house was at the end of a short street.

"We're here. Let me help you out of the truck and get inside first. Then I'll get your suitcase."

Jenny felt stiff, and she was beginning to shake. She took Marc's hand and eased herself out of the seat. It was an effort to make it up a few stairs and onto a porch. There were a couple of rocking chairs with an orange cat asleep in one. Marc unlocked the front door, and they entered. He put Jenny's handbag on the floor and helped her lie down on a couch with a pillow behind her head. Marc switched on a ceiling fan and opened windows. Then he went out to his truck and brought in his suitcase and Jenny's. He started a tea kettle heating on the kitchen stove.

"I've been gone for a couple of days," he said as he sat down in a chair. "My father passed away yesterday in Maryland."

Jenny's eyes had been closed.

She opened them and expressed her sincere condolences.

"Thank you, Jenny. I'll make some herbal tea for you. Drink it and rest."

"Thanks, Marc."

She closed her eyes and drifted off. Marc set the tea cup and two aspirin beside her on a coffee table. He unpacked and, in a moment of indecision, shoved the thick, black binder under his bed. Jenny was drinking the tea and had taken the aspirin when he returned.

"Oh, this is good," she said and smiled.

He sat down again and looked at her. She was pretty. Dark, curly hair, a pert nose, blue eyes, high cheek-bones, medium height, and trim.

A warm feeling began to stir in his heart. *"No,"* he said to himself and quickly averted his eyes.

Jenny looked at Marc. He was handsome in a rugged way: tan, and clean-shaven, with short, blond hair and green eyes. Tall, maybe six feet, and muscular with a relaxed smile and an easy way about him. He seemed to be a nice person. She became aware that a faint sensation had begun to grow in her heart. *"No,"* Jenny said firmly to herself. *"I'm not ready."*

The tea helped to calm her, and she soon became drowsy. Marc noticed.

"I'll bring a blanket in. You may want to use the bathroom now. Let me help you up off the couch."

Jenny washed her face and hands, brushed her teeth, and looked in the mirror. A sizable black and blue mark had formed on her forehead over a large lump. The pain was intense and throbbed. She wiped away tears, sighed, and returned to the couch.

"You've been through a very rough time, Jenny. I put some ice cubes in a ziplock bag. Place it on your forehead and get a good night's sleep."

Marc turned off the light. He finally took a shower, went to his bedroom, and slept.

Jenny smelled bacon, and her stomach growled. She opened her eyes. Marc was in the kitchen silhouetted against a sunlit window. She felt much better and realized she hadn't eaten anything since noon yesterday.

Marc turned and saw her get out from under the blanket, slowly stand up, and rub her eyes.

"Do you eat bacon?" he asked.

"You bet. I love bacon!"

"Great. Breakfast's soon."

Jenny walked to the bathroom. Her legs seemed to be working okay, but they were very stiff. When she looked in the mirror, she almost fainted. A huge reddish, purple bruise covered her entire forehead. She found the aspirin bottle in the medicine cabinet and took four more because the pain was still intense. "But, thank God, I'm alive," she said aloud. She washed up, got a change of clothes from her suitcase, and joined Marc at the table. He'd made eggs, bacon, toast, coffee, and orange juice.

"I always offer a prayer," said Marc.

"Please."

Marc placed his palms together.

"I give thanks to Jesus for my

life on this beautiful day, for my blessings and opportunities, for my good and improving health, and all that I have, all that I give, and all that I receive. And for Jenny's company. Amen."

"Amen," echoed Jenny.

"Food is neat. Let's eat!"

Jenny laughed and ate a piece of bacon. She was impressed that Marc had mentioned Jesus in his prayer. She'd been raised as a Roman Catholic in Queens, a borough of New York City.

"Where did you grow up, Marc?"

"Everywhere. My father was an admiral in the Navy and we moved around a lot. I went to different schools on US bases around the world. As a result, I didn't live in any one place for very long until I went to college. How about you?"

"New York City, mostly. I went to NYU and studied criminal justice.

I got a law degree at Yale, but never practiced. I was more action oriented and decided to take placement tests for the FBI. I passed and did my initial training at Quantico, Virginia. I worked at one of our New York City field offices."

"How did you end up in Arizona?"

"Luck, I guess. I love it. My technical computer skills were needed here, and my specialty is in missing persons cases. I applied for a transfer and started at the Phoenix field office just over two years ago. How about you, Marc?"

"Should I tell her that I know why people have been disappearing?" he thought. He decided to wait for the time being and answered her question.

"I've always had an interest in archaeology. I used to visit ancient ruins and temples in Greece and other European countries during school vacations, but the Native Americans of the Southwest have always intrigued me. I went to the University of Arizona and got both my undergraduate and graduate degrees there. Now I teach at Northern Arizona University in Flagstaff."

"If you teach there, then why are you living over three hours away in Keams Canyon?"

"An FBI agent's question if I ever heard one!"

Jenny laughed.

"Sorry, I just can't help it," she said and smiled.

Marc smiled back. He carried their dishes to the sink. The orange cat meowed and looked up.

"Oh, so you're hungry, too."

He spooned cat food in a small bowl and set it down.

"I'm on a six month sabbatical to write a book about the ancient Anasazi people. The Hopi call them *Hisatsinom* or "Ancient Ancestors". I'm nearly done, and I've found many sites in this area and recently made some pretty cool discoveries."

"I'm fascinated by the ancient *Puebloans*. I've done some reading about them."

Jenny brought the empty cups and glasses to the sink. She then patted her stomach and smiled.

"Thanks, Marc. That was so good.

I hadn't eaten anything since yesterday afternoon."

"How's your forehead? That's quite a bruise you've got."

"It hurts like you know what. I must have slept for twelve hours, and I'm feeling a lot better. The only thing is that I'm not sure if I can walk for any long distance, and I'd like to go to the Catholic church I saw on the way. Could you please give me a ride?"

"Sure. Let me know when you're ready."

Marc turned to the sink and began to wash the breakfast dishes.

ST. JOSEPH'S MISSION CATHOLIC CHURCH

Marc pulled up in front of the red-brick church. Two arched windows flanked the front door. A bell tower with a cross stood above the peaked roof. Marc helped Jenny slowly make her way up a flight of stone stairs and declined to go inside because he understood that she needed her privacy.

"I'll be here by the door if you need me."

Jenny dipped her hands in the open font of holy water. She then crossed herself and prayed.

"By this holy water and by Your precious blood, wash away all my sins, O Lord".

She entered the small church and took a seat in the first pew in front of the altar. There was no one else present, and Jenny shivered in the cold morning air despite her sweater. She placed her palms together and closed her eyes. Her forehead throbbed with such pain that it brought tears to her eyes. Scenes from yesterday's attempt on her life and Marc's timely rescue played in her mind. She knew she was protected and that his appearance had been no accident.

Jenny sighed and began to speak aloud in a strong voice.

"I choose this day to give thanks for saving my life to Marc Prentis and to my mother and queen, O Blessed Virgin Mary. And I give myself entirely to Your sacred heart, and to Your Son, my Lord, Jesus Christ. I will be more faithful to You than I have ever been before. Use me according to Your good pleasure and for the greater glory of God. Amen."

Her eyes remained closed. Then she thought of the smiling faces of the two men who had tried to kill her.

A wave of empathy swept through her.

"I forgive them both," she said.

Upon speaking those words, the unmistakable fragrance of roses filled the chapel accompanied by a rush of heated air. Jenny Spadaro's heart unfolded as she was overcome by pulses of love. Her eyes opened wide, and she gasped aloud.

The figure of a beautiful woman looked down on her. She had dark hair and wore a light-blue cloak, which covered her head and fell about her shoulders. Twelve glowing, silver stars formed a halo around her head. Her gown was pink and tied with a sash at the waist. She wore sandals and floated in the air about three feet above the floor. The woman smiled at her and spoke.

"My dearest child. Please call your friend, Marc, and ask him to join us."

Jenny sat, stunned. Tears streamed down her cheeks. She tried to speak, but was unable to utter a sound.

"Please."

Jenny took in a deep breath and released it slowly. Then she turned her head toward the door.

"Marc, would you please come in here?"

He entered the chapel and stopped short. Marc's eyes went wide, and he sat beside Jenny. Tears quickly formed, and he sobbed as powerful waves of love pulsed through him.

"Oh, my Blessed Virgin Mary."

She gazed down on them and spoke.

"My dear children, I have been asked to deliver the following message from The One God, and have chosen both of you to hear it:

Men have not changed their warlike ways and bettered themselves. The One God has decided to inflict a severe punishment on all humanity.

It will be a punishment more terrible than the Great Flood and one that will never have been seen before. Blue fire will fall from the sky and destroy a great part of humanity.

Death will come to both the good as well as the bad, sparing neither the priests nor the faithful. Those who survive will find themselves so devastated that they will envy the dead."

"But why?" asked Jenny. "I don't understand. There is so much more good and beauty in the world than evil. What is the punishment?"

"A blue comet is coming that will completely destroy Earth."

Marc at last found the words to speak.

"He must not do this! Please! There has to be a way to change His mind!"

"My husband, Joseph, after whom this church is so named, My Son,

Yeshua, and Myself, have implored, petitioned, and pleaded with The One God. He has reluctantly agreed to spare humanity, but only if a certain task is successfully completed, one that is nearly impossible to complete."

"Please, my Blessed Mother," implored Jenny, "tell us please. What is the task? And why, out of everyone else on the planet, have you chosen Marc and me?"

"The task so states that a golden disc must be placed on the out-stretched left hand of a gilded statue that represents Me. It stands atop the cathedral of Notre Dame des Doms in Avignon, France. And I have chosen you because of your

combined skills and knowledge, your deep faith and belief in Me and My Son, and your ability to overcome personal tragedies and to find forgiveness. I can also see that you will work well together as a team."

"Who is The One God you speak of?" asked Jenny.

"The One God who created the entire universe and our world. He or She is known by many names. Catholics say, *The Holy Father,* Jews *say Yaweh,* Muslims say *Allah,* Hindus say *Krishna,* Buddhists *say Brahma."*

Marc and Jenny absorbed Her words.

"What happens when the golden

disc is placed on the statue's left hand?" asked Marc.

"Once the disc has been set in place, The One God will create a miracle and cause the blue comet to miss Earth."

"Where is this golden disc?" asked Jenny. "How are we to find it?"

"I am aware of its location. However, The One God has forbidden Me to reveal it to you. Both of you must find it yourselves."

"How are we supposed to find it?" asked Marc. "And how much time do we have?"

"My answer to your first question is quite simple. You must have faith. I will do all that I can to assist and guide you in every possible way that

I can. The answer to your second question is less than four weeks."

Marc and Jenny bowed their heads as waves of love radiated through every cell and atom of their beings. When they finally raised their eyes, The Blessed Virgin was gone. Jenny gingerly touched her forehead with a finger and then rubbed it with her whole hand because there was no longer any pain.

They sat in stunned silence for a long time. Marc was the first to stir. They looked at one another for a moment, and smiles lit their faces. Marc stood up slowly. Jenny quickly got to her feet. She didn't need him to help her descend the stairs, but bounded down them and jumped in the truck. Marc drove back to his house, and joy filled his heart.

Jenny took a seat on the couch. Marc sat across from her in a chair.

"If the end of the world is coming, how are we supposed to stop it?" she said. "How can we succeed at the task set by The One God?"

"My father's last words echoed Mother Mary's. He said, *'Remember to always have faith'.*"

Marc looked over at Jenny and smiled.

"Your bruise is gone."

"What? Really?"

She ran to the bathroom to look in the mirror.

Marc got up and went to his

bedroom. He returned with the thick, black binder.

"Oh, Marc, you're right. It *is* gone! We really *did* see the Virgin Mother, after all. It all seems like a dream, but she *was real*!"

Then she noticed the black binder.

"My father gave this to me before he died. I was going to give it to you when you felt ready to return to Phoenix, but we're running out of time. I thought you'd better have a look at it now."

He set it down on the coffee table. "What is it?"

"All the answers to your questions regarding the missing people are in there."

Jenny leaned forward and began

leafing through the binder. She stopped to read one page, then another, and yet another. Then she read whole sections and looked up.

"Is this for real?"

Marc nodded and sat beside her.

"I read most of it on the flight home. My father was one of forty people who knew about the blue comet. In there you will find out about a secret space program and an underground base on Phobos, a moon of Mars. That's where all the missing people are being taken to build and maintain a sustainable living environment. They plan on having one thousand four hundred and forty-four people from among the world's wealthiest and most powerful elite escape to Phobos in two large triangular spaceships just before the comet strikes Earth."

Jenny slowly shook her head and looked skeptically at Marc.

"Yes, I know it sounds crazy, but this is for real. My father's last words were for me to stop these evil people and to find a man named Colonel Jason King. He's the pilot of one of the two triangular ships. He's had a change of heart and will help us. His private cell phone number is in the binder."

"As crazy as all this information seems, I must believe what's in this binder. If it's indeed true, then I'm almost certain that these people took my twin sister, Janey. She's a hydroponics engineer and went missing five days ago from Albuquerque. She must be at the base on Phobos."

"I'll find her, Jenny. I promise you."

"No, Marc. You and I are going to find her together."

SUB ROSA BASE, PHOBOS, MARS

The darkness gave way to blinding light, and Janey Spadaro stumbled and fell forward. She lay sprawled on the ground. A pair of hands grabbed her around the waist and lifted her to a standing position. Her eyes blinked in the harsh lights, then focused on a group of people standing around her. She turned and looked wildly at each face, then stopped. The tall, pretty blond woman and the imposing man with dark-gray hair from the Christmas party stood before her.

The man addressed her.

"Welcome to our growing community, which we call Sub Rosa. Your expertise in hydroponics is greatly needed here. I am the Director and my name is Michael Dryer. I believe you've met my wife, Andrea."

"You hit me on the head with a wine bottle and have taken me against my will. I demand that you return me immediately. You've got no right to do this to me!"

"You will be housed, well-fed, and all of your needs will be taken taken care of in exchange for your work," said Andrea.

"This is wrong!" shouted Janey. "I don't want to be here. I want to go home!"

She turned back toward the Jump Gate and tried to run between two armed men, who blocked her. One of the men spun her around.

"You are now half-a-mile below the surface of a moon named Phobos, which orbits the planet Mars three times a day," said Michael. "Phobos has no atmosphere to speak of, and the average surface temperature is four hundred and sixty degrees below zero Fahrenheit. Sub Rosa, Ms. Janey Spadaro, will be the place you call home for the remainder of your life. There is no escape."

CHAPTER THREE

Southern Peru, 1533 AD

Atahualpa was the last Incan emperor. The Spanish, under the leadership of *Francisco Pizarro*, executed him in the city of *Cajamarca*. His most loyal friend and general, *Ati Ruminahui,* brought his remains to *Sigchos* for burial. *Ruminahui* then based his fight for survival in this place against the Spanish intruders. *Sigchos* is about forty-five miles south of *Quito*, located on a hill dotted with brush. Archaeological excavations there have found a complex of walls, aqueducts, and remarkable stonework. A walled walkway starts at the *Machay* River, and one can still see the shape of an *ushno,* or staircase, which rises on one side of a pyramid. The pyramid is thought to contain the emperor's tomb. Nearby, a tiny, cut channel of water in a rock wall spilled out a small waterfall into a pool nicknamed, "the Inca's Bath."

When the Spanish conquistadors arrived in Peru, they looted gold along with silver and precious stones from the Inca tribes. One Incan priest of the Temple of the Seven Rays, named *Amaru Maru,* fled from *Sigchos* along with General *Ruminahui.* The priest carried a sacred golden disc known as, "The Key of the Gods," and they hid in the mountains of southern Peru, known as the *Hayu Marca*.

They eventually came upon the *Punku Hayu Marca*, a dimensional doorway portal carved into a sheer rock wall. *Q'ero* shaman priests watched and guarded the closed portal. *Amaru Maru* showed them the golden disc. A ritual was then performed, and the disc was set in a round indentation to the right of the closed door. The doorway opened, and an intense, brilliant, blue light issued forth. *Amaru Maru* smiled at General *Ruminahui* and then passed through the open portal, which closed after him. He was never seen again.

There was a meeting among the priests. What should they do with the sacred golden disc? They couldn't allow the Spaniards to capture it.

They prayed to *Inti*, the Sun God, and *Pachamama*, the Earth Mother.

In a flash of blinding light, a golden rain began to fall on their arms and upturned faces. The entire area reverberated with the voice of *Pachamama*.

"The golden disc must be hidden high in the Hayu Marca Mountains. Follow my light. I will lead you to a secluded and hidden valley. Our journey begins at sunrise."

General *Ruminahui* and the other priests set out the next morning. They walked over rough terrain with their llamas for many hours. Above them shone a bright, golden beam of light that led them in the right direction.

Eventually, in the late afternoon, they began to ascend a steep hill. A wide river came into view, and they followed it westward. A forest appeared, and a small tributary stream flowed north. The men walked along its sand and rocky banks, which brought them to a large waterfall cascading into the stream. *Ati Ruminahui* and the priests led their llamas around and behind the falls.

The view before them was stunning. A deeply green, hidden valley lay between two lofty mountains. On the mountain to the right stood a tall pillar of black stone. *Ruminahui* and the others watched, open-mouthed, as *Pachamama's* golden beam of light sculpted the pillar into the shape of a giant condor with its wings folded along its sides. Then, on the side of the mountain to the left, She used Her beam of light to draw an undulating *amaru*, or snake, onto a sheer rock wall. A natural crack, or fissure, curved vertically up and down, and the form of the snake exactly matched the contours of the fissure. At the bottom was the head of the snake.

Pachamama's voice suddenly spoke loudly and echoed throughout the valley. The priests fell to their knees, but the general remained standing. She directed them to descend to the valley floor. They carefully made their way down and stood before the massive rock wall.

"Ati Ruminahui, My blessed child, insert your hand into the jaws of the snake."

He did so and felt a handle.

"Pull the handle toward you."

A loud, grinding, groaning noise filled the air, and once again the priests fell to their knees in fright. General *Ruminahui* released the handle and stepped back as a sizable section of the tall, rock wall slid sideways and revealed an open doorway. *Ruminahui* and the priests stepped through and found themselves inside a small chamber. In the center lay a stone altar, on which sat a gleaming, golden bowl. The voice of *Pachamama* spoke once more.

"Place the Key of the Gods, otherwise known as the Sun Disc, inside the bowl and depart."

As the last priest made his way outside, a tremendous noise filled the air, the rock wall slid sideways, the doorway vanished, and the large undulating snake appeared once more.

Twilight bathed the sky in hues of cobalt blue and magenta. General

Ruminahui and the priests fed and watered their llamas and made camp for the night. They prepared a meal and offered blessings to *Pachamama* before they slept.

The next morning they followed the golden light beam of the Earth Mother and safely returned to the *Punku Hayu Marca* in the late afternoon. The men rested, and, as the sun became low on the horizon, a sound, subdued at first, then louder, filled the air with the sweet song of birds and the joyous voices of many hundreds, no thousands, of people singing. The figure of a tall, beautiful woman appeared before them. She wore a long, flowing robe and floated three feet above the ground. Her smiling face was framed by long, dark hair, and Her eyes were blue. A circle of twelve silver stars formed a halo around Her head. The priests and General *Ruminahui* cried as one and prostrated themselves before Her. *Pachamama* raised Her arms and spoke in a melodious voice filled with love.

"I ask of you a favor and set a task. The Golden Sun Disc will be needed at a time in the far, distant future. It will be a time in which the entire Earth, our world, will face complete and utter destruction."

The men stared up at *Pachamama,* and tears flowed from their eyes.

"How will the Golden Sun Disc prevent the destruction of the world?" asked a priest named *Hualpa.*

"When it is used properly, the pachacuti, the long-held Q'ero prophecy of great change, will take place.The world will be turned right-side-up and unified. Harmony and order will be restored. Evil and chaos will be ended once and for all. Hualpa, you are a master stone carver. Will you carve a map showing the location of the Golden Sun Disc onto a stone at Sacsayhuaman? I will select the stone."

"Yes, of course. I will do as You ask."

General *Ati Ruminahui* trembled and looked up at *Pachamama*. Her long, flowing robe was moving, changing, and transforming before his eyes. Wide blue rivers coursed and emptied into oceans and gray mountains upthrust from the oceans. Green tropical jungles became brown deserts and then returned to jungles once again. Fiery volcanos erupted, lightning lit the horizons, flowers blossomed, and rainbows filled the air. Beneath Her breasts lay an area of darkness in which a large blue sphere floated, wreathed in white clouds. Suspended above Her upturned right palm was a grayish, white sphere the general identified as the Moon. Then the thought came to him that the blue sphere must be the whole Earth as seen from a very long distance. He closed his eyes and shook his head in awe and wonder.

"General Ruminahui. your considerable powers of observation will be useful to Hualpa in carving the map stone, which must be accurate and contain identifiable landmarks. Depart in the morning for Sacsayhuaman."

Again the air was filled with the songs of birds and the joyous voices of multitudes of people singing.

Pachamama smiled at them, and in a flash of golden light, She was gone.

The general accompanied *Hualpa* to his house, while the other priests returned to their homes. They agreed to meet that evening just after sunset.

Hualpa hugged his wife, *Niqa*, and his six-year-old son, *Cusi*. He introduced *Ruminahui,* and the two men recounted their adventures. *Niqa* prepared a meal, and the two men departed as the sun grew low on the horizon. They carried unlit torches, and *Hualpa* brought along his stone-carving tools in a sack he carried on his shoulder.

The other priests arrived and looked down from the hill onto the city of *Cuzco* far below. The others had brought torches, as well. Though the Spanish rarely ventured forth at night, the general cautioned to leave them unlit since they may draw their unwanted attention.

"Let us find a comfortable place to wait for *Pachamama*," *Ruminahui* said.

They sat on the ground with their backs to a stone wall. The first stars and a half-moon appeared in the night sky. The men dozed.

"Look! To the west atop that great wall," the general shouted.

They stood as one and walked toward a golden beam of light shining down from above. A pathway led to various rooms used to store Incan weapons of war. The light beam illuminated the doorway of one such room, and they entered. The golden light focused on a medium-sized stone block set in a corner one course above the floor. The men approached it, and *Hualpa* lit his torch along with the others. The golden light went out, and the men knelt and examined the stone. It was no different from those surrounding it.

"We must carve an accurate map of the way to the hidden valley onto this stone.

"How should I proceed?" asked *Hualpa*.

"I have the ability to place myself above an area in my mind and look down upon it," said the general. "Allow me to describe what I see and begin to carve the stone accordingly."

And so the men met, and an aerial topographic map was carved onto the stone over a period of four nights.

The map stone, or *t'aslara muruk'u* in *Quechuan*, was done. The men prepared to return to their homes when the form of *Pachamama* appeared before them. They fell to their knees.

"You have pleased me beyond measure. There is one more carving to be done by Myself. Cover your eyes, and, I caution you, do not look up."

The men complied. A brilliant light filled the room and lasted for many minutes before darkness returned. *Pachamama* was gone. Torches were lit, and the men saw that along with the aerial map there were now two lists of words, which they were unable to read or understand.

Pachamama had inscribed two lists of place names beginning with the *punku,* or door, where they had begun their journey. She knew *Quechuan* was an unwritten language at this time in human history. However, She also knew that, far in the distant future, there would be those who would be able to read and translate the two lists, which read as follows:

punku Hayu Marca
(door *Hayu Marca*)

karu (far)

inti chinkanan (west where the sun sets)

bisjana (to climb)

hatun kalki (big hill)

simchi wichay (difficult ascent)

jatun runa (higher)

jalca (lofty region)

anqas mayu (blue river)

q'umir sacha (green forest)

yaku (water or stream)

fajcha (waterfall)

yaykuna (enter)

q'umir yunga uray (green valley below)

chaupipi (between)

iskay hayun urku (two big mountains)

urku alleq (mountain on the right)
yana rumi (black rock)
kuntur (condor)
urku lluq'e (mountain on left)
rumi perqa (rock wall)
amaru (snake)
maki (hand)
ukhunta simi (inside mouth)
pakalla punku ukhunta (secret door inside)
kuri muyu inti p'ulu (gold round sun ball disc)

The *t'aslara muruk'u* was now complete, and *Hualpa* spoke.

"We are *Q'ero* shaman priests and believe that our world is made of living energy. All of us create everything around us. *Despacho* is a prayer offering to *Pachamama* that I will now make. It has various flowers, medicinal herbs, the wool from llamas, and a little wine." *Haulpa* smiled at that.

"To ask is to receive. We bless and give to *Pachamama* and in return we receive our heart's desire and bring harmony to the universe."

A golden light suddenly appeared and lit up the *t'aslara muruk'u. Pachamama* stood before them once again.

"Thank you for your despacho, Hualpa, My beloved child. It is your young son, Cusi, who will one day be in a position of trust and authority. It is he who will see to it that the map stone is placed and concealed in the

*city below. It will remain there until
the time when it will be found and
used to avert the total destruction of
the world.*

*I now ask all of you to make a
pledge to me that your knowledge of
the Golden Disc of the Sun's location
and of this map stone will remain
a secret, never to be revealed to
anyone. Do I have your word?"*

All the men nodded and bowed
their heads.

*"Go forth and proceed with My
undying Love."*

The light on the stone faded out,
and *Pachamama* was gone. The
men sat silently in the dark for a
long time until General *Ruminahui*
stood up and lit his torch. He and

the others moved stacks of spears and shields in front of the stone to conceal it, closed the door, and left.

CUZCO, PERU 1535 AD

Ati cringed upon hearing the sound of boots on the cobblestone floor. His tormentor had returned. He had been blind-folded, spread-eagled, and chained to a wooden table. The Spanish had captured him after he lost the Battle of Mount *Chimborazo* near *Quito*. Their superior guns, mounted horseman, and cannons had prevailed.

"And will I learn the location of the Treasure of *Llaganatis* today, General *Ruminahui*?" asked the voice of *Don Francesco*.

Upon the death of Emperor *Atahualpa*, rumors that the general had hidden a huge trove of gold, silver, and precious stones in a mountain cave had spread throughout Peru.

He had been relieved to discover that the Spanish knew nothing of the Golden Sun Disc.

Ati heard the sound of bellows and groaned. He had been stuck and prodded with hot metal pokers for days. Open sores covered his body.

"Ah, a groan! Perhaps with a little more encouragement, you will reveal what I wish to know, yes?"

Ati screamed as the searing metal was placed on his abdomen. He gritted his teeth and then spat in the direction of the voice.

"Now, now, General. I will remove your blindfold and offer you one last chance to live. Give me the location of the treasure, and I will allow you to spend the rest of your days in a prison dungeon."

"How can you expect me to believe you? Your people promised *Atahualpa* his life if he filled a room with gold and another room with silver. He did as was asked of him, yet he was executed anyway. I tell you once again that there is no treasure."

"I have now grown impatient. I wish for you to see my face before I kill you."

Don Franceso removed the blindfold.

Ati Ruminahui looked up at a dark-haired, bearded man, whose face was deeply scarred. He had a furrowed brow, and many gold teeth showed when he opened his mouth to speak.

"Last chance."

He drew a sharp dagger and held it against the general's throat. *Ati* looked over his tormentor's right shoulder and saw the image of *Pachamama* appear. She smiled at him and held Her arms out wide.

He shook his head sideways in defiance. As the dagger began to slit his throat, he looked into the face of *Don Francesco* and saw that his brown eyes had now become a fiery crimson.

Ati spoke his last words.

"I forgive you."

CUZCO, PERU 1547 AD

Cusi was twenty years old when *Hualpa* packed a lunch, and they led their llamas up the hill to *Sacsayhuaman*. They entered the storage room and found that others had dutifully concealed the map stone behind a pile of wooden stakes.

"I am not long for this life," he said and smiled. "I will soon join your mother, *Niqa*."

"But, your health is good," protested *Cusi*.

Hualpa held up his right hand, palm out.

"Perhaps it is good today, but soon will be gone. I have brought you up here for a reason. First, to impart you with the sacred task of protecting the map stone. Second, to compliment you on your integration into Spanish culture and society. Last, but not least, to explain why you must continue to be of value and gain the respect of those in authority. For one day, *Cusi*, you must see to it that the map stone is removed from here and positioned in a prominent place, yet somehow hidden from sight. That will be difficult, I know, but I have faith that you will find a way."

"Please, Father, tell me again why this is so important."

Hualpa related the instructions *Pachamama* had given to him on this very spot. One day, in the far, distant future, someone would need to find the map stone and use it to locate a sacred Incan golden disc to prevent the complete destruction of Earth.

Hualpa unpacked their lunch, and they ate in silence. He looked at his son with love in his heart. *Cusi* was tall and handsome. He had become fluent in Spanish and worked along with the architects and builders as a supervisor. Many buildings were going up as the city expanded. *Cusi* had adopted the Spanish religion, been baptized, and had become friendly with many of the Catholic priests.

"Promise me that you will not entirely abandon our Incan ways."

"I promise, Father. The Spanish religion has already begun to incorporate our beliefs. For example, the Earth Mother, *Pachamama*, has become the same as the Virgin Mary, the mother of their God, Jesus."

"How will you remember our ways as you grow in age?"

"I have many Incan friends. We worship in secret. Our knowledge and history are shared with the children. We teach them of *Manco Capac* and *Mama Occlo*, who rose forth from Lake Titicaca to found the Incan Empire and the city of *Tihuantinsuyo*. We instruct them about the three realms: *Hanan Pacha* is the celestial realm of the sky. *Uku Pacha* is the inner Earth. And *Cay Pacha* is the world of us humans."

"And what of *Inti*?"

"*Inti* is the most important of all, the Sun God. Unfortunately, the summer festival honoring Him, the *Inti Raymi*, has been banned by the church. We will continue to worship *Pachamama*, the Earth Mother, and *Mama Quilla*, the Moon Goddess."

"What else?"

"We always revere *Kon-Tiki Virachocha Pachayachachic*, the

first God creator and the Father of the Sun God, *Inti*. Everything in the world is alive and connected to *Inti* and to each other."

Hualpa was very pleased. His son and others would see that their ways lived on. They finished their lunch, took a good look at the map stone, made sure it was well hidden, and then led their llamas down the hill.

CUZCO, PERU 1569 AD

Cusi was now forty-two years old. He had long since taken a Spanish name and was known as *Ricardo Vallejos*. However, all his Incan friends knew him by his given name. He had played a major role in the plans for the Cathedral of *Santo*

Domingo, which was shaped like a Latin cross, and he had supervised the transportation of building stones from *Sacsayhuaman*. They had been used in the cathedral's construction begun ten years earlier. Work was now underway to build a magnificent and permanent altar to replace the temporary one.

Cusi met with the bishop, *Matias Pineto*.

"I want to have large stone walls built on either side of the main altar, which will have wide stairs leading up to it. A statue of Our Lady of Ascension is being transported from Spain. Local painters have completed two oil portraits of famous conquistadors and noblemen. I wish for these paintings to be prominently displayed upon each of the two walls."

"I will see to it, Your Excellency," said *Cusi* as he genuflected.

SACSAYHUAMAN

Cusi knelt in front of the *t'aslara muruk'u.* His assistants, *Juan* and *Carlos*, carefully removed the four stones laying on the upper course. Then they pried up the stones on either side. The three looked around furtively. *Juan* and *Carlos* were the sons of two of the *Q'ero* shamans who had accompanied *Cusi's* father, *Hualpa*, in the journey to the hidden valley.

"We must take special care not to damage the map stone," said *Cusi*.

"Once we take it from the wall, we will cover it and come back tonight."

CATHEDRAL OF *SANTO DOMINGO*

The walls were nearing completion on either side of the main altar. *Cusi* and *Juan* stood on ladders while *Carlos* set the map stone on a wooden plank. Pulleys lifted it, and the two men above carefully placed it in the center of the left wall two-thirds of the way up. The rest of the stone wall was completed by the end of the day. Now it was time for *Cusi* to see that the map stone, the *t'aslara muruk'u,* was properly concealed.

"Tell me, *Monsignor Rivera*, who are the two men portrayed in the oil paintings?" asked *Cusi*.

"Brave conquistadors who valiantly defeated the Incas."

"Who is this painting of?"

"Why, *Ricardo*, that is General *Sebastian de Belalcazar*, who defeated the enemy forces led by the Incan General *Ruminahui* at the Battle of *Mount Chimborazo*."

"And this painting?" *Cusi* said and pointed to an ornately gold-framed portrait of a dark, bearded man with deep scars on his face.

"That is one of *Pizarro's* original conquistadors and a grand contributor of funds for the building of our cathedral. He died some sixteen years ago. The name of this great man was *Don Francesco*."

"Then I suggest that his portrait be

hung in a place of honor. Why don't I have my assistants put it high on the wall to the left of the main altar? And General *Belalcazar* can go on the right-hand wall."

"An excellent suggestion, *Ricardo*. See that it is done."

Cusi smiled and genuflected.

Juan and *Carlos* stood on a ladder and hung the large painting on metal stakes driven into the stone wall above the map stone. *Cusi* directed them from below, made sure the painting was level and completely covered, and hid the stone. Then *Juan* and *Carlos* descended and removed the ladders. The three men made certain the painting was squarely in front of the map stone. They walked up the aisle of the cathedral. Behind them, for the briefest of moments, the eyes on the portrait of *Don Francesco* glowed a fiery crimson.

CHAPTER FOUR

Cusco, Peru-Present Day

Dr. *Louis Carillos* shouted angrily.

"*Rosa*, for the tenth time today, tell *Arturo* to turn down the volume on his music. I'm in the middle of an important phone call."

He sighed and spoke into his cell phone.

"Sorry, Archbishop *Perez*. Teen-agers."

The archbishop laughed.

"As I was saying, *Louis*, we removed the painting from the wall for cleaning and restoration after centuries of candle and incense smoke had totally darkened it. That is when we saw the carved stone behind it."

"In your estimation, how long has the painting been hanging in front of the stone?"

"Since the painting has, to my knowledge, never been removed, my best guess is approximately four hundred and fifty years."

"I will be there in ten minutes."

Louis checked his emails before he left. There was one from his new archaeologist friend in America, Dr. Marc Prentis, whom he'd met at the International Federation of Rock Art Organizations (IFRAO) Conference in Mexico City. There was a photo attachment of three, dark hooded figures on a canyon wall. *Louis* had done his doctoral dissertation on the ancient rock art petroglyphs of *Pusharo*, Peru. The glyphs were thought to have been created by Amerindian shamans centuries ago, but some thought there was an Incan element to the designs. He attached four photos of heart-shaped faces, spirals, suns, and curled x's and sent them to Marc.

Louis took his right hand off the steering wheel and brushed brown hair off his forehead. At forty years old, he was already becoming gray above his ears. He drove down *Cuesta San Blas* toward the *Plaza de Armas* and the Cathedral of *Santo Domingo*. His two-story house was situated on a steep hill to the east in the historic *San Blas* neighborhood in the city of Cusco, which had an altitude of eleven thousand five hundred feet. The day was one of bright sunshine and cloudless blue skies.

Louis parked and walked across the plaza. The cathedral, with its imposing twin stone towers, dominated the square. He crossed himself and entered. Archbishop *Perez* was standing to the left of the main altar, directing assistants in the placement of a tall stepladder. He turned and smiled.

"I am so glad you have arrived to see this amazing stone."

"Thanks for calling me. I brought my camera."

Louis carefully climbed the ladder and reached the top. He gazed at the stone with wide eyes. The carving clearly depicted an aerial map, and beside it in two rows were what appeared to be place names written in *Quechua*, the language of the Incan Empire. In his nearly sixteen years as an archaeologist, *Louis* had never seen a single example of written *Quechua* because it was an unwritten language at the time. Yet here were words carved onto a stone. He took several pictures, then carefully climbed down.

"This is an extraordinary

discovery," exclaimed *Louis* to the archbishop. "I will download the photos and attempt to translate the words."

"Please let me know what they say when you have finished. I am curious."

"Absolutely. I thank you again."

Louis drove back up the steep hill to his home. He turned on his computer and downloaded the photos. Then he took a *Quechuan* dictionary off the bookshelf. It had been a work in steady progress for many years.

Loud music came from *Arturo's* room and distracted him. He got up and knocked once on the door. No response. He knocked again three times. The door opened, and *Louis* looked past his eighteen-year old son to see a pile of books on the desk and a lit computer screen. There was also a black light in one corner illuminating some vivid art posters.

"I bought you a pair of headphones. Why don't you use them?"

"Because I like to get up and move around, and the cord is way too short. Sorry, Father, I'll turn it down now. I'm studying for my college entrance exams next week."

"I don't understand how you can concentrate with such loud music, but to each his own. Just keep it down."

Louis returned to his desk and began translating the *Quechuan* words, which had been painstakingly derived over many decades from native speakers into Spanish and then into a dictionary. The words on the two lists corresponded to the aerial map and began with the words *t'aslara muruk'u,* or map stone, followed by *Punku Hayu Marca. Punku* means "door". The *Hayu Marca* mountain range lies in the southern end of Peru near the border with Bolivia, and many of the peaks ascend over twenty thousand feet.

His excitement began to build as he translated the words in the two lists. They described an arduous journey taken to find a remote, hidden valley lying between two lofty mountains. His heart raced as the words took on meaning, and when he reached the final translation, *Louis* leaned back in his chair and shook his head in wonder. What had he found? He went over the last ten listed words and rechecked his translation.

urku alleq (mountain on right)
yana rumi (black rock)
kuntur (condor)
urku lluq'e (mountain on left)
rumi perqa (rock wall)
amaru (snake)
maki (hand)
ukhunta simi (inside mouth)

pakalla punku ukhunta (secret door inside)

kuri muyu inti p'ulu (gold round sun ball disc)

The last words "gold round sun ball disc," were intriguing, to say the least. Could this be a map leading to an undiscovered Incan site? Did the word *kuri* refer to a golden treasure? Perhaps it was the Treasure of *Llaganatis* itself, which had never been found.

He called his father, *Manuel*, who lived in *Puno* on the shores of Lake Titicaca. The city was about a six-hour drive south from Cusco, but only a half-hour to the *Hayu Marca* mountains. Its elevation was twelve thousand three hundred and fifty feet above sea level.

"*Buenos dias*, Father. *Louis* speaking."

"Oh, Son, it is so good to hear from you. *Que pasa*?"

"There are wonderful things happening. In fact, I'm calling to ask you a favor. I need to stay with you for a few nights. I want to find a guide to take me into the *Hayu Marca* mountains. Maybe you know someone."

"Of course you may stay here. What is it that you seek to find in the mountains?"

"Of that I am not certain. However, I possess a map detailing the location of a hidden valley. The map dates back to over four hundred years."

"Tell me some details. I may know someone who can act as a guide."

Louis told his father about the various place names translated on his computer screen.

"I'll go ask my *Jaqi* friend, *Kawki*. He herds llamas, grew up in the mountains, and knows them well."

Louis knew that the the *Aymara* Indians had used the word '*Jaqi*" to describe themselves.

"Okay," he said. "Should I call you back again later?"

"No, he lives next door. Hold on, and I'll be right back."

Louis waited and re-read his

translation. He soon heard his father's voice on the phone.

"Yes, he says that he knows of a hidden valley where there is a huge black stone shaped like a condor. He has agreed to lead us."

"Us?"

"You don't think I would miss out on a real adventure, do you? I may be in my late sixties, but I am as strong as an ox."

"How old is *Kawki*?"

"I'm not sure, but I guess in his eighties."

"Very well then, but I warn you both. The journey will be strenuous and take us to high elevations."

"No problem. I have sturdy hiking

boots. We will bring llamas as pack animals to carry our provisions."

"*Esta bien*. I'll leave first thing in the morning and should arrive at your house in mid-afternoon."

KEAMS CANYON, ARIZONA

Marc fixed breakfast, and Jenny came in and sat down at the table. They ate in silence. Both were in a state of awe over their vision of The Blessed Virgin and the words She had spoken.

Jenny insisted on washing the dishes while Marc checked his emails. There was one from a Peruvian archaeologist, Dr. *Louis Carillos*, and another from Dr.

Thompson, his family doctor. Marc read it and spoke to Jenny.

"My father's funeral is in two days. It's at the Arlington National Cemetery in Virginia. Do you think that, I mean, would you like to go with me?"

"Yes, Marc, I would," she said without hesitation.

He made plane reservations online for both of them. Then he opened the black binder and found the phone number for Colonel Jason King.

"I wonder what the time difference is between here and the tip of South America?" he said.

"We don't know where in the world he is. Go ahead and call him."

Marc dialed the number.

"Jason King here."

"Colonel King, my name is Marc Prentis."

"Good to hear from you, Marc. Your father and I had a good conversation two weeks before he passed. I've been expecting your call. I'm staying at the Arlington Court Suites about half a mile from the cemetery."

"I'll make reservations for my friend Jenny and me. We both look forward to meeting you, sir."

"Same here. Be sure to bring lots of warm clothes. We've got snow on the ground, and it's mighty cold outside."

ARLINGTON, VIRGINIA

Marc called Jason King from his hotel room.

"Meet me in the lobby in five minutes," King said.

"What do you look like?" asked Marc.

"Six-four, suit and tie, gray hair, crew cut. You can't miss me."

Marc phoned Jenny's room across the hall and asked that she meet him downstairs. Jenny brushed her hair, applied some lipstick, and took the elevator to the lobby.

Jason stood by a window. He'd given Marc an accurate description. The man was large and solidly built. He turned and smiled as they approached. Marc introduced himself and Jenny.

"Nice to meet you. At least we have a bright, sunny day for the funeral," Jason commented. "My condolences on your father's passing, Marc. He was a great man, and we were good friends."

Marc thanked him. The three of them looked out at snow-covered trees and blue sky with white scattered clouds.

"Good to meet you too, sir," Marc said. "We'd better get going. Both of us look forward to talking with you at length when we get back."

"Yes," said Jason. "Same here. I suggest we take our own cars and not be seen standing together. I'm under surveillance. We all are."

Marc and Jenny looked at one another and nodded in agreement. They returned to Marc's room.

"I'm so happy to be here," Jenny said. "I mean, not for your father's funeral, of course, but because we're going to get some answers from Jason. Maybe we can figure out a way to free my sister and the other people at the base. Why do you think he's being watched?"

"I've no idea. From reading the black binder, I can see that this is a highly organized and secretive program, and the people who run it must have their reasons. The word *paranoia* fits well."

Jenny went to her room and dressed for the occasion with long pants, boots, gloves, a heavy parka, and a blue woolen hat with a matching scarf.

Marc also put on warm clothes. They met in the hallway. He smiled at Jenny, but inside he was experiencing a profound sense of emptiness and grief at the loss of his father. He locked his hotel door.

"Let's go," he said to Jenny.

"I'm freakin' freezing," Jack mumbled as he tugged down the earflaps on his hat. He and Augi trudged through slush and snow toward the large crowd gathered up ahead.

"I'm cold, too," said Augi. "We'll

be out of here soon. Let's do as the boss asked, okay?"

"You mean Victor?"

"We're not supposed to ever say his name."

"Screw that, Augi." Jack glanced around. "No one is nearby. Victor Spoils. There, I said it. To the victor go the spoils. Ha!"

"Well, the boss is paying us good. And we're on the evacuation list. We'll be nice and safe at the base on Phobos when the comet takes the planet out. So quit your griping, Jack."

They made their way to the edge of the crowd and looked around.

"There must be over a hundred people here," said Augi as he

squinted through his sunglasses. "See if you can spot Colonel King."

"Remind me again why we're here?"

"We're supposed to keep an eye on him. That's all. Watch who he speaks with and where he goes, I guess. He was supposed to be at the spaceship base in Chile and the boss..."

"You mean Victor?"

"Yeah, okay, Victor, was surprised to discover he was going to this funeral. Turns out he and the dead guy were Navy friends. And the dead guy was none other than Admiral Bill Prentis, one of the top people in the entire Evacuation Program."

"No shit?"

Jack and Augi made their way toward the front. They watched as the crowd parted, and two men in Navy dress uniforms walked forward, followed by six men carrying a casket draped with the American flag. A ceremonial band played, "Anchors Aweigh". Then an escort party fired three volleys into the air, and a bugler sounded taps. All the men and women dressed in uniforms saluted.

A single battalion consisting of two companies stood to one side of the crowd. Four enlisted men led by an officer carried flags and a pennant. The casket was lowered into the grave, and an admiral walked up to a young, blond-haired man and presented him with the flag from the casket. Then a Catholic priest conducted the funeral service. All bowed their heads.

Augi spotted Colonel King standing in the second row to his right. He nudged Jack.

"There he is."

"I guess the blond-haired guy is the dead man's son," observed Jack. "Wish I could see the chick standing next to him. I bet she's a looker."

Jenny Spadaro shivered in the cool breeze. Her woolen hat was pulled down tightly. Her scarf covered the lower part of her face. She glanced up as the casket was lowered, and her eyes widened. Standing on the other side of the crowd were the two smiling men who had run her car off the road. She re-played the scene, and her FBI-trained mind ID'd them instantly.

Marc received the flag from a three star admiral. She saw he was crying and handed him a tissue. He smiled and thanked her. Jenny was unwilling to call his attention to the men she'd just seen and decided to wait. Without thinking she found that she'd taken hold of Marc's hand.

Jason King welcomed Marc and Jenny at the door to his hotel room and ushered them inside. They sat on the couch while he served them cups of hot tea. Then Jason lifted one side of a curtain by the window and peered out. He recognized two men as they got out of a car and began walking toward the front lobby.

"Wait here," he said curtly. "I'll be right back."

Jason got something from the closet, put on a dark, gray trench-coat, and hurriedly left the room.

Jenny looked at Marc who shrugged, but she knew what was up.

Jack and Augi approached the front of the hotel. The blue sky had clouded over, and snow began to fall. Before they could react, Jason King stormed out of the lobby and stood towering over them, his face twisted in anger.

"You tell Victor to call you two

dogs off, you hear? I'll be back at the spaceship base on Wednesday. Now get the hell out of here!" he shouted and reached inside his coat. His hand came out with a revolver.

Jack and Augi quickly turned, walked back to their car, and drove away.

Marc put his tea-cup down as Jenny returned from the window and sat beside him. A minute later, Jason unlocked the door and stepped inside. He returned the gun to the closet and hung up his trench-coat. Then he sat down in a chair. He wiped his forehead with a handkerchief and audibly sighed.

"I had a couple of unpleasant characters to deal with out there.

As I said before, all of us are being watched."

"Those same two unpleasant characters tried to kill me in Arizona by running my car off the road," Jenny said. "Marc saved my life. That's how we first met."

She produced her gold FBI badge.

"Agent Jenny Spadaro. I'm the only one with that last name in the Phoenix phone book."

"How do you spell it?" asked Jason.

Jenny told him.

"Can I get both of your cell phone numbers and email addresses?"

They wrote them down for him, and he entered them into his cell phone.

"I'm sorry to hear you had a run-in with them," he said sincerely. "I'm glad you're on my team. Now, why don't we get down to business?"

Marc handed him the thick, black three-ring binder.

"My father gave this to me minutes before he died. Jenny and I have both read it thoroughly and understand the overall evacuation program. What you can provide us with are the details. We have information we'll share with you, too. Together we may be able to figure something out."

"They took my identical twin sister, Janey, about a week ago. I guess she's at the base on Phobos."

"I'm sorry to hear that, Jenny.

They're holding my wife, Chloe, and my two young daughters up there, too. Olivia is seven, and Meredith is ten.

My wife is a medical doctor. Because of my position as one of two spaceship pilots, they're being held as insurance. The top people want to be certain that I stay with the program. At first, I figured that if God was going to destroy Earth, why shouldn't the wealthiest and brightest survive? But they began taking people against their wills to run the base. Then they took my wife and kids. I'm telling you that I've had a change of heart. What these elite people are doing isn't right. You said you have information to share with me. What is it?"

Marc and Jenny looked at one another.

"Were you brought up in a Christian religion?" asked Marc.

"Yes," answered Jason. "Episcopal Church."

"What we're about to tell you may lead you to question our sanity," said Jenny, "but I assure you that it's the truth."

"Well, you've certainly got my full attention now. Please proceed."

The two of them recounted their vision of Mother Mary and their ensuing conversation with Her.

Jason wore a stunned expression.

"Then there *is* a way to save the

Earth. Do you have any idea where this golden disc is located?"

"No, we don't. From what I can remember, Our Lady said that She does, but She wouldn't tell us. She said that She would help us, though," said Marc.

"We have strong faith," said Jenny.

"I have no doubt that we will find the golden disc in time to complete the task given to us by Our Father."

Jason sighed.

"We have less than four weeks; closer to three and a half. The blue comet will soon become visible, even to amateur astronomers. The evacuation program is ramping up. I return to the spaceship base next week. I know this is hard to believe, but we have a Space Fleet that is extensive and known by the code word, "Solar Warden". Besides our two ships, there are dozens of space shuttles and freighters. So let me take a moment to brief you on some important things.

I am able to see my wife and two daughters in person when I am at the base. Jenny, you said your sister is up there. I can deliver information to her from you and vice versa. Recent arrivals at Sub Rosa, including your sister, indicate the Jump Gate in the Grand Canyon remains operational. Each ship can carry seven hundred and twenty-two people plus the crew and cargo. I land in a smaller impact crater within Stickney Crater, which is six miles across and takes up a full third of the tiny moon Phobos. Picture a very large gate boarding area at an airport with rows upon rows of chairs. The ship lands in an enormous air lock. A huge platform is then lowered from the bottom of the ship on hydraulics and travels half a mile to the base below where the passengers disembark and the cargo is unloaded.

There are Collection Points on four continents. They're all in extremely remote areas so as not to attract attention. They are located north of Wright, Wyoming, in the Great Sandy Desert, in Western Australia, at the *Taoudenni Basin* in *Mali*, West

Africa, and at *Campo Gallo*, in The *Pampa,* Argentina. When the comet gets to within ten days from Earth, large-capacity cargo planes will begin to transport the elite and their families to the four Collection Points.

My space ship is named the USS *Excalibur,* and the other ship is the USS *Concord.* We're going to have to make two trips to Phobos. Each ship will pick up ninety people at the four locations, or three hundred and sixty-one people on each ship. Then we'll take them to Phobos. Once there, we'll return to Earth and repeat the process. The trip takes three days. And make no mistake; when those people get to Sub Rosa, they will be in complete control, and everyone else up there will essentially become their slaves and be forced to do their bidding."

"Then we must rescue all of the people," said Marc earnestly.

"And then bring those responsible for their abduction to justice," added Jenny.

Colonel Jason King's face broke into a big smile.

"I have a plan. Suppose you were to go through the Jump Gate in the Grand Canyon and walk out at the base on Phobos. Your twin sister is there, and we can use her to our advantage. You can pave the way for an armed force. What do you think?"

"Sounds dangerous, but we just might make it work somehow. You can count me in. I'll do it," answered Jenny.

Marc and Jenny rode the elevator up to their rooms. He told her he felt the need to get some sleep and would make dinner reservations at the hotel restaurant for seven p.m.

"With snow falling outside, the last thing I want to do is drive anywhere."

Marc used the card key, opened the door to his room, and called the restaurant. When he lay down on the bed, the the tears came quickly. He would miss his father dearly. Many thoughts swirled through his mind, and the last was of Jenny holding his hand at the funeral. Marc fell asleep with a smile on his face. His dreams came and went in fast succession until one vivid scene remained. He was standing in the central area of the Anasazi site he had recently discovered. Jenny stood by his side. Rubble covered the ground. He knelt in the center and pushed aside rocks, pebbles, and decayed tree branches and uncovered the flat stone. Once again he used his knife, carefully running it along the edges of the stone and lifting it at the same time. Marc pried the stone up and put the knife away. He reached into the cache and carefully removed a necklace lying in a small, open *olla*, or decorative bowl. The necklace was strung with turquoise, hematite, and onyx beads of various sizes. He turned toward Jenny, lifted it over her head, and placed it around her neck. She gasped at the beauty of the stones and kissed him with great passion. The dream ended abruptly when the clock radio alarm buzzed loudly, startling Marc awake. He knew he'd been dreaming, but he could still feel Jenny's kiss on his lips.

Jenny returned to her room and undressed. She picked out an outfit to wear to dinner along with her gold cross necklace and a pair of rhinestone earrings. Each was in the shape of a heart with an open center. She set them atop the dresser, lay down, and soon fell asleep. At some point, she became conscious of a bright light penetrating her closed eyelids. She opened her eyes and observed a golden glow coming from the corner of the room. Jenny got up and cautiously approached the dresser. To her total amazement, the golden light was coming from her cross. As she stood transfixed, Jenny clearly heard the loving voice of Mother Mary resonate throughout the room.

"Open your heart, My dearest child."

The golden light from the cross went out, and the room returned to darkness. Jenny sat down on the bed. She put her face in her hands and wept. Her mind was unable to explain what had just happened, yet she knew with certainty that it *had* happened. She couldn't go back to sleep and decided to take a shower and get ready for dinner.

Marc and Jenny were seated at a corner table. The decor was colonial American and featured paintings of Revolutionary War battles and heroes. A candle burned in an antique-looking glass holder in the center of their table. The waitress brought water and rolls, took their orders, and departed.

Marc noticed that Jenny seemed to be troubled and pre-occupied.

"Are you feeling okay?"

Jenny looked at Marc. She felt disoriented, confused, and still in a state of shock over the incident in her room. She decided to share her feelings, took a deep breath, and began.

"Your father's funeral has brought up many painful memories for me, Marc. I buried my late husband, Mitch Schauer, just about two and a half years ago. He was forty-one years old."

Jenny took a sip of water and continued.

"He was with the FBI's elite Critical Incident Response Group hostage rescue team and fell to his death while participating in a counter-terrorism training exercise off San Diego. He and two others were rappelling down a rope from a helicopter to a ship when the helicopter ran into some kind of mechanical trouble. We'd been married for six years and were very happy together."

She paused to wipe away tears with a tissue Marc had handed her.

"Sometimes it's hard for me to accept the fact that he's really gone. I took the transfer to the Phoenix FBI field office from New York as soon as it became available. I thought a change like that would be good for me. It has been in a lot of ways, but I must admit that I haven't been interested in even thinking about meeting or dating anyone in all that time. That's my story."

Their meals were served, and they ate in silence. Marc didn't know how to respond and was saddened to hear about the death of Jenny's husband. When he'd finished his dinner, he put his hands, palms down, on the table, looked across at Jenny, and smiled.

"Well, I guess it's time for my own tale of woe. I met my ex-wife in graduate school. We were both going for our doctoral degrees in archaeology. She was beautiful and brilliant. But what I didn't know for a long time was that she was bipolar. We dated, then lived together, then got married. Her name was Chelsea. It took a while, but living together made me pay closer attention to her mood swings. Her highs were in the clouds, and just as suddenly her lows would bring her crashing down.

She was taking a lot of prescription psychotropic drugs. I found that it was very difficult to live with her. I really loved her."

Marc used a tissue to dab at some tears and continued.

"I didn't know what to do. I finally filed for divorce and moved out. She tried to change my mind. We briefly got back together, but I could see she was mentally stressed and unstable. It wasn't going to work out for us. That was around five years ago. About the time when the divorce became final, my mom, Iris, was diagnosed with a brain tumor. She became critically ill and died shortly thereafter. So I had a double-barrel shotgun blast fired at me.

Chelsea is much better now, and the drugs seem to be working. The fact that she never told me about her bipolar problems when we first began to date, that she'd kept her mental condition hidden from me, made me angry for a long time. But I've finally found forgiveness toward her. And I haven't considered dating anyone in all that time, either. That's my story."

Jenny suddenly had a clear picture appear in her mind of Mother Mary in the church explaining why She had singled out Marc and her to accomplish the task set by The Father.

"I have chosen you because of your combined skills and knowledge,

your deep faith and belief in Me and My Son, and your ability to overcome personal tragedies and to find forgiveness. I can also see that you will work well together as a team."

Jenny felt tears begin to well up. She looked across at Marc and gazed deeply into his eyes. He was a good, decent man, and her heart began to open toward him.

Marc offered to buy Jenny's dinner, but she insisted on paying for her meal. They rode the elevator up and walked down the hall. Jenny took out her card key and was about to insert it in the door when she experienced a searing, hot pain on her chest. She glanced down and saw that her gold cross was glowing a bright red. She began to cry. As her tears fell, they sizzled as they rolled down the length of her cross. Then the burning stopped, the redness faded, and her cross returned to normal.

Marc inserted his card key and opened the door. He switched on the room lights and turned to close the door behind him. Jenny stood in the open doorway. She took two steps forward, pulled him toward her, and kissed him on the lips.

"I want us to be together, Marc. Make love to me."

Marc stirred in his sleep as a dream slipped away. He slowly opened his eyes to see Jenny's face inches away from his. She was asleep and her right arm was around his shoulder. Marc noticed tiny freckles on the bridge of her nose and smiled. He matched his breathing with hers and drifted back to sleep. Jenny woke and kissed Marc on the lips, waking him. He kissed her back. She lay her head on his shoulder, looked at him, and held his hand.

"My whole life has suddenly changed," she said. "I don't know if I'm going to return to the FBI or not, and you know what? I honestly don't care right now. I officially have twelve days of vacation left. I didn't know how I was going to spend it. Now I'm here in Virginia with you. Meeting you, I mean, the very circumstances of meeting you, have been simply unreal. But they *are* real, Marc, and we saw The Blessed Virgin Mary together. We may not have much time left, but I have faith that we will succeed."

Marc squeezed her hand. He turned his head away as tears rolled down his cheeks. His own marriage had been brief and volatile, ending in divorce. He'd chosen to be alone for the last five years through fear of being hurt again. Now he didn't have a choice. Jenny had walked right into his life. Her head remained on his shoulder, and he saw that she was softly crying. Marc ran his fingers along her cheek and kissed her on the nose, which caused her to smile.

He took a deep breath, held it, and slowly exhaled. Somehow he found the words.

"I'm in love with you. Are you in love with me?"

Jenny was silent. Marc held his breath.

"My heart was closed," she said, "but I've had a special friend assist me in opening it up. Yes, Marc, I am in love with you."

They kissed and held each other. The world may be coming to an end, but for the moment, none of that mattered or made any difference to either of them.

KEAMS CANYON, ARIZONA

Marc and Jenny climbed out of his truck and carried their suitcases up the stairs and onto the porch. Jenny reached down and stroked the orange cat on her head, while Marc unlocked the door. *Mansi,* which means *"plucked flower"* in the Hopi language, lay on a rocking chair, purred contentedly, stretched, and went back to sleep.

"I'm so glad to be home," exclaimed Marc.

He opened some windows and the back door to air the place out. Then he got two bottles of beer from the fridge.

Jenny sat on the couch with her

head on a pillow and her legs up on the coffee table.

"I'm exhausted," she said. "I don't know how you can sleep on a plane. I've never been able to do that very well. And yes, I'm glad to be back, too."

Marc sat on the couch and handed her a cold beer.

"Here's to the future, whatever it may bring."

They clinked their bottles together.

"I guess I ought to check my emails," said Jenny.

"Me, too," agreed Marc. "But let's drink the beers first."

Jenny finished her beer and slowly got up. She took her laptop out of her suitcase and sat down at the kitchen table. There was an email from Susan, her assistant, basically saying everything was okay and that she missed her. She asked where Jenny was spending her vacation. There was another one from Jenny's mom and dad in Queens, wishing her a very Merry Christmas.

Marc was surprised to get an email from Robert Montoya, the son of *Cheveyo*, the Hopi elder and shaman at First Mesa. He knew Robert, whose Hopi name was *Kwahu* (eagle), and his son, *Tewa*. The email was an invitation from his father to attend *Soyal*, the winter solstice ceremony.

It was to be held in the *kiva*, underground ritual chamber, that evening. For Marc, as a *pahana* or "white person," this was a great honor. He emailed Robert back and asked whether his friend, Jenny, could accompany him. He was pleased to get a fast reply, saying she was also welcome. He told Jenny, who expressed her excitement at the prospect of witnessing and learning about an ancient sacred Hopi ceremony.

KIVA AT FIRST MESA

Jenny followed Marc as he climbed down a ladder, which descended from a square hole in the roof of the *kiva.*

"This is the time when *Hotomkam* begins to hang down in the sky,"

Marc commented as he looked upward. He saw the three belt stars of the Orion constellation and faintly the seven stars of *Chuhukonor,* the Pleiades.

She breathed in the strong fragrance of burning sage and wood smoke. Voices below were singing and chanting. Jenny stepped off the last rung of the ladder and turned around. She looked into the face of *Cheveyo* the Hopi elder she had met at the town hall meeting. He stared at her with great surprise.

"Agent Spadaro! What are you doing here?"

Jenny explained her near-fatal encounter following the meeting and how Marc had saved her life. Marc smiled at *Cheveyo* and said,

"Robert invited me here tonight and agreed to have Jenny come along as my guest. We both have vital information regarding the missing people that we want to share with you. I guess he didn't mention Jenny."

"There are other tribal elders present here. We will have a meeting after the ceremony. Please find places to sit. I will join you shortly."

Marc spotted Robert and *Tewa*. They found seats nearby, and he introduced them to Jenny. She looked around the room and noticed that, although the structure's outside was round, the room was square. A fire blazed in an *abobe* walled fire pit behind the ladder. Sparks and smoke rose in the updraft through the hole in the roof. Men, women, and children sat on wooden benches lining the north, south, and east walls. Everyone was dressed in his or her finest clothes.

A group of children smiled shyly at her, and she waved and smiled. A few waved back at her.

There was a large altar on the west wall, upon which many ears of corn, husks, and stalks had been placed. In the center of the altar stood a very large gourd. A thick adobe pillar in the middle held up the roof, and she observed regularly spaced vents in the walls to provide fresh air. Then Jenny noticed a four-foot-square sandbox with wooden sides about a foot tall in one corner. The sand inside was level and smooth.

Jenny looked over at *Tewa*. He was in his teens and had a bright smile. He got up and returned with a willow stick, which had a cotton piece of string tied to one end. The stick was decorated with a painted face, feathers, and pinyon needles. He offered it to Jenny, who saw that everyone had these sticks, and many were tied in people's hair.

"This is called a *pahos*," said *Tewa*. "They are gifts to our community, including our homes, animals, and plants. After the ceremony, we will decorate the *kiva* with them. Tomorrow we will sacrifice them by planting them in the ground in return for the blessings of life."

Jenny smiled and thanked him as *Cheveyo* approached and handed her two more brightly colored *pahos*.

"May I tie them in your hair, Jenny?" he asked.

She smiled and nodded.

"Please allow me to give you an explanation of our winter solstice ceremony, which we call *Soyal*.

We call this *tawaki*, or the winter "sun house". Through prayer, dance, and song, we symbolically assist *Tawa*, the Sun God, on his journey northward from his southernmost position on the horizon. We perform the ceremony to bring the sun back from its winter sleep. It is a time for purification."

Jenny took in the information.

"What is the purpose of the sandbox in the corner?"

"When the Sun God *Tawa's* footprints appear in the sand, we will know that our ceremony has been a success and that He will return to shine."

An old man walked up to them. His deeply wrinkled face was framed by shoulder-length, silver-white hair. He presented Marc and Jenny with two *pahos*, bowed to them, and smiled.

"My name is *Honaw*, which means 'bear' in our language. I am now one hundred and two years old. I warmly welcome you two *pahanas* to our *Soyal*," he said. "*Cheveyo* tells me that you have some information you wish to share. I look forward to hearing from you both."

He returned to his seat across the room.

"*Honaw* is a greatly respected elder," said *Cheveyo*. "I have asked him and eight other elders along with me to join us later. I see that our ceremony is about to begin."

A powerful, barefooted figure began to descend the *kiva* ladder.

"Who is that," Jenny asked *Cheveyo.*

"*Muy'ingwa*, the God of Germination."

Jenny observed that the man

was painted with white dots, which resembled stars on his arms, legs, chest, and back. He had a crook on his belt, upon which was tied an ear of black corn.

"That is *Masau'u's* corn signifying the Above," said *Cheveyo*. *Masau'u* is The Creator God. In an ancient legend, he is called the "Star Man," supposedly because of his headdress, which is made of four white corn leaves representing a four-pointed star, perhaps symbolizing Aldebaran in the Hyades constellation."

Jenny heard the sound before she saw the source. Six young men entered from a far corner, wearing costumes, shaking rattles, and sporting green cottonwood leaves in their long, black hair. They danced and circled the *kiva*. Then they formed a circle around *Muy'ingwa* as he began to stomp on a board in the center of the floor with his right foot.

"What is he doing?" asked Jenny.

"He is stomping on a board that covers a shallow hole, called a *sipapu,* that is symbolic of the portal through which our ancestors first emerged. It symbolizes the entrance to the underworld, from which our people came from the Third World into this, the Fourth World," answered *Cheveyo*. "Stomping on the board is a signal to the *katsina* spirits that the ceremony has now begun."

"What is he holding in his hands?"

"*Muy'ingwa* carries a sun hoop covered in buckskin in one hand and a sun shield with red horsehair fringe in the other. The shield has a dozen or so eagle feathers tied around it. Its lower half is painted blue. The upper half is divided in half. The right side is red, and the left side is yellow. There are two horizontal black lines for the eyes and a small, downward-pointing triangle for the mouth. They are painted on the lower blue half to form the striking face of *Tawa*, the Sun God."

Muy'ingwa began to dance faster as the young men shook their rattles. He twirled the sun hoop around and around in a clockwise motion.

"What is he doing now?" asked Jenny.

"He is trying to bring the sun northward from its southward position. Remember, Jenny, our Hopi ceremonies are not solely for us, but are for maintaining the harmonic balance of Earth."

She felt excited as many people around her began to shake rattles and chant. The six men took their seats as an older man with gray hair worn in a braid began to walk around the *kiva,* holding what looked like a large snake.

"What is that?" asked Marc.

"It is an effigy of *Palulukonuh*, also called the 'Plumed Snake'. He is the bringer of rain," answered *Cheveyo*.

"We carve it from the woody stalk of an agave plant. I'll explain the symbolism in a while."

Jenny's eyes took in the scene all around her. She smelled the sweet fragrance of burning sage, smiled at the voices of the Hopi as they sang, and found herself filled with happiness to be among these people. They were continuing to practice a traditional, ritualistic ceremony whose origins had begun in the ancient past.

She watched as the six young men rose from their seats. Three of them took positions on the north side and three on the south. They carried shields painted with dark clouds and rain, dying corn, fire, and falling snow. They began singing loudly as the older man entered holding a large shield emblazoned with a bright, orange, and yellow sun. They rushed at the older man on the north side, then the south, clashing their shields against his and shouting loudly. Both times the older man drove them back.

Jenny was shaken by what she saw and turned to look at *Cheveyo*.

"Please explain what's going on."

"The men symbolize the attack of hostile spirits on *Tawa*, the Sun God. Fire, drought, cold, and darkness influence whether the sun will shine and bless our crops." He paused and pointed. "Look over there."

The Plumed Snake effigy began to

rise from the large gourd in front of the altar on the west wall. The black-painted snake moved up and down.

It had a large, long, red tongue. The six young men stood and threw corn and pinyon nuts at the snake, which roared and hissed. Most nuts fell on the ground, but some made it into the gourd. The men continued to throw more until the sounds stopped and the snake withdrew its head.

"The black snake is symbolic of the evil influences. By throwing a meal at *Palulukonuh*, we attempt to persuade him not to swallow *Tawa*," explained Cheveyo. "When the roaring stops, we know that the sun will return and we will have rain and plentiful crops to feed our people."

Although Jenny knew the snake wasn't real, she had to admit that she'd felt uneasy. She had been afraid of snakes since childhood.

"I used to be small enough to hide in the gourd and be the snake puppeteer," said *Tewa*. His statement caused Robert, his father, and *Cheveyo*, his grandfather, to smile.

Jenny had been vigilant throughout the ceremony. She'd kept her eyes on the sandbox as much as possible, so she was amazed and gasped at the sight of a set of fresh footprints in the sand. She got up and walked over to inspect them. *Cheveyo* got up, as well.

"But, how is this possible?" she

asked. "I was watching closely. Where did they come from?"

The elder smiled at her.

"We Hopi know that *Tawa's* presence is always with us. His spirit form cannot be seen by mortals. With each *Soyal,* our faith is renewed by the appearance of the footprints in the sand."

Jenny returned to her seat. She held Marc's hand and put her head on his shoulder. The footprints were evidence of a deep, spiritual understanding and acceptance among the Hopi. She felt humbled and sighed deeply.

Everyone stood and began to mingle. Jenny and Marc were handed willow branches and, following the example of others, attached their *pahos* onto them. The sticks were then collected from each person. They were tied among the ceiling rafters of the *kiva* room, which became adorned with colorful feathers and carried the aromatic scent of pinyon needles.

When the last person had climbed up the ladder, *Cheveyo* brought Marc and Jenny over to a corner of the *kiva*. A group of nine elders, both men and women, sat on benches. The two of them sat on the floor beside *Cheveyo*, Robert, and *Tewa*. Someone had placed ten lit candles in a half circle around them. The flames cast shadows, which played across the adobe walls. Jenny took Marc's hand in hers and squeezed it.

"My name is *Hehewuti*, which means, "warrior mother spirit", in our Hopi language. She wore her long, white hair in a single braid, silver bracelets on both wrists, and her dark eyes spoke of great wisdom. She smiled and bid them both welcome.

Cheveyo then introduced them to the others. In all there were four elder women and five elder men including *Ahote*, who said his name meant, "restless one", and *Chu'a*, meaning "snake. One of the women addressed them.

"We are eager to hear your information," said *Chu'mana*. My

name means "snake maiden." She
had gray streaks in her dark hair,
which fell about her shoulders. She
wore a turquoise and coral necklace
and matching earrings. Her face
was wrinkled, and her large brown
eyes were kind. "This is my husband
Pavati, or "clear water."

"We are both eighty-six years old,"
he said. "Our lives have seen the
face of change sweep across the
land, yet we remain unchanged. The
old ways serve our people as they
always have."

"And my name is *Lenmana* or
"flute girl," said a tall woman with
long, braided gray hair and many
bead necklaces. I began playing the
flute before the age of two."

"Please tell us more of yourself, young woman," said *Pamuya* (water moon). "We know of your friend, Marc, who has worked to bring knowledge of the old one's to all people. Do you remember us? You spoke with my wife, *Mongwau* (owl) and me at the town hall meeting about our grandson, *Honovi*. He has been missing for three years now."

"Yes, I do remember you. What can I say about myself? I head the Missing Person's Division at the FBI field office in Phoenix. I've only lived in Arizona for a couple of years, but I'm drawn to the open land. I'm originally from New York." She paused and looked directly at *Honaw*. "But all that has no importance. What is important is the information Marc and I have to share with you."

"Then," said *Honaw,* "let us talk story."

Jenny recapped her attempted murder and how she had met Marc. Then Marc spoke of the deathbed confession of his father and summarized the contents of the black binder. The elders' faces were hard to read, and he was unsure whether they believed him or not. Jenny began to recount their vision of Mother Mary at the church, and Marc joined in. They spoke of the task set by The Father and of the golden disc. When they finished speaking, there was a long, uneasy silence broken when *Honaw* spoke at last.

"We have no reason to doubt your words," he said. "*Cheveyo* has told us you speak the truth. Your information answers many questions."

"My sister is among the missing," said Jenny. "I believe she was taken to the Jump Gate in the Grand Canyon about a week ago. I think she is now at the elite's secret base on Phobos."

"I'm pretty sure I saw her," said *Tewa*.

"What?" exclaimed Jenny. "Where?"

He related his frightening experience at Isis Temple and spoke of seeing a woman wearing a red, white, and green sweater being forced to walk into a large square structure.

"I gave her that sweater for Christmas two years ago!" cried Jenny.

Cheveyo clapped his hands together.

"We have heard your words, Marc and Jenny. Now hear ours. He looked at *Tewa*. Listen carefully, young one."

Jenny squeezed Marc's hand again.

"The history of the Hopi people is based on the concept of two horns. All of our knowledge, legends, and traditions are viewed this way.

Knowledge that lies ahead is seen by the horn on the right. Knowledge that has passed is seen by the horn on the left.

Our people know with certainty from where we came, and we know where we are headed. Our legends tell us how the world was first formed. The horn on the right tells us how the world will be destroyed. And, I am sorry to say, that time is not far off.

The ninth and last sign of the Hopi prophecies states:

You will hear of a dwelling-place in the heavens, above the earth, that shall fall with a great crash. It will appear as a blue star. Very soon after this, the ceremonies of my people will cease. When the Blue Star *Kachina* appears, material matters will all be destroyed by spiritual beings, who will remain to create one world and one nation under one power, that of the Creator, *Taiowa*.

We here, all ten of us elders, have kept what I will now tell you as a secret. In our own private *Wuwuchim* ceremony, held for sixteen days last month, a *Saquasohuh Kachina* dancer removed his mask. As prophecy foretells, the time is near. The world will end in the fires of a blue comet."

All were quiet. Everyone stood in a circle and held hands. *Honaw* cleared his throat and spoke.

"The greatest thing we possess for healing is the human spirit itself. We Hopi are children of the Sun. We know in our hearts that spiritual love is ultimately the answer. And we have learned that true knowledge exists beyond words. If there is to be an Armageddon, know that it lies within each of us. The End Time may also be viewed as the Beginning Time because we are creating, at this very moment, what our tomorrow will be. We Hopi are a strong people, and we will endure.

The other elders here, along with myself, have decided to take you to a Star Door. The Jump Gate you speak of in the Grand Canyon is of modern technology. We Hopi know of three others that have existed on Earth since ancient times. There may be others, but we are not aware of them. Some say that these three Star Doors were here even before there was man. One is in southern Peru near Lake Titicaca. Another is in France at a place called *Rennes le Chateau*. It has been said that they are linked to one another."

"And the third Star Door?" asked Jenny.

"It is but five and a half miles east of here in Steamboat Canyon. Meet us at the *kiva* tomorrow morning just after sunrise. We will take you there. Perhaps it will prove useful to you."

"What is inside the Star Door?" asked Marc.

Honaw looked at the faces of the nine other elders. One by one they nodded, and *Honaw* spoke.

"Within is the Light of the Sun, the Moon, the Stars, and the Magic of the Great Spirit."

CHAPTER FIVE

Sub Rosa Base, Phobos, Mars

"Ms. Oliver," said Michael Dryer, "please escort Ms. Spadaro to her new living quarters."

Janey turned her head and saw an older woman, who smiled at her.

"My name's Sharon. Let's get out of here."

They approached a high wall topped with barbed wire. Two armed guards stood on either side of a steel door. Michael Dryer used a remote control device which lifted a heavy bar and swung the door open. He nodded at Sharon, and they walked out. Janey heard the door close behind her, accompanied by the sound of the bar being dropped back in place.

Sharon led her across a street to a park. They took seats on a bench under a tree. Janey looked around and noted green grass lawns, a stream with a wooden bridge, and cement walkways. Quite a few people rode past them on bicycles. A few waved at Sharon, who waved back. Rows of tall buildings stood on the left side of the park. Janey clasped her hands and tried to smile at the older woman as tears began to fall. Sharon let her cry for a while, and then reached out and held Janey's right hand.

"I can understand how you're feeling because I went through it myself a year and a half ago. You're most likely angry, confused, disoriented, and hoping that all of this will turn out to be a bad nightmare. I'm sorry to tell you that it won't."

"It's so unfair," cried Janey. "They criminally abducted me! I don't want to be here!"

Sharon nodded in agreement.

"Look, Janey, all I can tell you is that it took me three months to adjust to life here. At this moment the best thing I can offer you is that you'll make friends and eventually find that your anger has lessened."

She let go of Janey's hand and stood up from the bench.

"I'm here to do all that I can to help you. Come with me now, and I'll take you to your apartment."

Janey walked beside Sharon along the left side of the park toward a group of buildings. She looked up and saw that high rock walls rose on all sides of the base.

"Why are we here? What's the purpose for all of this? Just what in the hell is going on?"

"All I know is someday about fifteen hundred people are expected to arrive here at the base."

They walked through the open

front doors of Complex E and took an elevator up. Sharon unlocked the door, and, much to Janey's surprise, her small second-floor apartment was fully furnished. Sliding glass doors led onto a balcony patio with a view of the large park below. There was a queen-size bed, dressers, and closets. The living room had a comfortable couch, matching chairs, end tables, lamps, and a coffee table. The bathroom had a sink, mirror, toilet, and shower. But she noticed that, while there was a sink and a small refrigerator in the kitchen, there was no oven range, hot plate, or microwave. Janey looked at Sharon with a quizzical expression.

"There's no cooking allowed in the apartments. All meals are served in the Complex E dining hall downstairs with set hours. Breakfast is between seven and nine, lunch between one and three, and dinner is served between six and eight. The dining hall is on the first floor and easy to find. We'll go to the Free Store in a little while."

"What's that?"

"You wouldn't believe me if I told you. But first I think it's a good idea for us to get acquainted. I didn't have anyone to talk to when I first got here, you know, someone to explain what's going on. I wish I'd had someone to guide me because

I had a very rough time of it in the beginning,"

Sharon sat on the couch and motioned for Janey to join her. Janey took a seat, smiled, and smoothed her red, white, and green, knit sweater.

"Nice sweater," commented Sharon. "And its got Christmas colors, too."

"Thanks. My sister gave it to me for Christmas two years ago. I've been wearing it for three days now and I really need to take a hot shower and change into something else."

Sharon nodded. Then her face took on a serious expression.

"Janey, you're about to begin to

experience a brand-new life here at Sub Rosa. The best advice I can give you is to go with the flow and don't spend your time trying to fight it. The ancient Chinese philosopher, *Lao Tzu,* once wisely said:

> *"The world is run by letting things take their course."*

Janey sighed deeply.

"I'm familiar with him. I took a class in comparative religions in college. I guess my appreciation for nature and all living things is Buddhist. It was the driving force behind my interest in gardening and hydroponics."

"Good. My own interest was in caring for people who had health problems. That led to a degree in nursing. I'm now fifty-eight years old. My husband, Jerry, passed away five years ago. My married name is Oliver, but my maiden name is Ryan; a good Irish name from Chicago. We moved to Arizona over twenty-five years ago. Before I was taken, I was director of nursing at the Mayo Clinic Hospital in Phoenix."

Janey studied Sharon and saw a woman with a pleasant face; graying hair, kindly, deep blue eyes, a plump body, and a nice smile.

"I never re-married," she continued, "and stayed in our house with my two cats. How about you?"

"Me? Well, let's see. I grew up in New York City. I have an identical twin sister named Jenny. I got my BS degree in botany at NYU and a minor in general engineering. Then an MS and doctorate in environmental science from MIT with an emphasis on hydroponics. But I always wanted to see the western states and accepted a job to teach at the University of New Mexico in Albuquerque. I was in a long-term relationship. His name was Tom. Eventually we drifted apart, and I found that we'd developed different ways of viewing life that weren't at all compatible. I've been single for three years or so, and, to be honest, I haven't really wanted to get involved with anyone."

"Where's your twin sister?" asked Sharon.

"Jenny's in Phoenix. She's an agent with the FBI and moved there a couple of years ago after her husband, Mitch, died in a training exercise. That was a big reason for her moving from New York City to Phoenix. She needed a change of scenery. Jenny gave me this sweater for Christmas a couple of years ago." She paused and looked into Sharon's blue eyes. "Oh, I already told you that. Would you please tell me how you were taken?"

"Sure. I drove home after my night shift. Two big guys with crew cuts dragged me out of my car. They must have followed me from the hospital. I was bound, gagged, and blindfolded. Four nurses from other Phoenix hospitals were taken the same night. They flew all of us in a helicopter. We landed somewhere and were made to walk through what I now know is called a Jump Gate. End of story. What's yours?"

"I went to the wrong Christmas party. Andrea Dryer hit me on the back of my head with a wine bottle."

"Great, just great."

"Sharon, tell me about your feelings when you first got here."

"My feelings? Probably identical to yours. I was in a blind rage. I felt confused, afraid, helpless, and found myself ranting against the unfairness of it all. Why me? I just kept asking that question until Andrea Dryer finally sat me down. She told me that this base was being made ready for a large group. That someday one thousand four hundred and forty-four people were expected to arrive. That my life and the lives of everyone here were dedicated to building, creating, and maintaining a sustainable living environment for ourselves and for those people."

"One thousand four hundred and forty-four? That sounds biblical!"

"Yeah, I know. So far they've taken almost a thousand people with specialties to run this place like nurses, doctors, cooks, carpenters, electricians, plumbers, teachers, all kinds of engineers, many farmers, and hydroponics experts. It took me three months to come to the realization that this was it for me. From then on, I began to lighten up and came to accept the situation. My past life was gone. I was lonely and began to make friends, and, after a while, I just made the best of it. I've been here for sixteen months."

Janey let out a big sigh and wiped some tears away with the sleeve of her sweater, a gesture that caused Sharon to nod.

"I know exactly how you're feeling. Come on. Let's go to the Free Store."

The two women took the elevator down, and Janey followed Sharon into a large building that looked like a department store.

"Pretty much everything you need for your apartment is here. Let's get you some clothes first. Then we can get bedding and toiletries."

"But, Sharon, how do I pay for it? I don't have any money!"

"We don't use money here. Take whatever you want. It will be delivered to your apartment."

"Really? Are you kidding me?"

Sharon shook her head.

"No money? Wow!"

Janey chose four pairs of long pants, shorts, T-shirts, a dozen blouses, eight dresses, lots of underwear, five pairs of shoes, some silk stockings, and pajamas.

"This is unbelievable!"

Sharon laughed. She gave Janey's

apartment number in Complex E to a store clerk.

"Come over here, and let's get you some things for your bedroom."

Janey chose printed sheets, bed pillows with matching cases, a comforter, and a digital alarm clock. She got items for her bathroom like a hair dryer, shampoo, conditioner, makeup, lipsticks, hair-brushes, soft soap, deodorant, a loofa, towels, and various cleaning supplies.

"Since we can't cook, choose stuff like crackers, cookies, chips, pretzels, raisins, peanut butter, dried fruit, beef jerky, candy, and granola bars. There is a small refrigerator in your kitchen, so I suggest you get some juice and bottled water."

"I could drink a beer or two right now. Maybe three or four."

"That's one good thing about Sub Rosa. Alcohol, cigarettes and drugs are totally non-existent."

"Really?"

"Really. Everyone gets clean and sober after a while. And in some ways, we're living in what it must have been like in early 1900s America."

"What do you mean?"

"We have electricity, but there are no televisions, radios, computers, telephones, cell phones, or i-Pads. We've had to learn to live without any kind of electronics. Let me amend that. Only the administration center, the Eco Farm's central office, engineering, the hospital, and the nuclear reactor have computers."

"But, that must be awful! I mean, how do you communicate? How do you know what's happening on Earth? No Internet?"

"We don't ever get any news about Earth. We've learned to talk to one another. There are many gatherings and events all the time like music concerts, art shows, plays, bridge, chess, tennis clubs, interesting lectures, and old movies."

Sharon led Janey to an area in a corner of the large store.

"Over here you can choose some things to decorate your walls."

The area had many pieces of art displayed in every media including paintings, sculpture, ceramics, and photography. There was also a large variety of musical instruments. Janey chose a wooden flute along with several framed paintings and photographs. Sharon handed her a CD player, and Janey picked out six CD's and another digital alarm clock for the kitchen. She signed for everything, and the store clerk told her that her items would be delivered to her apartment number #217 in Complex E. Then Sharon brought her to another building, which contained the library.

"None of the books or magazines in here have any news from Earth. That means there are no publications about politics or current events of any kind. The spaceships bring new books and periodicals regularly, but they are carefully selected and censored."

Janey chose a number of fairly new paperback novels and a variety of science and nature magazines. Then the two women walked outside, and Sharon pointed out the apartment complexes along the left side of the base.

"Those are the five living areas. Complexes A/B, C/D, E/F, G/H, and I/J. Each complex has four floors and a total of four hundred and eighty apartments with their own dining hall, fitness center, movie theater, music room, library, laundry room, and medical clinic. I'm the nurse in Complex C."

They walked over to the park and sat down on a bench. Janey looked up and noted long rows of what appeared to be halogen lights far above her head. The air temperature was pleasantly warm with a slight breeze.

"Notice anything unusual? Anything at all" asked Sharon.

Janey glanced around and listened. She noticed there were no flowers on the trees and bushes or in the lawn. Many people walked by them. Some rode on skate-boards and bicycles. A few of the people were joggers, who waved and smiled at them.

"Yes, Sharon. A couple of things. First, there are no insects or animals of any kind that I can see or hear."

"You're right. Nothing. No dogs or cats, squirrels, chipmunks, birds, mosquitos or flies, either. Only the Eco Farm has a tightly enclosed area for honey bee pollination. They also have coops of laying hens for eggs, hutches for rabbits, and ponds of fish to provide all of us with food protein."

"Second, how am I able to breathe?"

"Look straight up."

Janey complied.

"Do you see the many rows of large circles directly underneath the banks of lights?"

"Yes, I do. What are they?"

"This is incredible," said Sharon. "Humans breathe oxygen and exhale CO2. Plants take in CO2 and emit oxygen. The trees and grass lawns help, but what you're looking at up above are artificial organic leaves that produce oxygen just like regular leaves on Earth. The leaves consist of chloroplasts extracted from the fibers of silk. They are suspended in a matrix made out of silk protein. The chloroplasts from plant cells are placed inside this silk protein. They stabilize the molecules. It is the first photosynthetic material that is living and breathing just as a leaf does. The lights activate the photosynthesis process."

Jenny leaned her head back on the bench and shook her head. Despite her situation, she actually found herself smiling.

"I'm finally starting to calm down, Sharon. No flies or mosquitos? Maybe this place isn't so bad, after all. Thanks for being here for me."

"You're welcome, Janey. Let's go back to your apartment and get it set up."

The supplies from the Free Store had been delivered and sat in the hall outside her door. Sharon helped her bring everything in, make the bed, place the food items in the cabinets and fridge, organize the bathroom, and put the clothes in the closet and dresser drawers.

"It's mid-afternoon now. You've had a lot of trauma. I suggest that you try to get a few hours of sleep. Dinner is between six and eight o'clock. The dining hall is on the first floor. I'll be there, so look for me."

"Shower first, then sleep," Janey said aloud to herself after she'd let Sharon out.

"Oh, my God, I needed that shower!" exclaimed Janey as she began to blow dry and brush her hair. She chose a red and blue floral blouse and black slacks, put on some makeup, slipped on a pair of shoes, and took the elevator downstairs. The dining hall was large, but there were only about forty people there. She found Sharon sitting among a group of eight others at a large table.

"Hi, Janey. Go get your dinner and join us. Food is served buffet style."

She put a plate, bowl, napkins, and tableware on a tray and stood in line.

The main course was stew with some kind of meat, carrots, potatoes, celery, and spices. You could also make your own hamburger with fresh buns, ketchup, mayonnaise, pickled relish, mustard, onions, and tomatoes. There were fresh green salad with a variety of lettuce, spinach, and sprouts along with rolls. Famished, she filled her bowl with stew, put two hamburgers and salad on her plate, got a cold bottle of water, and sat down beside Sharon.

"Why is the dining hall so empty? Where is everyone?" she asked Sharon.

"Complex E has less than fifty people living in it. The rest of it is unoccupied. So is the other side, Complex F, as well as Complex G/H and I/J. They'll be full when the others arrive."

"What happens when the population exceeds the housing available at Sub Rosa?"

Sharon answered.

"There are two large underground bases on Mars that are currently inhabited by small populations, and there is another one on the dark side of the moon. They can all be made sustainable for larger communities."

"Other bases on Mars and the moon, besides this one? Are you kidding me? How do you know that, Sharon?"

"Good question. And it's true. Apparently, they've been there for a long time. And I've become friends with a man who works in engineering and he told me. He's from the Hopi tribe of northeastern Arizona. There are quite a few Hopi men here. Anyway, he learned a lot of information from a group of engineers who first excavated and built the base. We'll meet him tomorrow."

Janey nodded and ate some stew.

"What kind of meat is this? It's really delicious!"

"Rabbit," said Sharon. She looked at the other diners. "Janey, please allow me to introduce you to these nice people. This man's name is Jamie Glasgow. He has a very important job at the Eco Farm."

Jamie sat across the table from Janey. He had dark, curly hair, and a bright smile.

"What do you do there?" asked Janey.

"I'm a beekeeper and manage the pollination of various crops in the greenhouse. I'd be glad to give you both a tour of the farm."

"Thanks, Jamie," said Sharon. "How about tomorrow morning?"

"Great. Meet me in front around nine thirty."

"My name's Latona de Jahn," said a young African-American woman, who extended her right hand. Janey shook it and smiled.

"What do you do, Latona?"

"I was a school teacher in Scottsdale, Arizona, before I was taken. But, since there are only two children here, I've been assigned to work at the food processing facility. I helped prepare the rabbit your eating, and I work in the bakery, and do general clean-up."

"Who are the two children?" asked Janey.

"Meredith and Olivia. They're Dr. Chloe King's daughters. Her husband is one of the pilots of our two supply ships from Earth. But I've been told there will be plenty of kids to teach when the others get up here."

"Nice to meet you, Janey. My name is Donna Bailey. I'm the nurse in Complex B. I was taken from Phoenix along with Sharon and two other nurses. Life here is, I don't know what words to use to describe it, maybe challenging and interesting? I did deliver the first new-born healthy baby girl two weeks ago named Susie."

Janey smiled at that and caught the eye of a rugged-looking man with dark blond hair.

"I'm Jimmy Jaffe, and I work

on lighting, air temperature, and dehumidifiers."

"Hi, my name is Annie O'Neal," said a tall, dark-haired woman, whose smile lit the room. "I'm a groundskeeper and landscaper, and I take care of the trees, lawns, and shrubbery."

Another man named Steve Peterson was a delivery van driver, who picked up processed food and brought it to the inhabited complex kitchens.

"And this is John Spencer," said Sharon, "our plumber, whom we couldn't do without."

John had bright red hair, freckles, and green eyes. He smiled at Janey.

"In case Sharon hasn't mentioned

it, anytime you have a leaky faucet or a stopped-up drain, just leave a note for me on the bulletin board in the lobby by the front door."

Janey finished her dinner and joined everyone in bringing their plates to a row of tubs filled with hot water and suds.

"It's been a pleasure meeting all of you," she said and waved goodbye.

"I'll meet you in the dining hall around nine o'clock in the morning," said Sharon.

Janey rode the elevator up and entered her apartment. She turned on a table lamp, sat down on the couch, briefly leafed through a nature magazine, and then lay back against the cushions. She placed her hands on her knees and began rocking back and forth as tears began to stream down her face.

"Why, dear God? Why am I here?" she wailed between sobs. "I believe everything happens for a reason, so would You please tell me why I am here?"

Restless, she got up and brought a box of tissues from the bathroom. Agitated, she began to pace rapidly back and forth while she dabbed at her eyes.

"I have faith," she said aloud to herself. "I must believe that I've been brought here for some purpose. But I miss my home in Albuquerque, my lab and my students, my sister, Jenny, and my friends. My whole life has suddenly and completely changed."

Janey got a bottle of water from the fridge and drank half of it. She placed it on the coffee table, settled back on the cushions, and closed her eyes. She began to breathe slowly and steadily to calm down.

"If my being brought here is for my best and highest good, then so be it," she said aloud. "I will make the most of it. I will, as Sharon advised, go with the flow and make friends. My old life is gone."

Janey got undressed, set the alarm clock, and lay in her bed.

"My first night at Sub Rosa," she thought as sleep began to overtake her. Then she got a clear image of

her sister, Jenny, in her mind. She was lying in bed and there was a man asleep beside her. Words formed in her mind, and she sent them out.

KEAMS CANYON, ARIZONA

Jenny lay in bed next to Marc. He was asleep and lightly snoring. She began to drift off herself when she suddenly heard her sister, Janey, speak clearly and distinctly in her mind.

"Jenny, if you can hear me, know that I love you, and that I'm okay."

"Janey, where are you?" she shouted, waking Marc.

She sat straight up in bed and looked wildly around the room because her sister's voice had been so loud. Then she realized it must have been a dream. Marc put his arm around her, and Jenny cried herself to sleep.

SUB ROSA

Janey woke to the sound of her alarm clock. Eight a.m. She opened the sliding glass door and stepped out onto the balcony. People were already jogging and riding bikes in the park below. She took a deep breath.

"My first real day at Sub Rosa. And I'm going to make the best of it!"

She went back inside, washed up, changed, and went down to the dining hall. There were only a couple of dozen people, and she didn't recognize anyone from last night. She sat by herself and ate.

Janey was impressed with the food selection. She had two veggie omelets, hash browns, toast, blueberries, strawberries, and soy milk, but she was disappointed that there was no coffee or tea. She finished breakfast just as Sharon walked into the dining hall.

"Ready for the tour?" Sharon said. "First, we'll visit the Eco Farm, then the hospital, and finally engineering."

"Does everyone get a tour like this?"

"No. But the Director said to give you a grand tour of the base because you're the last person to be taken from Earth and brought to Sub Rosa."

"Some honor," said Janey.

"Oh, come on, Janey, this is going to be fun and interesting, especially the Eco Farm. I mean, they're able to provide three meals a day for almost a thousand people!"

The two women walked along a road running through the park and approached the front of the farm. Jamie Glasgow smiled as they drew near.

"Right on time! Good morning, ladies. Please follow me."

They entered a rectangular room, and Jamie firmly closed the front door behind them and opened yet another door.

"It's an air lock system. The interior is a sealed, controlled environment unto itself."

The two women walked behind him, and Janey's jaw dropped as she gazed out at acres upon acres of plants growing in neat rows with lights above them.

"The Eco Farm occupies an area of one square mile or six-hundred and forty acres and is divided into four different sections. The largest section is for hydroponic and aeroponic vegetables and berries. That's where my team and I work. I'll take you there now."

Janey and Sharon walked down a gravel path and through yet another air lock set of doors. Before them lay a huge greenhouse, the sides of which were completely covered with fine mesh screens.

"This is the area for managed bee pollination of crops," explained Jamie.

"How large is it?" asked Janey.

"Thirty-thousand square feet or the size of half a football field. The other sections of the Eco Farm are for the aquaponics raising of fish, hutches for rabbits, and coops for laying hens and roosters, and vertical farms. There are storage sheds and engineering buildings throughout the farm, a dining hall for workers, and restrooms are located in many places out in the fields. And there is an area for washing and preparing harvested plants to be delivered to the food processing facility and there is a central office."

Jamie handed Janey a binder.

"This is a manual all about the farm. Inside you will find maps of each section and lots of very useful information. You can leave it here. Take it with you after the tour."

"What kind of plants are grown in the greenhouse?" asked Janey.

"That information is in the binder. It's easier to read it than my telling you."

Janey looked at the table of contents and quickly located the correct page to answer her question. She read the following:

Fruit and vegetables grown in

the enclosed greenhouse for bee pollination are the following:

cucumbers, tomatoes, eggplants, four varieties of onions, celery, mustard, broccoli, cauliflower, cabbage, Brussel sprouts, red chilies, red, yellow, and green bell peppers, cantaloupes, varieties of squash including zucchini, lemons, limes, carrots, strawberries, cranberries, blueberries, raspberries, boysenberries, kidney and string beans, and clover.

Janey turned the page and read that the rest of the acreage was divided into four sections:

Section A-

Kale, spinach, beets, soy beans, radishes, Irish, russet and sweet potatoes, yams, and four types of lettuce.

Section B-

Five varieties of corn, black and brown lentils, snap and pod peas.

Section C-

Wheat, oats, barley, alfalfa, and rye.

Section D-

Rabbits, laying hens, aquaculture, aeroponics, and vertical farms.

"This is unbelievable! I mean, who was it that put this all together? And how long has it been in operation? And how many people work here?"

"Again," said Jamie, "the answers are all pretty well explained in the manual. But I can answer some of the questions. The farm has been operating for over two and a half years. I think there are around seven hundred and twenty-five people who run this amazing place. And a man named Brad Lambert directs the entire farm."

"Dr. Brad Lambert? The expert and professor in hydroponics from MIT?"

"Yeah, that's right."

"How did they get *him* up here?"

"You'll get to meet him soon enough, and he'll tell you himself.

But, I've heard that he was taken while speaking at a conference at the University of Arizona in Phoenix."

"Now that you mention it, I recall hearing about his disappearance on the news about two years ago."

"Lots of top people were brought up here to run the farm," said Sharon. "It's like they looked for specialists they needed and just took them."

"Everyone except me. I kind of walked right into being taken," said Janey and sighed.

"Let me tell you a little bit about what I do here," interrupted Jamie.

I have a team of thirty people. The plants in our greenhouse must have bees to pollinate them. We have solitary bees like miners. They really do not sting and are very beneficial to gardens. Also we have Japanese horn-faced bees, blue orchard bees, and mason bees. All of them have docile dispositions. And we also have alfalfa leaf cutter bees. They do not build colony hives like the others, so we constructed an entire section of drilled blocks of wood for them. We maintain an optimal air temperature for foraging between seventy-five and seventy-seven degrees Fahrenheit. In all, we have twenty bee-hives situated around the sides of the greenhouse, not including the alfalfa leaf cutter's wooden homes."

"And you grow enough to provide

food for everyone at the base? That's incredible," exclaimed Janey.

"So far you've only seen a small part of it," said Sharon.

"That's right," agreed Jamie. "Let me show you the other sections and introduce you to the heads of each division."

Jamie led the way.

"Janey, could you give me a basic idea about hydroponics. I mean, all our food is grown that way, but I'm not sure how it's done," said Sharon.

"Well, the major thing to know is that plants don't need soil to grow in. Instead, mineral nutrient solutions are introduced into the plant's water supply. There are different growing methods, but that's pretty much it."

"What sort of nutrients do plants need?"

"Mostly nitrogen, phosphorus, and potassium or NKP. There are others, too, like magnesium, phosphates, iron, and calcium. It depends on the types of plants."

"I thought we'd start in Section D and work our way around the farm," said Jamie. "This is our aquaponics area." He led them to a group of people standing next to a long row of water-filled pools with plants growing on the surface. "Sean, I'd like to introduce you to Janey Spadaro. I believe you know Sharon Oliver."

"Nice to meet you, Janey. He nodded at Sharon. What's your specialty?"

"Hydroponics."

Sean Bennett was a man in his forties with dark hair and bright-blue eyes.

"I'm sure we can use your expertise here. Let me show you around our area. We have a team of forty-five people. We employ a water raft trough system in the pools that are relatively shallow."

"What sort of plants and fish are grown here?" asked Janey.

"Chinese cabbage, two types of lettuce, basil, watercress, and taro. We have two types of fish. *Tilapia* is an herbivore from Africa and reaches an edible size in about three months.

The white *amur*, also an herbivore

fish prized in China, can grow to over a foot long in less than a year. Plant wastes are ground up and fed to the *tilapia* and *amur* fish. Ours is a closed-loop system that grows plants that filter wastes from the water in the fish pools. We rely on a symbiotic relationship between fish and plants to maintain stable nutrient and oxygen levels along with dense blooms of chlorella algae for feeding the fish."

Sharon looked at Janey and rolled her eyes, a gesture that brought on a smile.

"What you're doing here is really cool, Sean" Janey said. "Thanks so much for the information."

Next Jamie took them to the area

of rabbit hutches and introduced them to Vicki Hagar, a slim young woman with blond hair and dimples.

"Welcome to Rabbit Land! We have figured out how to supply all of us with meat that is low in fat, is mild-flavored, and can be cured like ham or made into sausage or rabbit burgers."

"I had two burgers last night with dinner," said Janey, "and some in my stew. They tasted great! But, just how do you raise rabbits?"

"Alfalfa is grown in Section C. It gives good yields of protein, but has way too much fiber, and people can't digest it. But when we add a little salt, it makes alfalfa a complete feed for the rabbits. They love it!"

"I like rabbit meat, too," said Sharon. "I've been here at Sub Rosa for a year and a half and eat it almost every day. How do you make it so available?"

"I know this will blow your minds, but rabbits grow so rapidly that a herd, which numbers twelve, can produce five times its initial weight in edible meat in one year! We've got eight hundred rabbits."

"Wow," exclaimed Janey. "How fast do they reproduce?"

"A doe has a litter averaging seven kittens every two months."

"Thanks, Vicki," said Janey as she shook her head in amazement. She followed Sharon and Jamie to an area down the path.

"This is where we raise chickens on the farm," explained Jamie. There were twelve long, neat rows of white coops raised above the ground. Each had stairs and an open doorway. Jamie motioned to a big man wearing coveralls and a straw hat, who came over and shook hands with Sharon and Janey.

"My name's Dave Duncan, and this here is our outer space chicken colony," he said and laughed. "I've got eighty-five people in my division, and the work never ends."

"What do you feed them?" asked Janey.

"Do you mean my staff or the chickens?"

Everyone laughed.

"Mostly leftovers from the apartment complex kitchens and dining halls along with waste from rabbit butchering at the food processing facility."

Janey looked down the long rows of coops. A group of seven roosters walked by.

"Ah, here's some of our big guys," Dave said. "Let's see, we've got Bubba, Vito, Casanova, Bogart, Valentino, Brad Pitt, and Romeo!"

Janey and Sharon laughed aloud.

"Can you explain how I was able to eat omelets for breakfast?" Janey said.

"Sure. We decided not to grow chickens for their meat because it's messy and labor intensive. Rabbits and fish are much easier. We've got about about six hundred chickens housed in raised wire cages above a concrete floor. Hens share the cages and are each allotted eighty square inches of space. Each row of coops has three levels of cages with conveyor belts running in front of the pens for food and underneath to collect manure. The bottoms of the pens are slightly angled so eggs roll out the front of the pens into a collection tray. Open windows allow for ventilation. We maintain an ambient temperature of sixty-eight degrees inside the coops. The cages all have nest boxes, litter, perch space, and some scratching materials, and each houses up to ten hens. The wastes brought here provide enough feed for the chickens to lay an average of three eggs a day for every person at the base to use in cakes, waffles, omelets, and mayonnaise."

"I've always wondered about the eggs. I mean, I knew we raised laying hens, but I didn't know how it was done. Thanks," said Sharon. Janey nodded at Dave.

"You're both welcome," Dave said.

"Now," said Jamie, "I'm going to take you to the area for washing and preparing harvested plants to be delivered to the food processing facility."

They walked along the path for a

good distance and came upon a row of buildings.

"Bonnie Thompson," said Jamie. "I'd like to introduce you to our newest base member, Janey Spadaro. Do you know Sharon?"

"Yes I do. Hi. Nice to meet you Janey."

"Nice to meet you, too, Bonnie."

"Allow me to explain what we do here. People from the four sections bring their produce to our division by trucks in ventilated plastic totes. The plants are then placed on a wash line and put onto a conveyer belt system, where they move through a series of wash tanks filled with cold water. Personnel inspect the greens as they move through the conveyer belt. After gathering, the greens are dunked into a large three-hundred gallon livestock tank. The next step is to spin the clean plants dry. Almost all water must be removed from the plant's surface. We use industrial-size drying machines that have an enameled basket inside. While in the machine, the plants are held in mesh bags, typically holding about six pounds of greens each. Two ten-pound bags, one on each side of the machine, are loaded for one spin cycle. It's a very efficient process, and we've got it down to a science. I've got eighty people on my team," said Bonnie.

"We are so grateful for your

work," said Sharon. "You do an amazing job!"

"I agree," said Janey. I mean, having fresh, clean produce is vital. I thank you."

Jamie now took them to see the large building where plants were grown by a method called aeroponics. They walked through an air lock set of two doors and entered.

"Oh, my God! It's as big as an airplane hangar," exclaimed Janey.

A tall, red-haired man walked up to them and smiled.

"My name is Aaron Cooper. Hi, Jamie. Hi, Sharon. May I please be introduced?"

"This is Janey Spadaro, who is an expert in hydroponics," said Jamie.

Janey and Aaron shook hands.

"Great!" Aaron said. "I'm sure we'll have lots of information to share and apply. Let me show you around our division."

"I'd heard about vertical aeroponic farms being started around the country before I was taken," said Janey. "I'm much more familiar with hydroponics."

"The principles of aeroponics are based on cultivating fruit and vegetables whose roots are in containers filled with flowing plant nutrition, and the roots can find the best conditions for oxygen and moisture. It's a form of hydroponics."

Jenny looked around and noted that there were hundreds of vertical towers in rows that receded in the distance.

"How do you grow the plants and harvest them?"

"Plant containers can be mounted on top of one another, and because they are light and handy, they can be easily moved," answered Jason. "Plants are mounted in vertical columns within our greenhouse with fourteen per column. Nutrients are allowed to trickle down through the growth columns and are contained in solution in a closed-circuit water supply system. The composition of the nutrients is controlled automatically. The roots of the plants absorb only the required nutrients."

"Okay. How do you harvest them?"

"The plant containers are periodically displaced. Young plants are placed at the highest level of the growth column. Afterward, they are progressively lowered, utilizing a rotational mechanical system. The rotation is periodically repeated. This permits constant harvest production without any interruption."

"This is a pretty big greenhouse. How many plants are you currently growing?"

"Let me explain something to you first. Climate controls within the greenhouse ensure optimal growing conditions assuring high yields. Our facility is ten thousand square feet. The vertical plastic plant-holding columns are eight feet high and fitted with rotation motors under a grid-beam structure with nets that run along the top of the walls to allow for air circulation."

"I've got so many questions, Aaron! Can we get technical?" asked Janey.

Sharon turned to Jamie. "Want to go for a walk?"

Jamie laughed.

"Let's go eat some strawberries!"

"To answer your last question, Janey, electric peristaltic pumps deliver nutrients to flexible distributors fitted to each of one thousand three hundred and fifty planting tubes. We are currently growing over nine thousand plants in the greenhouse."

"Tell me how it all works, Aaron."

"Our aeroponics division comprises high-pressure device hardware and biological systems that include enhancements for extended plant life and crop maturation, effluent controls, precision timing, and nutrient solution pressurization, heating and cooling sensors, forty-eight inch diameter propeller, belt-driven exhaust fans, thermal control of solutions, photon-flux light arrays, and spectrum filtration spanning."

"This is mind blowing!" Janey laughed. "Sharon would have fallen asleep by now! How did you get your knowledge about all of this? What's your story?"

"I got am MS in botany from

Louisiana State University and was involved in one of the first vertical column farms in New Orleans.

A good friend of mine turned me on to a book titled, *The Vertical Farm: Feeding the World in the 21st Century.* He had started a vertical farm in Mesa, Arizona, and he invited me to join him out there. I was home one night. There was a knock on the door and..."

"Two big guys with crew cuts?"

Aaron nodded.

"But, I'm happy to be here, I guess. I'm doing what I love, but I have to admit that in some ways it's like being in a prison. I can't go home. I wish I could."

Janey nodded.

"But, if we ever get out of here, I mean really go back to Earth, I'd apply our knowledge and experience to start vertical farms in cities all over the world. Vertical farms produce no agricultural runoff, use only a small amount of water, and we could grow enough vegetables and rice to feed the entire planet!"

Sharon and Jamie walked up to them with their mouths stained red.

"Wow, those are some plump, delicious strawberries," said Jamie.

"Thanks. And they're all organic, too!" exclaimed Aaron. "Janey, I'd like to have you working here, at least part of the time, if you want to, I mean."

"Thanks for the invite. You're on."

They left the greenhouse, and Jamie led them down to Section C, where a middle-aged, dark-haired woman named Abbie Larson met them.

"Janey is our newest farmhand," said Jamie.

They laughed aloud.

"Welcome, Janey. We grow all our hydroponic plants in three sections. The section you see here is mainly for cereal crops like wheat. We also grow barley, oats, alfalfa, and rye. The alfalfa is for the rabbits. We maintain so much acreage that electric carts and trucks are used by our workers to travel down roads that circle and intersect the growing areas. My division has two hundred and fifty people."

"What hydroponic systems or methods are you using?"

"Both static and continuous flow solution cultures are employed."

"Okay, Abbie," Sharon said with a sigh. "Please explain what the difference is between them to my ignorant self."

Abbie laughed along with the others.

"It's pretty simple, Sharon. Static systems make use of containers lined with black polytene film, beakers, pots and glass jars. The roots are suspended in a nutrient solution. In a continuous flow culture, the nutrient solution constantly flows past and under the roots in the plant beds."

A cart drove toward them and stopped.

"Great," said Jamie. "Now you can meet the head of our farm engineering and maintenance division."

A slim woman with long, light brown hair stepped out of the cart.

"Hi, my name is Laura Neal."

"This is Janey Spadaro. You may know Sharon Oliver, a clinic nurse in Complex C," said Jamie."

She nodded at Sharon.

"Yes, Sharon, I've seen you around the base. Are you new here, Janey?"

"Brand new. I was taken because

of my knowledge of hydroponics, and Sharon tells me that I'm the last person to be brought up to Sub Rosa."

Abbie, Laura, and Jamie were all visibly surprised.

"That means the others will be arriving soon," commented Laura.

"Is the Eco Farm ready for them?" asked Janey.

All three of them nodded.

"We're as ready as we can be," said Bonnie. "Our plant harvests can easily be multiplied to meet the increased demand."

A cart drove up and parked next to the other one. A heavyset man with short dark hair, and a big smile got out.

"Can I join the party?" he said.

"Sure," said Abbie. "May I introduce John Sanders? He supervises the Nutrient Division. This is Janey Spadaro, who's going to be working with us on hydroponics."

"Nice to meet you."

"Same here," said Janey. "Laura, I didn't get to ask about your division. Can you explain what you do? Then I'd like to hear from John, if that's all right."

"Well, our Division has a lot of different types of engineers. We maintain the lighting, air temperature, de-humidifiers, and general maintenance for the farm with a computer-controlled network of sensors, motors, and plumbing. And I have over a hundred and twenty-five people who make it all happen."

"I've noticed that the air temperature and humidity inside the farm are very comfortable," said Janey.

"Most of the moisture comes from the plants as water evaporates from their leaves in a process called 'transpiration'. The farm dehumidifiers are designed to remove a specific amount of moisture from the recirculated air stream."

"How do you light the farm?"

"We have a variety of lighting bulbs that include T5 fluorescent, high-pressure sodium, and metal halide. We use timers to simulate day and night. There is a set time of sixteen hours of bright artificial light, followed by eight hours of darkness. Plants need dark down-time, just like you, to metabolize and rest. You'll notice the lights overhead along with rows of three-foot diameter ceiling fans. We maintain all of it and more!"

"Wow! So your team basically makes the farm run, Laura."

"Thanks. We do our best."

Janey turned to John Sanders. "Okay, your turn."

John smiled.

"I have a team of eighty people in my division. We supervise the nutrient solution flow systems and nutrient spraying of crops throughout the farm for healthful vegetable crop production. Our division makes sure that a well-balanced nutrient solution is maintained to meet all plant demands consistently to accommodate and promote the three phases of vegetable development, which are: initial growth, flowering, and fruiting. We make adjustments of nitrogen and potassium, magnesium, and trace elements to the nutrient solution on a continuous basis.

Jamie Glasgow clapped his hands together.

"Thank you all for helping to bring Janey up to speed. Now she's going to meet with Dr. Brad Lambert and get her assignment. Then let's go get some lunch, okay? I'm getting hungry!"

"Me, too!" said Sharon.

Jamie led her and Janey toward a two-story building with rows of large plate glass windows.

"This is our central office and computer control base for the farm," commented Jamie as they walked through the front door.

A short man greeted them. He had laugh lines around his blue eyes, thinning dark hair and a big smile.

"Hi, Jamie."

"Hi, Dr. Lambert. Allow me to introduce Janey Spadaro. I believe you know Sharon."

"Yes I do," he said as he nodded at her and shook Janey's hand. "Please excuse us," he said and opened the door to his office. Janey followed him inside.

The office was large, and shelves were crammed with many books. More volumes were piled on tables, on which sat six large computer screens. Brad took a seat behind his desk and indicated Janey take a seat in a chair facing him.

"I am familiar with your research at UNM and am glad to have you here. Of course, I wish the circumstances were different, but here we are, so I bid you welcome."

"Thanks, Dr. Lambert."

"Brad, please."

"Brad. I got an MS in hydroponics and a doctorate in environmental science at MIT, so I was shocked when I read about your disappearance. It was headline news for a while; "MIT Professor Suddenly Vanishes". Want to talk about it?"

"I'm glad to hear you graduated from our great university, but there's not much to talk about. I attended a hydroponics conference at the University of Arizona in Phoenix. After my opening speech, I was hustled off stage by two big guys, who dragged me out a side door and into the back seat of a car. That's about it. They must have drugged me. When I woke up, I was in a helicopter. How about you?"

"Very much the same. Did the two big guys have crew cuts?"

"Yes, now that you mention it, they did."

"Well, we're here, Brad, and it doesn't look like we'll ever see planet Earth again. Sharon's been a good guide and a friend to me. She says not to fight it and to go with the flow."

"Good advice. I wish we could return to Earth and reproduce the Eco Farm all over the planet. We have a great team of people here and have achieved a lot in two and a half years, and I'm certain that we can train others. Duplicates of the Eco Farm could be started all over the Earth because we don't necessarily need to have sunshine or be hampered by growing seasons and weather. We could feed people in the northern latitudes like Alaska, the Northern Territories, Scandinavia, Siberia, and in high mountain regions like the Andes and Himalayas. And I can see no reason why we couldn't have Eco Farms in major cities inside large buildings or on rooftops. Did you meet Aaron at the vertical farm section?"

"Yes, I was so impressed!"

"A colleague of mine at Columbia University Medical School, Dr. Dickson Despommier, invented the term and has written a book on the subject and taught many classes on vertical farming, which have inspired so many people that there are now vertical farms all over the planet."

"That's fantastic! We could change

the world. With private funding and government assistance, I bet we could improve the health of the planet and make a big dent in famine, malnutrition, and disease," said Janey. "But I have a question. No, two questions."

"Ask away."

"Do you grow GMO's here at the farm?"

"Absolutely not. In fact, Michael Dryer told me in no uncertain terms that everything must be organically grown, and no GMO crops are allowed."

Janey looked around his office at the banks of computers and plasma screens.

"Who finances all of this? I mean,

the farm, my apartment came fully-furnished, and then there's the Free Store."

"I have no idea. All I've been told is that someday we're to expect quite a lot of new people and to have the farm able to feed all of them. Whenever I request things, they're usually delivered within two weeks."

"It's incredible!"

Brad Lambert stood up, walked around his desk, and shook her hand.

"Janey, I'm glad to have you on the team. I want you to be an all-around assistant. You'll be given daily assignments in various divisions on the farm in all sections. Your work schedule will be posted on the bulletin board by the front door. I'm sorry to tell you that there are no day's off at Sub Rosa. We all have to work every day and even on Saturday, though it's Christmas. Be here tomorrow at nine a.m."

"Would it be okay to get your cell phone number? I mean, I'd like to have it if we ever get out of here."

Brad laughed. "Fat chance of that happening! I'm sure that my cell phone number is no longer working after two years."

He wrote something down and handed it to her. Janey put it in her pocket. "That's my office number at MIT. I have it drilled into my brain!"

Brad stood up and led Janey

outside. Jamie and Sharon sat on a bench.

"If Janey is indeed the last one to be brought up here, I'm glad they got someone who will be essential to the farm," he said and returned to his office.

"I hope you've enjoyed the tour of the Eco Farm," said Jamie. "Now, let's get some lunch."

"Thanks. I feel like I can make a contribution here. I look forward to it."

The three of them ate in the central office mess hall. The place was crowded since around a hundred people worked in the building. Janey had two rabbit burgers, green salad, and fresh berries for dessert.

"Well, I've got to get back to my bees," said Jamie. He bid them goodbye.

"Where to now?" asked Janey.

"The hospital.

They walked along the road on the right side of the central park. Many electric delivery trucks and small vans passed them by. Sharon opened the front door, and they stepped into the reception area.

"We're here to see Dr. Chloe King. She's agreed to give my friend Janey a tour of the hospital," she said to a young woman who sat behind the counter.

"One moment please while I page her."

At that moment an elevator opened, and Dr. King emerged along with her two young daughters. Her girls had long, blond hair like their mother and blue eyes. Janey offered her hand.

"It is so nice to meet you, Dr. King."

"Chloe, please. And these are my girls. Meredith is ten, and Olivia is seven."

Janey shook their hands. They shyly smiled at her. Both had on pretty dresses and ribbons in their light-blond hair.

"My husband, Jason, will be landing soon, and I always make

sure they wear dresses. The rest of the time it's jeans and T-shirts. Let me show you around. We have three floors, and everything in our facility is state-of-the-art."

Sharon and Janey followed Chloe and the girls, and she showed them the first floor, which mainly had examination rooms and an ER. They took an elevator to the second floor.

"Here's where we have our ICU and rooms that contain an MRI, CAT scan, dialysis center, X-ray, and various other types of testing equipment. The third floor is where our patient rooms are located and a cafeteria for our patients and staff."

"How many types of doctors are there?" asked Janey.

"We have an orthopedic surgeon, a neurosurgeon, an oncologist, and I'm a general practitioner. There's an optometrist, an ophthalmologist, a podiatrist, an orthodontist, and an oral surgeon. We also have two chiropractors and an acupuncturist as well as twelve RN's like Sharon."

"Wow! Are you that busy? Why are you staffed so well?"

"We do have a steady stream of people coming here. The apartment clinics handle mostly minor wounds. We handle accidents from the food processing facility or the farm. Our first baby girl was born two weeks ago. But we're expecting a very large influx of people in the near future, and that's why we're so prepared."

THE USS *EXCALIBUR*

Colonel Jason King prepared to land inside the smaller impact crater within Stickney Crater on Phobos. The red surface of Mars loomed below him as he maneuvered the USS *Excalibur* over the moon and guided her on the landing approach to the air lock. Arnie Weber was his co-pilot. Intelligent and capable, he was five nine and wiry, with dark hair. Jason was glad to have him in the right seat.

"Reduce speed and bring the ship to a hover position."

"Yes, sir."

Jason momentarily closed his eyes and recalled a scene from three days earlier just before their taking off from the secret base at *Hoste Island*. The base was located in *Tierra del Fuego* at the southernmost point in Chile. This inhospitable, sub-polar region was one of immense beauty and was completely uninhabited. An icy plateau lay between some of the island's snow-covered mountains and was the perfect place to construct an underground space base for the two large ships under a thick cover of ice and rock.

Then he'd thought about his meeting with Marc and Jenny. They'd given him an idea. He would take pictures of the ships at the base in their underground hangars. At Sub Rosa, he would photograph the entire place. That would be his insurance and maybe a way to get his wife and daughters back to Earth. Blackmail? Why not?

He'd bought a Nikon Coolpix SO1. The digital camera was very small and thin, only three inches wide by one inch, easily hidden, and it took remarkably clear pictures. He had demanded and been allowed to have his private jet at the base. Jason planned on flying to *Point Arenas,* where he could safely email the photos to Jenny and Marc. He'd walked around the perimeter of his ship, taking photos. The walk had taken him over half an hour because each side of the triangular craft was two hundred and thirty-two feet long. He also made certain that the security guards didn't notice he was taking pictures. Jason had gotten good shots of the impulse engines and the cockpit from the outside. He'd photographed the sides of the ship, which were thirty-eight feet tall to accommodate three decks. He'd also gotten good shots of the USS *Concord* parked farther down the hangar from his ship along with shots of two medium-size shuttle craft and three larger space freighters. The shuttles carried scientists, engineers, and medical personnel to bases on the moon and Mars, and the freighters brought construction materials, electronics, and food supplies along with medical equipment.

He duct-taped the camera to the inside of his captain's hat, put it on, and prepared to taxi outside and fly to Phobos. The trip would take three days due to the variable-specific impulse magneto-plasma rocket engines and an electromagnetic device which acted as an anti-gravity force-field and provided inertia-free acceleration and deceleration.

Another scene formed in Jason's mind. He had the beginnings of a plan to rescue the people at Sub Rosa. Could he trust his co-pilot? What about the six other crew members, who took care of loading and unloading cargo? He'd gotten his answer unexpectedly when on day two his co-pilot had turned to him.

"Captain, I've got to get something off my chest. I may get into a heap of trouble for speaking to you, but it's been bothering me since our last trip ten days ago."

"Go ahead, Arnie."

"I saw one of my first cousins at Sub Rosa. His name is Dr. Jeff Simmons, and he's an oral surgeon. He disappeared from Provo, Utah, about two months ago. I didn't talk with him and I don't think he saw me. But he's got a wife and three kids. I tell you what's happening just isn't right."

Jason wrote on a notebook, "Let's

have this conversation in a safe place while the ship is on auto-pilot because the cockpit may be bugged."

Arnie nodded, and they went to a cargo hold down on Deck One.

"I've been developing a plan to rescue all the people who've been taken against their will like your cousin," Jason said. "My wife and two girls are at the base to keep me in line. Maybe we can make use of this ship."

"What about the other ship?"

"Out of the question. The pilot's Brad Dryer Michael and Andrea's son."

"Too bad, Captain. You can count me in on the plan."

"Thanks. Call me Jason when we're talking one on one from now on, okay?"

"You got it, Jason."

"What about the six crew members?"

"One of them is a Hopi from northern Arizona named *Kele* and he's got a good friend in engineering named *Honovi.*"

"I know *Honovi.* He and I have been here since the beginning three years ago. What about the other five?"

"I've spoken with all of them, and they agree that abducting the people isn't right. One's an African-American man named Ben

Anderson. He's a former Navy Seal, who's got a girlfriend at the base."

"But we're only there for three days and nights before we take off for Earth again! How's that possible?"

Arnie shrugged

"He works fast, I guess. I'll talk to both him and *Kele* privately."

"Okay. But just sound out how they feel and don't mention anything about an escape plan understand?"

Arnie had nodded, and they'd returned to the cockpit.

Now Jason's reverie was interrupted.

"We're hovering over the air lock and in a controlled descent, Capt…, I mean, Jason."

"Prepare the ship for landing

in four minutes. Countdown begins now."

ADMINISTRATION CENTER PHOBOS, MARS

Victor Spoils gazed in awe at the ship bearing down on Phobos. Even though he'd seen it many times, the sheer size of it always blew his mind.

Barry Dukov, deputy head of security at Sub Rosa, stood beside him. The Dryer's sat at a table. All watched the ship approach on an immense projection screen.

Barry glanced at Victor. The light from the screen reflected off his shaved head, and his crossed arms were covered in tattoos. The screen suddenly went black, and then

Xavier del Mundo appeared sitting at his desk in New York City. Barry had once asked how this was possible, and Victor had explained that there were three relay communication satellites. One was in Earth orbit, a second was at the mid-point at two and a half million miles, and the third was in Mar's orbit.

"I have initiated the escape operation. Expect one thousand four hundred and forty-four people to arrive in two weeks on our two ships. The USS *Concord* will bring an additional two dozen security guards in one week, and I will be aboard. Have my apartment cleaned, supplied, and made ready for my arrival."

"Yes, sir," said Michael Dryer.

The screen returned to the view of the ship as it settled neatly upon the air lock.

Jason and Arnie shut down the engines and ran through their post-flight check list. They unbuckled and joined the crew on the landing platform. The six men had loaded all the cargo onto large electric carts and stacked it in rows on the left side. Ramps had been built into the platform for unloading. The right side contained ten rows of seventy-two chairs, each for passengers. The large platform descended on hydraulics for half a mile, and the trip took approximately twenty minutes. They reached the bottom and were met by four security guards, who conducted a cursory pat down to make sure there were no cigarettes, booze, or drugs. The men emptied their pockets, and their bags were X-rayed.

Jason worried about his camera. His captain's hat and visor were black. Above the visor in real silver was an American eagle, and underneath were the words *Space Fleet Command.* The X-ray buzzed as he passed through the body scanner, but the guard, Jeff Leonard, was accustomed to that happening because of his hat and waved him on through.

Jason headed for the hospital.

It had been ten days since he'd

last seen his wife and girls. He walked in just as an elevator door opened, and Chloe, Meredith, and Olivia exited along with a nurse he knew named Sharon and a woman who looked exactly like Jenny Spadaro. Then he recalled that she had an identical twin sister named Janey at the base and smiled.

He bent down and lifted Meredith and Olivia in each arm. They kissed their daddy, and he kissed them back. He carefully set them back down and embraced Chloe. They looked into each other's eyes and kissed.

"I missed you so much," she said. "We don't want to be here

any longer. We want to go home to Earth."

"I'm working on it," whispered Jason. "Right now I want to have a conversation with these two ladies. Then we can go up to the cafeteria and have lunch."

"Okay. I love you."

Jason kissed her again and turned to Sharon and Janey.

"We must talk. Please follow me."

They took the elevator to the second floor, and he led them to the X-ray room.

"It should be okay to talk in here. The walls are lead lined." He paused and looked at Janey. "I recently met your sister, Jenny."

Janey felt tears form. She

attempted to speak, but couldn't. Finally, she rasped out two words.

"How? Where?"

He motioned for them to sit down. Then Jason relayed his meeting with her sister and Marc Prentis in Virginia. He told her about the attempt on her life and Marc's subsequent rescue of her. He then told them about their vision of Mother Mary in the church near Marc's house and the task set by The Father. Janey instinctively crossed herself.

"We're running out of time," said Jason. "I'm formulating a plan. Sharon, you've been here for quite a while and know a lot of people. I need your help. I want to bring

Jenny up here through the Jump Gate in the Grand Canyon. I'm not sure how at this point. She'll bring some weapons, explosives, and a communication device with her so we can speak through a secure channel on my ship. Then she'll go back to Earth through the Jump Gate. We've got to blow the steel door in the wall that leads into the base. I'd like to have an FBI SWAT team storm in and overpower the guards. We can get over seven hundred people on my ship, and the rest can go through the Jump Gate. It'll be touch and go, but I think we can pull it off."

"But, Jason," said Sharon. "That's

assuming Jenny and Marc will be able to complete their task in time."

"You're right. We all must operate on complete faith that they will. The comet is fast approaching Earth. We've got about two weeks. But we must try. Will you help?"

"Of course I will." Sharon said. "All of us would like to return to our lives on Earth. I'm taking Janey over to engineering next. There's a Hopi man there named *Honovi*. We're both from Arizona and have become friends. One of the security guards is also a Hopi. Maybe we can enlist him to get Jenny through the door somehow."

"*Honovi* and I are friends, too," said Jason, "and I'm sure he'll help us, but I must ask you to limit talking about the plan to those whom you can trust. I'm staying at Chloe's apartment #324 in Complex B, for the next two days and nights. Keep me up to date."

Both women nodded, and they left him and rode the elevator down to the lobby. They walked along the road and passed by two tall buildings. Sharon said one of them contained the nuclear reactor that ran the base, but she didn't know what was in the other one. She led Janey into engineering. The place was alive with people in front of computer screens, walking quickly across the room or in some cases running. Machinery hummed, and bright lights overhead illuminated everything below.

"What do all these people do here?" asked Janey.

"They run the lighting, sewage waste disposal, water filtration, temperature control, air circulation, and dehumidifiers for the base," answered Sharon.

She located *Honovi* and headed in his direction. *Honovi* was in a conversation with another engineer. They waited till he was free. When he turned to look at them, Janey's heart did a somersault, and her reluctance to be involved with someone again quickly vanished. The man was very handsome with long raven-black hair, reddish-brown skin, a flashing white smile, and piercing brown eyes. He was about six feet, muscular and well-toned.

"Please meet Janey Spadaro, our newest and last addition to the base."

The name *Honovi* means 'strong deer' in the Hopi language, and his heart leaped like one when he saw Janey. She was pretty with dark, curly hair, a pert nose, blue eyes, and high cheekbones. Her height was medium, and she was trim.

"He said, "nice to meet…"

"It's a pleasure to make…"

They spoke over each other, and both of them laughed along with Sharon, who then addressed *Honovi.*

"We passed by two buildings on the way here. One's the nuclear reactor, but I don't know what's in the other one."

Honovi signaled to three men, who came over and joined them.

"These two ladies have some questions I'm not qualified to answer. Allow me to introduce Janey and Sharon."

"My name is Brian Stern, and my two colleagues are Glen Horn and Aaron Levin. What are your questions?"

"We'd like to know about the nuclear reactor and also what's in the building next to it," said Sharon.

Aaron answered. He was a nuclear engineer.

"The building contains a Stirling radio-isotope power system generator or SRG for short. I'm not sure I can explain its function in an understandable way, but I'll make an attempt. Our SRG uses free-piston Stirling engines coupled to linear alternators to convert heat into electricity."

Sharon's eyes glazed over, but Janey understood.

"Can you achieve greater efficiency by increasing the temperature ratio between the hot and cold ends of the generator?"

Aaron was surprised, and his expression showed it.

"Why yes, Janey, we can. Also, we use non-contacting moving

parts and non-degrading flexural bearings in a hermetically sealed environment."

"Without appreciable degradation, your SRG should continue running for decades without major maintenance," said Janey.

"True. I'm impressed. How do you know about this topic?"

"I have a doctoral degree in hydroponic systems and a bachelor of science in general engineering from the Massachusetts Institute of Technology, or MIT. What's in the other building?"

Glen Horn answered.

"A collection of ninety-eight percent of Earth's DNA biological genome. The library is stored in six specially designed cylinders, and the contents of each are listed. They are kept at four degrees below zero Fahrenheit."

"What for?" asked Janey.

Glen shrugged.

"We don't know."

"How was the base first excavated?" inquired Janey.

Brian Stern took this question on.

"Because we would be working in an airless environment, one of the big ships parked on top of a small impact crater within the larger Stickney Crater. We constructed an air lock around it first. Once that was sealed and functioning, we began to go deep. Side-scan radar imaging revealed several large cavities beneath us, and we began to carve out and down through a half mile of rock layers."

"What did you use to cut through the rock?" asked Janey.

"High-powered laser diggers that not only cut through the rock, but actually vaporize it."

"Wow!" said Janey. I didn't know such a thing existed."

Brian and the other two men laughed.

"Technology is way beyond what the average person knows. We used one hundred megawatt lasers inside the laser diggers as a laser light source which were powered by a 1.5GWe nuclear reactor. Multiple laser diggers were used for redundancy in case one broke down because we could not wait for spare parts to arrive."

"How was the base itself constructed?" asked Sharon.

"Once we had the air lock system in place, a space freighter delivered the SRG. We began to put the hydraulic elevator system in place and constructed the platform. Then we put up the building to house the SRG and made sure it was fully functioning. We then started at the top and put in all of the lighting, fans, temperature controls, and the oxygen-producing plant leaves," answered Glen. "We needed lots of electrical engineers for that part."

"That's where I came in," said

Honovi. "At least four hundred men and women built what you see around you. And we did it all in about three years. A couple of hundred others put together the entire Eco Farm. Once the apartments were in place, we created a large park in the center of the base. It was my idea to have a wooden bridge crossing over a stream."

Aaron spoke up.

"We were recruited to the project. The thrill and adventure of working on a moon of Mars and building an underground base appealed to us. However, we were told that once the base was built, we'd be able to return to our families on Earth and we were flat-out lied to."

Brian cleared his throat.

"I think I speak for the others when I say that we are very bitter. We cannot leave and are stuck here for the rest of our lives."

"Would you please excuse us for a moment?" asked Sharon.

She led Janey a dozen steps away, where they could speak privately.

"What do you think? Should we ask them to help in the rescue plan?"

"Let's discuss that in a minute. I want to know if *Honovi's* single. Does he have a steady girlfriend or live with someone?"

Sharon grinned.

"Not that I know of. I've never seen

him with a woman, a least not in public."

Janey smiled at Sharon.

"Thanks." She paused. "Okay, I think we must include these men. Jason said he'd like a SWAT team to storm the steel door by the Jump Gate. What if all the lights in the base suddenly went out?" "I wonder if you can simply turn off the nuclear power generator?" asked Sharon.

"Let's find out," said Janey. She turned and began to walk back.

"Wait," said Sharon. "I think we ought to limit what we tell them to just the escape plan and keep the comet and other things to ourselves for now."

"I agree."

They returned to the men, and Janey posed Sharon's question. Aaron Levin answered.

"We can briefly put the SRG on standby mode whenever we need to do routine maintenance. That takes about twenty minutes. Then we turn the power on again. What's your reason for asking?"

Janey looked at Sharon who nodded.

"Is there someplace we can talk where we won't be overheard?" asked Janey.

"Follow me to my office in the SRG building," said Aaron.

They sat at a table in the center of the room surrounded by desks, banks of computers, and large plasma screens.

"This room is like a Faraday Cage and is shielded from radiation. We can speak freely in here."

"Colonel Jason King, the pilot of the USS *Excalibur*, has confided in us that he's putting a plan together for rescuing all of the people at the base," said Janey.

"How?" asked Brian Stern.

"We're working out the details. He knows my identical twin sister, Jenny, who's an FBI agent. If we can figure out some way to get her up here through the Jump Gate in the Grand Canyon, she can help us."

"I have a friend who's a security guard assigned to the gate area. His name is *Tuwa*, which means 'Earth ' in the Hopi language," said *Honovi*

"That's great," said Sharon. "Ask him if he'll help us."

"There's almost a thousand people at the base. How can you hope to rescue them all?" asked Glen Horn.

"Jason can take over seven hundred of them in his ship, and everyone else will have to go through the Jump Gate," explained Janey.

"How do you think we can help?" inquired Aaron.

"I'm not sure at the moment. Jason wants this to happen in two weeks. We have to coordinate everything. The first thing is to get my sister up here."

"I'll speak with *Tuwa*," said *Honovi*.

"Good," said Janey. "In the meantime, let's keep this to ourselves. Do I have your word?"

All answered yes.

Honovi walked beside Janey on their way back to engineering.

"I'd be honored if you would join me for dinner tonight. My apartment is in Complex A."

Janey nodded.

"What time?"

"Around seven p.m."

"I'll be there." Sharon gave Janey a wink as they began to walk across the park in the direction of the apartment complexes.

"That wasn't exactly an

enthusiastic response to *Honovi's* invitation."

"Sorry. I look forward to having dinner with him, but my mind is numb from the tour of the Eco Farm, all the information Jason gave us, on top of the meeting we just had. I think my brain's shutting down."

"Me, too. We've got some time. Let's go to your place, relax, and talk about it.

The voice of Michel Dryer resounded loudly throughout the base on the public address system.

"Attention. Attention. Be on notice that one thousand four hundred and forty-four newcomers will be arriving at Sub Rosa in two weeks time. I want everyone at Sub Rosa to be prepared to receive them."

The two women walked into the lobby of Complex E and took the elevator. Janey got two bottles of water from the fridge and set a bowl of chips and salsa on the coffee table. She sat beside Sharon.

"You go first. Then I'll go second. What are you feeling?" asked Janey.

"Scared," said Sharon. "That's first. Excitement is second, and

I guess, sad comes in third."

"Care to explain?"

"Well, what if we try to escape and somehow are stopped? Will we be punished? And what if your sister and her boyfriend are successful and the comet misses Earth? Will we still be stuck up here? And if so, what does that mean for us? I'm excited at the prospect of returning to Earth. And if everything works out and I actually get to go home, what will it be like trying to put my life back together? Will I get my old job back after a year and a half? And finally,

I know this may be hard for you to understand, but I feel sad because I'll miss the life I've built here and the friends I've made. Does any of that make any sense to you?"

"Yes, it does," answered Janey. And I'm feeling afraid, too, but we have to remain positive and do all that we can. Given the chance, I think everyone wants to get out of here. Sure, I understand that people are justifiably proud of what they've done at the base, but we've all been taken against our will. I've only just arrived, so I haven't had much of a chance to build a life here like you have. But the possibility of getting out of here is one I'll put everything I've got into. I'm super excited about seeing my sister, Jenny, and I'm scared, too. What if something goes wrong, and she's hurt? And, you know, if we do pull it off, I'll be kind of sad at having missed the opportunity of working at the farm. But if we do pull it off, excuse me, I mean, *when* we pull it off, I want to be part of starting Eco Farms like this one all over the planet. And what about Dryer's announcement? He said the people are coming in two weeks. We've got to put all the pieces in place before then and make our escape. Thanks for coming along on the tour with me today, Sharon."

"You're welcome. A nurse from the hospital filled in for me. It's around four o'clock. Get some rest. I hope you have a fun dinner with *Honovi*."

Janey nodded and let her out. She felt an overwhelming need to lie down. It had been a long day, and she was emotionally drained. She set the alarm clock for six p.m., undressed, washed up, and lay down in her bed. With her eyes closed, she formed an image in her mind of her sister.

"Jenny, if you can hear me, know

that I'm okay. Jason King told me that you're coming up here. Try to contact me just before, okay? I can't wait to see you."

KEAMS CANYON, ARIZONA

Marc and Jenny sat side by side on the sofa in the living room.

"What are you thinking?" he said.

"About my sister. I hope she's okay."

Marc put his arm around her. She snuggled against his shoulder and closed her eyes.

"Jenny? Know that I'm okay. Jason King told me that you're coming up here. Try to contact me just before, okay? I can't wait to see you.."

Jenny opened her eyes wide and sat bolt upright. She shook her head and looked at Marc.

"My sister! I swear I just heard Janey distinctly and clearly in my mind! She must have met with Jason because she just told me that she knows about the plan to send me to the base. Oh, Marc. We've got to rescue her and everyone else."

"There's not much we can do until we hear from Jason."

"As soon as we do, I want us to meet with my Special Agent in Charge. We've got to convince him to help us."

SUB ROSA, PHOBOS

Janey showered, dressed, put on some makeup, and walked over to Complex A right at seven p.m. *Honovi* was standing at the door to the mess hall and greeted her. They sat across from each other at a nearby table. *Honovi* hoped he didn't appear visibly nervous, but he was shaking. Janey's heart was beating fast, too. *Honovi* wore a blue denim shirt, tan slacks and a turquoise and silver pendant. His black hair was tied back in a pony tail.

"You look beautiful, Janey."

"Thanks. You look very handsome." *Honovi* smiled.

"Let's get some food." They stood in line and filled their plates. The main entree was spaghetti with rabbit meatballs, tomatoes, green bell peppers, and onions. They put their salads on separate plates and returned to the table. *Honovi* left and brought two glasses of cold water.

"Wow! I could get used this," she said.

"Hopefully, you won't have to get too used to it. I spoke with my friend, *Tuwa.* He said he'd help us and figure out a way to get your sister through the gate."

"Oh, that's good news. I guess it will be about five or six days before Jason returns to Earth."

"In the meantime, some of us can talk to others and enlist them in the escape plan."

Janey smiled at him. He was very handsome, but she's learned that good looks weren't always an accompaniment to intelligence. She knew very little about him.

"Where did you grow up?"

"On the Hopi reservation at First Mesa in northeastern Arizona. A charitable organization that helped poor kids get a good education chose me. I eventually attended the University of Colorado, where I studied architecture and got a degree in structural engineering."

"How did you end up here?"

"I was a supervisor and consultant for a big bridge that was being built. One night I'd stepped outside of my trailer to look at the stars. The next thing I knew, two big guys were in my face. I was knocked out, and I woke up in a helicopter. How about you?"

"A similar story," said Janey. "I like your pendant with a deer silhouetted against a full moon."

"Thanks. My grandmother made it. Her name is *Mongwau*, which means "water moon" in our language."

He paused. "And I really miss her along with my grandfather, *Pamuya*, and my mother and father, *Yamka* and *Tocho*. How about you? Where did you grow up?"

"In a place that's probably the exact opposite to yours. New York City. Loud, crowded, polluted, but always exciting. I went to NYU.

and then MIT. Before I was taken, I was an instructor in the science of hydroponics at the University of New Mexico in Albuquerque."

"I was very impressed with your engineering knowledge about our nuclear reactor when talking with Aaron Levin this afternoon."

"Thank you." Janey patted her tummy. "The dinner was really good."

They finished their meals and dropped their plates in the washing tubs. *Honovi* invited her to come up to his apartment, and Janey agreed.

"But just for a little while. I've got to be at the farm by 9 am."

"Same here. I start at nine, too."

Honovi unlocked the door, and they entered. Janey's eyes took in his apartment. The layout was identical to hers, but displayed on the walls was a wonderful collection of southwestern art. While *Honovi* went into the kitchen, she walked around and admired various framed photos, paintings, and prints. There were also Native American bowls and various sculptures on the coffee and end tables. But the painting that caught her eye was one titled, *"La Virgen con Christo"*.

She stood before it and crossed herself. *Honovi* appeared with two bottles of water, a bowl of tortilla chips, salsa, and two plates. He saw Janey crossed herself and smiled.

"Why do you have this painting?" she said.

"I guess to honor His original message, which was one of peace and brotherly love. And to honor my parents. They converted to Catholicism, and I was raised in the religion. My grandparents are traditional in the Hopi ways. In fact, only about five percent of Hopi's converted to Christianity. I must admit that over the years I've found that my own worldview coincided with that of my Hopi ancestor's way of looking at the world."

Janey nodded.

"I saw a lot of art at the Free Store, but nothing like this. You've got good taste."

"Thanks. There are individual buyers for art, music, clothing,

apartment furnishings and so forth.
I asked Jason to see if he could
persuade the art buyer to get pieces
that reflected the southwest since
most of the people here are from
Utah, New Mexico, Arizona and
Nevada."

"Why is so much provided to us at
no cost? I don't get it."

"Whoever's financing the base
wants to make sure people are not
only happy, but also productive."

They took seats on the sofa and
put chips and salsa on their plates.

"My sister, Jenny, is a devout
Catholic, but I guess I've lapsed over
the years like you. I still retain some
core beliefs, but I've also found
my own view. I don't know much

about the Hopi. What is their way of looking at the world?"

Honovi smiled.

"In the beginning, the Creator, *Taiowa*, gave us His plan for our lives. He created the land of the peaceful one's, the Hopi; a place of balance and harmony. The world at large and us, as individuals, must grow, but we must do so in a balanced way. When we act in this way, we set positive energies in motion. We Hopi believe that the true path will always be found through both prayer and meditation, where you are in a state of total reverence, have respect for all things, and become at peace with those things."

"Do you believe that everything has a spirit and an awareness?"

"The Hopi view encompasses the total web of the cosmos including animals, the plants, the land, Earth, the stars, and indeed, the entire universe. The Great Spirit guides all of it. How He does what He does is what we refer to as The Great Mystery."

They put their plates down, and *Honovi* opened the sliding glass door leading to the balcony. Like Janey's it faced the park. They stood silently looking out at the bridge, stream, and grass lawns intersected by bike paths and roads. Their hands rested on a metal railing.

Honovi turned to Janey.

"The web of the cosmos has been broken here. This state is called *koyaaniqatsi* in the Hopi language and means, "a collective life out of balance". Our people feel we are obligated to do all we can to repair the cosmic road so life progresses. Something is amiss. I can sense it when I relax my mind and meditate. Dryer's announcement that many people are coming and Jason's escape plan both happening on the same day is no mere coincidence. In fact, I don't believe in the concept of coincidence."

Janey gazed at *Honovi* and made a firm decision.

"You're correct. My sister, Jenny, and her friend, Marc, told Jason that they both had a vision of Mother Mary at a Catholic church in Keams Canyon."

"That's St. Joseph's, the church my parents and I attended. I went to Sunday school there. Please continue."

Janey relayed the message from The Father and the task that had been given to both of them.

"The Blue Star *Kachina* is on its way. How much time do we have?"

"Maybe two weeks," she said.

"We must escape and return to Earth. I will do all I can to help your sister. Pray that she and Marc are successful. The fate of our planet is completely in their hands."

"Mother Mary said She would

assist them. They have Her Love with them."

They were silent for a while. Then *Honovi* placed his hand over Janey's. She quickly withdrew hers and took two steps backward.

"Is this something you do often? Invite newly arrived women up to your apartment and put the moves on them?"

She glared at him. *Honovi* looked shocked and surprised.

"I plead innocent to the charges! As a matter of fact, you're the first woman I've ever asked to join me for dinner and the very first one to ever come up here!"

"Do you mean to tell me I'm the first, in what, three years? Why am

I so special? Sharon said that she'd never seen you with any women before. Are you gay?"

Honovi laughed.

"Hardly. I don't know what to say, Janey. I work a hard, long shift. I have to crawl into tight, dirty places, fix broken machinery, climb ladders, and study blueprints all day. When I get back here, I'm bushed. I take a hot shower, go downstairs for dinner, and come back up here to meditate. Then I go to sleep. Pretty boring, but that's my basic daily schedule."

"Did you have a wife, or did you live with a girlfriend before you were taken?"

"No. I returned to First Mesa after college to care for my parents and grandparents. Women who possessed some degree of intelligence and ambition had left the reservation, and I found that I couldn't relate to any of the women who lived there. I was able to find some jobs working on various construction projects, and a number of years later, I landed the job at the bridge. How about you?"

"We broke up three years ago. We had became incompatible. So I was not in a relationship when I was taken."

"I'll be honest with you, Janey. I was very attracted to you when I saw you today. Then I was even more attracted to you because I could see how intelligent you are. We don't know what's going to happen now. I must have faith that everything will work out. When your sister comes up here, we can start the rescue operation. In the meantime, would you have dinner with me tomorrow night after work?"

Janey put her hand out, and *Honovi* shook it. She had decided to decline his invitation, but surprised herself.

"Yes. I would."

KEAMS CANYON, ARIZONA

Jenny shivered in the cold Tuesday morning air despite her jacket, wool hat, and scarf. They stepped off the porch and walked down the stairs toward Marc's truck.

Mansi meowed from one of the rocking chairs. The sun was just beginning to rise. Marc drove to the *kiva*, and *Cheveyo*, Robert and *Tewa* greeted them.

"Where are all the others?" asked Jenny.

Robert pointed in the direction of the *kiva*.

"Inside. They are meditating and will join us shortly."

The sun grew higher in the sky and cast a warm glow on bands of cirrus clouds. The figure of *Honaw* emerged on the rooftop, *Cheveyo* and eight others soon followed.

"We are ready," announced *Honaw*.

Robert and *Tewa* rode in the back

of Marc's truck and followed the other two trucks onto Route 264. Marc drove east five and a half miles and stayed behind them when they pulled off onto a dirt road for a quarter of a mile and parked.

A large sandstone outcropping stood before them. *Cheveyo* and Robert walked toward a craggy, rock wall. Marc and Jenny watched as they lifted and carried many old dry mesquite tree branches and set them aside. A four foot by five foot entrance was revealed. One by one they crawled through a tunnel about twenty feet long. When they exited, Marc and Jenny stood up in a narrow corridor about eight feet wide between sheer rock walls rising high above them.

"This way," said *Honaw*.

Hehewuti turned and smiled at Jenny, and Marc got a wink from *Cheveyo* as they moved forward. *Honaw* motioned for everyone to stand in a group. Marc and Jenny looked up to see that the rock wall they faced was covered with many petroglyphs. They observed that directly in front of them was the outline of a doorway cut into the stone. Marc noticed that there was a round indentation on a ledge to the right of the door and gasped.

"This looks exactly like photos I've seen of the *Punku Hayu Marca* in Peru," he said. "Look at the two petroglyphs on either side. I've never seen anything like them and I've studied rock art for years. They look like butterflies. See, each of their heads has two antennae, and their wings are patterned."

"They symbolize flying through the Star Door," commented *Honaw*. "The Old One's are said to have used this as a means of travel in ancient times."

"What do you mean?" asked Jenny. "Used it how?"

"When you travel through the Star Door," answered *Honaw*, "you can journey to the other worlds. Inside the Star Door, only '*now*' time exists where past, present, and future all co-exist in the same space.

One may pass through other Star Doors and visit many parts of the universe and even other dimensions. In this way, one may experience enlightenment and greatly add to one's perspective and understanding of *Taiowa's* Great Plan."

As the sun rose, a red-tailed hawk circled lazily overhead, and its cry pierced the sky.

"We will return here next Tuesday afternoon around four. That is one week from today. My inner sense tells me we will all be witnesses to an unveiling of The Great Mystery."

CHAPTER SIX

Sutton Place, Manhattan, New York City

Xavier del Mundo's face was contorted with rage. He switched off the *BBC World News* coverage of massive worldwide demonstrations against GMO's, racism, and the militarization of police forces. He rose from his chair and began to pace rapidly across the carpeted floor of his spacious office. *Xavier* clasped his hands behind his back and spoke aloud.

"My elite colleagues and I have

established a new world order which is a self-perpetuating form of mind-control based on the accumulation of money. We have, through media propaganda, successfully put the masses to sleep and made their lives boring. We have turned people into robots. And someone who is bored won't even be aware of our plans, or object very much, should he or she become aware. Why? Because we control his or her lives through a one world government that monitors all currencies, armies, banking systems, police states, and the domination of water, food supplies, and agricultural production. The ultimate plan is to implant chips into every person so they can be tracked. If you do not have a chip, you may not be able to purchase anything, and you will starve. Good. Less population.

The goal is a global world currency, a global police state, a completely centralized government, the use of starvation and famine as a weapon, and the total brutal repression of dissidents. The controls are being put into place so quietly, silently, secretly, unobtrusively, thoroughly, and utterly that the people won't be able to so much as wiggle when the strings are inevitably tightened around them."

Xavier stopped pacing and gazed at the New York City skyline. He was forced to admit that worldwide protests against autocracy, the World Trade Organization, climate change, GMO's, growing income inequality, and government spying were increasing. The ninety-eight percent were starting to wake up, and somehow their consciousness was being switched on. Many were calling for more taxes and environmental regulations on corporations and even for increasing taxes on the rich. *Xavier* reflected on how his plans to greatly decrease the world's population through wars and political upheavals had largely failed and were becoming transparent. There were still billions upon billions of totally useless eaters. He focused on a framed painting of Jesus sitting on the right corner of his desk for appearance's sake.

"It's your doing, isn't it?"

He felt his anger and frustration begin to rise and wanted to scream but held it. He clenched his fists instead and continued to pace back and forth. As his anger increased, his office became suffused with a harsh, crimson light. He quickly turned the painting of Jesus face-down. He had placed sheets of paper beneath four silver candelabra as a precaution. They now caught the hot wax as the candles melted and dripped on them. The fresh bouquets of roses he had placed in his office each day wilted and died as his anger peaked.

Xavier spoke aloud in a strong, firm voice.

"Soon the blue comet will destroy all life on Earth. My elite friends and I will be safe at Sub Rosa. Someday we will return, and then I will rule supreme."

The crimson light diminished and was replaced by the normal light of his office. *Xavier* sat at his desk, took a long, deep breath, exhaled, and mopped the sweat off his brow with a handkerchief.

His secretary buzzed him on the intercom.

"Cardinal *Perrizzi* is on line two from Rome," she informed him.

"*Buon giorno, Xavier.*"

"First code words?"

"Sub Rosa."

"Second code words?"

"Solar Warden."

"Speak".

"The European Space Agency's Herschel Telescope has detected the comet and issued a statement from its headquarters at *Mario-Nikis* in Paris. It will be visible in the sky in about a week. We must make certain that the second part of the third prophecy fails."

"Rest assured, my friend, I have sent our agents to Avignon."

Xavier ended the call. He sighed again as he rose from his chair and opened a safe, from which he removed a manila envelope. He returned to his desk and took out a document, which was the third prophecy of *Fatima* which the Vatican had officially released in the year 2000. But the Vatican's version spoke only of the end of communism in the Soviet Union and the attempted assassination of Pope John Paul II. *Xavier* laid it on his desk. Beneath it was the true third prophecy which only the highest ranking members of the elite knew about. They had all been sworn to the utmost secrecy. Only two members of The Vatican knew about the Sub Rosa base on Phobos, and they were Cardinal *Perrizzi* in Rome, and Archbishop *Perez* in Peru. The

Pope and everyone else in The Vatican and the leadership of the Catholic Church knew absolutely nothing of their plans.

The first part of the third prophecy of *Fatima* had spoken of a fiery-blue comet striking the Earth and described the utter destruction of the planet. It had ended with the words of Mother Mary:

"However, there is a second part to the Third Prophecy in which this terrible fate may be avoided."

The second part had been missing and long searched for, but never found. *Xavier* reflected on how he had personally managed to find the missing second part.

THE CARMELITE CONVENT OF SAINT TERESA, *COIMBRA*, PORTUGAL

In his younger days, *Xavier* had been an official emissary for the Vatican. He had met with Sister *Lucia dos Santos*. She was the last survivor of the three children who saw the vision of Mother Mary at *Fatima*.

Mother *Celina*, Prioress of the convent in *Coimbra*, led him to Sister *Lucia's* spartan quarters. After some pleasantries, *Xavier* asked her about the third prophecy. She had then recited the words of the first part:

"Fire and smoke will fall from the sky, and the waters of the oceans

will turn to steam, hurling their foam toward the sky, and all that is standing will be overthrown. Millions and more millions of men, women and children will lose their lives from one hour to the next, and those who remain living at that moment will envy those who are dead. Half of mankind will be killed in a matter of hours. It will be the time of times."

Xavier recalled how he had placed her in a hypnotic trance. He inquired about the second part of the third prophecy and taped her words. The tape recording was later transcribed. Sister *Lucia dos Santos* died a few years later at the age of ninety-seven.

The few furnishings in the room

had consisted of a bed, a dresser, a desk, a table lamp, and a large, framed oil portrait of Mother Mary and an adult Jesus. *Xavier* recorded Sister Lucia's words. She finished speaking and remained in a trance. The large painting suddenly came alive. Jesus's right hand extended from the painting and pointed directly at him.

"You shall be consumed by the fires of a great comet. Your body shall be incinerated by that of my own fiery breath. In that moment your vital essence, indeed your very soul, shall be utterly extinguished and cease to exist."

Xavier quickly left the convent. The tape recording of the second part of

the third prophecy spoke of a golden
disc, which, when found, must be
used in a task The Father had set as
told by Sister *Lucia*:

"*The task is to set the golden disc
upon the outstretched left hand of
a statue of Our Blessed Mother
Mary. The statue stands atop the
Cathedral Notre Dame de Doms in
Avignon, France. Once the task is
successfully completed, the comet
will miss the Earth.*"

Xavier was resigned to the fact
that he and select members of
the elite would escape and live
on Phobos. Many years, perhaps
generations, would pass before
it was determined that they could
safely return to and re-populate the

Earth. Then, as the Antichrist, he would be in charge.

Xavier remembered his past life in feudal twelfth century Brittany, where he had been a lord. He'd many vassals as tenants. The serfs who lived on his lands were obliged to pay homage to him through their labor, a share of their produce, and taxes. He intended to turn the future Earth into just such a feudal society. He'd have many barons with their own fiefdoms, and he would have unlimited power. *Xavier* smiled again and placed the secret document in his safe.

SUB ROSA BASE, PHOBOS, MARS

Janey met *Honovi* at the door to the mess hall at Complex A. They sat at a table with Jason, Chloe, Meredith, and Olivia. They were soon joined by his co-pilot, Arnie, and crew members *Kele* and Ben, who was with his girlfriend, Latona de Jahn. Janey greeted everyone and reminded Latona that they had met the other night at dinner in Complex E.

"Yes, Janey, I do remember," she said and smiled. "How are you adjusting?"

"Pretty well. Thanks for asking. This was my first day at the farm. I worked with three division heads and their staff. There was so much information that I went to the Free Store after work and got a fanny-pack, three four-by-six yellow note-pads, and a package of pens so I could record everything."

Janey then looked around the table, and Jason nodded at her. He put his fork down and spoke.

"All of us here are in on our plan to get out of this place and go home. Ben and Latona will help. Both *Kele* and *Honovi* have asked their friend, *Tuwa*, who's a security guard, to assist us. The details are still being put in place. My ship leaves early tomorrow. We land on Earth early Tuesday morning, so I want to wish you all a very Merry Christmas in advance."

Everyone smiled and wished him the same. They finished their meals, and Jason took Janey and *Honovi* aside to an empty corner table.

"I've taken extensive photos of this base and of the spaceport. I'll email them to your sister along with a letter. She plans to meet with her FBI Special Agent in Charge on Tuesday morning. We'll coordinate a time for me to call and speak with them on a secure line. If he agrees to help us, I mean, *when* he agrees to help us, we'll get your sister, Jenny, up here sometime next week and start the escape plans rolling."

"Seeing Jenny again would be the best Christmas present ever," said Janey.

Jason nodded and shook hands with them. Janey and *Honovi* walked out of the mess hall.

"Would you like to come up to my place for a while?"

Janey shook her head.

"I'm feeling pretty tired."

"Okay. Get some rest. You're welcome to join me for Christmas dinner and the dance afterward tomorrow night."

"You're on," said Janey and smiled.

AVIGNON, FRANCE

The Air France jet taxied to a stop at *Caumont* Airport in Avignon. Jack and Augi unbuckled their seat belts and stood up in the aisle. They'd wrestled their carry-on bags out of the overhead compartment and waited in line to get off the plane. They'd first flown to Paris and had to run to catch the flight to Avignon, which was in southern France, not far from *Marseille* and the Mediterranean Sea. The doors opened, and they made their way off the plane.

Victor had bought them first class tickets, and the meals had been great. So had been the wine. They caught a shuttle bus and were dropped off in front of the Hotel *Innova,* which was right in the center of the city, where they could keep a close watch. They had separate, but adjoining rooms, and the view looked down on a large, open plaza.

Once they unpacked, the two men took the elevator to the lobby and found a restaurant named *Ginette et Marcel*. They sat at an outdoor table and ordered a bottle of wine. The air was warm for late December, but the streets were mostly empty of people.

"Ever been to Paris?" Jack asked.

Augi raised his glass.

"A voter santé! A la voter! A la tienne!"

"What does all that mean?"

"Basically "to your good health"."

"Merci," said Jack. "I know that much. He drank some wine and asked again. "Well, have you ever been to Paris?"

"Yeah. A bunch of times back in

the late eighties, but I never really saw the city."

"How come?"

"I was an aircraft mechanic in the U.S. Air Force with the 377th Combat Support Group stationed at *Ramstein*, Germany. I'd go into Paris on leave and find me a hooker. We'd shack up in a hotel room, smoke dope, and drink wine. Then I'd go back to the base."

Jack smiled at the thought.

"Remind me again why we're here in Avignon, Augi."

"The boss..."

"You mean Victor Spoils," Jack said and laughed.

"Okay, Victor Spoils. We're supposed to keep our eyes open for any sign of someone messing with that statue there."

He pointed in the direction of a tall building with a golden statue of Mother Mary, which looked to be at least twenty feet high.

"What do you mean by 'messing'?"

"Look, Jack. We know that the comet's on the way. By now everyone's aware of it. The scientists are busy debating each other whether it'll miss the Earth or not. Victor told me in strict confidence that some people will try to put some golden disc on top of the left hand of the statue, and we're to stop them at all costs."

"Why?"

"Because he said that if they're

successful, the comet will miss the Earth."

Jack thought hard about that for a moment. He cleared his throat.

"Well, that'd be good, wouldn't it?"

Augi put his glass down and leaned forward till he was inches away from Jack's face and scowled.

"No, Jack. That would *not* be good. The boss told me that the base is ready, and we're all going to live a good life up there. Someday, we, or our descendants, will be able to return to Earth and start things all over, but things will be run the way *we* want them run."

"Well, how's someone supposed to get way up there? I mean, the building is a good six stories, plus the statue is huge!"

"Helicopter, I guess. We're going to meet with some guys tomorrow. They work for Victor. Now drink up and let's order dinner. I'm hungry."

SUB ROSA BASE, PHOBOS, MARS

Janey returned to her apartment. The realization that it was Christmas Eve took hold, and she began to cry. Why had she declined *Honovi's* invitation? She shook her head.

"I don't know," she said aloud and reached for a tissue.

Janey dried her tears and changed into shorts and a T-shirt. She glanced at a framed painting she had chosen at the Free Store. It depicted

New Mexico's *Sangre de Christo* mountains at sunset, a view that only intensified her feelings of loneliness, isolation, and despair. "I'm not doing too well," she exclaimed and then thought of Sharon who would advise acceptance and going with the flow.

She settled back on the sofa, closed her eyes, and brought up a picture of her sister in her mind.

"Jenny, I love you so much. I miss you. I wish you and Marc a Merry Christmas. I can't wait to see you."

Tomorrow was another workday. She showered, set the alarm, and fell asleep.

KEAMS CANYON, ARIZONA

Jenny and Marc lay on their sides and faced one another in bed. They kissed, and Jenny briefly closed her eyes.

"Marc. I just…"

"Heard from Janey?" Marc said, finishing her sentence. "And?"

"She wished us a Merry Christmas."

They awoke to the sounds of *Mansi* meowing for her breakfast. Marc spooned some cat food in her bowl. Jenny joined him in the kitchen. They put their arms around each other and kissed for a long time.

"Merry Christmas, Marc."

"Can you believe I rescued you only eight days ago?"

"Time flies when you're…"

"In a race to save the world," he said, finishing her sentence again.

SUB ROSA BASE, PHOBOS, MARS

Janey walked back to her apartment after work. She hadn't had time to go to the Free Store and get presents. After a nap and a hot shower, she dressed and headed over to Complex A. Christmas music played, and people were in a jovial mood. The dinner buffet was wonderful and offered fish filets, rabbit burgers and sausages, mashed and sweet potatoes, fresh peas and steamed carrots, broccoli, squash, and corn on the cob.

She joined *Honovi* at a table. Chloe and her daughters sat down along with Latona and the three engineers, Aaron, Brian, and Glen. The table had a big bowl of red and green Jell-O in the middle, and Meredith and Olivia laughed when they saw it. They spooned gobs of it onto their plates. No mention of the rescue plan was made although it was definitely on

everyone's minds.

After dinner the tables were moved along the sides of the room. A stage had been built, and six musicians played a variety of dance tunes.

Honovi and Janey enjoyed

dancing with one another and took turns dancing with others. When the music ended, they took the elevator to *Honovi's* apartment. They sat on the sofa, and he handed her a wrapped present. Janey opened it and gasped.

"I found it in the art section at the Free Store during my lunch hour. I think it must have recently arrived with the cargo on Jason's ship."

Janey held a framed painting of Our Lady of *Guadalupe*.

"It's so beautiful. I've seen Her image all around Albuquerque. Thank you so much."

"You're welcome, Janey. Do you know much about the story?"

"Just some that I learned in

Sunday school and further reading I've done. But it impressed me, and I still

remember it to this day; in 1531 Mother Mary appeared as a young girl to a man in Mexico City named Juan Diego. She asked him to petition the archbishop there to build a cathedral on a local hill named *Tepeyacin* in Her honor. Juan recognized Her as the Virgin Mary. The archbishop asked for some proof. She instructed Juan to go back to the hill, and there he would find *Castilian* roses growing, which are not native to Mexico. It was early in the month of December and very cold. He did so, and sure enough, the roses were there. He picked them and carried them in his peasant cloak, called a *tilma*.

When Juan brought them to the archbishop as proof, the roses fell to the floor, and miraculously impressed on the *tilma* was the image of the Virgin Mary. The archbishop and other people in the room were astonished. He agreed to erect the cathedral."

"That's how I first heard the story in Sunday school, too," said *Honovi*. "Years later I researched it further on the Internet and learned some totally amazing facts."

"Like what?"

"Well, for one thing, the image and the cloth have been in a state of high-quality preservation for nearly four hundred and eighty-five years. Modern science cannot explain it. The *tilma* was originally put on display and was completely unprotected from candle smoke and humid, salty air for at least one hundred and sixteen years with no signs of decay. At least two incidents have occurred that should have damaged or destroyed the image. The first one was in 1785 when a worker spilled a solvent of fifty percent nitric acid onto the right side of the cloth. The cloth showed no signs of damage."

"And the second incident?"

"A bomb exploded near the *tilma* in 1921. The explosion was so forceful that it blew out all the windows within five hundred feet and cracked the marble floor. But the glass in front of the *tilma* remained intact, and the cloth wasn't damaged in any way. And if that's not enough, the last fact is mind-blowing."

"Why is that?"

"The eyes of the *tilma* have undergone rigorous scientific testing, and it has been determined that the image in Her pupils is like that of a living person with corresponding distortions due to the curvature of the eye. Reflected in Her eyes on the *tilma* is the scene in the archbishop's room with him and numerous identifiable people present when the Blessed Virgin's image was revealed."

Janey cradled the small painting in her hands.

"I'm sorry, but I didn't have time to get a gift for you."

"You're being here now *is* my gift."

Janey put her arms around *Honovi* and they kissed passionately.

"Merry Christmas," she said.

KEAMS CANYON, ARIZONA

Marc and Jenny made Christmas dinner together and cooked a roast turkey, stuffing with oranges and spices, along with sweet potatoes, green beans, and fresh rolls.

On Sunday morning they attended services at St. Joseph's Catholic Church around the corner. Jenny and Marc found seats near the door since the chapel was full. The elderly priest, Father Bill O'Neill, gave a sermon and then asked all to pray that the comet might miss the Earth and spare humanity. They bowed their heads along with the others.

The fragrance of roses suddenly filled the chapel. Two large brass candelabra sat on either side of the altar, and each held six unlit candles. All those present raised their heads and stared in amazement as a bright ball of light appeared. The light hovered above each candelabra, and soon the wicks of the candles on both flamed brightly. Then the ball of light vanished. Father O'Neill fell to his knees, placed his palms together, and looked upward.

"Dear God, this is surely a sign from Our Lady that the Earth and all who dwell on it will be spared," he said.

Marc and Jenny held hands and cried along with everyone else.

The next day they drove to Jenny's house in Phoenix and arrived in the late afternoon. She opened doors and windows to air the place out, swept the floors, and turned on the ceiling fans. Then she checked her emails. There was one from Jason King. He gave a number where he could be reached on a secure line. There were two

attachments. One was a letter to her Special Agent in Charge (SAC), and another with sixteen photographs. She read the email out loud to Marc.

"Meet with your Special Agent in Charge. Show him these pictures and have him read my letter. Then have him call me and put it on speaker phone. I'm developing a plan. Part of it is to have you go through the Jump Gate in the Grand Canyon and get to Sub Rosa. Since, Janey, your identical twin is there, we'll figure out some way to make it work. If we can pull it off, you can bring weapons, explosives, and a communication device so she can talk to me on my ship. Maybe the FBI can send a SWAT team through the Jump Gate in the Grand Canyon and overpower the guards at Sub Rosa. We have to find a way to rescue all the people up there. That's it for my part. Then you'll return to the Grand Canyon. I have the utmost faith that you and Marc will be successful in the completion of the task set by The Father."

Jenny then called her Special Agent in Charge and made an appointment for the next day at eleven a.m. He was surprised to hear from her and thought she was on vacation in some exotic place. Jenny assured him that she was okay and had vital information to share. She then replied to Jason's email and told him that tomorrow's meeting would start at eleven a.m. Phoenix time, and to expect their call. Jenny printed the photos along with Jason's letter and put them in a folder.

"Remember, Jenny, that we have to be back in Steamboat Canyon with *Honaw, Cheveyo*, and the others by four o'clock tomorrow afternoon," said Marc.

"I'm aware of that, Marc, and we should just make it there on time."

OFFICE OF THE FBI
PHOENIX, ARIZONA

Marc and Jenny passed through security and rode the elevator to the third floor. She briefly stopped to say hello to Susan, her assistant, and then led Marc to the office door of her Special Agent in Charge. The name-plate read James Cararuscio. Jenny knocked, and James opened the door. He shook their hands and motioned them to take seats facing him. James sat behind his desk. Jenny introduced Marc and summarized the town hall meeting, her attempted murder, and his subsequent rescue.

"Why didn't you report it to me?" James said.

"I guess we both got swept up in a series of events that have finally brought us to your office, sir," Jenny said.

James leaned back in his chair.

"Spadaro. That's Italian like mine. Where are you from?" asked James.

"Queens."

"Let me re-phrase the question. Where are your ancestors from originally?"

"Oh, from Sicily. And yours?

"The Bronx by way of Naples. How about you, Marc?" asked James.

"Scotch-Scandinavian. Prentis on my dad's side, Heldig on my mom's side, which is Danish."

"Prentis. My dad served in the Navy," James said. "He was a Lieutenant Commander with DESRON 31 aboard the destroyer USS *Towers* based out of *Yokosuka*, Japan, where we lived during the 1980s. I remember the Fleet Admiral's name was Bill Prentis."

"That was my dad. He passed away last week," said Marc. "Jenny and I attended his funeral at Arlington National Cemetery."

"I'm so sorry, to hear that," James said. "My father always spoke highly of him. Now tell me, Agent Spadaro, why are you here in my office and not somewhere like Rome or Paris or London?"

"With all due respect, sir, before I begin to answer that question, I think Marc would like to describe his own experience."

Marc relayed the deathbed confession of his father. James looked skeptical. Marc placed the thick, black three-ring binder on the desk. He and Jenny had underlined key information in red and placed Post-it Notes on the most important pages. He began to look through the binder. Five minutes later, he looked up, and his face wore an expression of shock and surprise.

"I felt exactly the same way, sir," said Jenny. I know that it sounds like a sci-fi movie or something, but I swear all of it is true. And the worst part is that my identical twin sister, Janey, has been taken and is living at the base on Phobos. She was a hydroponics instructor at the University of New Mexico in Albuquerque. Marc and I are in contact with the pilot of one of the large triangular ships named the USS *Excalibur*. His name is Colonel Jason King."

"He was an F-15A Squadron Wing

Commander in my dad's carrier task force in Japan," said Marc. "They were good friends."

"We have a letter from him that he's written to you, sir," said Jenny.

She handed James the letter from Jason, which he placed before him on the desk. He proceeded to read it.

The letter summarized Jason's recruitment as a pilot, the taking of his wife and daughters to the base, and his subsequent change of heart.

"Colonel King is expecting us to call him from your office, sir, but first Marc and I'd like to ask you a personal question."

"And that is?"

"What religion do you follow?"

"Catholic."

James turned around a frame sitting on his desk. It was a painting of Mother Mary cradling an infant Jesus.

"We knew about the blue comet before anyone else," stated Jenny.

"How? Besides Marc's father's deathbed confession, I mean," said James.

They took turns and relayed their vision of The Blessed Virgin at the church and then spelled out the task given to them by The Father.

"We must rescue all those who have been taken against their will from the base," said Jenny. "Marc and I will, with the help of Mother Mary, go to Avignon and complete the task so that the comet misses Earth."

They then told James about the miraculous event at the Catholic church in Keams Canyon on Sunday morning.

"Before we call Colonel King, sir, we'd like to have you look at sixteen photos he's taken of the secret space facility and the base on Phobos," said Jenny as she handed him a manila file folder.

James took his time and carefully looked at each picture and held many of them up for a closer inspection. When he returned the last one to the folder, he wore a stunned expression.

"I'm completely overwhelmed by

these photographs, the information in the binder, and everything you've told me. Let's call Colonel King. I'll put him on speaker phone."

Jenny handed him a piece of paper with Jason's secure line. James called the number.

"Jason King here."

"Colonel King, my name is James Cararuscio, Special Agent in Charge, Phoenix, FBI."

"It is my great pleasure to speak with you, sir."

"I have Agent Jenny Spadaro and her friend, Dr. Marc Prentis, here in my office. They have patiently unfolded a most incredible story through verbal testimony, your letter, a black binder full of information, and the photographs you provided. My question is, what would you like me to do?"

"Fly Jenny in a helicopter to the Grand Canyon. There is a teleportation apparatus inside Isis Temple called a Jump Gate. You've read about it. What you can do is supply her with various weapons and a communication device tuned to a secure frequency channel code I will give you now so I can communicate with those leading the escape plan at the base."

"One of your photographs shows a high wall and armored door in front of the Jump Gate at Sub Rosa. I will provide Jenny with C-4 M122 blocks and blasting caps so the door can be blown open by someone in the escape group. And I'll provide her with a C.A.V.E.S."

"I had a hunch that you would have one," said Jason.

"The FBI has many things the public would find to be unbelievable."

"C.A.V.E.S.? What does that mean?" asked Marc.

"Continuous Analog Variable Encoded Signal," answered James. "It's a device that uses spatial positions to lock in on a coded channel so all communications between two sources is totally secure."

James wrote down the signal code as Jason read it aloud.

"You may want to have a SWAT

team back you up and fly to Isis Temple in two or three helo's," Jason said. "I'm almost certain that the Jump Gate has been abandoned, but let's not take any chances. The plan is to get Jenny to the base in late afternoon this Thursday. My ship will be landing at Sub Rosa on Saturday. That gives you four days from today. One of the gate guards has agreed to help us. He'll have to know when to expect her and be ready. Her twin sister, Janey, will put her in touch with others, who will set into motion a plan to pave the way for an armed group to enter the base and rescue all the people. My question is, will you help us?"

"Normally I'd have to contact

the Directorate of Intelligence in Washington, D.C. and go through proper channels to authorize something like this," James said, "but with the comet on the way, there isn't enough time. Not to mention the fact that we may all be dead if I don't act now. So, yes, I'll help you"

"Thank you, sir," said Jason. "Once we've rescued the people from the base, the rest will be up to Marc and Jenny. From what they've told me, Mother Mary will offer them Her Divine assistance."

James ended the call. He crossed himself, and so did Marc and Jenny.

Then all three broke out in smiles.

CHAPTER SEVEN

Puno, Peru-Present Day

"Buenos tardes, Louis. Como esta ustedes?"

"Estoy bien, Father. But I'm thirsty as…"

"Let me get you a cold *chicha*."

Louis brought his gear inside his father's modest house. His mother had died many years ago, and *Manuel* had never remarried. He handed his son a glass of *chicha*, beer made from maize, and sat down next to him on the couch.

"Ahh, that hits the spot. *Gracias*."

"*De nada.*"

Louis put his glass down and looked at his father. He was wearing a traditional, red full-length cloth woven poncho with gold embroidery down each side. He wore a hat *Louis* had bought him in Cusco five years earlier. It had a wide brim and was tan with a black band. *Manuel's* face was light brown with deep wrinkles and laugh lines. He still had all his teeth, and his brown eyes were bright. He smiled at his son.

"Not too bad for an old man, eh?"

He took his hat off and ran his hands through a full head of dark hair.

"I noticed that mine's getting gray above the ears," commented *Louis*.

"Too much stress. I live a simple life."

Louis drained his glass and lay back against a pillow. He closed his eyes and began to drift off to sleep.

"I'll tell *Kawki* and his wife *Nina*, that you've arrived. We can visit with them later."

Louis woke to find his glass of *chicha* had been refilled. *Manuel* walked out of the kitchen with a bowl of *chairo* on a tray. He set it on *Louis's* lap. *Chairo* is a traditional stew of the altiplano. It is made of potato starch, white corn, lamb, beans, squash, cabbage, wheat, and dried mutton.

"*Gracias*, Father. I am very hungry."

"Eat, and then we will visit *Kawki*."

Louis swallowed a heaping spoonful.

"Ahh, that tastes so good! Did you say *Kawki's* wife is named *Nina*? That doesn't sound like an *Aymara* name."

"I once asked *Kawki* that question, and it turns out that *Nina* in *Aymara* means "fire that will never be extinguished.""

Manuel laughed at that and explained that not only was she strong in character and had a positive energy, but she could also be very stubborn with a bad temper. But, he added, she soon calmed down and always apologized. *Louis* finished his *chairo* and lay the tray down on the coffee table.

"Let's go next door," said *Manuel*.

Kawki and *Nina* sat outside at a table in front of their house. They were eating their late afternoon meal. *Louis* smiled, and they both smiled back. *Nina* asked them both to have a seat. She and *Kawki* appeared to be in their late eighties. They wore clothing traditional to the *Aymara*. *Kawki* had on an a*gorro*, a multi-colored knit, wool, conical hat with ear-flaps. *Nina* wore a fantastic hat with red around the wide brim, with what looked like green and red flames standing up all around the edge, and a dark-gray center crossed by white stripes. Her gray hair fell in curls on either side of her face. She had a long nose, which was round at the end, and dark eyes. *Kawki* was wiry and muscular, with dark-brown eyes. He had a flat, broad face with high cheekbones. A gray beard covered the lower half of his round head under the a*gorro*. He and *Nina* wore matching dark-brown wool ponchos.

"What are you eating?" asked *Louis*.

"Everything on the table we grow ourselves," said *Nina*. "We have potatoes, beans, sweet peppers and guinea pigs."

Louis gazed at their house, which was rectangular, made of turf, and the gabled roof was thatched with wild grass laid over pole rafters. A herd of llamas and alpacas grazed in an adjacent field.

"We will haul three llamas in my trailer and ride in the truck," said *Kawki*. "Once we arrive at the starting point, the journey to the valley takes a full day. We will have to camp overnight and return the next day. The altitude will get up to sixteen thousand feet, and the night will be very cold. Some of the mountains and scattered peaks in the area have elevations of nearly twenty-one thousand feet, so I hope you brought warm clothes, *Louis*."

"Yes, I did. And I have a tent, as well."

"*Esta bien*. We will meet here

at sunrise. The drive takes about twenty-five minutes."

Manuel woke *Louis,* and the two men got dressed and ate a quick breakfast in semi-darkness. They walked outside in the cold morning air and observed *Kawki* leading three male llamas to his trailer.

"May I introduce *Aroya, Metiche, and Cliquot*?" he said, and the llamas snorted.

Aroya was mostly white with a brown band around his mid-section. *Metiche* was all white, and *Cliquot* was entirely light brown except for his head, which was white in front and black in back. They were each six feet tall.

Kawki lowered a ramp, and the three llamas walked into the trailer. *Louis* and *Manuel* loaded their gear, tent, and sleeping bags into the truck, and they traveled south with the lake on their left.

Kawki followed the shore and slowed down. He pulled off onto a paved area and parked.

"We have arrived at the starting point," he said and gestured toward gigantic natural rock walls. They helped *Kawki* bring the llamas out of the trailer and then spent about twenty minutes carefully loading all their gear onto the animals. When they were done, they led their llamas. There were already more than two dozen people standing in front of what looked like a doorway cut right into the rock wall. *Louis* couldn't believe his eyes.

Many people turned to look at them, and the llamas snorted as they led them past the crowd.

"That is known as the *Punku Hayu Marca*," said *Kawki*. "Our legends say that it is a doorway to the stars."

"That is the name on the map stone. How does one go through it?" asked *Louis*.

Kawki shook his head.

"I do not know. No one does."

To the southwest of Lake Titicaca, the character of the Andes changes to that of a high plateau region known as the Puna. There vast tablelands rise to elevations that exceed eighteen thousand feet, and large volcanos covered in snow dominate the horizon.

The men led their llamas for many hours through grasslands and scrub forests. In the early afternoon, the land began to ascend steeply uphill. *Louis* began to experience shortness of breath and estimated they must be at fourteen thousand feet or more. The sun was hot, and they stopped to change from their morning clothes and have something to eat. *Kawki* handed some *charqui* to *Louis* and *Manuel*. *Charqui* are salted strips of llama meat dried in the sun. They can be kept for long periods and are good to bring on treks in the mountains. They ate and drank *chicha* while taking in the beauty that surrounded them. *Kawki* pointed toward a mountain's sheer cliff. They watched an *Andean* condor as it soared across the sky. *Louis* consulted his *Quechuan* lists and photos of the map stone.

They led their llamas, and the going became tough as the narrow trail wound its way through fields of large rock boulders and brush. As they walked, the path continued to ascend. *Kawki* heard it first, the sound of rushing water ahead. They rounded a bend in the trail, and a wide river came into view. They let the llamas get a drink. *Kawki* pointed to trees with thick bark along either side of the river.

"They are called *quenua* and grow only at altitudes above fifteen thousand feet."

Louis read his lists.

"We follow the river westward," he said.

Kawki nodded.

"I know the way to the hidden valley from this point."

A forest of *quenua* trees appeared. The men halted when a small tributary stream came into view that flowed north. They led their llamas along the sand and rock-strewn banks. Cold water swirled around large stones in the stream. Soon they all heard a roaring sound and came upon a large waterfall that cascaded from a high cliff into a pool and sent clouds of spray into the air.

Kawki motioned for them to follow him, and he led his llama, *Metiche*, around and behind the falls. *Louis* and *Manuel* did the same. The view before them was one of stunning beauty.

A deeply green, hidden valley spread below and lay cradled between two lofty mountains with their peaks covered in snow. The mountain on the right had a tall pillar of black stone shaped like a giant *Andean* condor with its wings folded along its sides.

"We have arrived," said *Kawki*. "There is a steep path that leads to the valley floor. Please follow me and be careful."

They led their llamas along a narrow trail to the bottom. *Kawki* found a place to set up camp beside a small stream. Late afternoon light lit the upper reaches of the valley and illuminated the peaks of mountains surrounding them on all sides.

The men removed their gear from the llamas, which drank from the stream and began to graze. *Louis* set up his tent, which was large enough to accommodate the three of them. *Kawki* used a shovel to dig a fire pit. He found large stones in and along the stream and placed them around the sides of the pit. Then the three men went in search of firewood, which they arranged in the center.

The sun set lower in the sky, and a cold wind began to blow. They quickly put on their woolens, jackets, and hats. Their sleeping bags, pillows, and blankets were laid inside the tent.

"I brought all the ingredients for *kalapurka*," announced *Kawki*, "and I made sure to bring my big cooking pot along."

Kalapurka is one of the oldest traditional Peruvian meals. The stew is made of chicken meat, *chuno*, or dried potatoes, onions, and various chilies, cilantro, cumin, peanuts, and cloves. The stew is cooked by removing the large hot stones from the edge of the fire and placing them in the pot.

Manuel lit the fire, and *Kawki* led his llamas to a nearby *quenua* tree and tied them there for the night. The sun had now left the valley in darkness, and *Louis* saw the first stars appear in a clear sky. He sat by the fire and concentrated on breathing steadily in and out. He guessed the elevation must exceed sixteen thousand feet. *Manuel* handed him a bottle of *chicha*, while *Kawki* offered him some coca leaves to chew.

"It will help with your breathing," he said.

Louis accepted the leaves, as did

Manuel. The men greatly enjoyed their meal, and *Kawki* told them stories about growing up in the mountains and having first seen this valley when he was twelve years old. Then he doused the flames, and they turned in for the night.

Louis woke to *Kawki's* voice outside. *Manuel* was still asleep. Sunlight was just beginning to play on the east side of the tent, and the air was very cold. He slowly got out of his sleeping bag and quickly put on his jacket and wool hat. He unzipped the door and stepped out. *Kawki* was talking to his three llamas and had led them to the stream.

Louis looked past them, and his gaze took in the cliff of a massive sunlit mountain on the western side of the valley. He hadn't noticed it before because most of the cliff had been in deep shadow when they'd first arrived. His eyes now took in the form of a large, undulating snake that followed a natural fissure running vertically up and down a sheer rock wall. He got his map and the location lists from his tent and gently shook *Manuel* awake.

"Time to get up, Father. *Kawki's* already got the fire going, and water is boiling for coffee. Looks like we've got some exploring to do after breakfast."

Manuel sleepily rubbed his eyes and yawned loudly.

"And, of course, I was right in the middle of a fantastic dream."

"Sorry," said *Louis*.

He went outside by the fire, and *Kawki* handed him a cup of coffee and a papaya cut in half topped with yogurt.

"Muchas gracias."

"De nada."

Louis sat in his camp chair and concentrated on breathing steadily as he ate his breakfast. When he was done, he accepted some coca leaves from *Kawki* and chewed them while he finished his coffee. *Manuel* came out of the tent and stood in sunlight. He held his arms out, and the three of them said a prayer of thanks to God for the beauty around them.

"*Inti*," intoned *Kawki*. "He created everything we see, and it is *Pachamama* who sustains and protects the Earth."

Manuel sat down, and *Kawki* handed him a papaya, yogurt, and coffee. The air warmed as the sun rose, and the three men took off their jackets and hats. *Kawki* doused the fire, and *Louis* led the way toward the cliff face in the distance. The snake seemed to grow in size and appeared to move as they drew near. *Louis* took the page containing the two lists from the folder and consulted it. He read the section dealing with the undulating snake.

urku lluq'e	(mountain on left)
rumi perqa	(rock wall)
amaru	(snake)
maki	(hand)
ukhunta simi	(inside mouth)
pakalla punku	(secret door inside)
ukhunta	
kuri muyu inti p'ulu	(gold round sun ball disc)

Louis stood before the head of the snake. Its jaws were open wide with protruding fangs, and its large eyes stared straight at him.

"I'm supposed to put my hand in its mouth?" he said aloud and shuddered.

"It's not real," said *Manuel*.

"It sure *looks* real," countered *Louis*.

"I'll do it if you don't want to," *Kawki* said and shrugged.

"Oh, all right. Here goes."

Louis moved his right hand inside the jaws of the snake and felt a depression in the rock wall. He then reached farther inside, and his hand grasped the shaft of a wooden handle. He pulled it toward him.

A strong vibration moved through his wrist and then traveled up his arm. A low-frequency sound began to be heard and soon grew progressively louder. *Louis* let go of the handle, and the three men stepped back as the sound grew and intensified. It reverberated throughout the valley. *Kawki's* three llamas were greatly agitated and ran back and forth along the banks of the stream. Suddenly a sizable section of the rock wall slid sideways and revealed an open doorway cut into the sheer rock.

Dr. *Louis Carillos*, *Manuel*, and *Kawki* stared in wonder. They entered the doorway and found themselves inside a small chamber. In the center lay an altar, and on the altar sat a large, golden bowl. *Louis* looked into the bowl. Inside was a golden disc, about seven inches in diameter and half an inch thick. He reached in, removed it, and carefully examined it. He saw that it was entirely smooth and was quite disappointed to find there were no drawings or inscriptions on either side or around the edge of the disc.

Manuel tried to lift the golden bowl from the altar, but he was unable to move it. He and *Kawki* both tried with all their might, but it wouldn't budge. *Louis* looked about the small chamber for artifacts but found nothing.

"Looks like we came all the way here for this golden disc," he said and felt very let down. He'd had visions of finding a vast Incan treasure trove of gold and jewels. "I guess we may as well pack up the camp and head on back to *Puno.*"

As they stepped out of the doorway, a tremendous noise filled the air as the rock wall began to slide sideways. The three men jumped backward as the doorway vanished and the undulating snake appeared once more on the cliff face.

They returned to the truck in the late afternoon. The men unloaded their gear, and *Kawki* led the three llamas into the trailer. He threw in a bale of hay, put a bucket of water against a corner, and latched the door. Lake Titicaca reflected clear blue skies as they drove north and arrived in *Puno* twenty-five minutes later. *Louis* stayed the night at *Manuel*'s. They slept late and joined *Kawki* and *Nina* for a hearty lunch. He patted his stomach and bade them farewell.

Louis drove north and called Archbishop *Perez* on his cell phone. He made an appointment for 7:45 a.m. and arrived home early in the evening.

He told *Rosa* and *Arturo* about the journey to the hidden valley and showed them the golden disc.

"But there are no pictures or words on it, and there weren't any inside the chamber," he said.

Then he showered, ate dinner, and fell into a deep sleep.

When his alarm clock awakened him in the morning, a strong thought suddenly seized *Louis*. There had recently been a series of break-ins in the neighborhood. He felt compelled to wrap the golden disc in a bath towel, put it in the trunk of his car, and leave it there while he met with the archbishop. He was on his way to the bathroom to wrap the disc in a towel when pounding music suddenly erupted from *Arturo's* room.

"Not again!" he shouted and knocked on the door. *Arturo* answered.

"It's seven twenty in the morning! Don't you realize that you're mother's still asleep?"

"Sorry, father. I have an early class. I don't know why, but I like to walk around my room while I read, and as I explained to you before, the cord on the headphones is way too short for me to use. Let me show you, okay?"

Arturo demonstrated and headed over to the corner where a black light lit up various art posters. *Louis* followed him and as *Arturo* stopped, the headphones fell off his ears.

"See? The cord is too short." He paused. "Father! Look at the golden disc. I can see letters on it!"

Louis held the golden disc under the black light. There were words in *Quechuan* on both sides. He ran back to his room and returned with a notebook and pen and wrote them down. He was able to translate the words in under five minutes on his computer and learned the history and importance of the golden disc and instructions on how to use it to enter the Star Door at the *Punku Hayu Marca.*

He then returned to *Arturo's* room.

"Son, I'm going to what is called a Star Door. It's south of *Puno* and..."

"I know where it is, Father. The legend says that the Incan priest, *Amaru Maru,* went through it and was never seen again."

"How do you know about it?"

"News articles on the Internet. Lots of New Age people go there all the time to try to go inside it, but they're unable to."

"Well, the words on the golden disc tell me how to use it to go through."

"Father, please, don't go through it!

I'm afraid that you won't ever come back, and I'll never see you again."

"I have a strong feeling that I've been given no choice. I have to go through it. Please don't be afraid, Son. I give you my word that I'll see you again soon. I love you so much. I've got to go now."

Louis wrapped the golden disc in the towel and put it in the car trunk. He raced to the Cathedral of *Santo Domingo* and made it in time for his appointment.

He handed Archbishop *Perez* a manila folder.

"Here are photographs of the map stone and translations of the *Quechuan* words listed on it. I followed the directions, and my father, *Manuel,* another man named *Kawki,* and I found a hidden valley and discovered an Incan golden disc."

The archbishop's eyes grew wide.

"A golden disc, you say? Where is this gold disc? Do you have it with you?"

Dr. *Louis* Carillos sat up straight in his chair as strong pulses of love began to resonate from his heart and through his entire body, followed by the overwhelming fragrance of roses. Then *Louis* clearly heard the voice of a woman speak to him in his mind.

"My dearest child, do not show the golden disc to the archbishop."

Louis was stunned and desperately tried to collect himself.

"Am I going crazy? I'm hearing voices in my head!" he thought.

"Well?" said the archbishop. "I repeat. Do you have it? May I see it please?"

"Do not show it to him."

"It's in my safe deposit box at the Bank of Cusco," he quickly lied.

Louis could see from the archbishop's expressions that he was clearly disappointed.

"Well, can you go get it and bring it to me here? I really want to see it."

Louis heard the female voice again in his mind.

"Tell him no."

"I'm sorry, Your Excellency, but,

I have an early class I must teach at the university and many more all day. Perhaps tomorrow. Adios."

He stood up and left the office.

As soon as *Louis* had walked out of his office, Archbishop *Perez* immediately called Cardinal *Perrizzi* at The Vatican in Rome. He told him about the discovery of the golden disc. Cardinal *Perrizzi* then called *Xavier del Mundo* in New York.

"Call the archbishop back. Tell him I order him to get the golden disc at all costs!"

Louis walked toward the front door of the cathedral. He was lightheaded and questioned his sanity. What felt like two hands began to push against his side and guided his body to the left. He entered a small side chapel and knelt in front of a large painting of the Virgin Mary holding an infant Jesus. *Louis* closed his eyes and placed his palms together as a rush of warm air flowed around him. He smelled roses again and opened his eyes.

A beautiful young woman with dark hair floated about three feet above the ground before him. Her gown was pink, and she wore a blue cloak. Twelve silver stars glowed in a halo around her head. She looked down at him with love. Tears streamed down *Louis's* face, and he gasped.

"My child, you have placed yourself in great danger. I urge you to return to the Punku Hayu Marca as soon as possible and use the golden disc to open and go through the Star Door."

"Where will I go when I enter the Star Door, and where will I be when I walk out?"

"Have faith and trust in Me. You will be warmly received by friends who greatly need to use the golden disc to make the blue comet miss the Earth."

Louis felt more tears stream down his face, and he sobbed. He dried his eyes with a handkerchief and looked up. The Lady had gone. He left the cathedral and headed back to his house. He drove past the Bank of Cusco and saw more than a dozen police cars parked in front. Many policeman were running in and out of the front door.

His cell phone rang.

The call was from *Arturo*.

"Father, the police are here, and they're searching the house. Mother and I are really scared. They say that you stole the golden disc! Is that true?"

Es eso cierto? "

"That's not true. I can't explain right now. I'm going to the Star Door in *Puno*."

Louis hung up and made a quick decision. He drove straight to the *Alejandro Valesco Astete* International Airport, where he parked in the garage and got the disc wrapped in a towel, from the trunk. *Louis* bought a ticket on a LAN commuter flight to *Juliaca*, arranged a car rental, and ran to the boarding gate. He took his seat with just four minutes to spare.

"We thoroughly searched the home and property of Dr. *Carillos,* but the disc is nowhere on the premises," reported Sergeant *Jorge Ramirez.*

"What about his wife and son?" asked Captain *Reynaldo Vasquez.*

"His wife knows nothing. I will interrogate his son soon and get back to you."

Captain *Vasquez* made a call to Archbishop *Perez* and informed him that the golden disc wasn't in the safe deposit box of Dr. *Carillos* or at his house.

"He has stolen a sacred Incan golden disc from the cathedral. We must get it back! For the love of God, find it!"

"I'm going to ask you some questions, and I want answers," said Sergeant *Ramirez*. "What is your name?"

"*Arturo Carillos*."

"Where is your father?"

"I don't know."

"I think you do know. Again, where is your father."

"I tell you I don't know."

The sergeant turned to another policeman, who stood nearby.

"Handcuff him. We'll have to continue this interrogation at the jail."

"No, please, I can't go to jail! I'll miss my college entrance exams that begin tomorrow morning. That's if the comet is going to miss us, of course."

"We all hope that the scientists are wrong," said the sergeant. "Tell me where your father is, and we'll leave you alone."

Arturo told them that his father had gone to the Star Door around *Puno*.

"*Gracias, Arturo*," said the sergeant. "I wish you good luck on your exams."

Sergeant *Ramirez* called Captain *Vasquez,* who ordered a series of road-blocks set up along Highway

3S from Cusco to Puno. Forty-five minutes passed without a report of the car being stopped, and he grew impatient. Then a call came in from a patrolman at the airport. The suspect's car had been located in the parking garage.

Captain *Ramirez* called LAN airlines.

"LAN. My name is *Lupe.* How may I be of assistance?"

The captain introduced himself and asked whether a Dr. *Louis Carillos* was among the passengers on a flight to *Juliaca.*

"Yes, sir. He also rented a car."

"When did the plane leave Cusco?"

"At eight thirty-five a.m. It landed in *Juliaca* about an hour ago."

"How long is the flight."

"Fifty-five minutes."

"Do you know where the Star Door is located?"

"Yes.

"How far is *Juliaca* from it by car?"

"Forty minutes."

The captain ordered an APB on the suspect's rental car to all police in the area, on Highway 3S, and along the southwestern shore of Lake Titicaca.

Louis's flight landed at *Inca Manco Capac* Airport in *Juliaca*. He got in his rental car, drove south fast, and covered the distance to the Star Door in thirty-five minutes. As he approached the area of the Star Door, a police car turned on its lights and siren, and began to chase him. He laid his foot on the gas pedal and stepped on it.

Louis screeched to a stop in the parking area, grabbed the golden disc, and jumped out of the car.

"Alto!" ordered the two policemen who ran close behind him. "Stop!"

He raced to the Star Door and scattered a large group of people standing in front of it. *Louis* tossed the towel on the ground, inserted the golden disc into the round indentation to the right of the door, and stepped forward. A brilliant blue light issued forth. As the policemen ran straight for the door, they saw

Louis's hand reach out, take hold of the golden disc, and then vanish before their eyes.

Louis felt as if his body were in free fall, and he moved rapidly downward. A pulsating hum accompanied by a whistling sound surrounded him in the utter darkness. He was overcome by waves of fear, which quickly vanished with the emergence of multitudes of brilliant stars, tremendous vibrantly colored, gaseous, nebular clouds, and spinning spiral galaxies. He was overcome by the immense beauty that surrounded him. He noted that he was breathing normally.

The humming and whistling

sounds continued, but the rush of free fall was soon replaced by a resistance. His body felt like he was breathing in and swimming through thick syrup. Then he broke through and moved at a tremendous rate of speed toward a brightly intense, electric blue light, which shone in the distance. The light grew in size as he drew nearer it.

As he began to enter and merge into the area that surrounded the light, the humming and whistling sounds abruptly ceased, and *Louis* observed that straight ahead of him, and in the very center of the light, stood a large open doorway.

STEAMBOAT CANYON, ARIZONA

Marc, Jenny, Robert, *Tewa*, *Cheveyo,* and the other nine elders were gathered before the Star Door in Steamboat Canyon. Marc glanced at his watch and saw it was just after four in the afternoon. Barely audible at first, a deep rumbling, humming sound grew ever louder. Dirt and pebbles began to fall from above and were soon followed by larger rocks. Everyone threw his or her arms over their heads and took two steps backward. A brilliant blue light burst forth in front of the group, which blinded them, and they covered their eyes. The light slowly began to diminish, and they stared in astonishment as the figure of a man began to emerge from the outline of the door that had been cut into the solid rock wall.

Dr. *Louis Carillos* stood before a group of people. He blinked wildly as his eyes began to focus. Marc stared at him in utter astonishment. *Louis* then raised his right arm and held up the golden disc.

"Dr. Marc Prentis, I presume?" *Louis* said. He laughed aloud. "I have brought you a special, wonderful, belated Christmas present from The Blessed Virgin Mother Mary."

Marc and Jenny were both stunned and exuberant. *Cheveyo*, followed by each in the group, hugged *Louis* warmly.

They took *Louis* back to Marc's house. Jenny sat on the couch with the golden disc on her lap. It was the size of a cup saucer and a half an inch thick. She ran her fingers over its smooth surface and then around the edge. "It's heavy. Maybe three pounds," she observed. "I think its made of solid gold, but there's no writing on it."

Jenny looked at *Louis*, who sat in a chair in front of her, and then glanced at Marc, who sat beside her. He gave her a wink and then laughed.

"Actually there is, but it can be seen only under a black light," said *Louis*. "The words instructed me how to use the golden disc to go through the Star Door in Peru, and that's how I am able to be here with you now."

"We have the disc! Our Lady is indeed helping us. Now, *Louis*," asked Jenny, "tell us what must be an amazing story. How in the world did you get it?"

Louis rubbed his eyes with both hands in an effort to come back to reality. He shook his head and then finished the beer Marc had given him.

"Well, where to begin? I guess at the beginning."

For the next thirty minutes, he relayed the events starting with the phone call from Archbishop *Perez* about finding a carved stone on the cathedral wall, which turned out to be a map that led him to a secret valley, where he, his father, and another man, discovered the golden disc hidden inside a mountain.

"Is there any more to the story?" asked Marc.

Once more *Louis* summarized seeing the letters on the disc under his son's black light (which had directed him on how to use it), his meeting Archbishop *Perez*, hearing the voice of Mother Mary in his mind and urging him not to give the disc to him, and Her appearing in the chapel and urging him to travel through the Star Door.

When he had finished, Marc and Jenny told him about their vision of Mother Mary, the task set by The

Father, and how the golden disc would to be used to save Earth from the comet. *Louis* was deeply moved upon hearing that. He asked whether he may be allowed to lie down somewhere and sleep. Marc took him to his bedroom and made sure he was comfortable.

The phone rang. Marc answered and handed it to Jenny.

"It's your SAC."

James Cararuscio instructed her to meet him in the Crowne Plaza Hotel lobby on North Seventh Street near the FBI field office in Phoenix tomorrow at six p.m."

You're scheduled to go through the Jump Gate on Thursday afternoon."

Jenny then told him about the

appearance of Dr. *Louis Carillos* through a Star Door near Marc's house and that they were now in possession of the golden disc.

"You have the gold disc? Oh, thank God!" he shouted and then paused. "I'm so ashamed to admit to you that I have had my doubts, but now that you actually have it, my faith is stronger than ever."

CHAPTER EIGHT

Avignon, France

Jack looked at the golden statue rising above him. He sipped some wine.

"Man, that is way up there."

"Yeah," answered Augi. "I wonder if we can get onto the roof. Let's go over there after we talk with the helicopter guys. They should show up soon."

Jack glanced around. The two of them sat at an outdoor table shaded by a white umbrella. The ancient stone buildings at the *Place de l'Horloge* in the city center looked like castles with medieval ramparts, crenelated walls, arched windows, and two tall, round towers with pointed tops. Bright sunlight reflected off wrought-iron balconies, and pigeons begged for a morsel at their feet.

A group of men approached them. Jack and Augi stood up.

"We are here at Victor's request," one of them said. "My name is *Antoine.* My friends are *Bertrand, Philipe, and Claude.*"

"*Bon jour.* Good to meet you. My name's Augi, and this is Jack."

The four men found chairs and took seats around the table. Jack was clearly disappointed.

"How come no one's named *Pierre*?" he said and frowned.

Augi stepped hard on Jack's left foot under the table.

"Ow!"

"Please excuse my stupid friend.

"Veuillez excuser mon ami goujon."

The men laughed.

"You understand why we're having this meeting?" asked Augi.

"Oui," answered Antoine. "We are on the evacuation list. Some scientists say the comet may pass the earth closely, while others claim we will receive a direct hit. Quel sera."

"Whatever will be, will be," said Augi. "We'll all be safe at the base off-planet. What we have to do is make sure that these people fail to place this golden disc on the statue's left hand, because, if they do, I guess that'll cause the comet to somehow miss the planet. Sounds kind of weird and freaky to me."

"Oui, I agree, but those are our orders. Now let's get down to the facts. We have two Eurocopter Tigre HAD's available for the job."

"Holy shit!" exclaimed Augi. "Where in the heck did you get those?"

Antoine smiled.

"You do not need to know. They carry 20mm cannons and air-to-air missiles. We will make short work of them."

"My friend Jack and I will be

right here, watching for any sign of a helicopter flying by or near the statue."

Augi entered Antoine's number into his cell phone.

"Call me immediately, and we will be here in less than five minutes," said Antoine. "Au revoir."

The four men rose from their chairs and walked away.

"Okay, Jack. Let's go check out the cathedral."

The two men entered. Jack had been raised Catholic and unconsciously crossed himself as he walked inside. Rows of dark wooden pews filled the center with richly decorated gold and red arches along the sides.

"Welcome. Are you both here for the tour?" asked a young priest in English.

Augi and Jack nodded.

"You are just in time."

He motioned for them to join a group of a dozen and a half people.

"My name is Father Pierre Cordon. I will inform all of you about the history and art of this great cathedral."

Jack couldn't help smiling at the first name of the tour guide, who proceeded to take the group to the center of the richly decorated sanctuary.

"Notre Dame des Doms is a Romanesque structure built in the twelfth century. Please look straight up. The cathedral boasts a huge octagonal dome. Over there are two organs and a marble throne used by the popes. The beautiful mausoleum of Pope John XXII before us is a masterpiece of fourteenth century Gothic stone carving. But perhaps the most prominent feature is the gold, gilded statue of The Virgin Mary atop the western tower, which was built in the year 1859."

The priest led the group along the right side to the main altar.

"How do you clean and take care of the statue? I mean, is there any way to get up onto the roof?" asked Augi.

Father Cordon nodded.

"Oui. I don't know how the statue

is cleaned, but one can get on the roof."

He pointed to an ornately carved wooden door near them.

"One must ascend five long flights of stairs. I did it once, and that was enough! There is a door that opens to the roof."

Augi waited for the group to move ahead before he tried to open the door. It was locked. He and Jack turned, left the building, walked back across the plaza, and took seats at a table. They ordered a bottle of wine and resumed their watch.

"When the time comes, I'll fire a couple of rounds at the door's lock, kick it in, and we'll run up the stairs to the roof," said Augi. "Looks like the helicopter guys won't need our help, but we should be up there."

Jack lifted his wine glass, nodded, and smiled.

"Oui", he said.

SUTTON PLACE, MANHATTAN, NEW YORK CITY

Xavier del Mundo groaned as another past-life recollection began to form in his mind. He had long learned that it was useless to resist and had resigned himself to allow the recollections to take him wherever they wished to go.

"*Up periscope.*"

"*Bis Periskop.*"

"Yes, Captain."

"*Ja, Kapitan.*"

Xavier balled his fists in anger and gritted his teeth.

"Not this one again!"

He leaned back in his chair and closed his eyes.

NORTH ATLANTIC
SEPTEMBER, 1940

"She is still zig-zagging and appears dark to me."

"Sie ist immer noch fahrt und erscheint dunkel fur mich."

"May I have a look?"

"Darf ich einen Blick?"

Kapitanleutnant Helmet Juhnke nodded to his *Ober Leutnant zur See, Otto Sommer.*

Otto gripped the side handles and peered into the periscope.

"The afternoon clouds darken her. Her two masts and single funnel identify her as a passenger liner. With all due respect, Captain, I think we should let her continue on her way."

"Die Nachmittagswolken verdunkeln sie. Ihre zwei Masten und ihr einziger Trichter identifizieren sie als Passagierschiff. Bei allem Respekt, Captain, denke ich, wir sollten sie ihren Weg fortsetzen lassen."

"I strongly disagree. I have watched her for three hours. She is outside of normal shipping lanes. Why would she be zig-zagging? I say we sink her."

"Ich stimme überhaupt nicht

zu. Ich habe schon einmal fur drei Stunden. Sie ist oberhalb der normalen Schifffahrt swege. Warum wurden Sie sein fahrt? Ich sage Wir sinken."

U-133 was a Type VII C class Nazi submarine. Her home port was *Hamburg* on the River *Elbe* 110 kilometers from the North Sea. She measured two-hundred and twenty feet long and had four bow tubes, and two stern tubes, and she carried fourteen torpedoes. The submarine had an 88mm cannon deck gun and a 20mm flak anti-aircraft gun. She could do seventeen knots on the surface and eight knots underwater. Her crew numbered forty-four men.

Kapitanleutnant Juhnke looked

through the periscope again
and noted that many lights were
beginning to shine through the ship's
windows as she sailed west toward a
magnificent sunset. *Helmet Juhnke's*
eyes began to glow a fiery crimson.

James Carnhill had rarely seen
such a beautiful sunset in his
six years as captain of the SS
Parthenia. His ship had left Liverpool
two days previously and would,
God willing, safely cross the Atlantic
and dock in Nova Scotia, Canada.
She was a good, sound vessel at
530 feet long and 67 feet abeam.
Her twin propellers were driven by
powerful steam turbines, and she
was capable of fifteen knots. James
looked out the window toward the

port side and noted that a number of passengers sat on benches toward the bow, enjoying the view.

Dorothy McFall held her six-year-old daughter's hand as they gazed at the sunset. The wind blew their red hair.

"I wish Daddy could see the sunset, Mama," said Julia.

"So do I, darling, but your Daddy is feeling a wee bit seasick and is sleeping."

"The sky is all lit up with pretty colors," exclaimed Julia.

"A gift from God," Dorothy responded. She unbuttoned the top of her coat and fingered her gold cross.

"What is that, Mama?" asked her

daughter and pointed with her hand. "Is it a whale or a dolphin?"

Dorothy focused on the area to their left and saw the wake of a submarine's periscope heading straight for them.

Captain Carnhill saw it, too, and turned to sound general quarters.

Ober Leutnant zur See, *Otto Sommer*, walked down the passageway and motioned to *Karl Fromsdorf,* the *Leitender Ingenieur.* He led him to his tiny quarters and spoke quietly.

"The captain wishes to sink a passenger liner, Karl. I have seen it through the periscope, and it is not a war or a merchant ship."

"Der Kapitän will sink ein

Verkehrs-flugzeug, Karl. Ich habe erlebt wie das durch das Periskop, und es ist nicht ein Krieg oder ein Handelsschiff."

"Of this you are certain?"

"Von diesem sind Sie sicher?"

"Yes. I do not know what to do."

"Ja. Ich weis nicht was ich machen soll."

"Let us speak with him."

"Wir wollen uns mit ihm reden."

The two men approached Captain *Juhnke. Karl* asked if he may be allowed to look through the pericope."

"Of course."

"Ja, natürlich."

Karl clearly determined that the ship was a passenger liner.

"Both *Otto* and myself are strongly opposed to sinking this ship. She is a British passenger ship. Why do you want to sink her? There must be hundreds of women and children aboard, and they will all die."

"Beide Otto und ich sind stark dagegen, Untergang dieses Schiffes. Sie ist eine British Passagierschiff. Warum wollen Sie Ihr Waschbecken? Es muss Hunderte von Frauen und Kindern an Bord, und sie werden alle sterben."

Otto and *Karl* stepped back as the Captain's eyes began to glow crimson. He scowled and shouted in their faces.

"My father was killed in the First World War. British soldiers

The Domain of Arrogance

bayonetted him in the *Argonne Forest*. I hate all British and I'm going to sink that ship!"

"Mein Vater ermordet wurde im der Erste Weltkrieg. Britische Soldaten bajonettierte ihn *in der Argonne Wald. Ich hasse alle Britischen und ich sunk, Schiff!"*

"But, sir, Admiral *Doenitz* has ordered us not to sink passenger ships."

"Aber, Sir. Admiral *Döenitz* hat uns bestellt nicht Fahrgastschiffe zu sinken."

"No buts. I will have you both arrested for insubordination when we make port in *Hamburg* if you like. Now prepare tubes one and two for firing."

"Kein aber. Ich werde sie beide verhaftet fur Unbotmäßigkeit wenn wir machen in Hamburg Wenn Sie mochten. Jetzt bereiten sie dir Rohre ein und zwei zum Abfeuern."

"Forward torpedo tubes ready, Captain."

"Vorwärts torpedorohre bereit, Kapitän."

"Fire."

"Feuer."

Dorothy and Julia stood up from the bench along with the other passengers.

"What's wrong, Mama?"

There was no time to answer. Dorothy reached behind her neck, undid the clasp, raised her right arm, and held up her gold cross, which glinted in the sun as it dangled from its chain. She spoke in a loud, firm voice.

"Dear Jesus and Blessed Mother Mary, please, I pray to you both. Do not let them torpedo our ship. Please, for the Love of God, stop them!"

Kapitanleutnant Helmet Juhnke peered through the periscope and saw that both torpedoes were on target, a fact that brought a smile to his face.

"Look at that big cloud!" exclaimed a man standing to their right. "I swear it wasn't there a second ago."

Dorothy and Julia looked up and saw a great, circular cloud overhead that sparkled bright silver around the edges and shimmered golden yellow in the middle. The center began to part, and five gigantic fingers emerged followed by a hand, wrist, and arm.

The arm lowered itself until it lay above the waves, which splashed against its sides. The hand came down directly in the path of the torpedoes, and everyone on deck clearly heard two loud explosions.

Captain James Carnhill stared, open-mouthed, and was speechless. His first mate stood at his side. They both heard the sound of the torpedoes exploding behind the enormous hand, which then rose into the air. The arm ascended and withdrew inside the center of the golden cloud, which remained positioned over the ship. James finally found his voice and spoke as he wiped tears away.

"Sweet Jesus! Thank You, thank You, dear God, thank You!"

"A miracle," said the first mate between sobs. "A miracle!"

Dorothy grabbed the side of the bench to steady herself. Those around her were crying, as was her daughter.

"What happened, Mama? Where did the big hand come from? Whose hand was it? Was it God's?"

Dorothy somehow summoned her voice and answered.

"Yes, the hand was God's. He

heard my plea for help. He saved us all."

Those around her stood with heads down, palms together, and uttered prayers of thankfulness. Someone began to recite The Lord's Prayer, and everyone joined in.

Kapitanleutnant Helmet Juhnke's smile faded as a gigantic hand splashed down onto the waves before his eyes, and both torpedoes exploded against it. The face of *Yeshua* appeared in the periscope, looked directly at him, and spoke.

"You think that you are invincible, but once again the Forces of Light prevail. You shall be consumed by the fires of a great comet. Your body

shall be incinerated by that of my own fiery breath. In that moment your vital essence, indeed your very soul, shall be utterly extinguished and cease to exist."

Yeshua's face disappeared, and *Helmet* heard the voice of his *Ober Leutnant zur See, Otto Sommer.*

"Did the ship sink?"

"Hat das Schiff sinken?"

"No. Both torpedoes missed."

"Nein. Beide torpedos verfehlt."

"Perhaps it is for the best."

"Vielleicht ist es fur das beste."

"Perhaps."

"Vielleicht."

Xavier del Mundo slammed his fist onto his desk. The framed painting of Jesus toppled over and landed face up on the carpeted floor. *Xavier* stood up and bent over to pick it up, but changed his mind. He brought his right foot down on top of it, stomped on it, and crushed and ground the glass beneath his shoe. Then he threw the framed painting in the trash can. Housekeeping would vacuum up the broken glass. His private phone rang.

"Cardinal *Perizzi* here."

"What is the password?"

"Sub Rosa."

"Speak"

"The European Space Agency in Paris announced today that the blue comet is ten days away. They give the chances of it striking Earth at better than eighty percent. Our transport planes are on the way to all four evacuation collection spots, and everyone on the list will be picked up and brought to the one nearest their location within the next six days and taken to the base on Phobos."

"Excellent. I have received a report from our assets that anyone attempting to place the golden disc on the left hand of the statue in Avignon will be severely dealt with. *Arrivederci.*"

PHOENIX, ARIZONA

The shades were drawn in their hotel room, but sunlight still managed to filter in behind the curtains. Marc slowly traced his hands along the curve of Jenny's breasts and kissed her gently on the lips.

"Slower," she said. "Move with me."

Marc obeyed and matched her rhythm. They made love passionately and then drifted off to sleep.

"Ahh, that feels good," sighed Marc as he awakened to Jenny's fingers lightly massaging the back of his neck.

"That makes me happy to hear that. Did you know that I was trained by one of the best in martial arts? I know how to completely disable someone with a judo chop to this exact spot."

Marc reached behind him, placed

his right hand over hers, and ended her massage.

"Then I'm glad it's you who's going up there and not me. What was his name?"

"Who?"

"Your martial arts trainer."

"You mean *her* name. *Viviane d'Aqs*. She was a visiting instructor at Quantico when I was new to the Academy. She was a career agent with the DST, which is the French equivalent of the FBI. We became good friends in the year she spent there. My late husband Mitch, and I visited her once in southern France around five years ago. She was also present at Mitch's funeral along

with her husband, whose name is
Bastien."

"Do you still train in martial arts? I
mean, you're a computer geek and
sit at a desk all day."

Jenny touched her forehead
against Marc's. She looked deeply
into his eyes and smiled ever so
slightly.

"I'm an agent with the FBI. All of us
are constantly trained in all tactical
areas, and those include firearms
and hand-to-hand martial arts."

"Again, I'm glad the fate of the
world rests on your shoulders and
not on mine."

Jenny smiled, but Marc could see
she was nervous.

"That only applies while I'm up

there. Now that we have the golden disc, when I return, the three of us are going to Avignon."

Marc smiled and then got serious. "Are you afraid about going?"

"No, just starting to feel tense. Are you afraid? Are you afraid for me?"

Marc couldn't find the words.

"Don't be. I have full confidence in myself and my abilities and in yours."

She felt his biceps. "I'll tell you what, though. The fact that we have the golden disc speaks volumes. Our Lady is helping us. And, Marc, I'm really excited about seeing my sister, Janey! Knowing her, she's busy putting together a team of people I'll be able to work with so we can execute a plan to successfully rescue everyone."

Marc glanced at the digital clock radio. It was 11:40 a.m. The phone rang. Jenny reached over Marc's shoulder and picked it up.

"Hello?"

"Agent Spadaro. Meet us at the hotel's restaurant in fifteen minutes for lunch," said James Cararuscio.

"Can I have twenty?"

"Okay, but don't be late."

Jenny hugged Marc and gave him a lingering kiss.

"I love you, Marc."

"I love you, too, Jenny. With all my heart."

She kissed him one more time.

"We're having lunch with my boss soon. Let's get dressed quickly."

Jenny called *Louis'* room and told him to meet them downstairs in the restaurant in twenty minutes.

James was waiting at the door to the restaurant as the three of them approached.

"And this must be...?

"May I introduce Dr. *Louis Carillos*?" said Jenny. "This is my boss, James Cararuscio."

The two men shook hands, and the hostess led them to a corner booth.

"There's one more person joining us, but he's running late," James said. "Please bring him to our table when he arrives."

The hostess nodded and left.

When they were seated, Jenny handed James the golden disc. He gave it a good look, ran his fingers all over it, handed it back, and looked at *Louis.*

"Tell me how you got the disc."

Louis succinctly summarized the story.

"This is confirmation that Our Lady is certainly looking out for us, and I have renewed faith in our success," said James.

The waitress brought a basket of warm rolls and glasses of water. They chose their meals, and soon the hostess brought Mike O'Brien to their table. Marc introduced him to Dr. *Louis Carillos* and studied Mike as he took a seat at the table. The man was six feet tall and, stocky, with a wide chest, and dark hair graying on the sides and worn in a crew-cut. His slacks were black, and he wore a navy blue T-shirt with FBI in large yellow letters across the back.

"Tell me what you ordered," Mike asked James.

"Double cheeseburger with fries."

"I'll have the same," Mike said to the waitress.

Mike then opened a manila folder and laid three aerial photographs on the table. He pointed to the first one, which was of the entire area surrounding Isis Temple. The next one was a close-up.

"There's room to land two of our MH-47E's."

Jenny had only seen pictures of this twin-rotor helicopter known as a SOA or Special Operations Aircraft.

"Wow," she said. "What's the armament? I mean, if we need any, of course."

MH-47E's are armed with M134 7.62mm electrically-operated, air-cooled Gatling guns, fitted in firing positions on the left port and right cabin door behind the cockpit, and two M240 7.62mm belt-fed machine guns fitted to windows toward the rear, plus two M134 7.62 mini guns in front."

Jenny, Marc, and *Louis* gulped.

"I guess that ought to do it," said Marc, and the other two nodded.

Mike showed an even closer third photo, and they could clearly see a path leading from the landing pad to a large opening in the sheer rock wall.

"How long will it take to get us to Isis Temple from here?" asked Jenny.

"About an hour," responded Mike O'Brien. "We'll take our two MH-47E's. My SWAT team will land first, secure the area, and hopefully, we'll meet with no resistance. Then I'll radio James an all clear, and you can land beside us."

Mike saw the waitress bringing

their orders and quickly placed the photos back in the folder.

When everyone was finished and the table had been cleared, Marc handed the gold disc to Mike. He ran his hands over it on both sides.

"I must believe that we have divine help. How did you get it, Dr. *Carillos*?"

Louis briefly described the events. Mike smiled and nodded.

James then described the various items she would take with her to Sub Rosa.

"We don't know how many we're up against, so I'm giving your sister and others enough time to take out the guards and blow the door open for our men to enter. I figure that there must be some people up there who were in the service and are familiar with weapons. So I'm having you bring two Micro TAR-21 sub-machine guns. They each weigh six pounds and take a 9mm cartridge that fires thirty rounds."

"Isn't that the standard weapon of the Israeli Defense Forces?" asked Jenny.

James nodded.

"Two C-4 M112 demolition blocks with blasting caps. That should be plenty to blow the door wide open. I'm also including three Glock 17 9mm pistols. And, just in case they're needed, five 5.11 XPRT folding tactical knives that have a four-and-a-half inch blade, plus six compact tactical LED flashlights with eighteen hundred lumens of light output in case you need them. Finally, one C.A.V.E.S. communicator that's six by three inches. Everything fits neatly in a black duffel bag with a padded shoulder strap. The total weight including ammo is just over twenty-five pounds. I'm giving you exactly two hours up there, Agent Spadaro, and no more. We'll be waiting for you."

"Thanks, James. "I'll be on time."

Everyone stood. James paid the bill, and they exited the restaurant.

"Meet us outside in front of the hotel lobby in thirty minutes," said James.

Jenny took Marc aside and whispered in his ear.

"I need some quiet time to contact my sister, Janey. Maybe you and *Louis* can go for a walk or something, okay?"

Marc whispered, "Okay."

Jenny returned to their room and used the bathroom to wash her face and hands. She took a seat on the couch and closed her eyes.

"Janey, this is Jenny. If you can hear me, I want you to know that I will be arriving through the Jump Gate at Sub Rosa in about an hour and a half, so please be expecting me and have someone there meet me. I love you. We're going to

make this work, and I can't wait to see you."

Jenny deeply inhaled, held her breath for a few seconds, and exhaled.

Janey Spadaro was done for the day at the Eco Farm. Her shift ended at four, and she walked out the main entrance and headed across the park toward her apartment complex.

A voice in her mind made her stop, and she took a seat on a nearby bench. She heard Jenny's voice telling her to be prepared for her arrival in an hour and a half. Janey made her way to the gate in the wall leading to the Jump Gate and was fortunate to locate the guard, *Tuwa*, as he made his rounds. She alerted him to her sister's arrival time and returned to her apartment.

There was so much to do. The first thing was to find *Honovi* and then for the two of them to begin contacting various people involved in the escape plan like the three engineers. But first she needed to let Jenny know she'd received her message. She sat down on the sofa and closed her eyes.

Marc returned to his room. Jenny was sitting on the couch and opened her eyes as he sat down next to her. She reached over, pulled him to her, and kissed him.

"Everything okay?" he asked.

Jenny sighed.

"I sent Janey a message, and we can only hope that she received it."

"Well, I certainly…"

Jenny held her hand up.

"Wait a minute, Marc. I hear her voice in my mind."

She closed her eyes and relaxed.

"Jenny, this is Janey. Can you hear me? I got your message. A guard named Tuwa is expecting you. He'll take you to my apartment, where you'll meet others who are planning to get out of here and go home. I'll see you soon."

Jenny relayed the message to Marc. Then she changed into tan slacks, a blue, short-sleeved blouse, and white tennis shoes.

"Let's pack fast. We have to meet James downstairs in ten minutes."

ABOVE ISIS TEMPLE GRAND CANYON, ARIZONA

Jenny looked out the window of the helicopter as they neared the enormous sandstone formation. She gazed down and saw that the SWAT team's copter was about to land.

"Stay hovering here," she heard James say to the pilot over her headset.

The side doors of the SWAT's MH-47E swung open, and twelve heavily armed men dressed in black armored uniforms swarmed out and quickly ran straight down an incline along a path. She watched them fan out and take up firing positions upon coming to a wide opening in the sheer rock wall. Then six men rushed inside with weapons drawn.

"We have met no resistance", Jenny heard Mike O'Brien say over her headset.

"Affirmative. Let's land," said James.

Their twin-rotor helicopter set down behind the SWAT team's. The doors opened, and they climbed out.

"You four men, take Agent Spadaro inside. Marc and *Louis*, come with me," said James.

Jenny hefted the duffel bag onto her shoulder and followed the men. They walked through an opening and entered an area of flattened earth, a space as as big as a supermarket parking lot. Ahead of her stood a tall, square, steel structure she knew must be the Jump Gate.

James approached her.

"We'll be here waiting for you. I'm allowing you exactly two hours and no more. I don't want to have to send men after you, Agent Spadaro."

"You won't. I'll find my sister, meet with her friends, and return on time."

James nodded.

"Set your watch timer anyway and say your goodbyes."

He turned and walked over to speak with Mike O'Brien.

Jenny took the duffel bag off her shoulder and set in on the ground.

She tenderly kissed Marc and whispered,

"Don"t worry. I'll be back soon."

Jenny gave *Louis* a big hug.

She slung the duffel bag onto her shoulder and strode fast toward the Jump Gate without looking back. The sides gleamed as she stepped onto the platform. She saw a curtain of swirling, dark grayness before her, took a deep breath, and walked forward.

SUB ROSA BASE, PHOBOS, MARS

At first, Jenny felt like she was falling fast. Then a thickness surrounded her that caused her to move in slow motion. The darkness soon gave way to bright light. She took two steps straight ahead, blinked, and stopped. Above her she could see banks of lights and moving fans. Around her on all sides was a high wall topped with barbed wire. Ahead of her was a steel door, beside which stood an armed man.

"You must be Janey's sister, Jenny," said the man. "My name is *Tuwa*. I'll take you to her. She's expecting you."

Jenny sighed with relief. The man used a remote control to lift a heavy steel bar and opened the armored door. Then he held his right hand up and whispered,

"There's another guard approaching. Put the duffel bag down on the ground inside and stand next to me. Let me do the talking."

He quickly shut the door with the remote control.

"Hi, Gary," said *Tuwa.*

"What are you doing out here at this time, Ms. Spadaro?"

Jenny remained silent.

"She's been in a meeting with Andrea Dryer that lasted all afternoon. There's a serious technical problem with an area of the hydroponics system in Section A at the Eco Farm and special parts have to be brought up here from Earth ASAP."

Jenny nodded in agreement.

"Okay. Head straight back to your apartment complex now."

Jenny nodded again.

"I'll see that she gets there, Gary."

The other guard continued on his way along the perimeter of the wall. *Tuwa* opened the door, and Jenny picked up the duffel bag as soon as he'd rounded a corner. *Tuwa* used the remote control to close the door and reset the metal bar inside.

"I've been here for over two years and have attained a top position in security. There are only four remote controls for the door. I have one, Michael Dryer, the Director, has another, head of security, Victor Spoils, has one, and Barry Dukov, Victor's second in command, has the fourth. I must return mine to the administration center every day along with my revolver and have them checked in at the end of my shift."

Tuwa led her to Complex E, where Janey was waiting for her in the lobby. Jenny rushed into her sister's arms, and they embraced. Tears flowed from both of their eyes as they hugged.

"Oh, Janey, I was so worried, but I never doubted that you were okay. Then all sorts of amazing things started to happen and..."

Her sister cut her off.

"Jenny, we really need to get you upstairs to my apartment and out of sight right now."

She turned to *Tuwa.*

"We're having a meeting soon.

Get back here as soon as you can. Thanks for bringing Jenny here."

They took the elevator up, and Janey opened the door. *Hovovi* got up from the couch and smiled.

"Jenny, I want you to meet *Honovi*. He's going to explain the basics of the escape plan to you. But first, come here."

Janey hugged her sister again and took her outside to the deck. She slid the glass door closed. She kissed her on the cheek and wiped tears away.

"*Honovi* and I are lovers. He's a special man and has helped me a lot to adjust to living here. Soon my friend Sharon will arrive. She's been my mainstay in all of this, and she'll fill you in on why this place exists and how it works. I can't tell you how good it is to see you. I love you so much."

They went back inside and sat down on the couch.

"I have less than two hours, and then I've got to go back to where the FBI is waiting for me. So, *Honovi,* brief me on all of the details and let's see about getting a sequenced plan of action set in place," said Jenny. "But first let me show you what I've brought."

Jenny zipped open the duffel bag and placed the contents on the carpet. She took out the C.A.V.E.S. and handed it to Janey.

"This is tuned to a secure channel

on Jason's ship," explained Jenny. She showed her how to turn the power on, and a green light glowed. "You'll be able to talk directly to Jason and vice versa. He's on his way here as we speak."

"Wow," exclaimed Janey. "We can coordinate things down to the minute!"

"This should do it," exclaimed *Honovi*. He cradled one of the Micro MTAR-21 machine guns in his arms.

Honovi then told Jenny and Janey that he'd spoken with Colonel King before leaving for Earth. Jason, his co-pilot, Arnie, and six crew members would be armed and take care of the guards when the platform reached the bottom. Their ship was due in around two o'clock in the afternoon on Saturday. The three engineers would have to put the nuclear reactor on stand-down around that time. They'd warned him that they must put it back on line within twenty minutes.

"So I'd say anywhere around two fifteen would be the time for me to blow the door. I have lots of experience with C-4, and Steve Peterson will be with me. He was in the Marines and will have one of these machine guns. I'd like one of these LED lights. The engineers have some, too, and will give one to Janey in case she needs one. As soon as the lights go out, I'll set the charges and blow the steel door."

"I'll be with the engineers to receive the call from Jason confirming that the guards have been overpowered," said Janey.

"How many guards are there? What kind of opposition will the FBI face?" asked Jenny.

"The USS *Concord* just brought up two dozen new security guards. I guess there were that many already. So, maybe fifty men, and they'll be armed. And some big shot was aboard the ship, too," said *Honovi.*

There was a knock on the door.

Janey opened it, and *Tuwa* walked in.

"My shift just ended. The others will begin to arrive soon, and I expect at least ten more people. I'll bring them up a few at a time so as not to arouse any suspicion," he said.

Sharon Oliver entered along with Donna Bailey, the nurse in Janey's Complex E. They took seats on the couch. Jimmy Jaffe, who oversaw the electricity, air temperature, and humidity in the apartment complexes, showed up with Jamie Glasgow, the bee keeper at the Eco Farm. They took the two remaining seats on the couch. *Honovi* brought in some chairs from the deck. Janey placed bowls of chips, salsa, and bottles of water on the coffee table.

Steve Peterson, the delivery van driver, Annie O'Neal, the groundskeeper, and John Spencer, the plumber for the complexes, arrived and were soon followed by Latona de Jahn, who worked in the food processing facility, and the three engineers; Brian, Glen and Aaron. *Tuwa* walked in, closed the door, and joined those who had found seats on the floor. *Honovi*, Janey, and Jenny remained standing.

"I'd like everyone to meet my sister, Jenny Spadaro. She's an agent with the FBI at their Phoenix field office."

Jenny smiled, cleared her throat, and took a deep breath.

"I welcome all of you here. We have a limited amount of time before

I must return, so let's get down to it right away.

The basic plan is for the door in the wall by the Jump Gate to be blown open simultaneously with all of the lights in the base going out. Colonel Jason King's ship will have landed, and he and his men intend to disable the guards when the landing platform reaches the bottom. When the door is blown open, an FBI SWAT team will rush through the Jump Gate and, with your help, overpower the guards. We want to seal off any remaining bad guys inside the administration center. Then about seven hundred people will ride up on the platform to Jason's ship above, while around three hundred people will go through the Jump Gate. Please ask me any questions you have, and together we'll start to figure things out."

Latona de Jahn raised her hand.

"How are we supposed to over-power the guards?"

Jenny zipped open her duffel bag and laid the contents on the floor.

"I couldn't bring a lot, but this ought to be enough until the main force arrives. The most important item is called a C.A.V.E.S. Could you show it to everyone, Janey?"

Janey held it in front of her.

"This is a secure communications device," said Jenny. "My sister will be able to talk directly to Jason King on a secure channel, and that will be a great help in making the escape successful."

"Does anyone know what the security guards have as weapons?" asked Jenny.

"All I've ever seen are revolvers on a belt like the one I carry," said *Tuwa.* "I really don't think there are any heavier weapons."

"Good," said Jenny. "How does everyone feel about actually having to shoot the guards?"

There was a moment of silence, which soon broke into many individual conversations.

"Look," said Latona de Jahn, "these people snatched us right out of our lives. It's too bad for them if we have to do whatever we can to get out of here. I want to go home. I'd shoot at them."

There were murmurs of agreement from everyone present.

"I'd shoot one of them for a beer." commented John Spencer, drawing lots of laughter and applause. "I can't tell you how much I'd like one now."

"Okay,' said *Honovi*. "Let's try to see if we can ask some more questions and get answers. My question is, how are we going to tell almost a thousand people that there's an escape attempt underway and that they should all be ready to grab some things and leave the base at a moment's notice?"

"Good question," said Sharon. "While I can't see anyone wanting to warn the Dryer's, it's just possible that some people like it here enough to want to stay and would be against an attempt to escape."

"People will only be able to bring whatever they can carry," remarked Jenny. "They won't have much time."

"Well, how would you feel if suddenly all the lights went out and you heard explosions and gunfire?" asked *Tuwa*. "I think we must have a number of people in each complex, the Eco Farm, engineering, food processing facility, and the hospital to warn everyone. Maybe we can let them know what's going to occur ten minutes before so as not to jeopardize the escape. What do you think?"

"Won't that cause people to panic and rush to their apartments?" asked Annie O'Neal.

"You're right," Janey said. "I guess we'll have to figure something out. Could we somehow get into the administrative center and make an announcement on the public address system?"

"Possibly," said *Tuwa*. "The P.A. system is in a room to the right of the front door. It would be risky, but as a guard maybe I can get into the room and lock the door. Maybe someone else could hold off the guards while I make the P.A. announcement."

"I was in the Marines with *Tuwa* and I volunteer," said John Spencer.

Janey turned to Glen, Brian, and

Aaron and asked them to explain how the lights would go out all over the base. Then she shook her head.

"That means we'd have to somehow get into the P.A. room and make the announcement, then blow the steel door, and shut off the electricity," said Janey.

"This is getting complicated," said Jenny. 'Let's take a break for five minutes and then get back to it."

Janey re-filled the chips and salsa and brought out more bottles of water.

Jenny went out onto the deck, and Sharon followed her.

"Thank you for being a good friend to my sister," Jenny said. "I can't imagine what it must have been like for her at first."

"My pleasure. She's returned the favor to me. Both of us will do everything we can to get out of here."

"Safely, please", said Jenny.

"Of course."

"She's adjusted well. Better than me when I first got here," said Sharon. "Her meeting *Honovi* has been a good thing for both of them. Do you really think we can pull this off?"

"Being able to talk directly to Jason will be vital. I've been thinking hard, and I've come up with a plan."

"Sounds good."

The two women went back inside.

When everyone had returned, Jenny announced that she'd figured it out.

"Maybe Jason can let Janey know on the C.A.V.E.S. that he and his crew have arrived on the platform and overpowered the guards. Then she'll ask the three engineers here to give her fifteen minutes to walk back across the park and tell *Tuwa*, along with John, to get into the P.A. room to make the general announcement. As soon as the engineers hear it, they can put the reactor on standby. All the lights will go out, and *Honovi* can blow open the door for the SWAT team."

"That will work," said *Honovi.*

"Once the base is secured

and the lights come back on, we can proceed to have an orderly evacuation. We have to figure out who goes on the ship and who goes through the Jump Gate," said Janey. "We only have a day and a half from now, so let's assign positions and responsibilities when we meet here tomorrow at the same time."

After everyone had left, Janey handed her sister a wide-brimmed hat. Jenny glanced down at her watch.

"I must return to the gate in twenty minutes", she said.

"*Tuwa* will be there to open it for you," said Janey. "The hat should help to disguise you. I wear it often."

The three of them caught up on

each other's lives. Jenny told them about how and why she had first met Marc Prentis; she also described their vision of Mother Mary, and how Dr. *Louis Carillos* had brought them the golden disc. She made it clear that the three of them were going to go to *Rennes le Chateau* through a Star Door near First Mesa and then end up in Avignon. She explained the task set by The Father and spelled out exactly what they intended to do.

Janey was stunned by what Jenny told her. She shook her head a few times.

"Oh, my God. Can you do it?"

"We have the help of Our Lady. Yes, I believe we can."

Then it was time for her to leave.

Tuwa was waiting as Jenny approached. He quickly opened the steel door with his remote control. When Jenny walked through, he closed it behind her and reset the metal bar, the inside of which fell into place with a thud.

Jenny walked straight ahead and stepped into the Jump Gate. Once more she felt like she was falling fast, then like she was moving very slowly and with great resistance. Then she found herself standing on the platform inside Isis Temple.

"Nice hat," remarked James.

She walked up to Marc and hugged him. They kissed passionately. Then Jenny shook hands with *Louis* and nodded at Mike O'Brien, who gave her a salute and smiled. Jenny smiled back and returned the salute.

"Let's fly the helicopters back to our FBI office in Phoenix for your debriefing," said James.

"Okay," said Jenny. "I have lots of important info to share, so let's get the heck out of this creepy place."

KEAMS CANYON, ARIZONA

"Are you ready for what's ahead?" asked Marc.

Jenny and *Louis* nodded.

"I must call my wife and son before we leave," said *Louis*.

"You can use the cell phone in my bedroom," offered Marc.

"Gracias."

Louis waited for the international call to go through and heard *Arturo* answer.

"Arturo? Como esta ustedes?"

"Padre?"

"Father?"

"Yes."

"Si."

"Mother and I have been beside ourselves with worry. The police have searched the entire house and are now looking everywhere for you."

"Madre y he estado junto a nosotros con la preocupación. La policía se revisaron toda la casa y ahora están buscando por todas partes".

Louis realized that the phone was probably bugged.

"I can't tell you how good it is to hear your voice, *Arturo*. Did you pass your entrance exams?"

"No puedo decirles lo bueno que es escuchar tu voz, Arturo. Le hizo pasar sus exámenes de ingreso?".

"Yes, I did. Where are you, Father?"

"Sí, yo lo hice. ¿Dónde estás, Padre"?

"I cannot tell you. The police are listening. Know that I love you and that everything will be okay."

"No puedo decirle a usted. La policía está escuchando. Sabes que te amo y que todo va a estar bien".

"How can you say that? The comet

is going to hit the Earth and kill us all!"

"*¿Cómo puedes decir eso? El cometa se va a golpear la Tierra y matar a todos nosotros!*".

"Not if my friends and I can help it, *Arturo*. Now, put your mother on the phone."

"*No si mis amigos y yo puedo ayudar, Arturo. Ahora, poner a su madre en el teléfono*".

"*Louis*? I am so mad at you! Where are you? Why did you leave? Come home. When the comet hits, I want us to die in each other's arms."

"*Louis? Estoy tan enojado en usted! ¿Dónde se encuentra? ¿Por qué dejar? Llegado a casa. Cuando el cometa hits quiero morir en cada uno de los brazos de otra".*

"We're not going to die. I insist that you have faith. I love you, *Rosa*, and I give you my word that I'll see you again soon. I have to go."

"No vamos a morir. Insisto en que usted tiene fe. Te amo, Rosa, y te doy mi palabra de que te volveré a ver pronto. Tengo que ir".

Louis reluctantly ended the call. He joined Marc and Jenny in the living room and sat down in a chair.

"Today's Friday," said Marc. "We're about to use the Star Door to go to France. How do you feel? Personally, I'm kind of nervous. And, even though I know we have The Blessed Virgin on our side, I still don't know how we're supposed to get the golden disc on the hand of Her statue in Avignon. I guess we have to have faith."

Louis nodded.

"I have faith. We have Our Lady."

"Plus," added Jenny, "we have me."

Marc laughed, and *Louis* smiled.

Two pickup trucks pulled up in front of Marc's house, and *Cheveyo* got out of one and approached them.

"Ready?"

"We're ready," said Marc. "Let's go."

They followed the other two trucks out to Steamboat Canyon and drove through billowing clouds of red dust.

Jenny turned on the radio and heard an old Beatle's song playing. She'd just begun to sing along when the song abruptly ended. There was static followed by a long silence. Then a man's voice began to speak in a firm and strong voice.

"This is a message from The President of the United States.
To my fellow Americans and to all citizens of the world: The comet, which can now be seen in daytime skies, will not, I repeat, not miss Earth. I urge you to make peace with and pray to whatever God you worship and extend your love to all of your friends and your families. Scientists expect a direct impact with

our planet within the next five days. May God bless you all."

Marc's truck bumped and ground along the dusty, dirt road for a quarter of a mile with the windshield wipers on. He parked next to the other two trucks.

"Where are Robert and Tewa?" asked Jenny as she coughed.

"At work and school," answered *Cheveyo*. "We have no time to waste. Let's get going."

The group approached the large sandstone outcrop. *Cheveyo, Ahote, Pavati, and Mongwau* cleared the dry mesquite tree branches away from the tunnel entrance, and everyone crawled through. They stood up on the other side, walked through the narrow corridor between sheer, red rock walls, and stood as a group in front of the Star Door. Marc held the golden disc in his right hand and looked at the faces of the ten elders. He saw compassion in their eyes. *Honaw* took a step forward and looked directly at Marc, Jenny, and *Louis*. He held both of his hands over his heart and spoke.

"There is a concept in our Hopi world vision that defines our people, and that concept is balance. And the world has become unbalanced. So *Taiowa*, the Creator God, has decided to end *Tuwaqachi*, the fourth world, but has given us a chance. All of us elders, and the three of you, are strong hearted people who know the true path and walk with love, strength, and balance. Go forward now with the Mother Spirit by your side and successfully complete the task set by *Taiowa*. Go through the Great Spirit Gateway. The close brush with fire and death will serve to renew and purify us, and all the people of our planet will then find that their hearts and minds have opened. United, all of us together will experience the pure golden light of a new day on Earth. Go now, my children. Go with courage, love, and faith."

Louis marveled at the two butterflies etched into the rock walls on either side of the outline of the doorway. He noticed the round indentation on the ledge to the right.

Marc took a step forward. He inhaled deeply and slowly let it out.

"Ready?"

Jenny and *Louis* nodded.

"Hold hands," he said.

Jenny stood between the two men. She took hold of *Louis's* right hand and Marc's left. The golden disc was set in the indentation. The three of them walked straight ahead.

The elders all stepped back as a brilliant, electric-blue light burst forth from the doorway. *Cheveyo* saw Marc's right hand reach out and take the golden disc just before he and the others vanished. Then the light faded, and the rock wall returned to normal.

Jenny held tightly onto Marc's and *Louis's* hands. Like the Jump Gate in the Grand Canyon, she felt a rush of air taking hold of her body, and she began to accelerate and move rapidly through grayness. She was surrounded by a humming and whistling sound, and a wave of fear seized her. Soon she began to slow down and met a resistance, which was like moving through thick syrup. Then the similarity with that of the Jump Gate at Isis Temple ended as she began to speed up again. The sounds stopped, and her fear vanished as she burst forth into jet-black space sprinkled with countless stars of every color, spiraling galaxies, and vast nebular clouds in a myriad of brilliant hues expanding in every direction as far as she could see. Jenny gasped at the unfathomable beauty of it all.

Louis had a strong feeling of fear as he fought against and through a thick gray cloud which enveloped him. The fear was soon replaced by the thrill of excitement as he found himself surrounded by star-studded space. He noticed that the whistling and humming sounds had ceased. He floated in the vacuum, holding hands with Marc and Jenny, and found that he was somehow able to breathe normally. *Louis* felt compelled to turn his head and look to his left. Around him were the outer planets of the solar system. He felt tears run down his cheeks.

Marc was freed from squirming through a gray cloud of molasses and shot out into black space and millions of bright stars. He could breathe and the sounds had stopped. He held onto Jenny's right hand and turned his head to look behind him. His mouth opened wide as he recognized the Andromeda galaxy. To his left were Uranus and Neptune, and there, beyond them in the distance, was Pluto. He glanced around him and was able to identify the Pleiades, Altair, Vega, Sirius, Orion, and Aldebaran mostly because he'd spent many nights out in the Arizona desert with his telescope.

The sounds started once more, and the three of them began to quickly accelerate. Their speed increased as they moved downward. Soon they swept past the rings of Saturn and on past Jupiter. Within minutes they flew by Mars and then the moon. They had the extreme pleasure of seeing the full Earth from a distance.

As they grew closer, their speed began to noticeably decrease, and they headed toward the continent of Europe. They descended over Spain and then southern France. As they continued their descent, they perceived what looked like an intense, brilliantly lit, electric-blue doorway directly below them, and they realized they were headed straight for it.

CHAPTER NINE

Rennes Le Chateau, France

Marc, hand in hand with Jenny and *Louis*, felt a force push them through the blue-lit doorway. The light vanished as they stepped forward onto a semicircular platform with three stairs leading down into what looked like a medieval period chamber. Moss and lichen grew between the cracks of large gray stones beneath their feet. Jenny looked up to see that they stood under an archway. Across the chamber, four small rectangular windows were arranged along the top of the far wall and dimly lit the room. She turned around. The blue-lit doorway from which they had entered was now a solid stone wall with a door deeply carved into it.

She looked for and found the round indentation on the right side. Jenny walked down the three stone steps and turned around once again. She raised her right arm and pointed up.

"Look! Unicorns!"

Marc and *Louis* joined her. On either side of the archway were the head and front legs of two unicorns, who faced one another with their single horns jutting into the air.

Louis brushed cobwebs away as

he turned and looked across the chamber toward a massive wooden door, which stood on the far side of the room.

"It looks like that is the way out," he said and began to walk toward it. He stopped. "I can hear the sound of many voices on the other side of this door, but they are speaking in French, which I do not understand. What are they saying?"

The three of them climbed up three gray, ancient stone stairs. Jenny cupped her hand to her right ear and leaned against the door.

"They are praying."

Louis reached for the ornate metal door latch, which gave way in his hand and fell to the floor in pieces.

"Great!" said Jenny. "Now how do we get the door open?"

Marc carefully laid the golden disc on the second stair.

"Come on. Let's see if we can find something."

The three of them explored every inch of the chamber. In one dark corner, hidden behind a thick wall of cobwebs, they discovered an assortment of garden tools. Marc found a long metal stake and with great effort used it to pry three rusted metal hinges off the door. When the last one gave way, he and *Louis* strained and pushed against the massive door with all their strength. The right side of the door splintered, gave way, and fell forward. The wooden door landed with a loud crash and slid down three stone stairs on the outside startling a large group of people.

The three of them walked out into bright sunlight, which dazzled and blinded them. Marc held the golden disc up and used it to shield his eyes. Jenny and *Louis* put their hands over their faces to block the light, found their sunglasses, and put them on. They stood before the crowd and felt confused and very disoriented. Dozens of people were either standing or sitting in chairs and filled a large courtyard outside what appeared to be the entrance to a chapel on the other side. The crowd stared at them in great surprise. Then an older woman approached them and looked closely at Jenny.

"Jenny Spadaro? What are you doing here? Where did you just come from?"

"Jenny Spadaro? Que faites-vous ici ? D'où êtes-vous juste venus?"

"Viviane d'Aqs? Oh, My God! I can't believe that you are here!"

"Viviane d'Aqs? *Oh, mon Dieu! Je ne peux pas croire que vous n'êtes ici !"*

"I can't believe that this is really happening! That door has been closed for hundreds of years!"

"Je ne peux pas croire que ceci arrive vraiment ! Cette porte a été

fermée pendant des centaines d'années."

"Yes, *Viviane*. It is really me. My two friends and I must speak with you immediately."

"Oui, Viviane. C'est vraiment moi. Mes deux amis et je dois paler avec vous immédiatement." Viviane decided to speak only in English.

"I retired from the DST three years ago and volunteered as a guide here at Rennes le Chateau. The main chapel is filled to capacity, so all of these people you see must pray outside, and I am tending to their needs."

"May I introduce you to my companions?" asked Jenny. "This

is Dr. Marc Prentis and Dr. *Louis Carillos*."

Viviane shook their hands.

"I'll arrange for someone to fill in for me. Then I suggest that we all go back to my house in Lavaldieu, where we can relax and I can hear how you came through that door and the rest of what must be a truly amazing and incredible story."

SUB ROSA BASE, PHOBOS, MARS

The members of the escape plan met in Janey's apartment on Friday at five o'clock. She typed the secure channel's frequency numbers into the C.A.V.E.S.'s key board, breathed in deeply, and waited.

"Janey? This is Colonel Jason King. Can you hear me?"

Janey and everyone else in the room sighed with relief.

"Yes, Jason, I can hear you."

"My ship is less than one day out from Sub Rosa. Estimated time of arrival is tomorrow, Saturday, at two o'clock in the afternoon."

"Our plan has to be exactly timed. Call me as soon as you land. Then, and this is vital, Jason, call me again when you reach the bottom and your men overpower the guards. That will be our sign to take over the P.A. room, make an announcement, turn out all the lights, and blow open the armored door."

"Okay, I got it."

Janey addressed those present.

"How many of you have military or police weapons experience, please?"

"John Spencer, I served with the U.S. Marines."

"Annie O' Neal, U.S. Air Force, 82nd Airborne."

"Steve Peterson, I was also in the U.S. Marines."

Tuwa said he'd also been in the U.S. Marines. He and John had been in the same unit, and they'd become good friends. They gave each other salutes.

Honovi explained his expertise with C-4 explosives. Jimmy Jaffe, the electrician, had been an officer with the Tucson Police, and Donna

Bailey had been a nurse with the U.S. Army in Vietnam.

"We've got two machine guns and three revolvers with plenty of ammo clips for all of them, plus five knives and six tactical LED flashlights."

The weapons were distributed.

One machine gun went to John Spencer, and *Tuwa* got an LED light. Steve Peterson got the other machine gun. He was to accompany *Honovi*. Annie O'Neal, Jimmy Jaffe, and Donna Bailey each got revolvers and LED flashlights. Knives went to Janey, Jamie Glasgow, Annie O'Neal, and *Honovi,* who got also got an LED flashlight.

"There's one knife left," said Janey.

"I'll take it," said Latona de Jahn.

Janey handed it to her.

"I'm going to assign a position for the three of you with revolvers and LED flashlights," Janey said. "When you hear the public address, Annie, be standing outside the apartment complexes. Jimmy, stand outside the Eco Farm along with Jamie Glasgow, and Donna, you stand outside of the food processing facility. Stop anyone who tries to leave those places and be prepared to use your weapons against any security guards."

All three nodded their consent.

"We'll meet here at one o'clock sharp during the normal work lunch-time," said Janey. "Everything happens tomorrow when Jason's ship lands. Till then, keep the escape plan quiet and to yourselves."

LAVALDIEU, FRANCE

Viviane drove them to her home in *Lavaldieu,* which was less than ten minutes from *Rennes le Chateau.* The area is a country hamlet with organic gardens and horse pastures. It dates back to megalithic times and contains the vaulted foundations of an eleventh century church built by the Knights Templar.

Jenny recognized the two-story, beige house with white doors and forest green shutters as they pulled into the wide driveway beside two other cars. *Viviane* opened the front door, and they entered. Three men were watching the news on television, and their faces were glum.

"What's wrong?" asked *Viviane*.

"We just heard from the U.S. President. He said that all of us may as well kiss our *derrière's au revoir*," said *Bastien*.

Viviane fought to hold back her tears and composed herself.

"May I introduce my three dear friends? Dr. Marc Prentis and Jenny Spadaro from America. Dr. *Louis Carillos* is from Peru. *Bastien*, do you remember Jenny? We both attended her late husband's funeral.

Bastien nodded.

"These are my two sons, *Jacques* and *Jean-Luc*. My friends wish to tell us all an amazing story. Let's go out to the backyard. *Bastien*, help me get some drinks and refreshments. Then would you please show our guests where the bathrooms are and accompany them outside?"

Jenny stepped out the back door and saw a small green building with an overhanging roof. Inside were chairs, along with a sink and refrigerator. She sat outside at a long table in the sun and was soon joined by the others. Sunglasses covered her eyes, which were still light sensitive. She drank a glass of iced tea and made a sandwich of bread and cheese. The others did the same.

Jenny waited till they had satisfied their thirst and hunger, smiled, and began to speak. With many interjections from Marc and *Louis*, she relayed their entire story from the beginning. *Viviane's* face showed both surprise and astonishment when Jenny spoke of the vision of Mother Mary in the church and the task set by The Father. *Louis* told of having had his own vision of Her in the cathedral in Cusco resulting in his bringing the golden disc to Marc and Jenny. At this point, Marc hefted the disc off the table and passed it to *Viviane* who examined it and handed it to *Bastien*.

"Somehow we must get the golden disc to Avignon and place it on top of the left hand of the statue to prevent the comet from destroying Earth. Can you help us?" asked Jenny.

"*Oui.*" said *Viviane* and nodded.

"We must get there by tomorrow. How far is it from here?" asked Marc.

"Three hours drive," said *Bastien.* "But I am a pilot, and I will fly us there in my Cessna Skyhawk R. The flight will take about forty-five minutes."

"How will you be able to place the golden disc on the statue's hand?" asked *Jean-Luc.* "It is very high on the roof of the cathedral."

"We don't know," said *Louis.*

"I have a friend in Avignon named *Renard,*" said *Bastien.* "He has a helicopter tour business. I will call him and explain the urgency of the situation. Perhaps you can be lowered by a rope ladder and place the disc on the statue's hand."

"That sounds dangerous," commented *Jacques*. *Jean-Luc* nodded.

"The danger is expected," said Jenny, "and I'm ready to face it."

"There are bad people who will do everything they can to stop us," said Marc. "They will be taken to Phobos soon, and the rest of us will be left to die when the comet strikes."

"I will come along with you and do whatever I can," said *Viviane*. My son, *Jacques*, is a military helicopter pilot, and *Jean-Luc* flies a Mirage fighter jet. Both are in the French Air Force and stationed in *Orange* at *Arienne* Air Base 115, which is sixteen miles north of Avignon."

"We will both help you," said *Jacques*. "If there are bad people who try to stop you, we will take care of them."

Jean-Luc nodded in agreement. Jenny and *Louis* smiled, and Marc shook their hands.

"I am moved by your visions of Mother Mary," said *Viviane*, "I have a strong connection to Her and a special ancient family bond with Mary Magdalene."

"Really?" said *Louis*. "Would you please tell us about it?"

Viviane began to speak, and Jenny held up her hand.

"I have to do something first. What time is it right now?"

"Four thirty," answered *Viviane*.

Jenny quickly calculated the time difference.

"It's seven thirty a.m. in Phoenix. I have to call my Special Agent in Charge. He always gets to the office early."

"You have a long distance call from Europe on line two," said his secretary.

James picked up the phone.

"Agent Spadaro reporting, sir. We safely arrived in France and are preparing to go to Avignon tomorrow morning. I know you will find this hard to believe, sir, but the first person we met was a friend and former instructor of mine at Quantico, *Viviane d'Aqs*. We are currently at her home, which is near *Rennes le Chateau.*"

"Wasn't she a martial arts teacher and an agent with the DST?"

"Yes. I took classes from her."

"So did I. She was tough!"

Jenny laughed.

"Her two sons are French Air Force jet and helicopter pilots and have agreed to assist us in the event that the bad guys show up. *Viviane's* husband will fly us to Avignon, where he has a friend who runs a helicopter tour business. We hope he will take us to the statue of Mother Mary."

"I will keep you in my thoughts and pray for your success. Stay in touch."

"Thank you. God bless you, sir."
Jenny ended the call.

The food and late afternoon sun
had a calming effect on the three of
them after their journey through the
Star Door. *Louis* looked at *Viviane*.

"I'm very interested in your family
connection to Mary Magdalene.
Would you kindly tell us about it?"

"What I am about to relate," said
Viviane, "is very controversial and
essentially unproven."

"Please continue," said Jenny. "I
really like controversy!"

Everyone laughed aloud and then
quieted.

"My distant ancestors came from
Dax in *Aix-en-Provence*, west of
Avignon and twenty miles north of

Marseille. Mary Magdalene was pregnant when Jesus was crucified. Mary was from the tribe of Benjamin, and Jesus was from the House of *Judah* of King David. Of course, there is no proof that she and Jesus were intimate partners or married to one another. But, if she was in fact the bearer of a child, and Jesus was the father, then that child was of a royal bloodline. The Jewish *Sanhedrin* Council that saw to it that Jesus was tried and executed viewed Mary Magdalene and all the followers of Jesus as a great threat and began to persecute them. For the safety of her child, she and many others fled by sea to *Gaul*, the ancient name of France. There they found safe refuge with the Jewish community, and she gave birth to a daughter named *Thamar.*"

"So what is your family connection to Mary Magdalene?" asked Marc.

"I'm getting to that."

Jean-Luc, will you please bring us some more iced tea?" said *Viviane*.

She then continued.

"Mary Magdalene lived and preached throughout southern France. Her daughter, *Thamar*, grew into a lovely woman, who met a man and married him when she was in her mid-twenties. Her husband's name was *Guillard d'Acqs*. He was from *Dax,* near *Acque Sextlae*. There was a hot springs near there known as *Aix,* or *Acqs*, from which his name was derived. *Acqs* is a medieval form of Latin, *aquae*, or waters."

Viviane paused to drink some tea and eat some more bread and cheese. The others followed suit.

"What became of Mother Mary after the crucifixion?" asked *Louis*.

"While there are no records, it has long been thought that she and Joseph of *Arimathea* traveled to the port city of *Ephesus* in modern Turkey, where they lived out the remainder of their lives."

"What happened to Mary Magdalene?" asked *Louis*.

"She lived in a cave grotto to an old age. She eventually passed on and is buried in a tomb near the sea in *Provence*."

"What happened to *Thamar* and her husband?" asked Jenny.

"There were those who wished to put an end to the royal bloodline, and *Guillard* and *Thamar's* lives were in constant danger. They were carefully watched and closely guarded by the Jewish community. Eventually, their offspring were raised incognito in France and came under the protection of the Knights Templar. In the fifth century, Christ's bloodline intermarried with the French royal bloodline, and they then became known as the *Merovingians,* who claimed to be, like Jesus, of the house and royal lineage of the

Bible's King David. They produced famous kings like *Clovis, Dagobert* and *Childeric. Clovis,* was the first king of the Franks to unite all the Frankish tribes under one ruler and is considered to have been the founder of the *Merovingian* dynasty. The word *merovingian* can be broken down into *mer* and *vin* or 'Mary and wine'. The line of descent from Jesus and Mary Magdalene is known as the *Spirit of Aix*, or the Family of Waters, which became the House of *d'Acqs*. Somehow, over the many centuries, the letter *c* got dropped, and that explains my family connection and the reason why I have always insisted on keeping my maiden name, *d'Aqs*."

She glanced over at *Bastien* who smiled broadly, exaggeratedly shrugged his shoulders, and made a funny face. Everyone laughed.

"On a more serious note, we should count on meeting resistance," said Jenny, "and we are unarmed."

Bastien nodded.

"Follow me, please."

"Suivez-moi, s'il vous plait."

Bastien used a key to unlock a door, and they descended a flight of stairs to a basement. *Viviane* then used another key and opened the bottom and middle locks of a solid-looking wood and steel door. *Bastien* then used his key on the upper lock. He leaned heavily against the door and shoved it open.

Jenny and the others stood in a storage room lined with shelves. There was a rectangular table in the center. One wall consisted entirely of three glass cases. One case contained two sub-machine guns. The middle case had three semi-automatic rifles, and the last glass case had a number of revolvers.

Again, *Bastien* and *Viviane* used separate keys to open the cases. She carefully unstrapped two machine guns and laid the three semi-automatic rifles on the table along with the revolvers.

"The boxes on the shelves contain ammunition for all of the weapons," said *Viviane*. She lifted a compact machine gun from the table. "This is my favorite. It's an Italian Beretta PM 12S, 9x9mm and can fire up to forty rounds before reloading."

"I prefer the *Ruger Mousqueton* AMD Mini 14 used by the French police," said *Bastien*. "It has a wooden stock and fires up to twenty rounds."

"What are the rifles?" asked Jenny.

"These are the standard weapon used by NATO forces and are 9mm 5.56 caliber automatic rifles that will fire up to twenty rounds," answered *Viviane*.

"And the revolvers?" asked Marc.

"Ahh, they are SP 2022's used by the French police," said *Bastien*. "They are 9x19mm, with a snub nose barrel, and they also fire up to twelve rounds."

"Well," commented Jenny, "if I'm going to be hanging from a rope ladder, I think a revolver would be better suited than a rifle."

"I agree," said Marc.

"We will provide you with chest holsters," said *Viviane*. She then turned toward *Louis*.

"What about you, my dear?"

"I am a man of peace and will count on Our Lady to protect me and keep me safe from any harm."

"As you wish," said *Viviane*. "But *this* lady will keep her eyes on you."

"*Gracias*", said *Louis*.

Bastien and *Viviane* distributed plenty of ammunition for each of the weapons and placed the revolvers inside the holsters. They left everything on the table and exited the room. *Bastien* and *Viviane* locked the door, and everyone went upstairs where *Jacques* and *Jean-Luc* were preparing to drive to the air base.

"If *Renard* agrees to help us, be sure to call me at least twenty minutes before you lift off for Avignon," said *Jacques*. "That will give me just enough time to warm up my helicopter and *Jean-Luc* his jet and fly from our base to the cathedral, okay?"

"Okay," answered *Viviane*.

"We must leave now as the drive back to our base takes around three hours. We wish you success tomorrow, and we will be there to assist you," said *Jean-Luc.*

Viviane took Marc, Jenny and *Louis* to their guest rooms.

"Dinner will be ready in an hour. I suggest that you get some rest."

Jacques and *Jean-Luc* said goodbye to their parents and left. *Bastien* placed a call to his friend *Renard* in Avignon. After a brief explanation and a number of questions he answered, *Renard* agreed to fly them in his helicopter.

"Be at my office by the airfield no later than ten a.m. *Au revoir.*"

"Merci beaucoup."

"I sense that *Louis* would greatly

appreciate some company," Jenny said as she and Marc embraced.

"Okay, let's go see him."

They knocked on his door, and *Louis* opened it. His face revealed his anxiety.

"We thought we'd like to hang out with you for a while, okay?" said Marc.

Louis nodded.

"I'm glad you're here. I'm a man of faith, but I must admit that I'm feeling very nervous."

"I felt that you needed some reassuring," said Jenny as she and Marc sat on two chairs. *Louis* sat on the bed. "Look, we're in this together. You can help us get the disc onto the statue's hand."

"How? I choose not to have a weapon. How can I help?"

"I can't answer that question." said Marc.

"I will pray hard for you both."

"That ought to help a lot," said Jenny sincerely.

"Look, we don't know what to expect," said Marc "But I believe there will be those who will try to stop us. *Viviane* is an expert in all martial arts. We are well armed. And we have Our Lady, too."

"Yes, and my faith is strong," affirmed *Louis*. "I will pray with all my might. I give you my word."

"We know we can count on you," said Marc.

He and Jenny stood and each

gave him a hug. Then they returned to their room. *Viviane* knocked on their door soon after to announce that dinner was ready.

The five of them sat at the dining room table, and *Bastien* served the main course, which was *ratatouille*; a vegetarian dish with eggplant, onions, zucchini, and tomatoes. Jenny held Marc's hand under the table, while *Viviane* poured the wine and proposed a toast.

"Here's to our successful completion of the task set by The Father. Our Lady is at our side, and I know in my heart that we will prevail."

All clinked their glasses and drank.

The mood, which had been somber, lightened considerably.

"We must leave here for our local airport no later than nine in the morning," said *Bastien*. "Our flight should take about forty-five minutes, and *Renard* will be waiting for us in Avignon. The helicopter ride to the cathedral takes just about seven minutes."

"I will call *Jean-Luc* and *Jacques* as soon as we land in Avignon," added *Viviane*. "I'll let them know *Renard* will assist us in his helicopter."

"How do you know *Renard*?" asked Jenny.

"We were in the French Air Force together, assigned to NATO, and served in the Rapid Reaction Corps, which is located in *Lille*, France, on the north-western border with Belgium. I cannot discuss what we did there, you understand. I must admit that I am quite proud to see that my two sons are following in my footsteps."

Marc and *Louis* finished their meals. Jenny soon joined the two of them and helped wash and dry the dishes. When they were done, everyone wished one another a good night. *Louis* returned to his room and closed the door. Jenny wrapped her arms around Marc as they stood outside their room in the hallway. They entered the room and undressed. Jenny took his hand and led him to the bed, where they made love before falling into a deep sleep.

CHAPTER TEN

Lavaldieu, France

Marc and Jenny awoke to four rapid knocks on the door.

"Good day! Breakfast is ready. Please join us quickly," announced *Viviane* in a loud voice.

"Bon jour ! Le petit-déjeuner est prêt. Veuillez nous rejoindre rapidement."

They walked downstairs to find a table laden with bowls of fresh fruit, yogurt, croissants, scrambled eggs, orange juice, and coffee.

"We will need a good meal to give us maximum energy," said *Viviane*.

"I would like to offer a prayer before we eat," said Jenny. "May I?"

"*Oui*," said *Viviane*.

"And I would like to say a prayer, as well," added *Louis*.

Viviane nodded.

"O God, and Our Blessed Mother," began Jenny, "You are the preserver of all life, and the keeper of our lives. We commit ourselves to Your perfect care on the journey that awaits us. We pray for a safe and auspicious journey. Give Your angels charge over us to keep us whole in all our ways. Let no evil befall us. Bless us that we may complete our journey safely and successfully under Your ever watchful care. Amen."

Louis cleared his throat and spoke.

"Blessed Virgin Mary, Your light surrounds us, Your love enfolds us, Your power protects us, and Your presence watches over us. We are always in Your service. Amen."

After breakfast, *Bastien* and Marc wrapped the weapons and ammunition in a large tarp and tied them with bungee cords. They carried them upstairs and loaded them in the car. *Viviane* found space in the trunk for a case of bottled water and a first-aid kit. They drove to the nearby airport and parked near *Bastien's* plane. The place was completely deserted.

"There she is," said *Bastien*. He pointed toward a brightly painted red-and-white plane. "She's a Cessna Skyhawk 172-R with a fuel-injected engine, pilot seat, and four seats for passengers."

Marc and *Viviane* stowed everything in the cargo hold and climbed aboard. Marc sat beside Jenny and *Louis*. *Viviane* sat in the co-pilot seat. *Bastien* revved the engine and ran through a pre-flight check list. Then he tried contacting the control tower, but there was no response. He taxied down the runway and lifted off, and they headed east.

AVIGNON, FRANCE

Jenny looked at the French countryside below as they neared *Montfavet* Public Airport.

"How far is the distance to Avignon from here?"

"About five miles north," answered *Bastien* as he began his descent. He tried to contact the control tower, but there was no answer. The Skyhawk touched down on the runway and taxied toward a hangar at the end. A man stood beside a helicopter and waved at them as the plane came to a stop. The man approached *Bastien's* door when he climbed down, and the two men hugged one another. Jenny saw a tall, well-built, older man with close-cropped, gray hair. He had a neat beard and mustache. He hugged *Viviane* and she introduced him to Marc, *Louis*, and Jenny.

"How long will it take for you to fly us to the cathedral in Avignon?" asked *Viviane*.

"About seven minutes," answered *Renard*. He pointed at the helicopter. "This is my baby. She's a Bell 407GXP with a Rolls-Royce high-performance turbine engine, five club-passenger seats, and she will fly at one hundred and fifty miles per hour."

Viviane called *Jacques* and told him they were at the airport in Avignon and *Renard* would fly them in his helicopter to the cathedral.

Jacques said he would call her once they had taken off and were well on the way. He hoped they would all arrive at the same time.

Renard got his weapon from the cabin. It was an Italian Beretta PM 12S like the one *Viviane* used. He gave her three .50 BMG, forty round clips of hard-core cartridges. They were made of hardened steel, carbide, and tungsten. And they were used to penetrate armor and bullet proof glass. Viviane loaded a clip in her gun and put the other two in her jacket pockets.

"I have a thirty foot rope ladder you can drop when we hover over the statue," said *Renard*. "If some bad guys show up, I can fire from my window, and you can fire from the open doors on either side. Let us pray that your sons arrive in time."

"Oui," said *Bastien* and *Viviane*.

"At least we have a beautiful day," commented Marc.

"Blue skies and a few clouds," said Jenny. "But it's pretty windy."

"We need to give my sons at least twenty minutes before we lift off, " said *Viviane*."

"If this is to be our last day, let's make it a good one!" said *Renard.*

He climbed into the pilot's seat and began to run through his pre-flight check-list, which took ten minutes. *Renard* tried to contact the control tower, but there was no response. He revved the engine, and the blades began to whirl. He waited five more minutes, lifted off, and headed north for Avignon.

AERIENNE AIR BASE 115, FRANCE

Aerienne Airbase 115 is home for the *Escadron de Chasse* (Strike Wing) *"Ille de France,"* operating Mirage 2005 Mk2 jets and Fennec AS550 combat helicopters. The primary mission of the small, single-runway base is to provide general air defense, air policing (interception), and in-flight protection of strategic and conventional strike forces. The base is situated sixteen miles north of Avignon.

The drive from *Lavaldieu* to the

base took a good three hours, and it was nighttime as *Jacques* and *Jean-Luc* approached the guard station. They found it to be empty, and the front barrier gate was wide open. They drove to the barracks, parked, and got their gear out of the car. The entire base around them was dark, but they could see some light coming from within the barracks. They walked in the front door and surprised four men in the lounge area who were watching television.

"What are you doing here?" asked *Jacques* and *Jean-Luc.*

Jules, a pilot, explained that they had no families and that the comet had driven everyone else to be at home with his or her loved one's.

"What are you two doing here?" asked *Gabriel*, an aircraft mechanic. "Don't you have family near *Rennes le Chateau*?"

"Let us get settled first, and then we'll tell you why we're here," said *Jean-Luc*.

They each found an empty room upstairs, unpacked, and returned.

Paul, another mechanic, turned off the television. *Lucien*, a maintenance engineer, looked at them and nodded.

"What we're about to tell you may be hard to believe," said *Jacques*, "but, well, here goes."

He and *Jean-Luc* took turns and described the attempt in the morning to place a golden disc on the left hand of the statue of Mother Mary atop the cathedral in Avignon.

"Our mother and father, along with two Americans, a man from Peru, and a helicopter pilot from Avignon, are all going to try. If they succeed, and this is the hard-to-believe part, the comet is supposed to miss hitting the Earth."

"*Jean-Luc* and I are going to fly there to protect everyone because there are bad people who will probably show up and try to stop them."

The four men sat in stunned silence. Then *Gabriel* spoke firmly.

"If what you say is true, I will help to make ready your jet, *Jean-Luc.*"

"I'll help, too," said *Paul.*

Both *Jules and Lucien* said they would help, as well.

Then the men walked outside and watched the blue-colored comet as it blazed brightly against the night sky.

Jean-Luc used his cell phone in the morning to call his mother.

"We are on the way to Avignon and took off twelve minutes ago. Give us about seven or eight more minutes from right now for us to arrive," said *Jean-Luc.*

"*Reynard* just lifted off. Please hurry. I have a feeling that we'll need your help," said *Viviane.*

THE *PLACE DE L'HORLOGE, AVIGNON,* FRANCE

Jack and Augi walked out of the Hotel *Innova* and strolled over to the *Place de l'Horloge*. They took seats at an outdoor table, and Augi ordered two glasses of wine. The streets were empty and still but for the cooing of pigeons. Jack lifted his glass to take a drink when he heard a sound that caused him to look up. He saw a helicopter hovering near the statue. Augi immediately called *Antoine*.

"We'll be there in five minutes," he said and ended the call.

Jack threw some money on the table, and they both quickly ran toward the cathedral.

NOTRE DAME DE DOMS

Jenny looked out from her window as they approached the city. She took in the scene to the northeast.

"What is the name of the river, and why is half that bridge missing?" she asked *Renard*.

"The river is called the *Rhone,* and the *Pont Saint Benezet* bridge was engulfed by flood-waters sometime in the sixteenth century."

Marc grinned at her.

"Even at a time like this, you're still asking questions!"

Jenny shrugged and laughed aloud along with everyone else.

Renard flew over the city. Below them was a medieval walled complex of buildings he said was called the *Palais des Papes,* or Palace of the Popes, built in the fourteenth century. "And we are now flying over the cathedral *Notre Dame de Doms.*"

"*Oh, Dios mio!* Look at the size of the golden statue of Mother Mary," shouted *Louis* from his seat.

Jack and Augi ran across the street and into the cathedral. The priest, *Pierre Cordonne*, told them the tours had been cancelled. Augi ignored him and walked over to the ornate wooden door. He fired two rounds at the lock and kicked the door wide open.

"Stop! What are you doing?" cried the priest. Jack shot him in the chest, and he toppled over on his back.

"I always wanted to shoot a priest!" exclaimed Jack. "Especially one that was named *Pierre*!"

They raced up the stairs and soon began to slow down since each stairwell had twenty stairs. There were five landings to get to the top or a total of one hundred stairs. Augi and Jack were exhausted when they finally walked onto the roof. They were very disappointed to find that there was only a narrow walkway around all four sides surrounded by a high wall. The statue loomed forty feet above their heads. Three large steps rose above the walkway that served as the foundation for a high tower, on which the statue sat. They walked around the roof and determined that this was as close as they could get. Jack shouted to Augi and pointed up. A helicopter was hovering above the statue. They watched as a long rope ladder was dropped, and two people began to climb down. Both men ran to the northeastern corner of the wall.

"I figure that from here we'll have the best possibility of hitting someone with our revolvers, even though at this distance our chances are pretty slim," said Augi.

Jack nodded and aimed his gun upward at the two people.

THE USS *EXCALIBUR*

Colonel Jason King brought the large triangular ship over the air lock.

"Let's descend slowly, Arnie, and when she sets down, we'll disengage the engines and have a meeting with the crew. Prepare the ship for landing."

Arnie Weber brought the ship down precisely onto the air lock, and Jason shut off the engines. They exited the cabin. Jason carried a cardboard box. They walked down to the cargo hold, where the six crew members were preparing to load pallets onto the platform with forklifts. They stopped what they were doing as the two men approached.

"Let's have a meeting," said

Jason. "You won't need to unload any cargo because, if all goes as planned, this will be our last visit to Sub Rosa. We're going to free all the people here, and I need your help." He opened the cardboard box and removed his C.A.V.E.S. "I've brought along rolls of duct tape and eight M9 Beretta revolvers. I don't want to have to use them unless it's absolutely necessary. Do you understand?"

The six men nodded in agreement.

"We'll overpower the guards when we reach the bottom. Duct-tape their hands behind their backs and try not to hurt anyone. I'm going to get my wife and daughters. Stay here until I return, and then we'll see if our assistance is needed elsewhere."

Arnie spoke to the men. *Kele*, Ben Anderson, Chris, Don, Sam, and Pete listened.

"We're going to help get almost seven hundred people on the ship and fly them out of here. I expect we'll have to fill the platform and make at least two or three trips up to the ship's passenger cabin. Jason and I have stocked lots of food, water, pillows, and blankets in cargo hold four. Be ready to assist the people when they start arriving here."

The men took their revolvers and duct tape. They sat in chairs as the platform began its twenty-minute journey to the bottom.

Jason made a call to Janey on his C.A.V.E.S.

"We have landed and are headed down."

"Thank you," she replied.

There were usually four guards at the checkpoint, but with the reinforcements brought up to the base by the USS *Concord*, there were now two more. Jeff Leonard, the head guard, brought some plastic tubs over and set them down on the table next to the X-ray machine. He always had Colonel King and his crew empty their pockets and then walk through the machine.

Ben Anderson lovingly ran his hand over the revolver. He'd been a Navy Seal on many tours of duty and knew the weapon well. So did *Kele,* who had been in the Marines. The four other men had either been in the armed forces or served as policemen and were familiar with the M9 Beretta. As the platform reached the bottom, they stood as one.

"Okay," said Jason." Follow my lead. "Arnie, walk beside me, and remember, no one gets hurt."

The men walked off the platform and approached the security checkpoint with Jason and Arnie in the lead.

"Hi, Colonel King," said Jeff Leonard. "Welcome back."

Jason reached behind his back, brought out his revolver, and leveled it at Jeff. Arnie and the other men did the same to the other guards.

"Put your hands up in the air and don't move," commanded Jason.

"What are you doing, Colonel King?" asked Jeff.

"We are freeing all the people who have been taken here against their will and bringing them home to Earth."

"What about us?" asked Jeff.

"You can come back with us, but first I need all of you to carefully remove your weapons and place them on the ground in front of you. Move slowly and know we won't hesitate to shoot you."

The guards complied.

Arnie and Ben picked up their six revolvers. The crew members had the guards turn around and heavily duct-taped their wrists together behind them. Then they had them sit down on the ground.

Jason called Janey on his C.A.V.E.S.

"We have successfully subdued the guards. I'm going to get Chloe and my daughters at the hospital. Tell the engineers you and I both need about fifteen minutes. When they hear the public announcement, they can place the nuclear reactor on standby."

"Got it," said Janey.

"Daddy!" shouted Meredith and

Olivia in unison when they saw Jason enter the front of the hospital. Chloe embraced him.

"I've come to bring you back to the ship with me," he told her.

"But I have appointments with patients for the next few hours," she responded.

"You don't anymore. We're rescuing everyone at Sub Rosa, and I need you and the girls to come with me now."

"But what about our things in the apartment?"

"We don't have time. Take whatever you have with you here and hurry."

Chloe grabbed her purse, and she and her daughters followed Jason.

He brought them to the platform, where they saw the guards sitting on the ground and the crew keeping a watchful eye on them. Jason brought them inside, and they sat down in a row of chairs. He went to hold four and rolled a cart back filled with food, water bottles, sweat-shirts for the girls, a jacket for Chloe, blankets, and pillows.

"What's happening, honey?" asked Chloe. "What are these for?"

"If all goes as planned, we can expect the lights in the base to go out soon. We're going to get as many people aboard the ship as possible and head back to Earth. It will take three days and nights, so get as comfortable as you can. We may hear gunfire and explosions. Don't be scared. We'll be okay here. The FBI is sending men to rescue all the people."

Meredith and Olivia seemed ready to cry. Jason hugged and kissed his daughters, then sat down between them. The four of them held hands.

Janey sat at a table with Brian, Glen, and Aaron. The three engineers told her they could allow only twenty minutes before they must power the Stirling reactor back up.

"Okay, just give me fifteen minutes to get across the park. I think Jason King is getting his wife and daughters right now."

"Here's an LED flashlight in case you need it," said Aaron.

Janey shook their hands.

"Be ready to power up the SRG again once you hear the all-clear announcement and then get over to the ship's platform," she said.

The men nodded, and she walked out the door.

Janey carried her C.A.V.E.S. in one hand and checked that her tactical knife was firmly in her left back pocket. About halfway across the park, she stopped to sit down on a bench. She concentrated on an image of her sister and sent her a telepathic message.

"Jason's ship has landed, and his crew has overpowered and tied up

the guards. I'm now on my way to see that the steel door is blown open and the public announcement is made. Know that I love you and have faith in your success."

ADMINISTRATION CENTER
SUB ROSA, PHOBOS

Victor Spoils and Barry Dukov sat and looked up at the wall-sized projection screen along with *Xavier del Mundo* and the Dryer's. They watched as Colonel Jason King's enormous ship settled on the air lock.

"The first half of our friends are now about to be welcomed to their new home at Sub Rosa," said *Xavier.*

"And our son, Brad, has left Earth

and is mid-way to Sub Rosa with the second half," said Michael Dryer.

"Soon all of our friends will be brought here from Earth. When the comet destroys the planet, we will be safe at Sub Rosa," stated Andrea.

Victor and Barry nodded.

Janey reached the other side of the park and found *Tuwa* and John Spencer waiting for her inside the front lobby of Complex E. John held one of the machine guns.

"The engineers are ready to turn out the lights."

They nodded and headed toward the administration center. Janey went up to her apartment to find *Honovi* and Steve Peterson standing in the hallway by her door.

"It's time. Go blow the gate."

She kissed *Honovi* and gave Steve a big hug.

Tuwa and John Spencer stood outside the administration center long enough to make sure no one was entering or leaving the building. Then they quickly walked inside. *Tuwa* opened the door to the public address room on the right, closed it, and locked it. The two men dragged desks and filing cabinets against the back of the door. He turned on the amplifier and sat in front of the microphone.

INSIDE ISIS TEMPLE, GRAND CANYON, ARIZONA

Rows of black-clad, heavily armed, helmeted men stood in the area before the Jump Gate. Captain Michael O'Brien had a force of sixty ready to rush through.

"How will we know when to go?" asked Special Agent in Charge James Cararuscio.

"Instincts, I guess," answered Mike. "I've brought along some C-4 M112 demolition blocks and blasting caps, just in case we need them."

Mike glanced at his watch.

"Two more minutes."

James Cararuscio turned to his Assistant Special Agent in Charge, Fred Turner.

"I must believe our mission will be successful. I want you to connect with FEMA and see to it that they and our agents are ready to assist about three hundred people who will be coming out of the Jump Gate. We need to provide food, sleeping arrangements, and porta-potties for all of them."

'Yes, sir. I will see to it." said Fred.

SUB ROSA, PHOBOS

Hovovi and Steve took the elevator down and headed for the gate. He had the charges in a knapsack, and Steve carried his MTAR-21 machine gun. As they neared the gate area, they saw a guard named Gary walking straight toward them.

"What are you two doing here?"

Then he saw Steve's machine gun and reached for his revolver. Thinking fast, *Honovi* shone his LED flashlight in Gary's face, and Steve fired four rounds into his chest.

"Hurry. Other guards will have heard the shots," said Steve.

Honovi placed the C-4 blocks at the top and bottom of the door and attached the blasting caps.

"Let's stand way back," he said.

The force of the powerful explosion blew the entire door to pieces along with the adjacent walls. The two men stood and waited for the FBI to enter.

ADMINISTRATION CENTER

"What in the heck was that?" shouted Victor Spoils at the sound of the door being blown apart.

"I don't know," said Barry Dukov. "Let's go find out."

Then the two men heard someone's voice speak on the P.A. system.

Tuwa held the microphone and spoke directly into it:

"ATTENTION EVERYONE! ATTENTION EVERYONE!

This is an announcement to all at Sub Rosa. The explosion you've heard is because the armored door leading to the Jump Gate has just been blown wide open. At this moment FBI SWAT teams are entering the base in force to rescue everyone. We will no longer be held prisoners here. Please stay where you are.

REPEAT-DO NOT GO ANYWHERE!

Stay where you are and do not move. Again, stay where you are until you hear the-

ALL CLEAR ANNOUNCEMENT."

The three engineers heard the announcement and placed the Stirling nuclear reactor on standby. Sub Rosa base was plunged into darkness.

"I want everyone to make a big barricade. Drag every desk and table, couches, and chairs in here and turn them on their sides," yelled Victor.

Suddenly all the lights went out.

"There are ten boxes of LED flashlights in the storeroom," shouted Victor to one of his men. "Get some help and pass them out to everyone."

"Go lock the front doors and find something like a chain or ropes to tie them together," Michael Dryer commanded Barry Dukov.

"What about our men outside?" asked Barry. "They can't get in."

"They'll just have to fend for themselves," answered Victor.

Xavier del Mundo ran to the last room in the back of the building and closed the door behind him.

There were forty-eight security guards. They made a wall of overturned furniture that stretched from one side of the building to the other and crouched behind it.

Captain O'Brien gave the order for his men to move forward. He and James led the way. All his men had Heckler & Koch MP5 sub-machine guns; the standard automatic rifle of FBI SWAT teams. They were equipped with a flashlight in front and a red laser-pointer sight, and they fired thirty rounds.

Mike and James entered the Jump Gate. They were surrounded

by grayness and then moved in slow motion. Suddenly they found themselves inside a square area with walls topped with barbed wire. Before them stood the smoking ruins of what had once been the steel door and two men, who quickly made it clear they were both part of the escape committee and introduced themselves.

"The administration center is to our left. That's where most of the bad guys are. Follow us," said *Honovi*.

Captain O'Brien shouted an order to his men as they came out of the Jump Gate.

"Move out."

AVIGNON

Renard hovered about fifteen feet above the statue of Mother Mary as *Louis* looked out his window. He observed the golden-gilded statue below him and saw that Her head was angled downward and that Her eyes were half-closed. The look on Her face was serene, and She was slightly smiling. Both Her left arm and hand were held straight out.

Viviane and *Bastien* unfurled the rope ladder and let it drop down to the middle of the statue. Marc turned around. He had the golden disc in a satchel around his neck, and his revolver was firmly secured in its chest holster. He began to climb down. Jenny was prepared to follow him when she heard her sister's voice in her mind telling her about events at Sub Rosa and expressing her faith in their success.

As she started to climb down, thoughts of the death of her husband, Mitch, entered her mind, but they only steeled her determination to help Marc put the golden disc in place. Below her a flock of pigeons on the left arm of the statue took flight.

Renard opened his window and cradled his machine gun. *Viviane* took up a position in the open door on the left side. *Bastien* stood on the right with his gun ready, while *Louis* remained buckled in his seat and prayed.

Jacques flew fast in his Fennec AS550 C2 helicopter yet couldn't keep up with *Jean-Luc* in his Mirage 2000-5 Mk2 jet, although he was in visual sight of his brother. His helicopter had a wide assortment of weapons including a 20mm GIAT M621 cannon, Herstal twin 7.62mm and 12.7mm machine guns, and 68mm Thales Brandt rockets. He'd always felt confident during the many dangerous missions he had been engaged in.

Jean-Luc saw his brother Jacques' helicopter behind him. The Mirage jet was capable of reaching high supersonic speeds when necessary. If he encountered any bad guys, his jet was equipped with 2x30mm DEFA

554 revolver cannons that fired 125 rounds per gun and both AIM-9 and AIM-54 Sidewinder missiles. He could see the outskirts of Avignon up ahead and called his brother.

"We'll be there in less than three minutes," said Jean-Luc to Jacques. "Fly in ahead of me and gauge the situation while I circle around. Over."

The four Frenchmen grabbed their gear and helmets, and ran out to the two Eurocopter *Tigres*. *Antoine* and *Bertrand* climbed into one, and *Philipe* and *Claude* got into the other. After a brief flight check-list, they both lifted off and headed for the cathedral which was less than two minutes away.

"We will do quick destruction to

whoever is there," said *Antoine*. The *Tigre HAD* was fitted with a GIAT 30mm gun turret, 20mm machine gun cannons, and Mistral air-to-air missiles.

Marc held tightly to the rope ladder as strong gusts of wind rocked him back and forth. He looked up to see alarm on Jenny's face. Ten feet below him was the outstretched arm of the statue, glinting gold in the sunlight. The wind abated long enough for him to climb down another five feet. Marc shook his head because he could swear he'd just seen the statue's right eye wink at him.

He carefully climbed down a few more feet until he was even with

Her hand, unzipped the satchel, and removed the golden disc. Then a strong gust nearly blew him off the rope ladder. Marc held the golden disc firmly against his chest and waited for the wind to lessen.

Viviane looked down at Marc and Jenny as they clung to the ladder, which was buffeted by gusts of wind. *Renard* maintained his position over the statue.

Bastien suddenly shouted.

"Here come the bad guys!"

"Voici venir les méchants!"

Viviane looked back to see two Eurocopter *Tigre*'s approaching.

"Fire at them when they get in range," she yelled. *Renard* rested his weapon against the window frame.

Bastien stood in the open doorway as did *Viviane*. The *Tigre's* fired their machine guns and peppered the right side of *Renard's* helicopter. *Bastien* ducked against the wall.

Viviane frantically called her son, *Jacques*.

"Where are you? We are being fired on. For God's sake, hurry up!"

"Où es-tu? On nous a tiré dessus. Pour l'amour de Dieu, dépêche-toi !"

"I see them ahead of me. Fire back! We're almost there."

"Je les vois devant moi. Fire de retour ! Nous y sommes presque."

He spoke to *Jean-Luc* who made a bee-line for the *Tigres.*

Viviane fired a long burst directly at *Antoine's* helicopter from her side, and *Renard* and *Bastien* did the same. To their surprise, they saw the two copters fly back out of range.

"They are firing armor-piercing bullets at us!" *Antoine* spoke into his headset to *Philipe* in the other helicopter. Back off!"

"Ils sont tiré des balles perforant à nous !" Antoine parlait dans son casque à Philipe dans l'autre hélicoptère. Abandonner!"

He spoke to *Bertrand* and told him to fire a missile, but there was no response. He looked beside him. Bullets had shattered a sizable hole in the front glass on the right side of the cockpit and blown off the top half of *Bertrand's* head.

"Oh, my God!"

"Oh, mon Dieu!"

SUB ROSA BASE, PHOBOS, MARS

Captain Mike O'Brien peered through his binoculars and focused on the two front glass doors of the administration center.

"The doors have been chained together," he said. "I'll need the C-4 and blasting caps I brought. I want a body shield for myself and six men with body shields, three on either side of me, in a staggered phalanx."

Annie O'Neal stood outside of Complex A/B and heard the explosion of the armored door followed by the announcement. Then the lights went out. Janey came running toward her with her LED flashlight. Two security guards ran out of the park. Janey shined her light on them. Annie fired her revolver and shot them both. Then they heard some people out in front of the apartments. Annie and Janey ran with the aid of their LED's and confronted a small group.

"You must get back inside now," shouted Janey. "It's far too dangerous out here. Wait until you hear the all-clear announcement. Then you may come out."

The people obeyed her order.

Jimmy Jaffe was on station in front of the Eco Farm with Jamie Glasgow. They heard the sound of people walking, and Jimmy shone his LED in that direction, revealing a dozen people who had exited the front door.

"All of you must go back inside," shouted Jimmy. "Now!"

Three security guards appeared without warning and ran straight toward them. Jimmy handed his LED to Jamie, who shone it on the guards. He kneeled and fired his revolver, hitting two of them in their mid-sections. The third pulled his revolver and fired once, wounding Jimmy in his right shoulder. He fell to the ground. Jamie quickly threw his knife, which struck the guard in the center of his chest. The group of people stared at them in shock and horror.

"Get back inside right now," Jamie yelled, "and don't come out until we give the all-clear announcement. Move!"

They turned and ran back through the front door. Jamie helped Jimmy onto his feet. He took off his shirt and tied one end around Jimmy's neck, wrapped the other end under his right armpit, and tightly tied the ends.

"Place your left hand over the entrance wound and apply pressure. You're lucky. It looks like the bullet passed clean through you."

Using his LED flashlight, he led him in the direction of the food processing facility, where he knew they had well-equipped medical first aid kits.

Donna Bailey saw them walking toward her. Minutes before she had ordered a group of people who had come out the front door to go back inside.

"Good job on the tourniquet, Jamie.

Let's get Jimmy inside where we can treat him."

AVIGNON

Bullets ricocheted off the statue as Jack and Augi began to fire wildly at the two figures on the rope ladder far above them. One of their bullets grazed Jenny's right arm. She lost her grip on the ladder, cried out in pain, and began to fall. Marc reached out, grabbed her around the waist, and pulled her to safety.

The two men below continued to fire. Marc tried once more to place the golden disc on the statue's hand, but a gust of wind prevented him. A bullet whizzed past. He handed the golden disc to Jenny and removed his revolver from its holster. He sighted and fired down. One of his bullets hit Jack in his upper right arm and shoulder.

More bullets flew past them. They climbed down and used the statue to shield themselves. Jenny held the disc in her left hand. She removed her revolver from its holster, aimed, and fired four rounds. One of them hit Augi squarely in the chest.

"That's for one of you creeps who ran me off the road," she shouted. Then she looked up, crossed herself, and said, "Sorry."

Marc took the golden disc back from Jenny, reached up, and tried to place it on top of the statue's hand. Jack fired a bullet, nicking Marc in his upper left thigh. He grimaced in pain, held onto the disc, and managed to maintain a grip on the ladder.

At that moment, *Philipe* fired a long burst from his 20mm machine gun cannon and punched more holes along the right side of *Renard's* helicopter. *Renard* fired his Beretta PM12s from his window and entirely smashed open *Antoine's* cockpit window.

"Fire a *Mistral* missile at them!" shouted *Philipe* to *Claude*, his co-pilot.

"Un feu de missiles Mistral à eux !"

Claude extended his right hand and poised his index finger directly over the control switch.

"I have them in my sites," said *Jacques*. "They are both within range."

"Take out the one on the left, and I'll get the one on the right," responded *Jean-Luc* as he flew straight at them.

Philipe looked in his rear camera screen and saw a Fennec AS550.

It was the last thing he would ever see. *Jacques* fired a Thales-Brandt rocket, which smashed into the *Tigre*. The helicopter erupted in flames and plummeted to the ground.

"Oh, my God!" cried *Antoine*. *"Oh, mon Dieu!"*

He turned in a desperate attempt to escape as *Jean-Luc* fired a Sidewinder AIM 54 missile from his Mirage jet and destroyed *Antoine's Tigre* in an inferno of fire and black smoke. The helicopter spiraled to the ground and came to rest near the smoldering remains of *Philipe's Tigre*. There were cheers from all those aboard *Renard's* helicopter.

Viviane called her son, *Jean-Luc*.

"You arrived just in time. Thank you!"

"Vous êtes arrivé juste à temps. Je vous remercie!"

SUB ROSA

James Cararuscio watched Captain Mike O'Brien approach the front doors of the administration center. He held his body shield in front of him and had three men holding body shields on either side of him. As Mike began to place the charges, James caught some movement out of the corner of his eye. Two security guards had snuck up on the SWAT team from behind. They began to fire their revolvers. Three bullets hit the SAC's armored

Kevlar vest but failed to penetrate. James aimed his H & K machine gun at the guards and shot both.

Mike and his men quickly stepped backward. The charges went off, and the explosion of the doors echoed throughout the base. The six men with Mike O'Brien tossed smoke grenades through the gaping hole that had been the front entrance, and the SWAT team rushed forward en masse into the administration building.

AVIGNON

Jenny cried tears of relief as she witnessed the destruction of the two helicopters. She looked down at Marc, and her joy was tempered by his face, which revealed his pain. His pants were torn open over his left thigh and stained with blood. He held the golden disc tightly against his chest. Her right arm had a wide path of torn skin across it and was red with blood. She peeked around the statue and saw a man standing below on the roof next to the one she had shot.

Jack looked at the lifeless body of Augi and shouted in rage. He'd taken a bullet in his upper right arm and shoulder, and despite his intense pain, he began to fire once more at the two people above him.

Jenny held onto the rope and moved her body from behind the side of the statue. She aimed her revolver and fired five rounds. One bullet struck the man directly in the chest, and he fell onto the roof.

"And that's for the second crap face that ran me off the road," said Jenny. Then she looked up, crossed herself, and said, "Sorry."

SUB ROSA

Victor Spoils and four security guards tried to open the door of the P.A. room, but it was locked.

"I'm going to kill whoever made that announcement," he screamed.

He fired two rounds at the lock, and the four guards used their combined strength to open the door and push the desks and filing cabinets backward. John Spencer fired his machine gun and shot them all. Victor Spoils then stuck his arm around the doorframe and emptied an entire clip into the room. *Tuwa* died, and John Spencer was fatally wounded.

Captain Mike O'Brien and SAC James Cararuscio rushed forward into the cloud of gray, smoke firing as they ran. The entire SWAT team followed them, clad in black armor. The flashlights and red lasers on their H & K's began to find targets. The security guards tried to use LED flashlights and fire revolvers at them, but they were outmatched, and a great many died.

Honovi and Steve Peterson ran in with the SWAT team, so did

Annie O'Neal and Janey. One of the guards fired at Steve and wounded him in his right arm. He dropped his machine gun. *Honovi* bent down and picked it up. Annie fired her revolver at a guard who had stood up from behind an overturned desk and shot him. Victor Spoils fired at Annie and hit her in the upper left leg. She fell to the ground. Captain Mike O'Brien aimed his H & K at Victor Spoils, but Victor fired first. The bullet struck his machine gun and knocked it out of Mike's hands. Victor then pointed his gun directly at Mike. James Cararuscio quickly ran up behind Victor and loudly shouted.

"Hey, meathead!"

Victor turned his head, and James,

remembering a karate move *Viviane d' Aqs* had once taught him, whirled around and swung his right leg in an arc that connected with Victor's hand, causing his gun to fly through the air. Mike O'Brien dropped to his knees, picked up his gun, and fired a burst of eight rounds into Victor Spoil's chest.

Barry Dukov saw Victor die and grabbed hold of Janey. He held her in a headlock with his left arm and pointed his gun at her with his right hand.

Mike O' Brien, James Cararuscio, and *Honovi* trained their guns on Barry.

"Let her go," said Mike.

"No."

"What do you want?"

"I don't want to die. I want to get out of here with you."

"Drop your gun and let her go," said James.

Barry shook his head.

"Promise me that I can surrender to you and you won't shoot me, or I swear I'll kill her."

"Okay, I promise," said Mike. "Now drop your gun."

"No, you three drop your guns first."

Janey carefully reached behind and removed the knife from her left back pocket. She flicked it open and slashed the long blade deeply across Barry's left arm. He screamed out in pain, let go of her, and she was able to run away from him. Realizing his situation was hopeless, he dropped his gun and raised both of his arms in the air.

"I kept my promise," said Mike. He turned to one of his men.

"Cuff him. You three men, go with him and escort the prisoner over to Jason's ship. Apply first aid to his arm."

Janey and *Honovi* embraced. She was shaking, but managed to call Jason on her C.A.V.E.S. and tell him to expect a prisoner.

SWAT team medics went to work treating Annie O'Neal, Steve Peterson, and other wounded.

Andrea and Michael Dryer ran past the few security guards, still firing, and headed for the back room. Latona de Jahn saw them and opened her knife. She threw it at Andrea's back and the blade entered below her left shoulder blade. She screamed but kept up with her husband. They opened the door and locked it behind them. They found *Xavier del Mundo* sitting in a chair, staring up at the wall-sized projection screen at Jason's ship.

"They'll be gone soon, but where? said *Xavier.* The comet will destroy Earth. Your son, Brad, will show up tomorrow with the second half of our people. We'll all be okay up here."

Michael Dryer looked unconvinced.

Honovi and Janey entered the P.A.

room and found *Tuwa's* body. They heard a moan and discovered John Spencer lying on his side behind an overturned desk. *Honovi* bent down and leaned close to him so he could make out his words.

"I said I'd shoot one of them for a beer," he whispered. "I guess you'll have to drink one for me when you get back to Earth."

John laughed and closed his eyes for the last time.

Mike O'Brien entered the room.

"We've taken the building. There are no prisoners except for the one."

Janey called the three engineers on her C.A.V.E.S. and told them the battle was over.

"Just in time," said Aaron. "We

were counting down to the last minute."

The lights suddenly went back on all over Sub Rosa. Janey turned on the power for the public address system and spoke directly into the microphone…

"ATTENTION!"

"This is Janey Spadaro speaking to everyone at Sub Rosa. The fighting is now over, and it is safe to go outside.

REPEAT-IT IS NOW SAFE FOR EVERYONE TO COME OUTSIDE

At this time everyone must return to their apartments. Take only what you can carry and no more. All those in Complexes C. D, and E will go through the Jump Gate. All those in Complex A and B will go on Jason's ship. Make your way across the park to the ship's platform. Jason and his crew will be waiting for you there.

AGAIN-IT IS NOW SAFE TO COME OUTSIDE

Do not linger in your apartments. Grab some food and water, a few personal items, and then get going. Those who will be leaving through the Jump Gate, please follow instructions that will be given to you there from FBI SWAT team members. This is it!

WE'RE GOING HOME TO EARTH! MOVE QUICKLY NOW!"

Janey sat back in the chair and closed her eyes. She breathed deeply a few times and quieted her mind. Then she formed an image of her sister and telepathically sent her a message.

"Jenny, we have successfully taken over Sub Rosa and are beginning our evacuation process. Tell me what is happening with you and Marc?"

She was prepared to wait but received an immediate response.

"There were bad men who tried to stop us. They're all dead. Marc and I are hanging onto a rope ladder. He's

trying to place the gold disc on the statue's left hand. It's very windy."

THE USS *CONCORD*

"What is our current position?" Captain Brad Dryer asked his co-pilot.

"We are approximately seventeen point five million miles past the midway point, and our ETA is 1200 hours tomorrow from landing on Phobos," Darren Carter responded.

"Very good."

Brad called his first mate, Peter Walsh.

"How are the three hundred and sixty-one passengers doing? Any complaints?"

"No, sir. Everyone is looking

forward to arriving at Sub Rosa. We have plenty of food and sleeping accommodations. I overheard two men talking about their three-day wait for our ship to arrive. One man waited near *Campo Gallo* in The *Pampa*, Argentina. He spoke of the large amount he and his family had paid for their jet flight from Germany, but then he had to admit that it was the last money he would ever have to spend on Earth and laughed. The other man had flown to our ship's evacuation pickup in the *Taoudenni Basin*, *Mali*, West Africa, all the way from Brazil."

"I assume Colonel Jason King arrived at Sub Rosa yesterday. He picked up the first half of our friends at the other two evacuation centers in the Great Sandy Desert, Western Australia and in an area north of Wright, Wyoming."

"They sure chose four completely out of-the-way places! Do you know how the runways and housing facilities were built in complete secrecy?"

"No, I don't, but I understand that no expense was spared. Let me know if you need anything, Pete."

You got it, sir."

Brad asked Darren to take over the controls so he could get some sleep and left for his quarters.

AVIGNON, FRANCE

Jenny held tightly onto the rope ladder as a strong gust of wind swept past her. She looked down at Marc and shouted,

"Janey told me that the FBI has taken over Sub Rosa, and they're beginning to evacuate everyone up there. It's time to do our job, Marc. Please try one more time."

Marc looked up at the statue. The serene face of Mother Mary met his gaze. He began to pray.

"Blessed Virgin, as your humble servant, I ask, not for me, but for all who dwell on Earth, please allow the wind to cease long enough for me to place the golden disc."

Almost immediately the wind died,

and the air became very still. Marc extended his arm and carefully lowered the golden disc directly onto the top of Her hand. He inhaled, deeply exhaled, and spoke.

"This is for you, Dad."

As soon as the golden disc was set in place, a powerful voice reverberated throughout the entire area...

"DO NOT, I REPEAT, DO NOT LOOK AT THE GOLDEN DISC. CLOSE YOUR EYES. KEEP THEM CLOSED."

Viviane, *Bastien, Renard* and *Louis* aboard the helicopter, and Marc and Jenny on the ladder, heeded the warning. *Jean-Luc* turned his helicopter around, and *Jacques* did the same in his jet.

A halo of blinding, brilliantly bright light suddenly flashed from the golden disc atop the statue's hand and bathed the area surrounding the cathedral in a glowing circle that extended for over two miles.

Minutes passed, and the light stayed strong. Then it suddenly went out. Marc cautiously peeked with his right eye and determined it was now safe.

"It's okay, Jenny. Let's get back into the helicopter."

They climbed up the rope ladder, assisted by *Viviane* and *Bastien,* and everyone cried. Marc hugged *Louis*, and Jenny kissed *Renard's* cheeks.

ABOARD THE U.S.S. *CONCORD*

Peter Walsh's face showed great fear and alarm as he shouted at Brad Dryer.

"I've lost control of the ship. We're being turned around!"

In an instant, the ship landed at the *Taoudenni Basin*, *Mali*, West Africa, from where they had left for Phobos a day and a half earlier. In a daze, the crew and passengers slowly disembarked until everyone stood in large groups outside in the blazing sun.

Suddenly the sky was filled with huge bolts of white lightning and a powerful golden light. The Voice of The One God began to speak aloud, in their minds, and in their languages. Everyone fell to his or her knees and looked upward as the gigantic, forms of religious figures filled the sky and stood in a circle around the horizon. They held hands and began to speak one after the other.

AVIGNON

The loudest sound of thunder and the largest bolts of lightning any of them had ever heard or seen suddenly cracked and boomed from all directions and were accompanied by a dazzling golden light, which filled the sky. All but *Renard, Jacques,* and *Jean-Luc*, who remained in their pilot's seats, fell to their knees as a Voice emanating from everywhere outside and, at the same time, inside everyone's mind and in his or her language, began to speak in a comforting, melodious tone.

EUROPEAN SPACE AGENCY HEADQUARTERS PARIS, FRANCE

"We are the last two scientists here. Everyone else has left to be with their families," said *Henri*.

"Yes, and soon we'll join them. As an astrophysicist," said *Daniel,* "I just wanted to have a last look at the blue comet through our telescope."

Daniel sat in the seat and peered through the lens.

"The comet has stopped!"

"La comète a arrêté!"

"What do you mean?"

"Que voulez-vous dire?"

"It just stopped moving! Wait. I think it is turning around!"

"Il vient d'arrêter de bouger! Attendre. Je pense qu'il est en train de changer!"

"Really?"

"Vraiment?"

"Here. Come look for yourself."

"Ici. Viens voir pour vous-même."

"Oh, my God!"

"Oh, mon Dieu!"

"What?"

"Ce qui?"

"It's speeding away from Earth at an incredible velocity! I wonder where it is going?"

"C'est l'accélération de la Terre

à une vitesse incroyable! Je me demande où il va?"

"Let me work out a trajectory."

"Permettez-moi de trouver une trajectoire."

"Well? What have you got?"

"Eh bien? Qu'avez-vous?"

"My figures indicate that the comet is heading directly for Mars."

"Mes chiffres indiquent que la comète se dirige directement pour Mars."

Then the two men heard the voice of The One God aloud, in their minds, and in French. They hurriedly left the building and walked outside to join multitudes of people, who were on their knees and looking at the sky.

And all the people on Earth and also at the Sub Rosa Base on the Martian moon Phobos heard the Voice of The One God.

SUB ROSA BASE, PHOBOS

Janey and *Honovi* stood in one of three long lines and waited for the signal to begin moving toward the entrance to the Jump Gate. They both had just enough time to grab a change of clothes, water, hairbrushes, toothpaste, and toothbrushes, from their apartments. At the last minute, Janey took the small painting of Our Lady of *Guadalupe* off the wall. She grabbed a bag of chips, two bottles of water, and the C.A.V.E.S. and put them in her daypack. She met *Honovi* outside, and they got in line.

Janey heard Jenny speaking to her in her mind.

"We did it! Marc placed the golden disc on Our Lady's hand! Then a loud voice told us to close our eyes, and there was a really bright light around us that lasted for a few minutes. I believe that means the comet won't hit Earth."

Sharon Oliver ran up to them.

"I'm going on Jason's ship."

She handed Janey a small piece of folded paper.

"Here's my number at the Mayo Clinic hospital in Phoenix. I've had it for so many years that I've memorized it. Call and leave a message for me there, okay?"

Janey nodded.

She gave Sharon the good news.

"Oh, that is so wonderful! That means the comet won't hit Earth, and we can actually go home!"

"We both love you, Sharon," said Janey as she kissed her on the cheek.

They gave her hugs, and she headed across the park and joined the long lines of people waiting to board the ship that would take them home to Earth. Janey saw Dr. Lambert standing way in the back of the line, and they waved to one another.

The SWAT team handed each

person waiting in line a questionnaire and pens.

"I already have pens," said Janey.

"Okay, answer the questions as best as you can, and someone will be by to collect them."

Janie unzipped her fanny pack and took out pens and notepads for them to write on.

"Please ask Captain O'Brien to come here as soon as possible," she asked the SWAT team member.

A few minutes later, Mike walked up to them along with James Cararuscio.

"What's up?"

First, Janey explained about her having telepathic communication with her twin sister. Then she told them Marc had successfully placed the golden disc on the statue's left hand.

"Oh, thank God," Mike cried.

"If that's the case, then the comet won't strike Earth after all," said James. "We give thanks to Our Lady, and to Marc and Jenny."

Jason, Arnie, and the six crew members helped over seven hundred people form ten lines, and three dozen men from the FBI SWAT team assisted them. While the people stood patiently waiting to begin to board Jason's ship, The USS *Excalibur*, SWAT team members passed out questionnaires and pens to everyone waiting in the lines, then collected them.

Jason and his crew had brought plenty of food, bottled water, futons, blankets, and pillows for everyone. It would take hours before the last person boarded the ship. Then they would lift off the air lock and ascend from the moon into space for the three-day journey to Earth.

Sharon was lucky to find a seat on a bench and sat down with her few belongings. She'd brought some fruit and two bottles of water. She closed her eyes and began to doze off when she heard a Voice speaking in her mind and also aloud. Sharon opened her eyes wide to see that, based on their reactions, the many hundreds of people around her were hearing the Voice, as well.

Many began to fall to their knees.

Jason, with Chloe, their girls, and Arnie beside him, stood by the door to the cockpit cabin. Hundreds of people were waiting in lines to board the ship when the Voice began to speak aloud and also inside Jason's mind.

"Harken to MY Voice, My Children. I AM THAT I AM, the ONE and ONLY GOD, The Creator of the Universe. I AM the UNIVERSAL INTELLIGENCE and the Creator of DIVINE ORDER, I AM the Cosmic Mind. I AM the Cosmic Harmony that surrounds you and all living things great and small.

I am known by many names: God, Jehovah, Allah, Brahma, Adonai,

Zeus, Apollo, Odin, *Ahura Mazda*, the Great Spirit, and so on. Yet, it is I ALONE, who am the CREATOR SOURCE.

I AM beyond thought, I AM beyond form. I AM invisible."

The One God then caused the half of Earth normally in night to be in daylight.

"I ask that you leave your dwellings and places of work and venture outside to witness my Avatars, who are visible to all of you around the world."

At that moment eighteen towering, gigantic figures suddenly appeared on all four rock walls surrounding Sub Rosa and also encircling Earth.

Each held hands with one another, and their faces smiled down on all the people. Many of those standing in lines fell to their knees, awestruck, and gazed upward. Many cried.

"The DIVINE AVATARS who now encircle Earth are MY representatives, manifestations, and teachers. They have been sent over the ages by ME with a message that has been essentially the same. They have faithfully guided and served as MY teachers to guide the human race in love, justice, tolerance, happiness, harmony, peace, and truthfulness."

Each avatar then introduced His or Herself and spoke aloud, in everyone's minds, and in his or her language…

OSIRIS I was the chief envoy of *Amun-Ra* or The One God to the people's of Egypt, and I instilled in them reverence, worship, and Goodness to one another.

KRISHNA I am a teacher of The ONE GOD, and speak of compassion, tenderness, and love in the Hindu religion of India.

BUDDHA As an avatar of The One God. I teach only two things: the nature of suffering, and the cessation of suffering, which will result in the complete extinguishment of greed, hatred, and delusion and lead to liberation and happiness.

MOSES I often conversed

with God. He gave me the Ten Commandments which I then presented to mankind to teach about morality, ethics, and righteousness.

JESUS *I am of MY FATHER, The One God Almighty, and teach that man's basis of fear can and will be cured by love because there is no fear in love, but perfect love casteth out fear. Faith and trust in God will replace fear. Therefore, love one another as I have loved you. As MY FATHER hath loved Me, so I have loved you. Continue ye in My love.*

MARY MAGDALENE As a servant of The One God, I brought and taught the teachings of Jesus and His message of love to many people throughout *Gaul,* now known as France. Live in love.

MOTHER MARY The One God blessed Me with the birth of My Son, Jesus, who has brought teachings of love, kindness, brotherhood, harmony, and peace to the world.

THE DALAI LAMA As an Avatar of The One True God, I taught that the meaning of life is *happiness,* and what makes true happiness is compassion and a good heart.

MOHAMMED God revealed Himself to me, and I teach on Earth that each person's purpose or goal is to seek God's pleasure and heaven through faith, prayer, and charity. To worship The One God and to treat all of God's creations with equality and compassion.to

BAHA 'U' LLAH I am the founder of the Bahai religion, yet I am but a manifestation of THE ONE TRUE GOD. As His humble messenger, I teach the oneness of humanity, the equality of men and women, the elimination of prejudice, and the goal of world peace. The fundamental purpose animating Bahai's is their faith in The One God, spiritual solutions to economic problems, the harmony of science and religion, the promotion of the unity of the human race, and to foster the spirit of love and fellowship among men, women, and children.

LAO TZU I taught that living a

simple and balanced life in harmony with nature will bring one closer to the Nameless, The ONE GOD, who is the origin of heaven and Earth.

QUETZALCOATL I brought The One God's teachings of love, peace, and brotherhood to the people's of what is now known as South America.

ZOROASTER As an Avatar of The One God. I taught that the purpose of humankind, and of all creation, is to sustain truth by actively participating in life with the exercise of constructive, loving, thoughts, words, and deeds.

CONFUCIUS I taught Goodness and, "Do not do unto others what you would not want others to do unto you!" as a manifestation of The One God.

ABRAHAM I am the friend and servant of God. I brought ethics and righteousness to mankind and stressed a whole-hearted commitment to The One God through living lives of peace, compassion, and hospitality.

MOTHER TERESA I am but a servant of The One God and His appointed messenger. I call on everyone listening to my voice to carry God's love to others and so be His shining Light wherever you are.

GURU NANAK The fundamental beliefs of Sikhism include faith and meditation on the name of The One Creator, divine unity, and equality of all humankind. I am both a messenger and a teacher of The One God.

PARMAHANSA YOGANANDA
The One God instructed me to bring the ancient practice of yoga to the West and to spread His word of love, truth, and compassion through prayer, self-reflection, and meditation."

"I, THE ONE AND ONLY GOD, created Earth with the duality of Good and Evil. My intention was for Good to always triumph over Evil. I created my Avatars, or Christ's, and I also created Antichrist's at the same time. To MY great displeasure, the essential qualities of Goodness have been forsaken by mankind.

Prejudice, fear, intolerance, anxiety, jealousy, sorrow, selfishness, judgment, anger, and greed continue to prevail and dwell in many of MY blessed children's hearts. The Earth has become consumed with war, poverty, distrust, and hatred.

I therefore, declare this to be a

HOLY DAY

I AM THAT I AM now put an end to duality on Earth and by doing so eliminate the presence of, and the very concept of, evil from this moment forth. I now bring a true understanding and sweep away the age-long barriers that have divided the great religions of the world. I now unite all religions together in harmony and equality, for one religion is no better or worse than another. All, in their own way, worship ME, THE ONE AND ONLY GOD.

I now declare an end to evil. And with the ending of evil, so too shall end the chief causes of human suffering, which are separation and division, and their partners, hatred and conflict.

My children, you are ALL the same. You are one family. My heart beats with DIVINE Love for all of you and knows no tribe, no skin color, and no nationality. For there is only ONE human race. From this time onward, I now declare that ALL religions on Earth will be united as ONE COMMON FAITH and will become as the rays of ONE SUN created by your ONE GOD.

Go forth now, MY children, and live your lives in a world full of peace, love, happiness, and security with the full knowledge that YOUR ONE GOD loves each and every one of you."

NORTH OF WRIGHT, WYOMING

Over the next two hours Jason and his crew, assisted by the FBI, helped get all aboard the ship. Janey had called him on the C.A.V.E.S. to give him the good news that Marc had successfully placed the golden disc on the statue's left hand. Earth had been saved.

"Thank The One God, Blessed Mother Mary, and Marc and Jenny! But I wonder what happened to the blue comet?"

He spoke to Arnie.

"Engage retro rockets."

"Retro rockets engaged."

"Lift off the air lock slowly."

"You got it, Jason," said Arnie.

"We're above the surface now, sir. I'm doing the best I can right now, but I'm in a state of awe over what we just experienced."

"Me, too. Let's go home. I never want to see this place again," said Jason. "We'll go back to the base on *Hoste* Island where we left, but, where will we take the passengers after we land there?"

And then, in an instant, the ship landed at one of the four collection points north of Wright, Wyoming. Outside the cockpit windows, fields of grasslands stretched to the horizon as far as one could see. Jason and Arnie were stunned. They joined the other crew members and disembarked from the ship to stand outside in bright sunshine and cloudless blue skies.

"Well, it looks like The One God answered my question," said Jason.

The sky soon became filled with huge bolts of white lightning and the emanation of a powerful golden light as one by one each of the Avatars became transparent and vanished. The passengers began to leave the ship and walked out onto the ground in long lines. Hundreds of people were crying, while hundreds more were smiling and laughing with absolute joy.

Jason, Chloe, Meredith, Olivia, Arnie, Sharon, Ben and Latona stood together and wore dazed expressions.

"Was that Jesus, Mama?" asked Meredith. "Was that Mother Mary?"

"Yes, honey. They both spoke to us about loving one another."

"The voice we heard, Mama. Was that God?" inquired Olivia.

"Yes, that was the voice of The One God," answered Jason. "He said that He loves each and every one of us."

Sharon crossed herself and spoke.

"I saw Jesus, Mother Mary, Mother Theresa, Moses, Buddha, Mohammed, and Krishna all holding hands. And I heard the voice of The One God!"

They found places to sit down on the ground in the warm sunshine.

"I've never been an atheist or a church-goer, either." commented Arnie. "But I'm sure going to make a change now. God has given us all another chance to straighten up and live in peace with one another. God said there would be no more evil. I wonder what that will be like?"

"I guess we're going to find out,"

said Ben. "I've been a fighting soldier most of my life. I always wished that there was another way to live. Now it looks like we won't need to have any armies anymore."

"A great blessing has just been bestowed on us," observed Latona de Jahn. "It is a Holy Day, for sure."

"May we all love each other," said Dr. Chloe King, bringing smiles to everyone's face.

EUROPEAN SPACE AGENCY HEADQUARTERS, PARIS

Daniel and *Henri* got to their feet. Both men were crying.

"I've been an atheist my entire life," said *Daniel*. "A strict material scientist with no room for a spiritual viewpoint. And now, my life has been turned upside down and inside out. I am feeling freedom and joy I have never felt before."

"J'ai été athée toute ma vie." dit Daniel. Un matériel strictement scientifique avec pas de place pour un point de vue spirituel. Et maintenant, ma vie a été bouleversée et l'intérieur. Je suis un sentiment de liberté et de joie que je n'ai jamais ressenti auparavant."

"And I have been an atheist, as well. Now suddenly all has changed, and I know there is but The One God, who loves us and has removed evil from the world. I saw Jesus, Moses, and so many others speak to me in my mind and aloud and in

French! I am so happy. I must return home to my family now. Goodbye."

"Et j'ai été athée, aussi bien. Maintenant tout à coup tout a changé et je sais qu'il n'y a qu'un Dieu qui nous aime et a supprimé le mal du monde. J'ai vu Jésus et Moïse et et tant d'autres parlent de moi dans mon esprit et à haute voix et en français ! Je suis si heureux. Je dois retourner à la maison pour ma famille maintenant. Au revoir."

SUB ROSA BASE

James Cararuscio and Captain Mike O'Brien helped their FBI team organize nearly three hundred people into lines before the Jump

Gate. Then they found a place at the front and waited to go through.

"I have renewed and strengthened my faith in God and in The Blessed Virgin Mary," stated James. "She helped Marc place the golden disc on the statue's arm, and The One God caused the comet to miss Earth."

"I have to admit that what just happened completely blew my mind. I mean, I'm numb!" said Mike. "But at the same time, I'm realizing that we are about to enter an entirely new world without evil."

"We won't have any bad guys to chase and arrest anymore," observed James. "Looks like you and I will just have to find another line of work!"

The two men smiled at each other and burst out laughing.

INSIDE ISIS TEMPLE

Janey and *Honovi* made their way out of the Jump Gate. Six dozen members of the FBI and FEMA assisted the people. They were led to their designated area. Bowls of fruit and turkey sandwiches, bottles of drinking water, paper plates, and napkins sat on a table. There were folding chairs and two futons nearby with blankets and pillows. The same set up was repeated all around them.

A woman wearing an FBI badge stopped by to introduce herself.

"My name is Allison Matthews." She wiped tears from her eyes, blew her nose, and smiled at them. "I am assigned to this section. Please excuse me, but I'm overwhelmed by what happened. We heard The Voice of The One God and then saw the Avatars appear on the rock walls all around us. I've never been a religious person, but now I feel so happy, so thrilled, and so confident about the future of our planet."

Janey took her hands in hers and smiled, and *Honovi* gave Allison a big hug. She thanked them both.

"Helicopters will soon begin to transport people to the nearby airport in Flagstaff and then on to Phoenix over the next few days.

Please let me know how I can be of service here. The portable-potties are over there."

Allison left. They ate the turkey sandwiches and fruit, looked at one another, and smiled.

"I propose a toast," said *Honovi.*

They both opened a bottle of water.

"I wish to give my grateful thanks to The One God and especially to Marc and Jenny. Without their success, you and I would not be sitting here at this moment."

"And I," said Janey, "would like to tell you how humbled I feel by what just happened. To actually hear the Voice of God and then see the Avatars and their good message of unity is overwhelming. So I wish to offer a prayer to The One God and give thanks for the blessing of the end of evil and the beginning of peace for our world. And for this food."

Honovi smiled.

"At this moment, Janey, I would like to ask you a question."

Janey held her breath.

Honovi clasped her hands in his.

"Will you marry me?"

Tears formed in Janey's eyes, and she nodded.

"My answer is yes. Of course, I will marry you."

They kissed and hugged.

AVIGNON

Jean-Luc in his jet and *Jacques* in in his helicopter flew in circles while they listened to the voice of The One God and His avatars speak to them in French. *Renard* found a city park with enough room to land his helicopter, and everyone got out. All of them stood looking up at the enormous Avatars and heard their words in English, French, and Spanish. Jenny, Marc, *Viviane*, *Bastien*, and *Louis* were crying as they gazed up at Jesus, Mary Magdalene, Mother Mary, and the other Avatars. When the last word of The One God had been spoken, the entire sky remained golden, as one by one the form of each Avatar vanished.

Everyone took seats around a picnic table and sat in deep silence, absorbed by his or her thoughts. *Viviane* loudly sighed and softly spoke.

"We are entering a new world without evil and with the promise of lasting peace. I would like to thank you, Marc and Jenny, for your valiant effort to put the golden disc in place."

"And I would like to thank all of you for your assistance in completing the task set by The One God," said Jenny. "We never could have done it without you."

"At this moment," Marc said to

Jenny, "I would like to ask you a question."

Jenny held her breath.

"Will you marry me?"

Jenny burst into tears and smiled.

"My answer is yes. Of course, I will marry you."

The others cheered and clapped as bolts of white lightning cracked and boomed in the golden sky.

Renard went to his helicopter and returned with a medical kit. He and *Viviane* used bottled water and isopropyl alcohol to clean the wounds on Jenny's arm and Marc's thigh, then applied topical antibacterial cream and taped bandages in place.

"That will do until we can get you both to a clinic," said *Viviane*.

Renard gave *Bastien* a hug.

"It has been the greatest pleasure of my life to assist you today. Now I wish to be united with my family."

"Il a été le plus grand plaisir de ma vie pour vous aider aujourd'hui et maintenant, je tiens à être unis avec ma famille."

Renard walked around and closely inspected his helicopter. He noted the many bullet holes along the fuselage on the right side of the craft. Fortunately none had caused enough severe damage to affect his ability to safely fly. He climbed aboard and waved at everyone from his window as he lifted off.

ARIENNE AIR BASE 115

Jean-luc flew his jet back toward the base. He was stunned by what he had just witnessed and smiled as a feeling of intense happiness begin to fill his heart and his entire being.

In his helicopter, *Jacques* followed his brother. They both landed, and when they met on the runway, they hugged and laughed with sheer joy.

"That was incredible," shouted *Jacques*. "I saw it with my own eyes and heard The One God and the Avatars speak to me in French!"

"C'était incroyable," cria Jacques. "J'ai vu de mes propres yeux et entendu Dieu et les avatars me parler en français !"

"Me, too," said *Jean-Luc*. "Now we

will have a world without evil and live in peace with one another."

"Moi aussi," dit Jean-Luc. "Maintenant, nous aurons un monde sans le mal et vivre en paix les uns avec les autres."

Gabriel, Paul, Jules, and *Lucien* ran out of the bunkhouse and greeted them warmly.

"You did it! Come inside and tell us what happened," said *Jules.*

"Vous l'avez fait ! Venez à l'intérieur et nous dire ce qui s'est passé," a déclaré M. Jules.

The brothers related everything from their own perspectives about how they had arrived just in time to destroy two Eurocopters. Then *Jacques* told them he had seen the

American man place the gold disc on the statue's hand and described how he and *Jean-Luc* had to fly away from the cathedral to avoid a huge, blinding light that surrounded it in a wide area.

The four men told the brothers about their hearing the Voice of The One God that spoke to them in French and in their minds; then they saw the Avatars circling the sky with their message of love, unity, and peace.

"Now we must drive three hours back to our parent's house near *Rennes le Chateau*," said *Jean-Luc.* "We will see you again soon. Goodbye."

"Maintenant nous devons conduire

trois heures retour à notre chambre des parents près de Rennes-le-Château," dit Jean-Luc. *"Nous nous reverrons bientôt. Au revoir."*

Bastien flew his Skyhawk back to the airport, and they drove to his house in *Lavaldieu. Viviane*, Marc, *Louis*, and Jenny got to work preparing food and drinks for everyone and brought plates of sandwiches, potato salad, and chips to the table in the backyard. *Viviane* opened a bottle of wine, and *Bastien* poured glasses for all.

Viviane stood and spoke in English.

"I propose a toast to The One God, The Creator Source of all existence, and to all of the

Manifestations who have been our guides and teachers throughout human history. From this day on we will live in a world filled with peace and love."

All clinked their glasses and drank. When their hunger was satisfied, the enormity of what they had experienced began to take its toll, and all retired to their rooms to rest and sleep.

Marc and Jenny undressed and hugged for a long time. Then Jenny began to cry.

"I'm not crying because I'm sad, Marc, but because I'm so happy at the words of The One God and those of the Avatars."

Marc looked into her eyes.

"I love you, Jenny, more then words can say. My heart belongs to you. I want you to know that I could never have done anything without you."

"And I love you, too, Marc. Of course, Mother Mary's assistance and our strong faith helped."

"I agree, but you were incredible! Now let's get some rest."

Marc and Jenny fell asleep with their arms wrapped around one another. During the night, he had a dream. His mother and father stood before him amid white marble buildings, bathed in golden light. They were about the same age they had been when Marc was a teenager. Marc's father smiled and spoke.

"I wish to thank you for all that you have done. You fulfilled my request, and for that your mother and I are eternally grateful. Know that we are both fine. We love you and wish you and Jenny much happiness."

Marc stirred, woke briefly, kissed Jenny on the cheek, and fell back to sleep, but his kiss had awakened her from a dream. She lay half-asleep, and her mind returned to part of her dream. All she could recall was that she was inside the ancient room at *Rennes le Chateau* and looked down on the golden disc, which glowed like the light of the sun.

Bastien woke to the sound of

the doorbell. He dressed, went downstairs, and opened the door for his two sons. *Jean-Luc* and *Jacques* walked in and hugged their father. Night had fallen, and *Bastien* brought them food and drink at the dining table. *Viviane* and the others awoke and joined them. Marc and Jenny shared the news of their engagement. All gave toasts in celebration of the news and to The One God. Then J*ean-Luc* and *Jacques,* along with the others, went to their rooms to sleep.

TAOUDENNI BASIN, *MALI*, WEST AFRICA

Brad Dryer was shocked to find his ship and passengers back at the evacuation center they had departed from a day and a half earlier. His co-pilot, Darren Carter, and first mate, Peter Walsh, stood beside him in the hot African sun. The three hundred and sixty-one passengers began to exit stair ramps from the large ship and stood in groups, staring at the sky. Brad looked up to see bright golden clouds appear and then heard the crack of tremendous booms and saw ragged bolts of bright white lightning. Then a Voice began to speak out loud and also inside of his mind.

An hour later, he found himself on his knees as tears streamed down his cheeks. His heart had been totally opened wide, and he knew that from that moment, his life had been fundamentally changed forever.

SUB ROSA BASE, PHOBOS

There were three people left alive at Sub Rosa. They were Michael and Andrea Dryer and *Xavier del Mundo*.

"Ohhh, it hurts so much," cried Andrea as Michael carefully pulled out the knife blade from her left shoulder. He used a torn tablecloth as a tourniquet to staunch the bleeding and then poured sulfa powder he had found in a medical kit onto the wound. He removed the tourniquet, applied bandages, and taped them on.

"Brad should be here by

tomorrow," said *Xavier.* "Then we can go..."

"Where?" asked Michael. "Earth has been destroyed. We're stuck up here. All the people who built and ran this place are leaving. I don't know where they're going. But I do know that I have no idea how to grow anything. We're all going to starve to death."

They looked up at the huge projection screen and saw Jason's ship begin to lift off the air lock.

"Traitor," shouted *Xavier.*

Then, in an instant, the large triangular space ship just vanished.

"Where did it go?" asked Andrea.

"What's that in the distance?"

voiced Michael with alarm. "It looks like an enormous blue light!"

"Whatever it is it's moving fast and straight toward us!" yelled Andrea.

Within minutes the entire wall-sized projection screen was filled with the light of the blue comet. Then the face of *Yeshua* filled the screen. He looked directly at *Xavier del Mundo* and spoke to him in a stern and commanding voice:

"Our Father has decided to abolish the principle of duality for His children on Earth. From this moment onward, harmony and balance will be bestowed upon them. I, as His Son, Yeshua, now solemnly speak to You, My brother, the following words…

817

Your Darkness will now be utterly terminated. You shall be consumed by the fires of this great blue comet. Your body shall be incinerated by that of My own fiery breath. In this moment your vital essence, indeed your very soul, shall be totally extinguished and cease to exist forever. From this Holy Day onward, Our Father commands that evil in any shape, form, or thought shall no longer exist or be known to any of His beloved children who dwell on Earth. So be it, and so it is."

The comet struck the moon Phobos with such force that it splintered it into millions of rocky pieces, which joined the large asteroid belt already existing between Mars and Jupiter. The Dryer's. and *Xavier del Mundo* were vaporized.

CHAPTER ELEVEN

A New World

Jenny dreamed again that she was standing inside the small room at *Renne le Chateau*. Before her were the three aged stone stairs leading up to the Star Door. In the middle of the top stair lay the golden disc, which shone with an intense yellow light. The dream faded, and Jenny slipped back into a deep sleep.

There were three knocks on the door followed by *Viviane's* voice.

"Time to get up, sleepyheads! Breakfast is ready."

"Le temps de se lever, sleepy-heads! Le petit déjeuner est prêt."

Marc and Jenny groaned and groggily stood up. Their bodies ached and felt stiff after all they had gone through the day before. They got dressed, washed up in the bathroom, and went downstairs.

"Good morning," said *Bastien*.

"Bon matin."

Jean-Luc and *Jacques* greeted them, as well.

Louis smiled.

"A most wonderful good morning to you both, and it is the first day in a new world."

"Una buena mañana más maravillosa para ambos, y es el primer día en un nuevo mundo".

"De nada," said Marc and Jenny. *"Buenos dias."*

The kitchen table was laden with bowls of fresh fruit, yogurt, croissants, butter, and jam. There were mugs of hot coffee and glasses of orange juice for everyone.

Viviane spoke in English.

"I've made appointments for both of you with my doctor at the clinic this afternoon at two. She will tend to your wounds.

Now, I wish to say a prayer before we eat.

We are all so grateful to The One God and to the Blessed Mother Mary for our success yesterday as well as for the words of The One God and the Avatars. We look forward to living in a world where love, peace, and harmony fill the lives of those who live on Earth."

"Nous sommes tous très reconnaissants à l'unique Dieu et à la Très Sainte Mère Marie pour notre succès hier ainsi que pour les paroles de Dieu et les avatars. Nous nous réjouissons à l'idée de vivre dans un monde où l'amour, la paix, l'harmonie et de remplir la vie de ceux qui vivent sur la terre."

Louis spoke for all present and clapped his hands.

"Very well. Now let's eat!"

"Muy bien. Ahora vamos's comer!

After they finished and washed the dishes, Jenny calculated the time difference.

"I want to call my SAC now and later we can go to the clinic," she said and placed a call on her cell phone.

"You have an international call on line two, sir," said his secretary.

"Thanks. James Cararuscio speaking."

"Jenny Spadaro reporting in, sir."

"Well, well, well. And how are you and Marc doing, may I ask?"

"Quite full after a great breakfast. We are in France. How are things in Phoenix?"

"Fine. It's good to hear your voice."

"We'll be arriving in Keams Canyon sometime tomorrow. I'll call you when we get there."

"Very good. I'll look forward to

seeing you both and having you tell me how you were able to get the golden disc on the statue's hand!"

"It's quite a story! And we want to know how you rescued everyone at Sub Rosa!"

Jenny ended the call.

Viviane drove Marc and Jenny to the clinic, where the doctor removed the temporary bandages and applied antiseptic, thoroughly cleaned their wounds, and put on new bandages.

They returned to *Viviane's*. Still physically exhausted, Marc and Jenny slept the rest of the afternoon. Everyone enjoyed a fine dinner, and plans were made to go to the Star Door after lunch the next day. Jenny calculated the time and made a call to *Cheveyo*'s son, Robert. He answered.

"We plan on arriving at the Star Door in Steamboat Canyon sometime in the early afternoon your time. Can you please tell *Cheveyo*?"

He said he would be at work, but would let his father know.

She thanked him and they returned to their room. Jenny was in the bathroom when she heard Marc say,

"I can't find the golden disc anywhere. It was on the bed stand table, but it's not there!"

"Don't worry," said Jenny. "I know where it is."

Renne le Chateau was very quiet. A large plastic tarp had been put in place and covered the area where the ancient wooden door had once stood. Marc ripped open the right side of the tarp along with a few dozen staples and walked in. *Jean-Luc, Jacques, Louis, Viviane, Bastien* and Jenny followed him inside.

The entire room was bathed in bright-yellow light, which emanated from the golden disc lying in the center of the top stair. Marc picked it up. The light faded and went out.

"I don't know how it got here," he said. "I guess it's time go home."

He turned around, faced the others, and said,

"On behalf of myself, Jenny, and *Louis*, as well as all of the people on our planet, I would like to express my heartfelt gratitude for your assistance. Without your help, we could never have placed this golden disc on the statue's hand. And be sure to thank *Renard* for us, as well." Marc looked at *Jean-Luc* and *Jacques*. "And you showed up at the moment when we needed you the most and shot the bad guys down. We extend our utmost thanks to you both."

The two brothers bowed.

Jenny then spoke.

"We are going to go through the Star Door and intend to end up in Arizona. I will call you, *Viviane,* to let you know we have arrived safely."

"*Merci.* Just as long as it is not at three o'clock in the morning!"

Everyone laughed.

Jenny stood between *Louis* and Marc. She glanced up at the two unicorns on either side and smiled.

"*Au revoir,*" she said.

Marc placed the golden disc in the indentation to the right. There was a blinding flash of electric-blue light. Marc's hand grabbed the gold disc, and they were gone.

STEAMBOAT CANYON, ARIZONA

Marc, Jenny, and *Louis* walked out of the Star Door to be greeted by the Hopi elders and *Tewa*. After hugs all around and warm greetings, *Honaw* cleared his throat and spoke.

"You three have taken the heroes' journey and survived. You have been divinely assisted along the way, but clearly you and others accomplished the task and saved our world. To hear the true words of God and his Avatars cleansed my heart of any doubts. The One God's declaration of an end to evil and the coming of the Fifth World and a golden age of peace has brought great joy. You are blessed, my dearest children, and all of us here give you our utmost praise."

Marc, *Louis*, and Jenny were given a ride back to his house. Seeing them, *Mansi* meowed loudly, jumped out of her chair on the porch, and rubbed herself against Marc's right leg. Marc reached down and stroked her head. The windows and doors were opened wide to air the place out, and a pot of water was started for tea.

The three of them sat in the living room, and Marc handed the golden disc to *Louis*.

"You'll need this to travel home to Peru tomorrow," said Marc.

"*Muchas gracias*. If I may use your phone, I wish to call my wife and son."

Marc handed him the phone, and he went into Marc's bedroom for privacy.

"*Rosa*, this is *Louis* calling."
"*Rosa, este Louis llamando.*"

"Oh, my God! I've been so worried. Where are you?"

"Oh, Dios mío! Yo' he estado tan preocupado. Dónde estáis?"

"I am in Arizona and am safe. Please call *Manuel* and ask him to take his neighbors, *Kawki* and *Nina*, to meet me at the *Punka Hayu Marka*. Take *Arturo* and drive down there yourselves. He knows where it is."

"Estoy en Arizona y estoy seguro. Por favor llame a Manuel y pedirle que tome sus vecinos, Kawki y Nina, a reunirse conmigo en el Punka Hayu Marka. Tomar Arturo y conducir allá vosotros. Él sabe dónde está".

"When are you coming home?"

"Cuando tú vienes a casa?"

"Tomorrow afternoon at two o'clock your time. I can't wait to see you."

"Mañana en dos o'el reloj de su tiempo. Puedo't esperar a verte."

"I love you. Goodbye."

"Te amo, adiós."

Louis ended the call.

Jenny determined that there was a nine-hour difference between Arizona and France. The time was just after two o'clock in the afternoon, and she hoped that calling her at eleven would not be too late. She placed a call to *Viviane*.

"Hello?"

"Bonjour?"

"*Viviane*, Jenny here. I hope it"s not a bad time to call."

"Viviane, Jenny ici. J'espère que c''est pas un mauvais moment pour appeler".

"No, *Bastien* and I had a late dinner, watched a movie, and are enjoying a nice bottle of wine. I will switch to English, okay?"

"Non, Bastien et j'ai eu un dîner tardif, regardé un film, et jouissent d'une bonne bouteille de vin. Je vais passer à l'anglais, d'accord?"

"Okay. I wanted to let you know that we arrived safely. *Louis* will travel through the Star Door tomorrow to Peru. Marc and I are happy being back at his house and are just now beginning to realize all that has happened in the past month. It seems so amazing. Our faith is what kept us going, even when things looked hopeless. All we can do is sigh with relief that it's finally over."

"Our hearts are always with you both. Please let us know about your wedding plans."

"I will as soon as we get details."

"Goodbye, Jenny. Keep in touch."

Jenny ended the call, then immediately phoned her SAC on his personal cell number.

"James Cararuscio speaking."

"Jenny Spadaro reporting in, sir. Marc and I arrived safely and are at his house in Keams Canyon."

"Good to hear your voice, Jenny.

Plans are in the works for a complete overhaul of the FBI to re-write our mission. Let's meet next week. I'll let you know the time and date. Enjoy your life."

"Thanks. I have good news, sir. Marc and I are engaged. We still have to work out the wedding plans. It would be an honor to have you there."

"Thank you for inviting me, Jenny, and I, too, am honored. Take care."

STEAMBOAT CANYON, ARIZONA

The temperature was quite warm as they stood in the narrow channel running between rock cliffs. *Louis* faced the group of elders and bowed. He gave hugs to Marc, Jenny, *Cheveyo,* and *Honaw* and smiled at the others.

"It has been my great pleasure to know all of you and to have had your faith, prayers, and support. I believe that your positive thoughts guided us to success. I now return to my family and country. Let us remain in contact and know that you are always welcome to visit me in Peru."

Louis turned and placed the golden disc in the indentation to the right of the door. A wave of electric-blue light emanated from the Star Door, and as he stepped forward, he reached out, grabbed the disc, and vanished.

Stars, planets, and clouds of nebular gas of incredible colors surrounded him, and then he was hurtling down toward an electric-blue doorway. When *Louis* reached it, the figure of Mother Mary was waiting for him. His eyes filled with tears, and he sobbed with joy.

She reached out, and *Louis* handed her the golden disc.

"You have done all that I requested of you and more. No one will ever need to use this gold disc again."

Then *Louis* gasped as Her features began to transform into the figure of *Pachamama*. As a Peruvian archaeologist of the Inca, *Louis* knew Her well. She smiled at him and spoke.

"At last the Incan prophecy of the *pachacuti*, the long-held *Q'ero* prediction of great change, will now take place. The world will be turned right-side-up. Unity, harmony, and order will be restored, and all evil and chaos will be ended once and for all. And a golden age will now be brought about by The One God."

Pachamama smiled and *Louis* stepped forward and out of the Star Door. His wife, *Rosa*, son *Arturo*, father *Manuel*, *Kawki,* and *Nina* stood before him.

"Oh, my God! *Louis*, my love!"

"Oh, mi Dios, Louis, mi amor!."

The two embraced and kissed, and there were hugs all around.

"What happened to you, Father? Where did you go for so long?" asked *Arturo*.

"Lo que le ha ocurrido a usted,

padre? ¿Dónde ir durante tanto tiempo?" preguntó Arturo.

"It is a very long story that I will tell all of you at *Manuel's* house."

"Es una historia muy larga que les diré a todos ustedes a Manuel's casa".

ISIS TEMPLE, THE GRAND CANYON

FBI agent Allison Matthews walked up to Janey and *Honovi* as they sat at their table.

"You're with the next group to board an M-26 Halo helicopter. Three were flown here from Luke Air Force Base. They'll fly you to the airport in Flagstaff. From there

Greyhound buses will take you to Phoenix.

A group is forming over there."

Janey and *Honovi* stood in line and soon walked outside and up a steep path to the landing zone. The M-26 twin-rotor helicopter was enormous and could easily transport seventy-five people. After a short flight, they landed at Pullian Airport in Flagstaff and found seats at a boarding gate.

"I'm going to try to connect my mind with Jenny's," she said to *Honovi.*

PHOENIX

Marc helped Jenny air out her house. She checked her emails.

Her SAC requested their presence at a meeting at two o'clock in the afternoon. They relaxed on her sofa. Then Jenny heard Janey clearly in her mind and sat straight up.

"Jenny, Honovi and I flew out of Isis Temple on a really big helicopter, and we're at the airport in Flagstaff. I guess we're going to get on a bus down to Phoenix. I love you, and we'll see you soon somehow."

She relayed Janey's words to Marc. They then drove to the FBI office.

OFFICE OF THE FBI, PHOENIX

Present at the meeting were James Cararuscio, Captain Mike

O'Brien, and Jenny's assistant, Susan Johnson.

After she and Marc recounted their harrowing experiences and success in having two men firing at them, two armed helicopters firing at them, and gusts of wind preventing them from placing the golden disc on the statue's hand, James and Mike relayed their gunfight at the Sub Rosa base. When all questions had been asked and answered, James brought up something on his computer screen and began to read aloud:

"This is from the Director of the FBI:

Due to the Voice of The One God, there will be major changes in the purpose and direction of the FBI.

Now that there is no more evil, money traditionally spent on armies, law enforcement and prisons have now become available. That money will be used to rebuild infrastructure, education, and health care, restoring the environment, and erase poverty.

The new name for the FBI is now the FBA, Federal Bureau of Assistance.

The Phoenix Missing Persons Division will now become an assistance agency for the nearly one thousand people who were taken in four states to Phobos against their wills. It is my pleasure to announce that Agent Jenny Spadaro has been promoted to director of this new agency along with Susan Johnson, who is now her deputy director.

The FBI Directorate in Washington, DC, has agreed to allocate fifteen thousand dollars to each person to help get them re-established. Jenny's division will handle the complete operation along with co-operating FBA offices in Nevada, New Mexico and Utah. Congratulations to both you and Ms. Johnson. We look forward to working with you in the future."

Jenny had a big smile on her face as did Susan, Marc, James, and Mike.

"Where to begin? How do we start?" she asked James.

Captain Mike O'Brien spoke.

"At Sub Rosa we passed out a questionnaire form to every single person and then collected them.

They are being processed as we speak. The data-base will then be made available to you. Before I joined the FBI, I worked at HUD for a few years and have that experience to offer your new agency if you would accept it. In other words, I would like to work with you."

"Offer accepted," said Jenny. "What sort of questions were on the form?"

"The questionaries asked for their names, social security numbers, former addresses, cell phone or land- line numbers, dates of and places of birth, names of their last employer, names of banks where they had checking and savings accounts, and the names and telephone numbers of their close friends and relatives. These people will need our help. Most no longer have jobs. They have no ID, money, or even a place to live."

"When will we have the data base?"

"Within two days. I'll deliver a printed copy to you and send it to you digitally, as well."

James handed Jenny a new cell phone and charger.

"All of us are getting new phones

for the FBA. Call or text me and keep me up to date."

"Yes sir. Thank you. If I may, I would like to try calling Colonel Jason King on his cell phone. I don't know where he is, but I have his number on my old phone."

Jenny found it and made the call.

"Jason? This is Jenny Spadaro, calling. How are you?"

"Jenny! I'm just fine. So is my family. Somehow, I lifted off from Phobos, and in an instant my ship was someplace north of Wright, Wyoming, literally in the middle of nowhere! Once the word got out to the local authorities, a caravan of buses came from Laramie and Cheyenne and took everyone to the nearest city of Gillette. Buses pulled up by the ship for two days and nights! When everyone got to Gillette, the Red Cross provided food and water, and people found shelter in churches, auditoriums, and school gyms. We then boarded a plane and flew to Denver for a few days of relaxation. That's where we are right now. There are over seven hundred people in Gillette minus me and my family. Oh, and one other."

"Who's the other?" asked Jenny.

"Sharon Oliver. She asked me to loan her enough money to book a flight to Phoenix. If it weren't for her being such a good friend to Janey and being a leader in the escape plan, we never would have made it.

She really wanted to go home, and I was glad to help her."

"I understand completely. Thanks, Jason," said Jenny. "We'll see you soon. Keep in touch."

SKY HARBOR AIRPORT, PHOENIX, ARIZONA

Upon landing, Sharon asked the man sitting next to her on the flight from Gillette to Phoenix whether she could make a local call. He agreed, and she phoned her longtime neighbor whose telephone number she'd memorized.

"Is this Ellen Wilson?"

"Yes, who's calling?"

"Sharon Oliver. I'm at the airport. I have no money and no driver's license. Can you pick me up and take me to my house? I'll be standing in front of Arrivals."

"Of course. It's so good to hear your voice, Sharon! We've been so worried about you. Bob and I want to know where you've been for the last year and a half! I'll be there very soon."

Ellen Wilson pulled up and got out of her car so she could give Sharon a big hug. They got in, and Ellen drove toward their homes.

"Oh, Sharon, it's so good to see you. Bob and I feared the worst. We thought you had flown somewhere and taken a cab to the airport so you wouldn't have to pay for parking. That's why your car was left in the driveway. Then a week went by and then two weeks. We became very worried. So much has happened since we heard the voice of The One God.

I have a lot to tell you. But I want to know where you've been for a year and a half. Oh, your two cats are fine. I'll bring them over."

Sharon did her best to explain to Ellen about her being taken to Phobos and that her story, along with those of a thousand others, would soon be all over the news. They parked in Ellen's driveway, and Sharon walked over to her car.

"We decided to lock the doors after a week or so just to be safe," Ellen said.

"Were my purse and keys on the driver's seat?"

"No."

"The two men that abducted me must have taken them."

"Do you have a spare car key? What about a key to your house?"

"I hid one outside, and I have a spare car key inside. I'll see you and Bob soon. Right now I just want to lie down for a while."

Sharon found the hidden key and opened her front door. The house was dark except for some light from the windows. No power. She found a flashlight and walked into her bedroom closet. She pushed aside hanging clothes to reveal a wall safe containing her spare car key, her

U.S. passport, and $20,000 in cash. She walked outside, opened her car door, sat down, and said a prayer. Then she turned the key, and the engine started.

"Thank you, The One God!"

Sharon let her car run for five minutes and returned to her bedroom. A wave of fatigue swept over her, and she lay down with the flashlight beside her and began to cry. She felt a tangle of emotions; joy at being home in her bed, sadness due to the sudden separation from the friends she had made at Sub Rosa, and relief that the ordeal was finally all over. She audibly sighed and fell into a deep sleep.

Sharon slowly opened her eyes

and heard her stomach growling. She got some money from the safe and drove to a twenty-four hour Safeway at a nearby shopping center and bought a roast chicken, rolls, a half-pint of milk, one cube of butter, lettuce, vegetables for a salad, along with six candles and a package of lighters.

On the way back home, she passed by a large area of abandoned buildings in a complex that used to be a major electronics manufacturer, which had moved its business to Mexico. Oddly, many lights were on inside, even though it was now after eleven o'clock at night. Curious, she parked her car and approached the front door. It was unlocked. She entered an air lock, passed through a second air lock, and found herself staring at the area of bee pollination. She was looking at the Eco Farm!

Sharon drove back to her house in a daze. What was happening? Her mind just couldn't comprehend what she had just seen. Her stomach growled again. When she got home, she used her flashlight and placed the candles around the house and lit them. Then she opened a bottle of *Pinot Noir*, made a nice dinner for herself, and ate by candlelight.

The next day Sharon visited the power utility and phone offices. She paid them the amounts she owed, and everything was turned back on.

She went to the DMV and patiently went through the process of getting her driver's license reissued. When she returned home, her neighbor, Ellen Wilson, brought her two cats over, and they were reunited. She aired out her house and then drove to the Mayo Clinic hospital.

Everyone there was astonished to see her walk in. Sharon explained as best she could what had happened to her and many others. Everyone was so happy to see her.

"Soon you will hear it all over the news. Nearly one thousand people were taken."

Her assistant, Dorothy Wells, had become director of nursing but stated that she would now relinquish her position back to Sharon and become assistant director once more. She then handed Sharon her cell phone and told her someone had just called and left a message for her. Sharon listened, and the message was from Janey. She and *Honovi* were at the Greyhound bus station and requested that she come and pick them up.

Sharon parked and entered the bus station, where she located Janey and *Honovi*. They embraced, and she kissed them both.

"Come on. You both must be starving, and I am, too."

She took them to a local Garcia's Mexican restaurant, and they stuffed themselves and ended their meals with *pina* coladas. Without revealing the Eco Farm, Sharon headed back toward her house. When she got to the abandoned buildings she parked her car.

"Where are we?" asked Janey.

"Is this where you live?"

Sharon laughed.

"No, I live a few blocks away. I have a special surprise for you. Let's go."

They got out of the car and approached the front door, which was once again unlocked. They entered the first air lock and then went through the second air lock. Before them was the vast area of bee pollination.

Janey and *Honovi* stood there open-mouthed, and stared.

"What?" asked Janey.

"How?" wondered *Honovi* aloud.

"Oh. This has got to be the work of The One God! How much more of the Eco Farm is there?" asked Janey.

"I don't know. Let's go and find out," said Sharon.

They wandered through the area of aquaponics and discovered that the entire Eco Farm was there including areas for the fish, rabbits, and chickens. With their minds blown, they returned to Sharon's car, and she drove home and parked.

"Now *this* is where I live," she said.

"Please come in. I had the power and phone turned back on today."

"Oh, my God! We've got to go get Dr. Brad Lambert! I forgot. He's at the bus station," shouted Janey.

Sharon drove back to the Greyhound station. Janey ran inside and returned with Dr. Lambert. Sharon hugged him and then drove back to the Eco Farm. They walked through the air locks and into the vast area of bee pollination.

"I guess I didn't need your office number at MIT after all, Brad!" said Janey and laughed.

Dr. Lambert had a stunned, wide-eyed expression on his face.

"I can't...I mean...what is...how? I want to go see my office."

The four of them walked to the central office and entered.

"Everything is exactly as it had been when I left! This is amazing!"

"It is the work of and a gift to us from The One God," said Sharon.

Brad bowed his head. The four of them held hands and prayed.

Sharon returned to her house.

"May I call the FBI office?" asked Janey. "I want to get in touch with my sister."

"Of course," answered Sharon. "I have to get a new cell phone, but I'll look up their number in the phone book, and you can use my landline."

"Phoenix FBA."

"My name is Janey Spadaro, and

I would like to speak to your SAC, James Cararuscio."

"One moment, please."

"Janey?"

"Yes, sir. Have you seen my sister?"

"Yes, she and Marc were here a couple of hours ago."

"Can I get her cell phone number?"

"Sure. Let me look it up."

James gave her the new number.

"Thanks so much."

Janey immediately called Jenny.

"This is your twin sister calling."

"Janey! Where are you?"

"*Honovi* and I are at Sharon Oliver's house in Phoenix. I can't wait to see you and Marc. Here's Sharon."

Sharon gave Jenny directions to her house, and she said to expect them in about fifteen minutes.

"May I use your phone to call my wife and then my office?" asked Brad.

"Of course."

She, Janey, and *Honovi* walked outside to the patio and sat in lawn chairs in the afternoon sun.

"Claire?"

"Bradley?"

"Yes, darling."

"Oh, my God. Are you all right? Where are you! Oh, my God!"

"I'm in Phoenix, and I'm fine. I was one of almost a thousand people who were taken, and soon you'll hear all about it on the news. It's been two years. I hope you haven't remarried!"

Claire laughed aloud.

"Of course not. I didn't know where you were. Only that three witnesses described you being forced into a car."

"It's a long story. I'll be home soon.

Then I'll tell you all about where I've been and what I've been doing. Please tell our two sons that I'm okay. I love you so much."

Brad called his office at MIT and gave them the news that he was fine and looked forward to seeing everyone shortly.

There was a knock on the front

door. Sharon opened it and let Jenny and Marc inside. Janey ran from the patio and embraced and kissed her sister. Marc held out his hand, but *Honovi* put his arms around him and gave him a long hug.

"If you hadn't placed the golden disc on the statue's hand," *Honovi* said, "none of us would be here right now. I'm honored to know you."

Marc blushed, and they all went out to the patio and engaged in a lively conversation. Jenny told them about her new position of assisting everyone who had now returned to Earth. Janey, Sharon, and Brad then told them they had a surprise and asked that Jenny follow Sharon's car.

They drove into the parking area

and got out. Janey and *Honovi* saw a large number of abandoned buildings overgrown with ivy. They followed Sharon, who opened the front door, and they entered.

"This is what fed me for a year and a half on Phobos," said Sharon.

"And I was director of the Eco Farm for the past two years," said Brad. "Janey was here for a short time. What you're about to see is a miracle created by The One God."

They walked through the two air locks and into the Eco Farm. Jenny and Marc were astonished by what they saw as they walked throughout the farm.

When they returned to Sharon's house, Jenny explained that she had the authority to issue $15,000 to each person who had returned to Earth. Janey thanked her and said she now wished to gather as many division heads as possible and offer them an opportunity to move to Phoenix and work at the farm. Jenny told everyone about Mike O'Brien and the data base.

"I'm going to my office later this afternoon and will get the data-base. I'll see if any of the people who ran division sections at the farm are at the Greyhound station."

She told them about Jason's ship landing and all the people who were bused to Gillette, Wyoming.

"I wonder how many there are in Gillette," said Sharon.

"Over seven hundred," answered Janey. "Brad and I are going there. Four division heads are in Gillette." She paused and looked at her phone. "Mike just emailed me that five more are at the Phoenix Greyhound bus station. We'll bring all nine to the Eco Farm. Then we'll see how many of the people who worked at the farm on Sub Rosa want to work at it here in Phoenix."

FBA OFFICE, PHOENIX, ARIZONA

Mike O'Brien brought the hardcopy data-base to Jenny's office. He, Susan, and Jenny sat at a table and began to study it. Mike explained that 99 percent of the nearly one thousand people had been identified. Both FEMA and the new FBA were working together to distribute the money to everyone and assist in finding housing, rental cars, cell phones, and employment. He told them he had scoured the greater Phoenix area and found a decent rental rate on rooms with a half-year lease agreement at a Courtyard Marriott in west Phoenix with available parking for those who would work at the farm until they located housing for themselves. James Cararuscio signed a contract for the FBA with the hotel. Later that afternoon, Jenny and Dr. Lambert used their cell phones to take photos and videos of the entire farm. They flew to Gillette, Wyoming, the next morning, and FBA staff met them at the airport. They had a meeting and reunion with Dave Duncan, who had taken care of the chickens, Bonnie Thompson, who had been in charge of the plant washing division, Abbie Larson of hydroponics, and John Sanders, who had run the division of plant nutrient solution systems. She and Dr. Lambert showed them the photos and videos, to their great astonishment. All agreed to return to Phoenix and see the farm. Jenny issued them their $15,000 FBA cash allotments, and the FBA paid for their plane tickets. They checked into the Courtyard Marriott.

When Sharon got off work, she

and Janey drove them to the Eco Farm. Everyone was amazed, in awe, and jubilant.

Janey and Sharon found the five division heads at the Greyhound Station in Phoenix. They reunited with Jamie Glasgow, the bee keeper, Sean Bennett, who had run aquaponics, Vicki Hagar, who had been in charge of the rabbits, Aaron Cooper, who had managed the vertical farms, and Laura Neal, who had run the Eco Farm engineering and maintenance division.

Janey and Sharon drove them all to the Courtyard Marriott, where they checked into their rooms. Their $15,000 allotments were issued and Mike O'Brien and others with the FBA assisted all nine people in leasing rental cars, getting cell phones, opening bank accounts, and obtaining driver's licenses.

The FBA created a division headed by Mike O'Brien to sell the produce from the farm to three local organic food wholesalers. Dr. Lambert asked Janey to assist him in pursuing the opening of other Eco Farms in the United States and then all around the planet. She was indecisive because she looked forward to returning to her lab and the teaching position at the University of New Mexico in Albuquerque and told him so. He was sad, but understood.

Mike O'Brien hired a local

business management company. They sent a manager, Shelly Wagner, to run the farm as a business and see that the employees were paid. Everyone liked her, and she was astonished by the Eco Farm, especially when she was told that The One God had re-created it from where it had been located below the surface on a moon of Mars.

Dr. Lambert returned home and to MIT long enough to put his house up for sale and make arrangements for him and his wife, Claire, to move to the Phoenix area. Their two sons were adults and lived elsewhere with their families.

PUNA, PERU

Louis, *Rosa*, *Arturo*, *Kawki* and *Nina* returned to *Manuel's* house in *Puno*. Everyone sat outside in the sun with cold *chicha's*. *Arturo* was the first to speak.

"You told me not to worry, that the comet wouldn't hit Earth if you and your friends could help it. What did you mean?

"Me dijeron que no me preocupara. Que el cometa no golpean la tierra si usted y sus amigos pueden ayudar. ¿Qué significa?

Louis gave an overall answer to his question and then made a statement:

"I knew all along that Our Lady

was assisting us in every possible way She could. That gave me certainty that we would succeed."

"Yo sabía que la Virgen estuvo asistiéndonos en toda forma posible podía. Que me dieron la certeza de que tendríamos éxito".

Rosa spoke next.

"You insisted that I have faith, that you would see me again soon. All of us want to know what happened from when you walked into the Star Door and walked out today."

"Ustedes han insistido que tengo fe, que me vea de nuevo pronto. Todos nosotros queremos saber qué es lo que ha ocurrido desde el momento en que entré a la estrella puerta y salió hoy".

Louis spent the next hour telling the amazing story from his perspective. When he finished, *Manuel* and *Kawki* got more cold *chicha's* for everyone, and *Arturo* asked the one question on everyone's mind.

"Were you scared to walk through the Star Door?"

"Estabas asustada a caminar a través de la Puerta de Estrella?"

"Yes and no. Our Lady urged me to go through it, and when I got there, two policemen were running right behind me. I didn't have time to be scared. I just ran in and grabbed the golden disc. I was traveling in outer space with stars and galaxies all around me. I wasn't scared then. In fact, I cried at the beauty of it all."

"Sí y no. Nuestra Señora me instó a ir a través de él y cuando llegué allí dos policías fueron girando a la derecha detrás de mí! No tengo tiempo para estar asustados. Acabo de correr y agarró el disco de oro. Yo estaba viajando en el espacio ultra terrestre con estrellas y galaxias todos alrededor de mí. Yo no estaba asustado. De hecho, lloré por la belleza de todo."

Then *Louis* told everyone about Mother Mary meeting him upon his return to the Star Door and that She had taken the gold disc from him and told him he had achieved all She had asked of him and more.

"We have now entered into a golden age with an end to evil and the advent of a lasting time of peace and love. All of us on Earth have been blessed by The One God."

"Hemos entrado ahora en una edad de oro con el fin del mal y el advenimiento de un tiempo duradero de paz y amor. Todos nosotros en la Tierra hemos sido bendecidos por El Único Dios".

Everyone raised their *chicha's.*

"I'll drink to that," said *Kawki.*

"Voy a beber a eso," dice Kawki.

That caused all to laugh. *Rosa* hugged and kissed *Louis*, followed by *Manuel, Arturo, Kawki* and *Nina.*

FIRST MESA, POLACCA, ARIZONA

Janey and *Honovi* drove up from Phoenix to Keams Canyon early in the morning and arrived at First Mesa.

He'd had an emotional phone call with his parents to let them know he was okay and was coming home. He'd asked them to let his grandparents know, as well. When they arrived and parked the car, *Cheveyo, Honaw, Honovi's* mother, *Yamka* (blossom), his father, *Tocho* (mountain lion), his grandfather, *Mongwau* (owl), and his grandmother, *Pamuya* (water moon), hugged and kissed him. Then he introduced them to Janey.

A sizable crowd of people was

assembled in the shade of a large pinyon tree. Tables and chairs had been set up in an area swept clean of pine cones and needles. A colorful assortment of flower bouquets lay in front of the tree.

They walked over to the area and took seats in front, where they were introduced to Bob, John Spencer's brother, and his wife, Karen. *Honovi* noted that Bob had the same red hair and freckles as his late brother. They had driven from Flagstaff. *Honovi* then introduced Janey to *Tuwa's father, Wikvaya, (one who brings),* and his mother, *Chu'si, (snake flower).*

The day was warm, and sunlight

dappled the ground. *Honaw* and *Cheveyo* stood before all present.

"*Sonew talöngva*, (good morning),"
said *Cheveyo*. We are gathered here
to honor two men, John Spencer and
Tuwa, a member of our tribe. *Tuwa*,
John, and *Honovi* disappeared near
in time to one another. The great
mystery of where they went is now
known. One has returned to us,
but the others have not. The name
Tuwa in our language means 'Earth.'
He was a man of good heart, and
his nickname was *Patala,* which
means 'shining with water', as after
a rain shower. He and John served
together in the U.S. Marines, and
they were good friends. John would
come to First Mesa to visit him often,

and all those here who knew him found him to be a man with a good sense of humor. He always kept us laughing and repaired our plumbing problems, too."

Cheveyo stood to one side, and *Honaw* took his place. He nodded at *Chu'si*, who stood and carried a small basket, from which she withdrew many pieces of *pika,* a bread made from blue corn with the look and consistency of blue crepe paper; it was extremely fragile, paper thin, and it shattered into tiny pieces like a corn-flake when bitten into. It is considered sacred by the Hopi.

She placed the *pika* by the flowers and resumed her seat. *Wikvaya* put his arm around her.

Honaw held a large feather.

"I will now waive the *paho*, a prayer eagle feather, in the four directions and send prayers for *Tuwa* and John to *Taiowa,* the Great Spirit."

He did so, and then turned to face the gathering.

"Both men were virtuous and will follow the Sun Trail and *paki (enter)* the village of the Cloud People. Both men had a *loma* (good*) unangwa* (heart*). Honovi* explained to us that there wasn't enough time to bring the bodies back with them, so we are honoring them today in this memorial service. At this moment, I would like to invite Bob to say some words about his brother."

Bob stood and spoke.

"John was my big brother, and we fought a lot as boys will do, but in the end, we were good friends and had shared interests in the local history of Flagstaff and in the Hopi. Over the years I met *Tuwa* and later *Honovi* along with many others at First Mesa.

We were at a total loss when John disappeared, followed shortly by *Honovi* and *Tuwa.* All I can tell you is that I will deeply miss my brother and *Tuwa*, as well. Now that we have been spoken to by The One God, now that there is no more evil, their valiant deaths in an effort to free the people held captive have helped usher in a new world for all of us. I would like to say *kwakwha* (thank you) to everyone present."

Bob took his seat, and *Honaw* again stood in front with *Cheveyo* at his side.

"I would like to recite the 'Hopi Prayer' written by Mary E. Frye. I have changed it slightly to honor these two men," *Honaw* said and continued.

Do not stand at our sacred place and weep
We are not there. We do not sleep.
We are a thousand winds that blow.
We are the diamond glints on snow.
We are the sunlight on ripened grain.

We are the gentle autumn rain.

When you awaken in the morning's hush.

We are the swift uplifting rush

Of quiet birds in circled flight.

We are the soft stars that shine at night.

Do not stand at our sacred place and cry;

We are not there. We did not die.

Many openly cried at the end of the poem including Janey and *Honovi*.

A group of Hopi women brought platters of food and drink from the village and set them down on the tables. Janey and *Honovi* stood and faced those seated in the front row.

Each held a bottle of beer and five

plastic cups. They poured some beer into the cups and handed them to *Cheveyo, Honaw,* Bob, Karen, *Chu'si Wikvaya, Mongwau*, and *Pamuya.*

"I was at John's side as he lay dying,' said *Honovi.* "I had to bend down and lean close to him so I could hear his last words. He asked that we drink a beer for him on Earth."

All of them drank their beer and then joined all those present in honoring, praising, and celebrating John and *Tuwa's* lives.

DENVER, COLORADO

The U.S. Secretary of the Air Force publicly appealed to the pilot of the huge spaceship in Wyoming on all public and social media platforms to fly his ship to Edwards Air Force Base in California. Jason King responded to the appeal and contacted him. Then he called Brad Dryer's cell phone number.

"Brad Dryer speaking."

"This is Jason King, calling, Brad. How are you and where are you?"

"Jason! Good to hear from you. I'm fine and am at my vacation cabin in Idaho with my family. Where are you?"

"I'm in Denver with my family, too. Have you heard the appeal from the U.S. Secretary of the Air Force?"

"Yes, I just watched it on TV."

"Tell you what. My ship's near Gillette, Wyoming. Give Darren a call and ask him to join you. Then why don't you and Darren fly there? Arnie and I will meet you at the airport. Give me the flight info and ETA, and we'll pick you up. Then Arnie and I will fly you to your ship. By the way, where is your ship?"

"Believe it or not, it's in *Mali*, West Africa. It took me over a week to get a flight out of there with over three hundred and sixty people all trying to go home at the same time! I'll make the plane reservations and get back to you."

"Thanks. See you guys soon."

EDWARDS AIR FORCE BASE CALIFORNIA

General Bishop couldn't believe his eyes. Not one, but two, enormous triangular space ships were heading for the base and there were shouts of astonishment from all who stood around him.

The USS *Excalibur* and the USS *Concord* landed one at a time and taxied down Runway 5 at Edwards Air Force Base located on Roger's Dry Lake in the Mojave Desert of southern California. A large group of civilian and military people met Jason King and Arnie Weber, along with Brad Dryer and Darren Carter.

"Welcome to Edwards AFB, gentlemen. My name is General

Greg Bishop. All of us here have never seen anything like these spaceships in our lives except for maybe in sci-fi movies. They are huge!"

He turned and looked directly at Jason and Brad.

"How do your ships operate? Does it really take only three days for you to get to Mars from Earth?"

"In a nutshell, General, the ship employs a VASIMR electric propulsion system. VASIMR is an acronym for Variable Specific Impulse Magneto-plasma Rocket. The engines use radio waves to ionize and heat propellant, which generates plasma that is accelerated using magnetic fields to produce a relatively high thrust without the need for electrodes or most moving parts," answered Jason. "And yes, we can get to Mars in approximately thirty-six hours."

Brad explained,— "the engine design, encompasses three parts: turning gas into plasma via helicon radio frequency antennas; energizing plasma via further radio frequency heating in an ion cyclotron resonance frequency (ICRF) booster; and using electro-magnets to create a magnetic nozzle to convert the plasma's built-up thermal energy into kinetic force."

General Bishop had a blank look on his face, but quickly recovered.

"Well, I'm quite sure our team of

aerospace scientists will be looking forward to working with the two of you and your co-pilots. You and your families are our special guests at the base and are welcome to enjoy all privileges such as housing at the High Desert Inn, meals, and school for your children. Colonel King, I understand that your wife is a medical doctor. We will offer her a position with the 412th Medical Group, which is our family health care clinic on the base.

Jason and Brad both saluted the general who returned their salutes.

KEAMS CANYON, ARIZONA

Marc parked his truck and got out. The desert heat hit him like a wave, and he quickly took off his jacket. The afternoon temperature was unusually hot for mid-February. "*Must be climate change,*" he thought. He slipped on his day-pack. Inside was a liter of cold water, a cloth and cleaner, and his camera. Marc headed for the entrance to the Anasazi cache he had discovered. It seemed to have been a long time ago when, in fact, it had been only a month and a half.

He walked along the path and noted the petroglyph of three faded, robed figures on the rock wall. He removed his large knife from the holder on his belt and began to cut and clear the many branches of the bushes that had grown back and concealed the entrance. Once done he bent down, crawled through, and stood up on the other side. He followed the narrow path through a cleft running between two steep rock walls.

Marc continued down the path until he entered an open area. Many rocks, pebbles, dried wood, and old leaves covered the ground. As before, he knelt in the center and used his knife, carefully running it along the edges of the stone, and lifting it at the same time. No one had disturbed it, and he saw the chert arrowheads and covered bowls. And there, lying in a small open *olla,* was the beautiful necklace that had been finely made of turquoise, hematite, and onyx beads of various sizes. He carefully lifted it, took off his cowboy hat, turned it over, and lay the necklace inside. Marc used the cloth and cleaner he'd brought with him to thoroughly wipe off any visible dirt and dust on it. Then he replaced the necklace in the *olla*, set the flat stone back in place, and threw some rocks, wood and leaves on top. On the way out, he took some photographs of the area and one of the petroglyphs. As Marc drove down the dusty road, he sadly recalled the last time he'd been in this place and the news he'd received on his cell phone from Dr. Thompson about the imminent death of his father.

Marc sighed and felt in his heart a deep satisfaction that he had fulfilled his father's dying request by what he, Jenny, and his friends had been able to accomplish.

Janey and *Honovi* arrived, and Marc welcomed them to his house. Then a thought suddenly struck him. *"What am I going to do now? My sabbatical is over, and I've not finished my book. On top of that, I'm about to be married tomorrow!"*

"You look totally spaced-out," commented *Honovi*. "Are you okay?"

"Too much hot sun," said Marc. "What I need is a cold beer."

Jenny opened the fridge and handed him one. Janey sat on the couch with *Mansi* on her lap, who purred contentedly.

"I like your orange kitty," she said.

Marc smiled and drank some beer.

"Right now," he said, "I think it's a good time for us to have a conversation about the future."

"I agree," said *Honovi*. "What are we all going to do? So much has changed, and there are so many possibilities out there for us."

"With Jenny being a director with the FBA, I won't be teaching in Flagstaff anymore. Maybe I can see if there's a position available at the University of Arizona in Phoenix."

"And what am I going to do for work?" asked *Honovi*. "I need a job."

"I'm really hoping I can get my

teaching job back at the University of New Mexico," said Janey. "I think Dr. Lambert wants me to help him with running the Eco Farm in Phoenix and starting up other one's, but there's no way I can do both."

Jenny returned from the kitchen with cold beers for everyone.

"Let's drink to the future, whatever it will bring," she said. "I trust that The One God will undoubtedly have some surprises in store for all of us."

After dinner Marc and Jenny helped put sheets, blankets, and pillows on the couch in the living room for Janey and *Honovi*. Everyone used the bathroom and retired for the night.

Marc sat beside Jenny on the bed.

"Are you absolutely sure that you want to marry me?" asked Marc.

"Yes, I am. Absolutely."

"Why?"

"Well, you saved my life twice. There's that," stated Jenny.

"True. What else?"

"You have a curious mind, and we're both interested in archaeology. Also, the fact that you're not materialistic and aren't driven to make and have lots of money. That's not at all very important to you."

"Are you sure you want to marry me then? I am not exactly a well-financed guy, you know."

"Yes. I know, but with my FBA salary, we'll both be fine."

"What are some reasons that you want to marry me?" asked Jenny.

"I'm impressed with your strong dedication to upholding the truth and seeing that justice is done."

"Thank you. Anything else?"

"You give really good massages."

Jenny laughed.

"Okay. Is that all?"

"No. I love you because you have a good heart. You're capable of great empathy and compassion, and those are important values to me. And you're very smart. I also think you are quite beautiful."

Jenny kissed him.

"And I like hanging out with you."

They both laughed.

"What are you going to wear tomorrow?" Marc asked.

She took a dress off a hanger in the closet and held it up in the light.

"I bought this in Phoenix the other day. Do you like it?"

Marc saw that it was a solid off-white dress with colorful floral embroidery around the neck, the ends of the short sleeves, and also the hem.

"Yes, I think it's very pretty."

"Thanks, What are you going to wear tomorrow?"

"After my dad passed away, I searched his closet for a vest he had gotten in Japan that I had always liked. We were about the same size. Here it is. I'm going to wear long tan slacks and a white shirt along with it."

Marc put the vest on so Jenny could see it.

"Wow! It's very nice. I like the gold background, the pine-like needles and the white and dark orange daisies."

"Thanks, We'd better get some sleep now, or we'll be a wreck in the morning, and I want us both to be awake and present."

Janey and *Honovi* sat beside one another on the couch.

"Tell me why you want to marry me. I want to know," asked Janey.

"I like how you kiss me."

Janey laughed.

"No, seriously. Why?"

"Because you're not only beautiful physically, but spiritually, as well. That's important to me. You're also extremely intelligent and capable. And you have a good sense of humor. That's why."

"Anything else?"

"Yes. Your interest in growing plants," he said, "The Hopi culture is traditionally based on agriculture.

Your study of hydroponic science and teaching it at the university are both virtues. And you are ethical and know right from wrong. Now, tell me why you want to marry me?" he asked.

"I like your long black hair."

Honovi laughed.

"Also the fact that you are deeply

spiritual, meditate, and have a respect for your ancestors and their way of seeing the world. You're also very intelligent and have a gentleness about you that I love. We now know we will see great changes in the world, and I want to live the rest of my life with you as my husband."

They kissed, and *Honovi* got up and opened a duffel bag. He brought out a dress and held it up. The dress consisted of a red sash that wound around the waist of an all-white wedding dress with red stripes on the shoulders, neck, and hem. He told her that his mother and grandmother had hand-made the dress. She held it up to her body and determined it would easily fit her.

"It's very pretty. I like it a lot," said Janey. "Thank them both for me."

She carefully folded the dress and placed it back in the duffle bag.

Honovi put the pendant around his neck that his grandmother, *Mongwau*, had made and given to him. It was of a deer silhouetted against a full moon.

"That's the pendant you wore on our first date," she said. "I remember it, and how nervous I was."

"So was I." he said and smiled. "I'll wear it tomorrow at the wedding ceremony along with navy blue slacks and a white shirt."

"It starts at 10 o'clock," said Janey.

"We'd better go to sleep. I love you very much."

"And I love you very much."

Marc sat in a rocking chair on the front porch with *Mansi* on his lap. A car drove down the short street and parked. James Cararuscio got out.

"Welcome to Keams Canyon," said Marc as he stood. *Mansi* jumped onto a nearby chair. He and James shook hands. Then *Cheveyo* parked his truck in front. He and *Honaw* got out. Down the street walked Father Bill O'Neill.

"Looks like everyone's here," said Marc. "I'll see if the others are ready."

"Almost," came Jenny's voice through the bathroom door.

"Then it's my turn," said Janey.

"Well, please hurry. We want to get there and be done before noon, okay?"

"Okay, okay."

Marc returned to the porch with *Honovi* and everyone sat down.

"A big day for you both," said Father Bill. "I am honored to be here."

"Father, I am so glad to see you again. You were my Sunday school teacher at St. Joseph's," said *Honovi*."

"And I'm honored to be at Marc's and your wedding today."

"Thank you," they replied.

"It's a beautiful drive to Keam's Canyon," remarked James. "I must have passed the spot where Jenny's car got pushed off the road and you rescued her."

"Hard to believe its been less than two months since then," stated Marc.

"The world has changed for the better," observed Father Bill O'Neill.

James and Father Bill rode with Janey and *Honovi.* Marc and Jenny went in his truck, and *Cheveyo* rode with *Honaw* in his truck.

The mid-morning air was fresh, and the sun shone brightly when they reached the area. Marc led the way and pointed out the hooded figures petroglyph to the others. He bent down, and Jenny passed him the duffel bag. Then she crawled through and stood up on the others side. Janey passed her duffel bag and climbed through. All of them followed Marc as he led them to the clearing.

Jenny and Janey asked the men to please turn around while they both changed. In around five minutes they announced that they were ready.

"Wow! You both look very beautiful," exclaimed *Cheveyo*."

Marc and *Honovi* got their clothes out of the bags and changed.

"Okay, I think we"re ready now," said Marc.

Honaw, Cheveyo and Father Bill stood in front of Marc, Jenny, *Honovi* and Janey. James stood to one side.

"*Sonew talöngva*, (good morning)," said *Honaw*.

"It is a great honor for *Cheveyo*, Father Bill, and myself to conduct this wedding ceremony for four people who are responsible for saving our world.

Cheveyo waved a large eagle feather in the four cardinal directions and spoke a prayer in his Hopi dialect.

Honaw raised his arms.

"I invoke *Taiowa*, The One God, Who Art the Greatest of All, Who Created All, Who Generated It from Thyself, Who Sees All and is Never Seen. We ask Your blessing for Marc and Jenny and for *Honovi* and Janey as they enter into the cherished covenant of marriage.

We ask You to Bless this gathering

of friends, who pledge their love and support for these two couples, for whom we owe so much.

Infinite One,

Fly ahead of Them

Open the Way

Prepare the Path

Spirit of the Sun

Mother of the Light

Come to Them!"

Cheveyo held two medium-size wedding vases, each decorated with a thunderbird design and filled with holy water. He explained:

"The wedding vase has been part

of Pueblo life for centuries. The two spouts on the vase represent the separate lives of the bride and groom. The looped handle represents the unity achieved with marriage. The space created within the loop represents the couples' own circle of life."

He handed one vase to Jenny and Marc and instructed each to drink from either spout, while Janey and *Honovi* drank from the two spouts on their vase.

"This symbolically represents the blending of your lives. This ceremony is equivalent to the exchanging of wedding bands."

Upon hearing this, Father Bill O'Neill handed two rings to Marc and Jenny and two rings to *Honovi* and Janey. They slipped the rings on one another's fingers.

"In the power vested in me by the State of Arizona and in the name of The One God and His Avatar, Our Lord Jesus Christ, I now pronounce both of you couples to be legally married."

Jenny, Marc, Janey, *Honovi*, and James Cararuscio instinctively crossed themselves. Then all stood in a circle, held hands with one another, and prayed to The One God.

As he stood there, Marc's mind recalled the dream he'd had at the hotel in Arlington, Virginia, following his father's funeral:

He had been standing in the central area of the Anasazi site he recently discovered. Jenny had stood by his side. Rubble covered the ground. He knelt in the center and pushed aside rocks, pebbles, and decayed tree branches, and uncovered the flat stone. He used his knife, carefully running it along the edges of the stone, and lifting it at the same time. Marc pried the stone up and put the knife away. He reached into the cache and carefully removed a necklace lying in a small, open *olla*, or decorative bowl.

The necklace was strung with turquoise, hematite, and onyx beads of various sizes. He turned toward Jenny, lifted it over her head, and placed it around her neck. She gasped at the beauty of the stones and kissed him with great passion.

Then Marc returned to the present. He knelt down and used his knife to pry up the stone and take out the necklace. He turned toward Jenny, lifted it over her head, and placed it around her neck. And just like in the dream, she gasped at the beauty of the stones, and kissed him with great passion. Everyone applauded.

After he placed the necklace around Jenny's neck, *Cheveyo* explained that *Honovi's* family had planted blue, white, and sweet corn in their fields because one has to have corn to get married in the Hopi custom. The corn leaves and corn husks were used to make the traditional Hopi sweet blue corn bread, called *somiviki*. The bread was made using blue corn, juniper ashes, sugar, and boiling water. The dough was then rolled in the corn leaves or husk and steamed. Everything was done with prayers.

After the corn-bread was baked, the *piki* bread was made. *Cheveyo* brought out a basket filled with *somiviki* cornbread and *piki*. *Honovi* produced a bottle of champagne and plastic cups, and the others toasted both couples and drank in their honor.

KEAMS CANYON, ARIZONA

Marc hadn't checked his mail in weeks. He drove into Keams Canyon and found that his post office box was stuffed full of mostly junk mail, but one thick envelope caught his attention. The return address was from his father's law firm of Miller, Price, and Hill located in Bel Air, Maryland. Curious, Marc opened it and determined that it had something to do with his inheritance. He drove back to his house, and he and Jenny began to read the contents.

His father's house and property had been sold, and his extensive investment portfolio had been liquidated.

The law firm requested that Marc fly to Maryland and make an appointment with their office in Bel Air. Several documents required his signature before a substantial amount could be dispensed to him.

"Oh, my God," said Jenny.

"I wonder what 'substantial amount' means?"

"When you said that The One God will undoubtedly have some surprises for all of, you weren't kidding!"

"The wedding reception is in three days," said Jenny. "We'll both fly to Maryland after that."

CROWNE PLAZA HOTEL PHOENIX

Harold and Beverly Spadaro greatly enjoyed seeing their daughters and meeting their future sons'-in-law on the night before the wedding reception. They had a wonderful dinner together at the hotel's restaurant.

Afterward, Jenny and Janey accompanied their parent's to their hotel room, reminded them that the reception was at two o'clock, and wished them a good night.

Beverly smiled at her daughters.

"You've chosen well. I like both of them very much."

"I heartily agree," affirmed Harold.

THE RECEPTION AT THE CROWNE PLAZA HOTEL IN PHOENIX

Jenny and Janey walked into the ballroom around one thirty and spoke with the events manager, Kristin James. Everything looked great. The flowers they'd ordered were on all the tables, the place settings were done, and a stage had been set up for the local band Mike O'Brien had hired for dancing after the luncheon.

They went to the lobby and front desk, where they got room numbers for *Viviane* and *Bastien* and their sons, *Jacques and Jean-Luc*, and for *Louis, Rosa* and *Arturo*. They called and asked that they all meet them in the front lobby.

"Sorry, I'm early. Is there anything I can do to help?" said Sharon Oliver after she came in the front door.

Latona de Jahn and Ben Anderson had followed her.

"Us too," Latona said.

Jenny and Janey gave all three of them big hugs.

"Yes," said Janey. "We need to set up a table by the door to the ballroom. I bought plenty of name tags. When people enter, you can ask them to write their names and put the tags on."

"Okay," said Sharon. "Anything else?"

"Not that I can think of," said Jenny.

At that moment *Viviane, Bastien, Jean-Luc* and *Jacques* arrived at the lobby and *Louis, Rosa* and *Arturo* soon joined them. Janey introduced them to Sharon, Latona, and Ben.

"Where are your husbands?" asked Sharon.

"Marc and *Honovi* said they were going to have some cold beers at the hotel bar," answered Jenny just as they appeared.

"Almost time," said Marc as he glanced at his watch. "Quarter to two."

On cue, Bev and Harold Spadaro walked in and were introduced to all.

"Jenny, let's ask Kristen where we

can get a table for the name tags," said Janey.

"Okay. Please meet us at the hotel ballroom," said Jenny as she and Janey walked away. "Follow Marc."

Marc asked the woman behind the front desk whether she would help direct people to the ballroom, and she agreed. He began to lead the group when he heard a voice behind him.

"Wait for us!"

James Cararuscio, Mike O'Brien, Susan Johnson, Jason and Chloe King, and their two daughters entered the lobby.

Marc led them to the ballroom, where Sharon, Ben, and Latona had everyone fill out name tags and put them on as more people began to arrive. These included *Cheveyo, Honaw, Honovi's* mother, *Yamka* (blossom), his father, *Tocho* (mountain lion), his grandfather, *Mongwau* (owl), grandmother, *Pamuya* (water moon), along with Robert and *Tewa* from First Mesa, and the sheriff Jim Burch from Keams Canyon. Shelly Wagner, manager at the Eco Farm, Dr. Lambert and his wife, Claire, Aaron Cooper, who had run the vertical farms at Sub Rosa, and Abbie Larson, who had managed plant hydroponics, also joined them.

"How many are you expecting?" asked Kirsten James, the events manager.

"Fifty-six," answered Jenny.

"We'd better set up some more tables then," said Kristen. "I'll have that done right away."

Cheveyo approached them.

"If it's all right, I would like to say a few words before lunch."

"Also count me in," said *Honaw*.

"Of course." said Jenny. "Thank you."

A group of men from the hotel set up four more tables and left. People found seats, and the ballroom began to fill.

Jenny and Janey greeted the three engineers Aaron Levin, Glen Horn, and Brian Stern and many others from Sub Rosa including, Jamie Glasgow, the bee keeper, Dave

Duncan, who had taken care of the chickens, and two people who had been wounded in the battle. Annie O'Neal, who had been shot in her left leg, walked in with a cane. She had been a groundskeeper. Jimmy Jaffe, who had taken a bullet in his right shoulder, said he was wearing a Velcro brace under his shirt. He had been a delivery van driver.

Two long tables had been set up in front of the stage for Marc and Jenny, *Honovi* and Janey, *Louis, Rosa* and *Arturo*, Jason and Chloe King, their daughters, *Viviane, Bastien,* their sons, Sharon Oliver, *Cheveyo, Honaw*, James Cararuscio, Father Bill O'Neill, and Bev and Harold Spadaro.

When everyone had arrived and been seated, the two couples stood on the stage and thanked everyone for attending their wedding reception. Then they bowed deeply and returned to their table.

Cheveyo, Honaw, James Cararuscio, and Father Bill O'Neill stood on the stage. *Cheveyo* was the first to speak.

"We honor the wedding of Marc and Jenny, *Honovi* and Janey. As someone who was present from the beginning of their courageous journey, I am humbled by their faith and determination against imposing forces. That they prevailed is testament to the power of the prayers and intentions of many of us at First Mesa, who unfailingly stood with them."

Cheveyo took a seat, and *Honaw* faced the room.

"It was our greatest pleasure to marry these two couples to whom we owe so much. The Hopi traditional ways of looking at the universe are now joined with those of Father Bill's church as we both celebrate The One God common to all of us. This was possible only through the valiant efforts of Marc and Jenny, *Honovi* and Janey, and all those who assisted them. May The One God bless all of them."

Honaw stood aside, and Father Bill O'Neill related the miracle of the ball of light that had appeared and lit all

the candles in his church and that
he had known then, without a doubt,
that the comet would miss Earth.

Then James Cararuscio said,

"Everyone in this room knows
parts of the amazing set of events
that have brought us to this moment.
I am deeply honored to have been
present at the wedding ceremony
along with *Honaw, Cheveyo,* and
Father Bill O'Neill.

When Jenny and Marc presented
me with their information regarding
a secret space program and an
underground base on a Martian
moon, well, I thought it was the most
cockamamie story I'd ever heard.
But the evidence was overwhelming
as was a phone conversation I had

with Colonel Jason King, who was the pilot of one of the two space ships.

I decided to give them the complete assistance and resources of what was known then as the FBI. Janey, *Honovi*, Sharon Oliver, and many others, led the escape plan. Together we were able to rescue all those at the base on Phobos.

That was one part of the story. The second part involved Marc and Jenny, who successfully completed the task set by The One God. All of us here, and indeed, everyone on Earth, are alive today because of these two couples and the many who fought with them. I now offer them our sincere, deepest, and heartfelt thanks."

All in the room rose to their feet in a standing ovation in honor of those who sat nearest the stage.

The luncheon was served followed by dancing to the music of the great band Mike O'Brien had hired. Afterward, those at the table near the stage sat down, and *Louis Carillios* spoke.

"We are so happy to be here at your wedding reception. I just wish Our Lady hadn't asked me to give the golden disc back, because we could have used the Star Door to travel here and saved a lot of money!"

Honaw and *Cheveyo* laughed

along with *Rosa* and *Arturo*, Marc, Jenny, *Honovi,* Janey, and everyone else.

Ben Anderson and Latona de Jahn walked over to the table and announced that they were engaged to be married. Latona got her job back as a school teacher in Scottsdale. Ben said he had always loved to cook and was opening a restaurant there.

Marc checked his cell phone for emails. There was one from Dr. Thompson, who regretted that he couldn't attend the ceremony and sent his congratulations. There was also an email from *Renard* in Avignon, wishing them all the best.

Several people at the reception

who had worked at the Eco Farm at Sub Rosa now expressed their desire to see the Eco Farm that The One God had manifested in Phoenix. After the reception, Dr. Lambert and his wife, Claire, along with Shelly Wagner and Mike O'Brien, assembled a large group and brought them there.

BEL AIR, MARYLAND

Marc and Jenny flew to Bel Air, a few days after the wedding reception in Phoenix. They rented a car and checked into a hotel, where they had lunch and drove to the law offices of Miller, Price, and Hill. The three law partners had been Admiral Bill

Prentis' attorneys for many years, and they all knew Marc.

They took seats around a large, wooden table. Two stacks of folders sat in front of the three attorneys facing Marc and Jenny.

Herbert Miller, the senior partner said,

"Marc, your father consented to have our law firm sell his house and property, liquidate his extensive stock and bonds portfolio, and close his savings and checking accounts. In his last will and testament, he has directed us to designate all of his assets to you, his only son. The total, minus our firm's preparation fee, amounts to the sum of $16.8 million dollars."

Marc was stunned by the amount, and a clear memory appeared in his mind of being at his father's bedside and some of the last words he had spoken to him before he died.

"I see your mother standing over there in the corner. She's waiting for me to be with her in heaven. It's my time, Son. Know that I'm proud of you. You could have joined us in our business and made lots of money, but archaeology has always been your passion. I'm leaving my inheritance to you. I know you'll use it wisely."

Jenny watched as tears began to well up in Marc's eyes.

"Marc, are you okay?"

But Marc never heard her

question. He lay his head down between his arms on the table and began to sob uncontrollably. One of the attorneys, Margaret Hill, handed Jenny a box of tissues. Marc continued to cry for a few minutes. He deeply sighed and slowly raised his head. He used a wad of tissues to wipe his eyes and face.

"I loved him so much," he said with great emotion.

"We all did," said Paul Miller, one of the attorneys. "He was not only a client, but also a good friend."

"We will all miss him dearly," said Herbert Price, the senior partner.

"I agree. He was a wonderful man," said Margaret Hill.

Marc signed a stack of documents

and gave the law firm his banking information. Then he and Jenny left.

They drove back to the hotel in silence, each absorbed in his or her own thoughts. Jenny was the first to speak.

"What are you, I mean, what are we going to do with all that money, Marc? I never wanted to be a millionaire, and money has always provided a sense of security to me, but *this* much?"

'I've been giving it some thought. We can use some of it to start other Eco Farms. What do you think?"

"Yes! Maybe we can use the one in Phoenix and copy it."

"We could build them inside buildings or enclosed rooftops. We wouldn't need to have sunshine or be hampered by growing seasons and weather, and the farms would be environmentally friendly. Plus, we could employ lots of people, especially botanical scientists, like Janey."

"Janey! Oh, I can't wait to tell her and *Honovi,* too! He helped build the Eco Farm at Sub Rosa," said Jenny. "We could change the world."

"You're right. We can reproduce the Eco Farm all over the planet. We have a great team of people in Phoenix, and I'm certain we can train others. Maybe we could even start one in Albuquerque. Let's have a meeting of everyone involved in the farm when we get home," said Marc.

ECO FARM IN PHOENIX, ARIZONA

They met in the main dining hall at the Phoenix farm. Present were Dr. Lambert, Shelly Wagner, Mike O'Brien, Jenny, Marc, Janey, *Honovi*, and all nine of the division heads, including Jamie Glasgow, head of bee pollination, to discuss starting another Eco Farm.

Everyone sat around a couple of tables pushed together. Marc spoke first and explained about receiving an inheritance and how he and Jenny wished to use some of it to finance other Eco Farms. Dr. Lambert was quite excited at the prospect. Janey and *Honovi* then brought up the fact that, after speaking with Jenny and Marc, the next proposed Eco Farm would be in Albuquerque.

"We'll have to find a suitable site, of course," said *Honovi*. "And Marc has kindly offered me the position of superintendent overseeing the construction and hiring. Once built, we'll need to rely on all of you to spend some time there and get things up and running. Then we can find local people to take over."

"This is fantastic," said Dr. Lambert. "We will start there and gradually expand to other cities. As I once told Janey, there are many parts of the world like Scandinavia, Alaska, and Siberia that don't get sunlight half the year and also high altitude mountain ranges like the

Andes and Himalayas. We could make agriculture available year round for those who live there."

How are we doing at the Phoenix farm?" asked Marc.

"Very well," answered Shelly Wagner. "The three organic wholesalers are happy with our produce, eggs and fish. We haven't enough people to process the rabbits on site, so they are being sold to a local meat processing facility. Jamie has worked hard to make sure our bees are happy and doing their job. We showed a modest net profit during our first two months and are able to pay a growing staff of people. All in all, I believe we can show that the farm is profitable."

"How are we doing on staffing?" asked Dr. Lambert. "We had well over seven hundred people working at the farm on Phobos."

"We are steadily employing more people," answered Shelly, "and are being assisted by both the State of Arizona and Phoenix employment departments. We now have four hundred and thirty-six people working at the farm."

Mike O'Brien looked at those who sat around the table.

"We now have all of our division heads living in Phoenix. The money allocated to everyone by the FBA has helped people greatly with car rentals, cell phones, and enough to buy groceries and, pay rent and bills.

The Courtyard Marriott has agreed to extend our leased apartments for a full year, so all has worked out very well for everyone.

"And, let us not forget," said Jenny, "that all of this has been made possible through the love bestowed on us by The One God."

All held hands and bowed their heads in prayer.

SVALBARD GLOBAL SEED VAULT, NORWAY

On *Spitsbergen*, an Arctic island off the coast of Norway, lies the *Svalbard* Global Seed Vault, which is home to more than two billion seeds. The vault is buried so deeply in the surrounding sandstone bedrock that it could survive a nuclear strike. Its purpose is to preserve crops in the face of climate change, war, civil strife, natural, and cosmic disasters.

Dr. *Jarle Oddvar* and Dr. *Einar Asbjorn* sat beside one another in front of large computer screens in the vault's control room.

"Our security cameras are recording some large objects in Vault Three, Section H," said *Jarle*.

"Vår sikkerhet kameraer er opptaket noen store objekter i avsnitt H," sa Jarle.

"But Section H is empty!"

"Men avsnitt H er tom!"

"Not anymore," said *Einar*.

"Ikke lenger," sa Einar.

"What are you talking about?"

"Aktivert noe hva er det du snakker om??"

"Take a look."

"Ta en titt."

Jarle looked at the computer monitor display from the security cameras in Vault Three, Section H.

"We had better check it out," said *Jarle.*

"Vi hadde bedre sjekk den ut," sa Jarle.

The two men donned heavy parkas, ski masks, woolen hats, gloves, and blue helmets. They carefully made their way through the large frozen ice tunnel to Vault Three, opened the heavy wood and steel reinforced doors, and entered. Six cylinders stood in Section H.

They were each eight feet tall and five feet in diameter.

"What are they?"

"Hva er det?"

"There is a list. It says: 'Library of 98% of Earth's DNA Biological Genome'," said *Einar.*

"Det er en liste. Det sier:

'Bibliotek for 98% av Jorden's DNA Biologiske Genomet'," sa *Einar.*

"How did they get inside?" asked *Jarle.* "I have been here all day, and no one brought them in."

"Hvordan ble de få inne? Jeg har vært her hele dagen og ingen førte demi & aktivert noe."

Then *Jarle* looked upward.

"It must be a gift from The One God."

"Det må være en gave fra én Gud."

"Yes," said *Einar.* "The One God gave it to us in case we ever need to use it here."

"Ja," sa Einar. "Én Gud gav det til oss i tilfelle vi trenger å bruke det her."

"Here? No, not here," said *Jarle.*

"I am an amateur astronomer. The One God gave it to us to use as we explore space and establish bases and colonies on other moons and planets. We will bring the Earth along with us."

"Her? Nei, ikke her," sa Jarle. "Jeg er en amatør astronomen. Den ene Gud gav oss til bruk som vi utforske verdensrommet og etablere baser og kolonier på andre måner og planeter.

*Vi vil bringe Jorden sammen
med oss."*

*CATHÉDRALE NOTRE-DAME
DESDOMS, D'AVIGNON, FRANCE*

A flock of pigeons flew swiftly through the air and landed on the arms of the statue of Mother Mary high atop the cathedral. They were the only witnesses to see Her face break into a broad smile. They cooed loudly in response to Her booming, joyful laugh, which multitudes of people clearly heard as it echoed around the four corners of the world followed by the words everyone heard at the same time and in his or her's mind and language:

"Welcome to a New Golden Age of Light, Love, and Peace."

THE END